Hot Lead

The two streams of molten lead fell into the crowd, like hot water on snow. Screaming wretches fell, burned half to cinder; others lay moaning in agony. Above the flame, the two towers loomed. In the flickering light, the innumerable sculptured gargoyles and dragons on the cathedral seemed to be laughing at the spectacle.

And among those freaks thus awakened from their stony slumber, one was walking about. He could be seen passing in front of the blazing pile like a bat in front of a torch.

"........ringer. It's Quasimodo!" screamed the Duke.

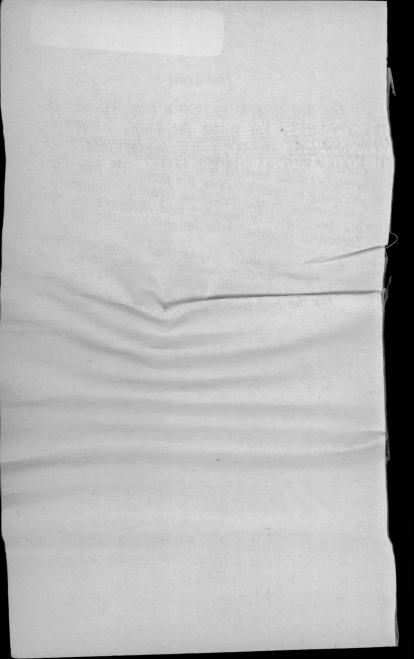

THE HUNCHBACK
OF NOTRE-DAME

Victor Hugo

A TOM DOHERTY ASSOCIATES BOOK
NEW YORK

This is a work of fiction. All the characters and events portrayed in this book are fictitious, and any resemblance to real people or events is purely coincidental.

THE HUNCHBACK OF NOTRE-DAME

All new material in this edition copyright © 1996 by Tom Doherty Associates, Inc.

A Tor Book
Published by Tom Doherty Associates, Inc.
175 Fifth Avenue
New York, N.Y. 10010

Tor® is a registered trademark of Tom Doherty Associates, Inc.

ISBN: 0-812-56312-3

First Tor edition: June 1996

Printed in the United States of America

0 9 8 7 6 5 4 3 2 1

Contents

Contents

Contents

BIOGRAPHY

Victor-Marie Hugo was born February 26, 1802, the third
son of Joseph-Leopold-Sigisbert Hugo, an officer in Napoleon's army, and Sophie Trébuchet, a sea captain's daughter. By the time he came into this world in Besançon,
France, Victor's parents' marriage was already in trouble,
although they did not formally separate until he was sixteen years old. His father traveled extensively with the
army; sometimes Victor, his mother, and his brothers, Abel
and Eugene, came along. When Victor was two years old,
however, his mother took him with her to live in Paris
while his father was away on military duty. Victor fell in
love with the city and later called Paris "the birthplace of
my soul." For most of his childhood, he was uprooted
again and again, traveling with his father to Italy and
Spain, but always returning to his mother and Paris.

Victor Hugo was given a solid education in Latin literature and even studied to be a lawyer, but by 1816 he had
already filled notebook after notebook with a myriad of
poems and several plays. In 1822, he published his first

book of poems, *Odes et poésies diverses*, and the volume was so well received that it earned him an award from King Louis XVIII. That same year, he married his childhood friend, Adele Foucher. Together they had five children: Charles, Francois, Leopold II, Leopoldine, and Adele.

Hugo continued to write prose, poetry, drama, and political commentary, producing works at an astounding rate. He established himself as one of the young writers who called themselves "Romantics." They challenged Classicism, the rigid literary structure that contemporary critics esteemed, and embraced a more emotional, free-flowing form of literature that the establishment deemed excessive. At the same time, Hugo, who was raised to share his mother's conservative, royalist politics, was becoming more and more liberal. His political convictions were strengthened by King Charles X's interference with the freedom of the press, including interference with Hugo's own work. In 1829, the production of his new play *Marion Delorme*, which painted a rather sour picture of one of the King's ancestors, was halted by the royal censor. In response, he wrote and produced another play, *Hernani*, about a passionate revolutionary. It was romantic in the extreme, and became the literal battleground between the Classicists and the Romantics. Every early performance ended in fistfights among the warring factions in the audience, but it was made clear by the play's enormous popularity that the Romantics had won the day.

Victor Hugo, a life-long opponent of capital punishment, consistently lobbied against it in his work. One of his early novels, *The Last Day of a Condemned Man*, was an impassioned plea for an end to the death penalty, but it was not a popular success. In March of 1831, *Notre Dame de Paris*, or *The Hunchback of Notre Dame*, as it is known in English, was published. It reworked the anti-execution theme in a more palatable manner. Hugo would continue to pursue this cause in subsequent works, but was unsuccessful. France abolished capital punishment in 1981, nearly a century after Hugo's death.

Notre Dame de Paris was an international success, and assured Hugo a place in the realm of French letters. In 1841, on his fifth nomination, he was elected to the Académie Française. But his prolific voice was about to be silenced for a time.

In February of 1843, his daughter, Leopoldine, married Charles Vacquerie. In September, the newlyweds were drowned in a boating accident. Hugo first learned of his daughter's death when he read of it in a newspaper. He was plunged into deep sorrow, and, although he continued to write, he published nothing for the next nine years.

In 1845, Hugo was made a Peer of France, but this honor was short-lived. In December of 1851, after Louis Napoleon took control of the French government and set himself up as its emperor, Hugo organized an unsuccessful resistance effort. He and his family had to flee France and live in exile, first in Brussels, Belgium, then on the Channel Islands of Jersey and Guernsey. Hugo had been offered amnesty by the French government in 1859, but refused to return to his native land until 1870, when the Franco-Prussian War restored the French Republic. By then his wife, Adèle, had died in Brussels.

While in exile, Hugo finally broke his publishing silence with a volume of verse entitled *Les Châtiments*, a literary stab at Louis Napoleon that still stands as one of the sharpest satires in the French language. This was followed by the deeply personal, spiritual volume *Les Contemplations*, in which he addressed the loss of his daughter. In 1862, still exiled from his beloved France, Hugo published his most famous novel, *Les Miserables*. Legend has it that he sent the manuscript to his publisher with a note that merely said "?." He received a telegram the next day that read "!."

When Victor Hugo returned to France, he was a revered both as a statesman and as France's premiere writer. He was elected Deputy of Paris in February of 1871, but resigned in March after his son, Charles, died. In 1876, he was again elected to public office, this time as senator for the Seine. On his 80th birthday, the street where he'd lived for years, Avenue d'Eylau, was renamed Avenue Victor Hugo in his honor.

On May 22, 1885, Victor Hugo died, the victim of a congestion of the lungs. Although he requested a simple pauper's funeral, his body lay in state under the Arc de Triomphe, and his funeral procession lasted for six hours. His body was interred in the Pantheon, a fitting honor for the man who was the heart and soul of France.

                                        —Elizabeth Massie

Foreword

Victor Hugo's early novel, *Notre Dame de Paris*, published in 1831 and set in medieval Paris of 1482, was the work that made his reputation outside his native France. First translated into English in 1833 by William Hazlitt the Younger as *Notre Dame of Paris*, the novel was released only a few months later in a second translation as *The Hunchback of Notre Dame*, and has been known to English speakers by this title ever since. Although not as acclaimed as Hugo's 1862 masterpiece *Les Miserables*, *The Hunchback of Notre Dame* nevertheless holds a special fascination. In addition to being a bestseller from its first publication, the novel has been the subject of many films. Who doesn't know the name Quasimodo, even if, upon hearing it, Lon Chaney, Sr.'s twisted visage comes to mind more readily than Victor Hugo's grandfatherly brow? What is it about this novel that compels us to identify with one of the most horribly deformed characters in all of literature? Why do we feel more than pity for Quasimodo? Why, once the dust has settled and the story is finished, do we come to respect him, to mourn his passing? Is there something to this outcast of outcasts that speaks to that part of ourselves that worries if we'll ever "belong?" In reality, *The Hunchback of Notre Dame* is the story of outcasts; Quasimodo, denied access to a normal life because of his many deformities, is only the most obvious.

Pierre Gringoire, based on a rather successful satirist of the same name who lived from 1475 to 1538, is, in this novel, a pathetic sort of fellow who becomes a poet because he's been a failure at everything else. Orphaned in childhood (a characteristic he shares with almost everyone else of importance in the novel), Pierre tries his hand at soldiering, attempts a religious life in a monastery, offers himself as an apprentice and as a schoolmaster. He isn't suited for any of these vocations. He could have easily become a truant—one of the beggars or petty thieves whom he eventually joins in the Court of Miracles—but it's too risky. He'd like to avoid the gallows if he can. He figures there is nothing left for him but to become a poet, and he's not very good at that, either. Even as he tries to make a name for himself with his ill-fated mystery play, he must face the fact that the masses would much rather watch a face-making contest than drink in the subtleties of his verse. When he stumbles mistakenly into the Court of Miracles and finds himself on trial for *not* being a criminal, he tries to proclaim himself one of them. That, he finds, is not good enough. He must prove himself worthy of the designation "truant," and, once again, he fails miserably. Only Esmeralda's intervention saves him.

We want to like the hapless Gringoire. Pierre is, like many of us, struggling to find a place for himself in the world. We lose patience with him though, when he shows himself over and over again to be a coward. He has several chances to save the innocent Esmeralda from the gallows, thus repaying her kindness to him, but he never quite gets up the gumption to see his schemes through. He's not a hero, and he is, perhaps, too much like us for us to take him to heart.

Esmeralda is as much a victim of her stunning beauty as she is of her gypsy caste. Hated and feared as sorcerers and baby-stealers, gypsies have been the pariahs of Europe since the dark ages. As one of the "Tribe of Egypt" (so called because of their swarthy complexions), Esmeralda would never be allowed into "respectable" society. She could never be a legitimate companion to Captain Phoebus, no matter how lovely her face or loving her character. And she is a very charitable young woman. In fact, it is her abundant goodwill and open heart that prove her undoing, as surely as her bewitching beauty. Yes, it is her kindness, her selfless charity to Quasimodo, bound and flogged for accosting her, that endears Esmeralda to him and to the reader. The fact of the matter is, though, that if Claude Frollo had not been enchanted by her outward charms, the chain of events leading to her downfall would never have been set in motion.

Esmeralda is too naive, too sheltered, even after her gypsy childhood, to hold her own against the forces of evil that abound in the streets and, especially, in the law courts of Paris. True justice does not exist in this medieval city, and life is very cheap—all life, including the beautiful Esmeralda's. She has somehow never been hardened into realizing that there is no "Prince Charming" out there to save her, should worse come to worst, as it does. She hopes her dashing Captain Phoebus will rush in and sweep her away to safety, but it is her ill-placed love for the scoundrel and her misunderstanding of his intentions that seal her fate. Quasimodo, in fact, is the only selfless savior she has.

Of course, Quasimodo, the deaf, one-eyed hunchback, so hideous that it pains "normal" people to look at him, is completely exiled from society. Even in today's "enlightened" times, we find it hard to accept deformity, to look at a misshapen body or a scarred face steadily and without revulsion. In the middle ages, the chances of a child such as Quasimodo being allowed to live were very slim. In fact, when he is left as a foundling on the shelf in Notre

Dame, everyone who sees him agrees that he would be better off dead. If Dom Claude Frollo had not adopted him, he would have most likely been taken outside the city walls and exposed to the elements, there to starve or freeze to death, and no one would have been shocked or dismayed. One can make the argument, along with the matrons of fifteenth century Paris, that death would have been preferable to the life Quasimodo led. Almost blind, bent nearly double, eventually deafened by the loud ringing of the bells, even Victor Hugo describes him as violent, ill-tempered, and dull. But his description of Quasimodo is superseded by the way the hunchback comports himself.

First of all, how "dull" is Quasimodo? Dom Claude taught him to speak French, which he still can utter despite his deafness. Once his hearing is lost, he is able, with the help of Claude Frollo, to develop a form of sign language so he can continue to communicate with his mentor. And he is inventive, as well. When the truants make a stand against Notre Dame, demanding Esmeralda's release, Quasimodo, knowing only that they are attacking his beloved cathedral, devises several successful means of staving off their advances. No, despite all the descriptions to the contrary, Quasimodo is not stupid. And, despite all the pain and ridicule he has suffered at the hands of the people of Paris, he is still able to love. His affection for Esmeralda is born of her kindness to him, not her outward beauty. He is well aware of how offensive his ugliness is to her, and he takes the greatest care not to offend her. His loyalty to Claude Frollo, too, is borne of the long legacy of kindness the priest showed him. It takes Quasimodo a very long time to admit to himself that Claude has betrayed him, and, even as the archdeacon meets his deserved end, Quasimodo is shattered by his loss.

So, here is a man, outcast in every way from a society that finds him good for nothing except as the butt of their jokes, so hideously deformed that he frightens even grown men, shut off from communication with all but his hateful mentor, who, nevertheless, has the capacity to feel a deeper and more selfless love than anyone around him. We like to feel we could show him friendship and compassion, for we have all felt some measure of isolation from society. And yet, confronted with so much ugliness, could we look past the shell to the inner man? Not even Esmeralda, try as she might, is able to ignore his horrid appearance. That his love will never be returned is not only his tragedy, but the tragedy of all mankind.

—Elizabeth Massie

1

It is this day three hundred and forty-eight years six months and nineteen days since that the good people of Paris were awakened by a grand peal from all the bells in the three districts of the City, the University, and the Ville. January 6, 1482, was, nevertheless, a day of which history has not preserved any record. There was nothing worthy of note in the event which so early set in motion the bells and the citizens of Paris. It was neither an assault of the Picards nor the Burgundians, nor a procession with the shrine of some saint, nor a mutiny of the students, nor an entry of our "most redoubted lord, Monsieur the king," nor even an execution of rogues of either sex, before the Palace of Justice of Paris. Neither was it an arrival of some bedizened and befeathered embassy, a sight of frequent occurrence in the fifteenth century. It was but two days since the last cavalcade of this kind, that of the Flemish Ambassadors commissioned to conclude a marriage between the Dauphin and Margaret of Flanders, had made its entry into Paris, to the great annoyance of the Cardinal of Bourbon, who, in order to please the king, had been obliged to receive this vulgar squad of Flemish burgomasters with a good grace, and to entertain them at his hotel de Bourbon with a goodly morality, mummery, and farce, while a deluge of rain drenched the magnificent tapestry at his door.

What set in motion all the population of Paris on January 6, was the double solemnity, united from time immemorial, of the Epiphany and the Festival of Fools. On that day there was to be an exhibition of fireworks in the Place de Greve, a Maytree planted at the chapel of Braque, and a mystery performed at the Palace of Justice. Proclamation had been made to this effect on the preceding day, with sound of trumpet in the public places, by the provost's officers in fair coats of purple camlet, with large white crosses on the breast.

That morning, therefore, all the houses and shops remained shut, and crowds of citizens of both sexes were to be seen wending their way toward one of the three places specified above. Be it, however, observed, to the honor of the taste of the cockneys of Paris, that the majority of this concourse were proceeding toward the fireworks, which were quite seasonable, or to the mystery which was to be represented in the great hall of the palace, well covered in and sheltered, and that the curious agreed to let the poor leafless May shiver all alone beneath a January sky in the cemetery of the Chapel of Braque.

All the avenues to the Palace of Justice were particularly thronged, because it was known that the Flemish Ambassadors, who had arrived two days before, purposed to attend the representation of the mystery, and the election of the Pope of Fools, which was also to take place in the great hall.

It was no easy matter on that day to get into this great hall, though then reputed to be the largest room in the world. To the spectators at the windows, the palace yard crowded with people had the appearance of a sea, into which five or six streets, like the mouths of so many rivers, disgorged their living streams. The waves of this sea, incessantly swelled by fresh accessions, broke against the angles of the houses, projecting here and there like promontories into the irregular basin of the Place. In the center of the lofty Gothic facade of the palace, the grand staircase, with its double current ascending and descending, poured incessantly into the Place like a cascade into a lake. Great were the noise and the clamor produced by the cries of some, the laughter of others, and the tramping of the thousands of feet. From time to time, this clamor and this noise were redoubled; the current which propelled the crowd toward the grand staircase turned back, agitated and whirling about. It was a dash made by an archer, or the horse of one of the provost's sergeants kicking and plunging to restore order—an admirable maneuver, which the provost bequeathed to the constabulary, the constabulary to the marechaussee, and the marechaussee to the present gendarmerie of Paris.

Doors, windows, loopholes, the roofs of the houses, swarmed with thousands of calm and honest faces gazing at the palace and at the crowd, and desiring nothing more; for most of the good people of Paris are quite content with the sight of the spectators; nay, a blank wall, behind which something or other is going forward, is to us an object of great curiosity.

If it could be given to us mortals living in the year 1830 to mingle in imagination with those Parisians of the fifteenth century and to enter with them, shoved, elbowed, hustled, that immense hall of the palace so straitened for room on January 6, 1482, the sight would not be destitute either of interest or of charm; and all that we should have around us would be so ancient as to appear absolutely new. If it is agreeable to the reader, we will endeavor to retrace in imagination the impressions which he would have felt with us on crossing the threshold of the great hall, amid this motley crowd, coated, gowned, or clothed in the paraphernalia of office.

In the first place, how one's ears are stunned with the noise!—how one's eyes are dazzled! Overhead is a double

roof of pointed arches, ceiled with carved wood, painted
sky-blue, and studded with *fleurs-de-lis* in gold; underfoot,
a pavement of alternate squares of black and white marbel.
A few paces from us stands an enormous pillar, then another, and another; in all, seven pillars, intersecting the
hall longitudinally, and supporting the return of the
double-vaulted roof. Around the first four pillars are
shops, glistening with glass and jewelry; and around the
other three, benches worn and polished by the hose of the
pleaders and the gowns of the attorneys. Along the lofty
walls, between the doors, between the windows, between
the pillars, is ranged the interminable series of all the
Kings of France ever since Pharamond; the indolent kings
with pendant arms and downcast eyes; the valiant and warlike kings with heads and hands boldly raised toward
heaven. The tall, pointed windows are glazed with panes
of a thousand hues; at the outlets are rich doors, finely
carved; and the whole, ceiling, pillars, walls, wainscot,
doors, statues, covered from top to bottom with a splendid
coloring of blue and gold, which, already somewhat tar-
nished at the time we behold it, was almost entirely buried
in dust and cobwebs in the year of grace 1549, when Du
Breul still admired it by tradition.

Now figure to yourself that immense oblong hall, illumined by the dim light of a January day, stormed by a
motley and noisy crowd, pouring in along the walls, and
circling round the pillars, and you will have a faint idea of
the general outline of the picture; the curious details of
which we shall endeavor to delineate more precisely.

One of the extremities of this prodigious parallelogram
was occupied by the famous marble table, of a single
piece, so long, so broad, and so thick, that, as the ancient
terriers say, in a style that might have given an appetite to
Gargantua, "never was there seen in the world a slice of
marble to match it"; and the other by the chapel where
Louis XI placed his own effigy kneeling before the Virgin,
and to which, reckless of leaving two vacant niches in the
file of royal statues, he removed those of Charlemagne and

Saint Louis, saints whom he conceived to possess great influence with Heaven as kings of France. This chapel, still new, having been built scarcely six years, was in that charming style of delicate architecture, wonderful sculpture, and sharp deep carving, which marks with us the conclusion of the Gothic era, and prevails still about the middle of the sixteenth century in the fairy fantasies of the revival of the art. The small rose mullion over the porch was in particular a masterpiece of lightness and delicacy; you would have taken it for a star of lacework.

In the middle of the hall, opposite to the great door, an inclosed platform lined with gold brocade, backed against the wall, and to which there had been made a private entrance by means of a window from the passage to the gilded chamber, was erected expressly for the Flemish Envoys, and the other distinguished personages invited to the representation of the mystery.

On this marble table, according to established usage, the mystery was to be performed. Arrangements for this purpose had been made early in the morning. The rich marble floor, scratched all over by the heels of the clerks of the Bazoche, supported a cage of woodwork of considerable height, the upper floor of which, exposed to view from every part of the hall, was to serve for the stage, while the lower, masked by hangings of tapestry, formed a sort of dressing-room for the actors. A ladder, undisguisedly placed outside, was to be the channel of communication between the two, and its rude steps were to furnish the only medium as well for entrances as for exits. There was no movement, however abrupt and unexpected, no piece of stage-effect so sudden, but had to be executed by the intervention of this ladder. Innocent and venerable infancy of the art of machinery!

Four sergeants of the bailiff of Paris, whose duty it was to superintend all the amusements of the people, as well on festivals as on days of execution, were stationed one at each corner of the marble table.

It was not till the great clock of the Place had struck the

hour of twelve that the performance was to begin—a late
hour, to be sure, for a theatrical representation, but it had
been found necessary to suit it to the convenience of the
ambassadors.

Now, the whole assembled multitude had been waiting
ever since the morning. Many of these honest sight-loving
folks had, indeed, been shivering from daybreak before the
steps of the palace; nay, some declared that they had
passed the night under the great porch, to make sure of
getting in. The crowd increased every moment, and, like
water that rises above its level, began to mount along the
walls, to swell about the pillars, to cover the entablatures,
the cornices, all the salient points of the architecture,
all the relievos of the sculpture. Accordingly, the weariness, the impatience, the freedom of a day of license, the
quarrels occasioned every moment by a sharp elbow or a
hobnailed shoe, and the tediousness of long waiting, gave,
long before the hour at which the ambassadors were to arrive, a sharp, sour tone to the clamor of the populace,
kicked, cuffed, jostled, squeezed, and wedged together almost to suffocation. Nothing was to be heard but complaints and imprecations against the Flemings, the provost
of the merchants, the Cardinal of Bourbon, the bailiff of
the palace, Madame Margaret of Austria, the sergeant-
vergers, the cold, the heat, the bad weather, the Bishop of
Paris, the Pope of Fools, the pillars, the statues, this closed
door, that open window—all to the great amusement of the
groups of scholars and serving-men distributed through the
crowd, who mingled with all this discontent their sarcasms
and mischievous sallies, which, like pins thrust into a
wound, produced no small aggravation of the general ill-
humor.

There was among others a knot of these merry wights,
who, after knocking the glass out of one of the windows,
had boldly seated themselves on the entablature, and
thence cast their eyes and their jokes alternately within and
without, among the crowd in the hall and the crowd in the
Place. From their mimicries, their peals of laughter, and

the jeers which they exchanged from one end of the hall to the other with their comrades, it was evident that these young clerks felt none of the weariness and *ennui* which overpowered the rest of the assembly, and they well knew how to extract from the scene before them sufficient amusement to enable them to wait patiently for the promised spectacle.

"Why, 'pon my soul, 'tis you, Joannes Frollo de Molendino!" cried one of them, a youth with a fair complexion, handsome face, and arch look, perched on the acanthi of a capital; "you are rightly named, Jehan du Moulin, for your arms and legs are exactly like the four sails of a windmill. How long have you been here?"

"By the devil's mercy," replied Joannes Frollo, "more than four hours, and I hope they will be counted into my time of purgatory. I heard the King of Sicily's eight chanters strike up the first verse of High Mass at seven o'clock in the Holy Chapel."

"Rare chanters, forsooth!" rejoined the other, "with voices sharper than their pointed caps! The king, before he founded a Mass to Monsieur St. John, ought to have ascertained whether Monsieur St. John is fond of Latin chanted with a Provencal twang."

"And it was to employ those cursed signers of the king of Sicily that he did it!" cried an old woman among the crowd at the foot of the window. "Only think! a thousand livres parisis for one mass, and granted out of the farm-rent of the sea-fish sold in the market of Paris into the bargain!"

"Silence!" ejaculated a lusty, portly personage, who was holding his nose by the side of the fish-woman; "how could the kind help founding a mass? Would you have him fall ill again?"

"Admirably spoken, sire Gilles Lecornu, master-furrier of the king's robes!" shouted the little scholar clinging to the capital.

A general peal of laughter from his comrades greeted

the unlucky name of the poor master-furrier of the king's robes.

"Lecornu! Gilles Lecornu!" cried some of them.

"Cornutus et hirsutus," said another.

"Ay, no doubt," replied the little demon of the capital. "What is there to laugh at? An honorable man, Gilles Lecornu, brother of Master Jehan Lecornu, provost of the king's household, son of Master Mahiet Lecornu, first porter of the wood of Vincennes, all citizens of Paris, all married from father to son!"

A fresh explosion of mirth succeeded; all eyes were fixed on the fat master-furrier, who, without uttering a word in reply, strove to withdraw himself from the public gaze; but in vain he puffed and struggled till he was covered with perspiration; the efforts which he made served only to wedge in his bloated apopletic face, purple with rage and vexation, the more firmly between the shoulders of his neighbors.

At length, one of these short, pursy, and venerable as himself, had the courage to take his part.

"What abomination! Scholars dare to talk thus to a citizen! In my time they would have been scourged with rods and burned with them afterward."

The whole band burst out, "Soho! who sings that tune? What screech-owl of ill omen is that?"

"Say; I know him," said one; " 'tis Master Andry Musnier."

"One of the four sworn booksellers to the University," said another.

"Everything goes by fours at that shop," cried a third; "the four nations, the four faculties, the four festivals, the four proctors, the four electors, the four booksellers."

"Musnier, we will burn thy books!"

"Musnier, we will beat thy serving-man!"

"Musnier, we will tear thy wife's rags off her back!"

"The good fat Mademoiselle Oudarde."

"Who is as fresh and as buxom as though she were a widow."

"The devil fetch you all!" muttered Master Andry Musnier.

"Master Andry," rejoined Jehan, still perched on his capital, "hold thy tongue, man, or I will drop upon thy head."

Master Andry lifted his eyes, appeared to be measuring for a moment the height of the pillar, estimating the weight of the wag, mentally multiplying this weight by the square of the velocity, and he held his tongue.

Jehan, master of the field of battle, triumphantly continued, "I would do it too, though I am the brother of an archdeacon."

"Pretty gentry those belonging to our universities! not even to enforce respect for our privileges on such a day as this!"

"Down with the rector; the electors, and the proctors!" cried Joannes.

"Let us make a bonfire tonight with Master Andry's books in the Champ Gaillard!" exclaimed another.

"And the desks of the scribes!" said his neighbor.

"And the wands of the bedels!"

"And the chair of the rector!"

"Down," responded little Jehan, "down with Master Andry, the bedels, and the scribes! down with the theologians, the physicians, and the decretists! down with the proctors, the electors, and the rector!"

"It must surely be the end of the world!" murmured Master Andry, clapping his hands to his ears.

"The rector! there goes the rector!" cried one of those at the window.

All eyes were instantly turned toward the Place.

"Is it really our venerable rector, Master Thibaut?" inquired Jehan Frollo du Moulin, who, from his position on the pillar within, could not see what was passing without.

"Yes, yes," replied the others, " 'tis he! 'tis Master Thibaut, the rector!"

It was, in fact, the rector and all the dignitaries of the university, going in procession to meet the embassy, and at that moment crossing the palace-yard. The scholars who had taken post at the window greeted them as they passed with sarcasms and ironical plaudits. The rector, who was at the head of his company, received the first volley, which was a sharp one.

"Good morrow, Mr. Rector! Soho! good morrow then!"

"How has he managed to get hither—the old gambler? how could he leave his dice?"

"Ho, there! Mr. Rector Thibaut, how often did you throw double-six last night?"

"How he trots along on his mule! I declare the beast's ears are not so long as his master's!"

"Oh, the cadaverous face—haggard, wrinkled, and wizened, with the love of gaming and dicing!"

Presently it came to the turn of the other dignitaries.

"Down with the bedels! down with the mace-bearers!"

"Robin Poussepin, who is that yonder?"

"It is Gilbert le Suilly, chancellor of the college of Autun."

"Here, take my shoe; you are in a better place than I am; throw it at his head."

"Saturnalitias mittimus ecce nuces."

"Down with these six theologians in their white surplices!"

"Are they the theologians? Why, I took them for the six white geese given by St. Genevieve to the city for the fief of Roogny."

"Down with the physicians!"

"May the devil strangle the proctor of the German nation!"

"And the chaplains of the Holy Chapel, with their gray mices!"

"Ho, there, masters of arts! you in smart black copes, and you in smarter red ones!"

"What a rare tail they make to the rector!"

"You would suppose it was the Doge of Venice going to marry the sea."

Meanwhile, Master Andry Musnier, sworn bookseller to

the university, inclining his lips toward the ear of Master Gilles Lecornu, master-furrier of the king's robes, "I tell you, sir," he whispered, "it is the end of the world. Never were known such excesses of the scholars; it is the cursed inventions of the age that ruin everything—artillery, serpentines, bombards, and, above all, printing, that other pestilence from Germany. No more manuscripts! no more books! Printing is cutting up the bookselling trade. The end of the world is certainly at hand."

"I perceive so," said the master-furrier, "because velvets have become so common."

At this moment the clock struck twelve.

"Aha!" said the whole assembled multitude with one voice. The scholars were mute; and there ensued a prodigious bustle, a general movement of feet and heads, a grand detonation of coughing and handkerchiefs; each individual took his station, and set himself to rights. Profound silence succeeded; every neck was stretched, every mouth open, every eye fixed on the marble table; but nothing was to be seen, save the four sergeants of the bailiff, who still stood there, stiff and motionless as four painted statues. Every face then turned toward the platform reserved for the Flemish ambassadors; the door remained shut, and the platform empty. The crowd had been waiting ever since morning for three things: noon, the Flanders Embassy, and the mystery. Noon alone had been punctual to its time. This was rather too bad.

They waited one, two, three, five minutes, a quarter of an hour; nothing came. Not a creature appeared either on the platform or on the stage. Meanwhile impatience grew into irritation. Angry words were circulated, at first, it is true, in a low tone. "The mystery! the mystery!" was faintly muttered. A storm, which as yet only rumbled at a distance, began to gather over the crowd. It was Jehan du Moulin who drew from it the first spark.

"The mystery, and let the Flemings go to the devil!" shouted he, with all his might, twisting like a snake about his capital. The crowd clapped their hands. "The mystery!" they repeated, "and send Flanders to all the devils!"

"Let us instantly have the mystery," resumed the scholar, "or I recommend that we should hang the bailiff of the palace by way of comedy and morality."

"Well said!" cried the people; "and let us begin with hanging the sergeants!"

Prodigious were the acclamations that followed. The four poor devils turned pale, and began to look at each other. The crowd moved toward them, and they saw the frail wooden balustrade which separated them from the people already bending and giving way to the pressure of the multitude.

The moment was critical. "Down, down with them!" was the cry, which resounded from all sides. At this instant the tapestry of the dressing-room, which we have before described, was thrown open, and forth issued a personage the mere sight of whom suddenly appeased the crowd, and changed, as if by magic, its indignation into curiosity.

"Silence! silence!" was the universal cry.

The personage in question, shaking with fear in every limb, advanced to the edge of the marble table, with a profusion of bows which, the nearer he approached, more and more resembled genuflexions. Meanwhile, tranquillity was pretty well restored; nothing was to be heard but that slight noise which always rises even from a silent crowd.

"Messieurs les bourgeois, and Mesdemoiselles les bourgeoises," said he, "we are to have the honor of declaiming and performing, before his eminence Monsieur the Cardinal, a very goodly morality, called *The Good Judgment of Madam the Virgin Mary*. The part of Jupiter will be enacted by myself. His eminence is at this moment attending the most honorable the embassy of Monsieur the Duke of Austria, which is detained till now to hear the speech of Monsieur the Rector of the university, at the gate of Baudets. The moment his eminence the Cardinal arrives, we shall begin."

It is very certain that nothing but the interposition of Jupiter saved the necks of the four unlucky sergeants of the bailiff of the palace. Had we even the honor of inventing this most true history, and were we in consequence responsible for it before the tribunal of criticism, it is not against us that the classic precept of antiquity, *Nec Deus intersit,* could at this moment be adduced. For the rest, the costume of his godship was very superb, and had contributed not a little to quiet the crowd by engrossing all their attention. He was attired in a brigandine of black velvet with gilt studs; on his head he wore a helmet, adorned with silver gilt buttons; and but for the rouge and the thick beard, which divided his face between them; but for the roll of gilt pasteboard, garnished all over with stripes of tinsel, which he held in his hand, and in which the practiced eye easily recognized the thunderbolt of Jove; but for his flesh-colored legs, and feet sandaled after the Greek fashion; he might have sustained a comparison for his stately port with a Breton archer of the corps of Monsieur de Berry.

2

While he was speaking, however, the universal satisfaction, nay, admiration, excited by his costume, was dispelled by his words; and when he arrived at that unfortunate conclusion, "The moment his eminence the Cardinal arrives, we shall begin," his voice was drowned by the hootings of the multitude.

"The mystery! the mystery! Begin immediately!" shouted the people. And, amid the tempest of voices, was heard that of Joannes de Molendino, which pierced through the uproar like a fife in a band of rough music: "Begin immediately!" screeched the young scholar.

"Down with Jupiter and the Cardinal de Bourbon!" vociferated Robin Poussepain and the other clerks roosted in the window.

"The morality immediately!" repeated the populace; "this instant! or the sack and the cord for the comedians and the Cardinal!"

Poor Jupiter, affrighted, aghast, pale beneath his rouge, dropped his thunderbolt, took off his helmet, and bowed trembling and stammering: "His eminence—the ambassadors—Madame Margaret of Flanders——" He knew not what to say. In good sooth he was afraid of being hanged—hanged by the populace for waiting, hanged by the Cardinal for not waiting; he had the same prospect on either side, that is to say, the gallows. Luckily for him, another person came forward to extricate him from this dilemma, and to assume the responsibility.

An individual who had stationed himself within the balustrade, in the vacant space left around the marble table, and whom no one had yet perceived, so completely was his tall slender figure screened from sight by the diameter of the pillar against which he had been leaning—this individual, tall and slender, as we have said, fair, pale, still young, though his forehead and cheeks were already wrinkled, with sparkling eyes and smiling lips, habited in black serge worn threadbare with age, approached the marble table, and made a sign to the horror-stricken actor, who was too much engrossed to notice him.

He advanced a step farther. "Jupiter!" said he, "my dear Jupiter!" Still the other heard him not. At length, the tall pale, man, losing his patience, called out almost under his very nose, "Michel Giborne!"

"Who calls me?" said Jupiter, starting like one suddenly awakened.

"I," replied the personage in black.

"Aha!" said Jupiter.

"Begin immediately," rejoined the other. "Comply with the wish of the audience. I undertake to pacify Monsieur the bailiff, who will pacify Monsieur the Cardinal."

Jupiter breathed again.

"Gentlemen citizens," cried he, with all the force of his lungs to the crowd who continued to hoot him, "we shall begin forthwith."

"Evoe, Jupiter! Plaudite cives!" shouted the scholars.

"Huzza! huzza!" cried the populace.

A clapping of hands that was absolutely deafening ensued; and, after Jupiter had retired behind his tapestry, the hall still shook with acclamations.

Meanwhile, the unknown personage, who had so magically laid the tempest, had modestly withdrawn into the penumbra of his pillar, where he would no doubt have remained invisible, motionless, and mute as before, but for two young females, who, being in the front rank of the spectators, had remarked his colloquy with Michel Giborne Jupiter.

"Master!" said one of them, beckoning him to come to her.

"Hold your tongue, my dear Lienarde," said her neighbor, a buxom, fresh-colored damsel, gayly attired in her Sunday bravery, "he is not a clerk, but a layman; you must not call him master, but messire."

"Messire!" said Lienarde.

The unknown advanced to the balustrade. "What would you with me, my pretty damsels?" inquired he, eagerly.

"Oh! nothing," said Lienarde, quite confused; "it is my neighbor, Gisquette la Gencienne, who wants to speak to you."

"Not so," replied Gisquette, blushing; "it was Lienarde who called you master, and I told her she must say messire."

The two young females cast down their eyes. The other, who desired nothing better than to engage them in conversation, surveyed them with a smile.

"Then you have nothing to say to me?"

"Oh, dear, no!" answered Gisquette.

"Nothing," said Lienarde.

The tall, fair young man was just retiring, but the two inquisitive girls had no mind to let him go so easily.

"Messire," said Gisquette, with the impetuosity of a sluice that is opened, or of a woman who has taken her resolution, "you must know that soldier who is to play the part of the Virgin Mary in the mystery?"

"You mean the part of Jupiter?" rejoined the unknown.

"Ah, yes!" said Lienarde; "she is stupid, I think. You know Jupiter, then?"

"Michel Giborne?" answered the pale man. "Yes, madam."

"What a goodly beard he has!" said Lienarde.

"Will it be fine—what they are going to say up there?" timidly inquired Gisquette.

"Mighty fine, I assure you," replied the unknown, without the least hesitation.

"What will it be?" said Lienarde.

"The good Judgment of Madam the Virgin, a morality, an't please you, madam."

"Ah! that's a different thing," rejoined Lienarde.

A short silence ensued; it was broken by the unknown informant. "This morality is quite a new piece; it has never been performed."

"Then," said Gisquette, "it is not the same that was given two years ago, at the entry of Monsieur the legate, in which three handsome young girls enacted the parts of——"

"Of sirens," continued Lienarde.

"And quite naked," added the young man.

Lienarde modestly cast down her eyes; Gisquette looked at her and did the same. He then proceeded, with a smile, "That was a pleasant sight enough; this morality today was composed expressly for the Princess of Flanders."

"Will there by any love-songs in it?" asked Gisquette.

"Oh, fie! in a morality!" said the unknown; "they would be inconsistent with the character of the piece. If it were a mummery, well and good."

"What a pity!" exclaimed Gisquette. "On that day there were at the conduit of Ponceau wild men and women who fought together, and put themselves into a great many attitudes, singing little songs all the while."

"What is fit for a legate," dryly replied the unknown, "may not be fit for a princess."

"And near them," resumed Lienarde, "was a band of musicians playing delightful tunes."

"And, for the refreshment of passengers," continued Gisquette, "the conduit threw out wine, milk, and hypocras, at three mouths, for everyone to drink that listed."

"And a little below the Ponceau," proceeded Lienarde, "at the Trinity, the Passion was represented by persons, without speaking."

"If I recollect right," cried Gisquette, "it was Christ on the cross, and the two thieves on the right and left."

Here the young gossips, warming at the recollection of the entry of Monsieur the legate, began to speak both together.

"And farther on, at the Porte aux Peintres, there were other characters magnificently dressed."

"And at the conduit of St. Innocent, a hunter pursuing a doe with a great noise of dogs and horns."

"And then, at the shambles, those scaffolds representing Dieppe!"

"And when the legate passed, you know, Gisquette, how our people attacked it, and all the English had their throats cut."

"And then the superb personages at the Pont au Change, which was covered all over with an awning."

"And as the legate passed, more than two hundred dozen of all sorts of birds were let loose upon the bridge. What a fine sight that was, Lienarde!"

"This will be a finer today," remarked the interlocutor, who seemed to listen to them with impatience.

"You promise us, then, that this mystery will be a very fine one?" said Gisquette.

"Certainly," replied he, adding, with a degree of emphasis, "I made it myself."

"Indeed!" exclaimed the young females in amazement.

"Indeed!" responded the poet, bridling up a little; "that is to say, there are two of us; Jehan Marchand, who sawed the planks and put together the woodwork of the theater, and I, who wrote the piece. My name is Pierre Gringoire."

The author of the Cid could not have said with greater pride, Pierre Corneille.

Our readers may probably have perceived that some time must have elapsed, between the moment when Jupiter disappeared behind the tapestry and that in which the author of the new morality revealed himself so abruptly to the simple admiration of Gisquette and Lienarde. It was an extraordinary circumstance that the crowd, a few minutes before so tumultuous, now waited most meekly on the faith of the comedian; which proves that everlasting truth, confirmed by daily experience in our theaters, that the best way to make the public wait with patience is to affirm that you are just going to begin.

At any rate, the young scholar Joannes did not fall asleep at his post.

"Soho, there!" he shouted all at once, amid the quiet expectation which had succeeded the disturbance. "Jupiter, Madam the Virgin, puppets of the devil, are ye making your game of us? The mystery! the mystery! Begin at once, or look to yourselves."

This was quite enough to produce the desired effect. A band of instruments, high and low, in the interior of the theater, commenced playing; the tapestry was raised, and forth came four persons bepainted and bedecked with various colors, who climbed the rude stage-ladder, and, on reaching the upper platform, drew up in a row before the audience, to whom they paid the usual tribute of low obeisance. The symphony ceased, the mystery commenced.

The performers, having been liberally repaid for their obeisances with applause, began, amid solemn silence on the part of the audience, a prologue, which we gladly spare the reader. On this occasion, as it often happens at the present day, the public bestowed much more attention on the dresses of the performers than on the speeches which they had to deliver; and, to confess the truth, the public were in the right. All four were habited in robes half white and half yellow, which differed in nothing but the nature of the stuff: the first being of gold and silver brocade, the second of silk, the third of woolen, and the fourth of linen. The first of these personages carried a sword in the right hand, the second two gold keys, the third a pair of scales, and the fourth a spade; and, to assist those dull perceptions which might not have seen clearly through the transparency of these attributes, there was embroidered in large black letters at the bottom of the robe of brocade "My name is Nobility"; at the bottom of the silken robe, "My name is Clergy"; at the bottom of the woolen robe, "My name is Trade"; and at the bottom of the linen robe, "My name is Labor." The sex of the two male characters, Clergy and Labor, was sufficiently indicated to every intelligent spectator by the shortness of their robes and the fashion of their caps, while the two females had longer garments and hoods upon their heads. Any person, too, must have been exceedingly perverse or impenetrably obtuse, not to collect from the prologue that Labor was wedded to Trade, and Clergy to Nobility; and that the two happy couples were the joint possessors of a magnificent golden dolphin, which they intended to adjudge to the most beautiful of women. Accordingly, they were traveling through the world in quest of this beauty; and, after successively rejecting the Queen of Golconda, the Princess of Trebizond, the daughter of the great Khan of Tartary, and many others, Labor and Clergy, Nobility and Trade, had come to rest themselves upon the marble table of the Palace of Justice; at the same time bestowing on the honest auditors as many maxims and apophthegms as could in those days have been picked up at the Faculty of Arts, at the examinations, disputations, and acts, at which masters take their caps and their degrees.

A ragged mendicant, who could make nothing by his vocation, lost as he was among the crowd, and who had, probably, not found a sufficient indemnity in the pockets of his neighbors, conceived the idea of perching himself upon some conspicuous point, for the purpose of attracting notice and alms. During the delivery of the prologue, he had accordingly scrambled, by the aid of the pillars of the reserved platform, up to the cornice which ran round it below the balustrade, and there he seated himself silently, soliciting the notice and the pity of the multitude by his rags and a hideous sore which covered his right arm.

The prologue was proceeding without molestation, when, as ill luck would have it, Joannes Frollo, from the top of his pillar, espied the mendicant and his grimaces. An outrageous fit of laughter seized the young wag who, caring little about interrupting the performance and disturbing the profound attention of the audience, merrily cried, "Only look at the rapscallion begging yonder!"

Reader, if you have ever thrown a stone into a pond swarming with frogs, or fired a gun at a covey of birds, you may form some conception of the effect produced by this incongruous exclamation, amid the general silence and attention. Gringoire started as at an electric shock; the prologue stopped short, and every head turned tumultuously toward the mendicant, who, so far from being disconcerted, regarded this incident as a favorable opportunity for making a harvest, and began to drawl out, in doleful tone, and with half-closed eyes, "Charity, if you please!"

"Why, upon my soul," resumed Joannes " 'tis Clopin Trouillefou! Hoho! my fine fellow, you found the wound on your leg in the way and so you've clapped it on your arm, have you?"

As he thus spoke, he threw, with the dexterity of a monkey, a piece of small coin into the greasy hat which the beggar held with his ailing arm. The latter pocketed, without wincing, both the money and the sarcasm, and continued, in a lamentable tone, "Charity, if you please!"

This episode considerably distracted the attention of the audience; and a number of the spectators, with Robin Poussepain and all the clerks at their head, loudly applauded this extempore duet, performed, in the middle of the prologue, by the scholar with his squeaking voice and the mendicant with his monotonous descant.

Gringoire was sorely displeased. On recovering from his first stupefaction, he bawled out lustily to the four actors on the stage, "Why the devil do ye stop? Go on! go on!" without even condescending to cast a look of disdain at the two interrupters.

At this moment he felt a twitch at the skirt of his surtout; he turned round in an ill humor, and had some difficulty to raise a smile, which, however, he could not suppress. It was the plump, handsome arm of Gisquette la Gencienne, thrust through the balustrade, which thus solicited his attention.

"Sir," said the damsel, "will they go on with the mystery?"

"Most certainly," replied Gringoire, not a little shocked at the question.

"In that case, messire," she resumed, "will you have the courtesy to explain to me—"

"What they are going to say?" asked Gringoire, interrupting her. "Well, listen."

"No," rejoined Gisquette, "but what they have been saying so far."

Gringoire started like a person with a wound which you have touched in the quick.

"A plague on the stupid wench!" muttered he, between his teeth.

Gisquette had completely ruined herself in his good opinion.

The actors had, meanwhile, obeyed his injunction; and the public, seeing that they had resumed the performance, began again to listen, but not without losing a great many beauties, from the abrupt division of the piece into two parts, and the species of soldering which they had to undergo. Such, at least, was the painful reflection mentally made by Gringoire. Tranquillity, however, was gradually restored; the scholar held his tongue, the beggar counted

the money in his hat, and the piece proceeded swimmingly.

It was, in truth, a masterly work; and we verily believe
that managers might avail themselves of it at the present
day, with some modifications. The plot was simple; and
Gringoire, in the candid sanctuary of his own bosom, admired its clearness. As the reader may easily conceive, the
four allegorical characters were somewhat fatigued with
their tour through the three parts of the world, without finding an opportunity of disposing, agreeably to their intentions, of their golden dolphin. Thereupon followed a
panegyric on the marvelous fish, with a thousand delicate
allusions to the young bridegroom of Margaret of Flanders,
at that moment sadly shut up at Amboise, and never dreaming that Labor and Clergy, Nobility and Trade, had been
making a tour of the world on his account. The said dolphin, then, was young, handsome, bold, and, above all—
magnificent origin of every royal virtue!—the son of the
lion of France. I declare that this bold metaphor is truly admirable; and that the natural history of the theater is not at
all startled, on an occasion of this kind, at a dolphin, the offspring of a lion. It is precisely those out-of-the-way and Pin-
daric medleys that are evidences of enthusiasm. Critical
justice, nevertheless, requires the admission that the poet
ought to have developed this original idea in somewhat less
than the compass of two hundred verses. It is true that the
mystery was to last from the hour of twelve till that of four,
according to the ordinance of Monsieur the Provost, and
that it was absolutely necessary to say something or other.
Besides, the audience listened very patiently.

All at once, in the midst of a quarrel between Mademoiselle Trade and Madame Nobility, at the moment when
Master Labor was delivering this emphatic line:

"More stately beast was ne'er in forest seen,"

the door of the reserved platform, which had hitherto remained so unseasonably closed, was still more unseason-

ably thrown open, and the sonorous voice of the usher abruptly announced, "His Eminence Monseigneur the Cardinal of Bourbon."

3

Poor Gringoire! the noise of all the big double petards at St. John's, the discharge of a hundred matchlocks, the detonation of that famous serpentine of the Tower of Billy, which, at the siege of Paris, on September 29, 1465, killed seven Burgundians by one shot, nay the explosion of all the gunpowder in the magazine at the gate of the Temple, would not have so shocked his ears at that solemn and dramatic moment as these few words from the lips of an usher: "His Eminence Monseigneur the Cardinal of Bourbon."

Not that Pierre Gringoire either feared or disdained Monsieur the Cardinal; he had neither that weakness nor that arrogance.

There was then, neither hatred of the Cardinal nor disdain of his presence in the disagreeable impression which it made on Pierre Gringoire. On the contrary, our poet had too much good sense, and too threadbare a frock, not to feel particularly anxious that many an allusion in his prologue, and particularly the eulogy on the dolphin, the son of the lion of France, should find its way to the ear of a most eminent personage. But it is not interest that predominates in the noble nature of poets. Supposing the entity of the poet to be represented by the number 10; it is certain that a chemist, on analyzing it, would find it to be composed of one part interest and nine parts vanity. Now, at the moment when the door opened for the Cardinal, the

nine parts of Gringoire's vanity, swollen and inflated by
the breath of popular admiration, were in a state of such
prodigious enlargement as completely to smother that imperceptible particle of interest which we must now discover in the constitution of poets; a most valuable
ingredient, nevertheless, the ballast of reality and of humanity, without which they would never descend to this
lower world. Gringoire was delighted to see, to feel, in
some measure, a whole assembly of varlets, it is true—but
what does that signify?—stupefied, petrified, and stricken
as it were insensible, by the immeasurable speeches which
succeed each other in every part of his epithalamium. I affirm that he participated in the general happiness, and that,
unlike La Fontaine, who, on the first representation of his
comedy of "The Florentine," inquired, "What paltry scrib-
bler wrote this rhapsody?" Gringoire would gladly have
asked his neighbor, "Who is the author of this masterpiece?" Now imagine what must have been the effect produced upon him by the abrupt and unseasonable arrival of
the Cardinal.

What he had reason to apprehend was but too soon re-
alized. The entry of his Eminence upset the auditory. All
heads turned mechanically toward the platform. Not another word was to be heard. "The Cardinal! the Cardinal!"
was upon every tongue. The unlucky prologue was cut
short a second time.

The Cardinal paused for a moment on the threshold of
the platform, with supercilious looks surveying the auditory. Meanwhile the tumult increased; each striving to
raise his head above his neighbor's to obtain a better view
of his Eminence.

He entered, therefore, bowed to the audience with that
hereditary smile which the great have for the people, and
proceeded slowly toward his armchair covered with scarlet
velvet, apparently thinking of something very different
from the scene before him. His train, which we should
nowadays call his staff, of abbots and bishops, followed
him as he advanced to the front of the platform, to the no

small increase of the tumult and curiosity of the spectators. Each was eager to point them out, to tell their names, to recognize at least one of them—Monsieur the Bishop of Marseilles, Alaudet, if I recollect rightly; or the Dean of St. Denis; or the Abbot of St. Germain des Pres, that libertine brother of one of the mistresses of Louis XI; but, as it may be supposed, with abundance of blunders and mistakes. As for the scholars, they swore lustily. It was their day, their feast of fools, their saturnalia, the annual orgies of the Baoche* and of the schools. There was no turpitude but was authorized on that day. Was it not then the least they could do to swear at their ease, and to curse a little in the name of God, on so fine a day, in the company of churchmen and lewd women? Accordingly they made good use of the license, and amid the general uproar, horrible was the clamor of the blasphemies and enormities proceeding from the tongues of clerks and scholars, restrained during the rest of the year by the fear of the red-hot iron of St. Louis. Poor St. Louis! how they set him at naught in his own Palace of Justice! Each of them had fixed upon a black, gray, white, or purple cassock for his butt among the new occupants of the platform. As for Joannes Frollo de Mollendino, he as brother of an archdeacon, boldly attacked the scarlet; and, fixing his audacious eyes on the Cardinal, he sang at the top of his voice, *Cappa repleta mero.*

All these circumstances, which we here reveal for the edification of the reader, were so smothered by the general tumult as to pass unnoticed by the reverend party on the platform; had it, indeed, been otherwise, the Cardinal would not have heeded them, so deeply were the liberties of the day engrafted on the manners of the age. He was, moreover, wholly preoccupied—and his countenance showed it—by another solicitude, which pursued him, and, indeed, entered the platform almost at the same time with him, namely, the Flanders Embassy.

*The company of clerks of the parliament of Paris.

He turned, therefore, toward the door, and with the best grace in the world—so well had he studied his part—when the usher, with his sonorous voice, announced Messieurs the Envoys of Monsieur the Duke of Austria. It is scarcely necessary to remark that all the spectators did the same.

The forty-eight ambassadors of Maximilian, of Austria, headed by the reverend father in God, Jehan, Abbot of St. Bertin, Chancellor of the Golden Fleece, and Jacques de Goy, Sieur Dauby, High-bailiff of Ghent, then entered two and two, with a gravity which formed a remarkable contrast amid the volatile ecclesiastical retinue of Charles of Bourbon. Deep silence pervaded the assembly, broken only by stifled laughter at the mention of the uncouth names and all the petty titles which each of these personages repeated with imperturbable solemnity to the usher, who then flung them, names and qualities pell-mell and cruelly mangled, among the crowd. There was Master Loys Roelo, echevin of the city of Louvain; Messire Clays d'Etuelde, echevin of Brussels; Messire Paul de Baeust, Sieur de Vormizelle, President of Flanders; Master Jehan Coleghens, burgomaster of the city of Antwerp; Master George de la Moere, and Master Gheldolf van der Hage, echevins of the city of Ghent; and the Sieur de Bierbecque, Jehan Phinnock, Jehan Dymaerzelle, etc., bailiffs, echevins, burgomsters; all stiff, starched, formal, tricked out in velvets and damasks, and ensconced in caps of black velvet with prodigious tassels of Cyprus gold thread; fine Flemish heads after all, with austere but goodly faces, of the same family as those which Rembrandt has brought out, so grave and so expressive, from the dark ground of his nightpiece; personages who all had it written on their brows that Maximilian of Austria had good reason "to place full confidence," as his manifesto declared, "in their discretion, firmness, experience, loyalty, and rare qualities."

There was, however, one exception. This was a sharp, intelligent, crafty looking face, a physiognomy compounded of that of the monkey and the diplomatist, toward

the owner of which the Cardinal advanced three steps with
a low bow, and whose name, nevertheless, was plain
Guillaume Rym, councilor and pensionary of the city of
Ghent.

Few persons there knew who this Guillaume Rym was.
He was a man of rare genius, who in times of revolution
would have raised himself to distinction, but was forced in
the fifteenth century to resort to the hollow ways of in-
trigue, and to live in the saps, as saith the Duke of St. Simon. For the rest, he was duly appreciated by the first
sapper in Europe; he wrought in familiar concert with
Louis XI, and frequently lent a helping hand to the king in
his secret necessities—circumstances absolutely unknown
to the crowd, who marveled at the respect paid by the Cardinal to so insignificant a person as the Flemish bailiff.

4

While the pensionary of Ghent and his Eminence were
exchanging a low obeisance and a few words in a
still lower tone, a man of lofty stature, with jolly face and
broad shoulders, stepped forward for the purpose of entering abreast with Guillaume Rym; they looked for all the
world like a bulldog beside a fox. His felt cap and leathern
vest were conspicuous amid the velvets and silks which
surrounded him. Presuming that he was some groom, who
had mistaken the way, the usher stopped him.

"No admittance here, my friend," said he.

The man in the leathern vest pushed him back.

"What means the fellow?" cried he, in a voice which
drew the attention of the whole hall to this strange colloquy. "Dost not see that I belong to them?"

"Your name?" asked the usher.

"Jacques Coppenole."

"Your quality?"

"Hosier; at the sign of the Three Chains in Ghent."

The usher was staggered. To have to announce bailiffs, and burgomasters, and echevins, was bad enough; but a hosier!—no—he could not make up his mind to that. The Cardinal was upon thorns. The whole assembly was all eye and ear. For two days his Eminence had been taking pains to lick these Flemish bears, in order to make them a little more producible in public, and his failure was galling. Meanwhile, Guillaume Rym, with his sly smile, stepped up to the usher, and, said in a very low whisper: "Announce Master Jacques Coppenole, clerk to the echevins of the city of Ghent."

"Usher," said the Cardinal, in a loud tone, "announce Master Jacques Coppenole, clerk to the echevins of the most noble city of Ghent."

Now it is very certain that Guillaume Rym, had he been left to himself, would have shuffled off the difficulty, but Coppenole had heard the Cardinal.

"No, by the rood!" cried he, with his voice of thunder, "Jacques Coppenole, hosier. Hark ye, ushers, neither more nor less. By the rood! hosier—that's quite enough! Monsieur the Archduke has more than once sought his gloves among my hose."

A burst of laughter and applause ensued. A witticism or a pun is instantly comprehended at Paris, and consequently sure to be applauded. Coppenole, be it moreover observed, was one of the people, and the assembly by which he was surrounded belonged to the same class.

Coppenole bowed haughtily to the Cardinal, who returned the obeisance of the high and mighty burgher, dreaded by Louis XI. Then, while Guillaume Rym, a "cunning man and spiteful," as saith Philip de Comines, looked after both with a smile of conscious superiority, they proceeded to their places—the Cardinal mortified and disconcerted; Coppenole, calm and proud, thinking, no doubt, that his title of hosier was as good as any other, and that

Mary of Burgundy, the mother of that Margaret whose marriage Coppenole had come to negotiate, would have felt less dread of him as a cardinal than as a hosier; for it was not a cardinal who would have raised the people of Ghent against the favorites of the daughter of Charles the Bold; it was not a cardinal who would have steeled the multitude by a word against her tears and her entreaties, when the Princess of Flanders proceeded to the very foot of the scaffold to beg their lives of her subjects; while the hosier had but to lift his finger and off went your heads, ye most illustrious gentlemen, Guy d'Hymbercourt, and Chancellor William Hugonet!

The poor Cardinal's probation, however, was not yet over; he was doomed to drink to the very dregs the cup of penance for being in such company. The reader has, perhaps, not forgotten the impudent beggar, who at the commencement of the prologue perched himself beneath the fringe of the Cardinal's gallery. The arrival of the illustrious guests had not dislodged him from his roost, and while the prelates and ambassadors were packing themselves, like real Flemish herrings, in the boxes of the gallery, he had placed himself at his ease, and carelessly crossed his legs over the architrave. Nobody, however, had at first noticed this extraordinary piece of insolence, the universal attention being directed to another quarter. Neither was he, on his part, aware of what was going forward in the hall; there he sat, rocking to and fro with the utmost unconcern, repeating as from mechanical habit, the ditty of "Charity, if you please!" To a certainty he was the only one in the whole assembly who had not deigned to turn his head at the altercation between Coppenole and the usher. Now, as luck would have it, the hosier of Ghent, with whom the people already sympathized so strongly and on whom all eyes were fixed, took his seat in the first row in the gallery, just above the mendicant. Great was, nevertheless, their astonishment, at seeing the Flemish ambassador, after taking a survey of the fellow nestled under his nose, slap him familiarly on the shoulder covered with tatters. The mendicant turned sharply round; surprise, recognition, pleasure, were expressed in both faces; and then, without caring a pinch of snuff for the spectators, the hosier and the scurvy rogue shook hands, and began to talk in a low tone, while the rags of Clopin Trouillefou, clapped against the cloth of gold with which the gallery was hung, produced the effect of a caterpillar upon an orange.

The novelty of this singular scene excited such a burst of merriment in the hall, that the Cardinal could not help noticing it; he leaned forward, and as, from the place where he sat, he had but a very imperfect view of the squalid figure of Trouillefou, he naturally supposed that he was soliciting alms; incensed at his audacity, he cried: "Mr. Bailiff of the Palace, throw me that varlet into the river."

"Cross of God! Monsigneur the Cardinal!" exclaimed Coppenole, "that varlet is a friend of mine."

"Huzza! huzza!" shouted the crowd. From that moment, Master Coppenole had "great influence over the populace at Paris, as well as at Ghent; for," adds Philip de Comines, "men of that kidney are sure to have it, when they are so beyond measure disorderly."

The Cardinal bit his lips. Turning to his neighbor, the Abbot of St. Genevieve, he said, in an undertone, "Right pleasant ambassadors these, sent to us by Monsieur the Archduke to announce Madame Margaret!"

"Your Eminence," replied the abbot, "is throwing away your civilities upon these Flemish hogs; *margaritas ante porcos.*"

"Say rather," answered the Cardinal with a smile, *"porcos ante Margaritam."*

The whole petty cassocked court was in raptures at this sally. The Cardinal felt somewhat relieved; he was now quits with Coppenole; he too had gained applause for his pun.

From the moment that the Cardinal entered, Gringoire had not ceased to bestir himself for the salvation of his prologue. At first he enjoined the actors, who were in a state of suspense, to proceed and to raise their voices; then, perceiving that nobody listened to them, he ordered them to stop; and for the quarter of an hour that the interruption had lasted he had been incessantly bustling about, calling upon Gisquette and Lienarde to encourage their neighbors to call for the continuation of the prologue—but all in vain. Not a creature would turn away from the Cardinal, the embassy, and the gallery, the sole center of that vast circle of visual rays. There is also reason to believe, and we record it with regret, that the audience was beginning to be somewhat tired of the prologue, at the moment when his Eminence arrived and made such a terrible diversion. After all, the gallery exhibited precisely the same spectacle as the marble table—the conflict between Labor and Clergy, Nobility and Trade. And many people liked much better to see them without disguise, living, breathing, acting, elbowing one another, in the Flemish Embassy, in that episcopal court, under the Cardinal's robe, under the vest of Coppenole, than talking in verse, painted, tricked out, resembling effigies of straw stuffed into the yellow and white tunics in which Gringoire had enwrapped them.

When, however, our poet perceived that some degree of tranquillity was restored, he devised a stratagem for regaining the public attention.

"Sir," said he, turning to a jolly citizen, whose face was the image of patience, "don't you think they had better go on?"

"With what?" asked another.

"Why, with the mystery," replied Gringoire.

"Just as you please," rejoined his neighbor.

This demi-approbation was quite enough for Gringoire. Mingling as much as possible with the crowd he began to shout with all his might: "The mystery! the mystery! go on with the mystery!"

"The devil!" said Joannes de Molendino; "what is it they are singing down yonder?" (Gringoire was, in fact, making as much noise as half a dozen persons.) "I say, comrades, the mystery is over, is it not? They want to begin it again; we'll not suffer that."

"No, no," cried all the scholars. "Down with the mystery! down with it!"

This only served to redouble Gringoire's activity, and he bawled louder than ever, "Go on! go on!"

This clamor drew the attention of the Cardinal.

"Mr. Bailiff of the Palace," said he to a stout man in black, stationed a few paces from him, "are those knaves in a holy water font, that they make such an infernal racket?"

The Bailiff of the Palace was a sort of amphibious magistrate, a kind of bat of the judicial order, something between the rat and the bird, the judge and the soldier.

He stepped up to his Eminence, and sorely dreading his anger, he explained to him, with faltering tongue, the popular inconsistency, how that noon had arrived before his Eminence, and that the comedians had been forced to begin without waiting for him.

The Cardinal laughed outright. "By my faith!" he exclaimed; "the rector of the university should have done the same. What say you, Master Guillaume Rym?"

"Monseigneur," answered Master Guillaume Rym, "we ought to be glad that we have escaped half of the play. The loss is so much gained."

"May those fellows continue their farce?" asked the bailiff.

"Go on, go on," said the Cardinal; " 'tis the same to me."

The bailiff advanced to the front of the gallery, and enjoined silence by a motion of his hand. "Burgesses and inhabitants," he cried, "to satisfy those who wish the piece to proceed, and those who are desirous that it should finish, his Eminence orders it to be continued."

The characters on the stage resumed their cue, and Gringoire hoped that at any rate the rest of his piece would be heard out. This hope, however, was destined, like his other illusions, to be very soon blasted. Silence was, indeed, in some degree restored among the audience, but Gringoire had not observed that, at the moment when the Cardinal ordered the mystery to be continued, the gallery was far from full, and that, after the Flemish Envoys had taken their seats, other persons forming part of the train kept coming in, and the names and qualities of these, proclaimed every now and then by the bawling voice of the usher, broke in upon his dialogue and made great havoc with it. Gringoire was the more incensed at this strange accompaniment, which rendered it difficult to follow the piece, because he felt that the interest increased as it proceeded, and that his work needed nothing but to be heard. Indeed, a more ingenious and more dramatic plot could scarcely be invented. The four characters of the prologue were bewailing their mortal embarrassment, when Venus appeared to them in person, attired in a robe embroidered with the arms of the city of Paris. She came to prefer her claim to the dolphin promised to the most beautiful female; it was supported by Jupiter, whose thunder was heard rumbling in the dressing-room, and the goddess had well-nigh carried her point, that is to say, without metaphor, established her right to the hand of Monsieur the Dauphin, when a child, in a dress of white damask, and holding a daisy—diaphanous personification of the Princess of Flanders—entered the lists against Venus. This unexpected incident produced an instant change in the state of affairs. After some controversy, Venus, Margaret, and the whole party, agreed to refer the matter to the decision of the Holy Virgin. There was another striking part, that of Don Pedro, King of Mesopotomia; but owing to so many interruptions it was difficult to discover its connection with the plot of the piece.

All these beauties were unfortunately neither appreciated nor understood. The moment the Cardinal entered, it was as if an invisible and magic thread had suddenly drawn all eyes from the marble table to the gallery, from the southern extremity to the west side of the hall.

What would he not have given for the return of that delicious moment!

The brutal monologue of the usher ceased at last; all the company had arrived; Gringoire breathed once more, and the actors proceeded with spirit. All at once, what should Master Coppenole the hosier do, but rise from his seat? Gringoire stood aghast to hear him, amid the breathless attention of the spectators, commence this abominable harangue:

"Gentlemen, burgesses and yeomen of Paris, I know not, by the rood, what we are about here. Down there, on yonder stage, I see some mountebanks, who appear disposed to fight. I cannot tell whether this is what you call a mystery; let it be what it will, it is not amusing; they bang one another with their tongues, and that is all. Here have I been waiting this quarter of an hour for the first blow; but nothing comes of it; they are cravens only who clapperclaw each other with abuse. You should have sent to London or Rotterdam for bruisers, and, by my faith! you would have had thumps which you would have heard all over the place; but these paillars are contemptible. They might have given us at least a morris-dance or some other mummery. To be sure nothing was said about that; they promised me that I should see the festival of fools and the election of pope. We have our pope of fools at Ghent too, and, by the rood, in this respect we are not behind your famous city. But the way we do is this—we collect a crowd, such as there is here; then every one that likes puts his head in turn through a hole, and grins at the others, and he who makes the ugliest face is chosen pope by acclammation—that's it. 'Tis a diverting sight, I assure you. Shall we choose your pope after the fashion of my country? 'Twill be more amusing at any rate than listening to those praters. If they like to come and grin through the hole, why, let them. What say you, gentlemen burgesses? We have here a sufficiently grotesque specimen of both sexes to raise a hearty laugh in the Flemish fashion; and we have ugly faces enough among us to expect a capital grimace."

Gringoire would fain have replied, but horror, indignation, stupefaction, deprived him of utterance. Besides, the motion of the popular hosier was hailed with such enthusiasm by the citizens, flattered with the appellation of yeomen, that resistance would have been useless. All that he could now do was to resign himself to the stream.

5

In the twinkling of an eye, everything was ready for carrying into effect the idea of Coppenole. Burgesses, scholars, and lawyers' clerks had fallen to work. The little chapel opposite to the marble table was chosen for the scene of the grimaces. Having broken the glass in the pretty little round window over the door, they agreed that the competitors should put their heads through the circle of stone that was left. To enable them to reach it, two hogsheads were brought and set one upon another. It was determined that all candidates, whether men or women—for females were eligible—should hide their faces, and keep them covered in the chapel till the moment of exhibiting them, that the impression of the grimace might be the stronger. In a few minutes the chapel was full of competitors, and the door was shut upon them.

Coppenole, from his place, ordered, directed, superintended all the arrangements. During the uproar, the Cardinal, not less disconcerted than Gringoire, having excused himself on the plea of business and vespers, retired with his retinue; while the crowd, which his coming had so strongly agitated, was scarcely aware of his departure. Guillaume Rym was the only person that noticed the discomposure of his Eminence. The popular attention, like the sun, pursued its revolution; setting out from one end of the hall, after pausing some time in the middle, it was now at the other extremity. The marble table, the brocaded gallery, has each had their moment; it was now the turn of Louis XI's chapel. The field was open to every species of fun; the Flemings and the populace alone were left.

The grimaces began. The first face that presented itself at the window, with its red eyes and wildly gaping mouth, and forehead puckered up in wrinkles, like hussar boots in the time of the emperor, caused such convulsions of inextinguishable laughter, that Homer would have taken these ruffians for immortal gods. A second and a third grimace succeeded—then another and another, followed by redoubled shouts of laughter and the stampings and chatterings of merriment. The crowd was seized with a sort of frantic intoxication, a supernatural kind of fascination, of which it would be difficult to convey any idea to the reader of our own days. Imagine a series of visages successively presenting every geometric figure, from the triangle to the trapezium—from the cone to the polyhedron—every human expression, from rage to lechery; all ages, from the wrinkles of the newborn infant to those of the hag at the point of death; all the religious phantasmagorias from Faunus to Beelzebub; all the brute profiles from the distended jaw to the beak, from the snout of the hog to the muzzle of the bull. Imagine all the grotesque heads of the Pont Neuf, those nightmares petrified under the hand of Germain Pilon, suddenly starting into life, and coming one after another to stare you in the face with flaming eyes; all the masks of the carnival of Venice passing in succession before your eye-glass—in a word, a human kaleidoscope.

The orgies became more and more uproarious. Teniers could have given but an imperfect idea of the scene. Fancy Salvator Rosa's battle turned into a bacchanalian piece. There was no longer any distinction of ranks and persons—no longer scholars, ambassadors, men, or women—all were lost in the general license. The great hall was one vast furnace of effrontery and jollity; where every mouth was a cry, every eye a flash, every face a contortion, every individual a posture; all was howling and roaring. The extraordinary faces which in turn presented themselves at the window acted like so many brands thrown upon a blazing fire; and from all this effervescent crowd issued, like vapor from a furnace, a sharp, shrill, hissing noise, as from an immense serpent.

Meanwhile Gringoire, the first moment of dejection over, had recovered his spirits; he had braced himself against adversity. "Go on!" said he for the third time to his speaking machines, the comedians, and then paced to and fro, with long strides, before the marble table. He almost felt tempted to exhibit himself in his turn at the round window of the chapel, were it but to enjoy the pleasure of grinning at the ungrateful populace. But no, said he, mentally, no revenge! that were unworthy of us. Let us struggle manfully to the last—the power of poesy is mighty over the populace—I will bring them back. We shall see which will conquer—the grimaces or the belles lettres.

Alas, poor Gringoire! he was left to be the only spectator of his play—every back was turned upon him.

I am wrong; the fat, patient man whom he had previously consulted in a critical moment was still turned toward the theater. As for Gisquette and Lienarde, they had long since deserted.

Gringoire was touched to the bottom of his heart by the constancy of his only spectator. He went up and spoke to him, at the same time gently shaking his arm; for the good man was leaning upon the balustrade and napping a little.

"Sir," said Gringoire, "I am exceedingly obliged to you."

"Sir," replied the fat man, with a yawn, "for what?"

"I see," rejoined the poet, "that you are quite annoyed by all this uproar, which prevents your hearing comfortably. But never mind; your name will be handed down to posterity; may I ask what it is?"

"Renauld Chateau, keeper of the seal of the Chatelet of Paris, at your service."

"Sir, you are the only representative of the muses in this assembly," said Gringoire.

"You are too polite, sir," replied the keeper of the seal of the Chatelet.

"You are the only one," resumed Gringoire, "who has paid any attention to the piece. What do you think of it?"

"Why, to tell the truth," answered the pursy magistrate, only half awake, "it is stupid enough."

Gringoire was forced to be content with this opinion; for thunders of applause, mingled with prodigious shouts, cut short their conversation. The Pope of Fools was elected. "Huzza! huzza! huzza!" cried the people on all sides.

It was in truth a countenance of miraculous ugliness which at this moment shone forth from the circular aperture. After all the faces, pentagonal, hexagonal, and heteroclite, that followed each other at this window, without realizing the idea of the grotesque which the crowd had set up in their frantic imaginations, it required nothing short of the sublimely monstrous grimace which had just dazzled the multitude to obtain their suffrages. Master Coppenole himself applauded; and Clopin Trouillefou, which had been a candidate—and God knows what intensity of ugliness his features could attain—confessed himself conquered. We shall do the same; we shall not attempt to give the reader any idea of that tetrahedron nose, of that horseshoe mouth, of that little left eye, stubbled up with an eyebrow of carroty bristles, while the right was completely overwhelmed and buried by an enormous wen; of those irregular teeth, jagged here and there like the battlements of a fortress; of that horny lip, over which one of those teeth protruded, like the tusk of an elephant; of that forked chin; and above all, of that mixed expression of spite, wonder, and melancholy spread over these exquisite features. Imagine such an object, if you can. The acclamation was unanimous; the crowd rushed to the chapel. The lucky Pope of Fools was brought out in triumph, and it was not till then that surprise and admiration were at their height; what had been mistaken for a grimace was his natural visage; indeed, it might be said that his whole person was but one grimace. His prodigious head was covered with red bristles; between his shoulders rose an enormous hump, which was counterbalanced by a protuberance in front; his thighs and legs were so strangely put together, that they touched at no one point but the knees, and, seen in front, resembled two sickles joined at the handles; his feet were immense, his hands monstrous; but with all this deformity, there was a formidable air of strength, agility and courage, constituting a singular exception to the eternal rule, which ordains that force, as well as beauty, shall result from harmony. He looked like a giant who had been broken in pieces and ill-soldered together.

When this sort of Cyclop appeared on the threshold of the chapel, motionless, squat, almost as broad as high, "the square of his base," as a great man expresses it, the populace instantly recognized him by his coat, half red and half purple, sprinkled with silver bells, and more especially by the perfection of his ugliness, and cried out with one voice—"It is Quasimodo, the bell-ringer! it is Quasimodo, the hunchback of Notre Dame! Quasimodo, the one-eyed! Quasimodo, the bandy-legged! Hurrah! hurrah!" The poor devil, it seems, had plenty of surnames to choose from.

"Let breeding women take care of themselves!" cried the scholars. The women actually covered their faces.

"Oh, the ugly ape!" cried one.

"And as mischievous as ugly," said another.

" 'Tis the devil himself!" exclaimed a third.

"I am so unlucky as to live near Notre Dame, and I hear him at night prowling about in the gutters."

"What! with the cats?"

"He is always on our roofs."

"The other night he came and grinned at me through my garret window. I thought it was a man; I was dreadfully frightened."

"I am sure he attends the witches' sabbath. He once left a broom on my leads."

"Oh, the ugly hunchback!"

"Faugh!"

The men, on the contrary, were delighted. There was no end to their applause. Quasimodo, the object of all the tumult, was still standing at the door of the chapel, gloomy and grave, exhibiting himself to the popular admiration, when Robin Poussepain came up close to him and laughed him in the face. Quasimodo, without uttering a word, caught him up by the waist, and hurled him to the distance of ten paces among the crowd.

Master Coppenole, astonished at the feat, approached him. "Cross of God!" he exclaimed. "Holy Father! why thou art the finest piece of ugliness I ever beheld. Thou deservest to be Pope at Rome as well as at Paris."

As he thus spoke, he sportively clapped his hand on the monster's shoulder. Quasimodo did not stir. Coppenole continued, "My fine fellow, I should like to have a tussle with thee, were it to cost me a new douzain of twelve tournois. What sayest thou?"

Quasimodo made no reply. "Cross of God!" cried the hosier, "art thou deaf?" Quasimodo really was deaf.

Presently, beginning to feel annoyed by Coppenole's manner, he turned suddenly toward him with so formidable a grin that the Flemish giant recoiled, like a bulldog from a cat. A circle of terror and respect, having a radius of at least fifteen geometric paces, was left vacant around this strange personage.

An old woman informed Coppenole that Quasimodo was deaf.

"Deaf!" cried the hosier, with a Flemish horse-laugh. "By the rood! he is an accomplished pope!"

"Ha!" said Jehan, who had at length descended from his pillar to obtain a closer view of the new pope; " 'tis my brother's bell-ringer! Good-morrow, Quasimodo!"

"A devil of a fellow!" sighed Robin Poussepain, aching all over from the effects of his fall. "He appears—he is hunchbacked. He walks—he is bandy-legged. He looks at you—he is one-eyed. You talk to him—he is deaf! And what use does this Polyphemus make of his tongue, I wonder?"

"He can talk when he likes," said the old woman. "He became deaf with ringing the bells. He is not dumb."

"He wants that qualification," observed Jehan.

"And he has an eye too much," added Robin Poussepain.

"Not so," rejoined Jehan, tartly; "a one-eyed man is more incomplete than one who is quite blind."

Meanwhile all the mendicants, all the lackeys, all the cut-purses, together with the scholars, went in procession to the storeroom of the Bazoche to fetch the pasteboard tiara and the mock robe of the Pope of Fools. Quasimodo suffered them to be put upon him with a kind of proud docility. He was then required to sit down on a party-colored litter. Twelve coiffers of the fraternity of fools hoisted it upon their shoulders; and a sort of disdainful exultation overspread the morose countenance of the Cyclop, when he saw beneath his feet all those heads of straight, handsome, well-shaped men. The roaring and ragged procession then moved off, to pass, according to custom, through the galleries in the interior of the palace before it paraded the streets and public places of the city.

6

We have great satisfaction in apprising the reader that during the whole of this scene, Gringoire and his play had maintained their ground. His actors, egged on by him, had continued the performance of his comedy, and he had continued to listen to them. In spite of the uproar, he

was determined to go through with it, not despairing of
being able to recall the attention of the public. This glim-
mer of hope became brighter when he saw Quasimodo,
Coppenole, and the obstreperous retinue of the Pope of
Fools, leaving the hall. The crowd rushed out after them.
"Excellent!" said he; "we shall get rid of all those trouble-
some knaves." Unluckily these were the whole assembly.
In the twinkling of an eye the great hall was empty.

To tell the truth, a few spectators still lingered behind,
some dispersed, others in groups around the pillars, old
men, women, or children, who had had enough of the uproar and tumult. Some of the scholars, too, remained,
astride of the entablature of the windows, where they had
a good view of the place.

Well, thought Gringoire, there are quite as many as I
want to hear the conclusion of my mystery. Their number,
indeed, is but small; but they are a select, a lettered audience.

At that moment a symphony, destined to produce a
striking effect at the arrival of the Holy Virgin, was not
forthcoming. Gringoire perceived that his musicians had
been pressed into the service of the procession of the Pope
of Fools. "Skip that," said he, with the composure of a
stoic.

He approached a knot of citizens who seemed to be
talking about his play. The fragment of their conversation
which he overheard was as follows:

"Master Chenteau, you know the hotel de Navarre,
which belonged to Monsieur de Nemours?"

"Yes; opposite to the chapel of Braque."

"Well! the exchequer has just leased it to Guillaume
Alexandre, the history writer, for six livres eight sols
parisis per annum."

"How rents are rising!"

"Bah!" ejaculated Gringoire, with a sigh—"the others
are listening at any rate."

"Comrades," all at once shouted one of the young

scape-graces in the windows, "La Esmeralda! La Esmeralda in the Place!"

This intimation produced a magic effect. All who were left in the hall ran to the windows, clambering up the walls to obtain a sight, and repeating—"La Esmeralda! La Esmeralda!" Thunders of applause arose at the same time from the Place.

"What can they mean by La Esmeralda?" said Gringoire, clasping his hands in despair. "Gracious heaven! It seems to have come to the turn of the windows now!"

Turning toward the marble table he perceived that the performance was at a stand. It was precisely the moment when Jupiter was should have appeared with his thunderbolt; but Jupiter was standing stock-still at the foot of the stage.

"Michel Giborne!" cried the incensed poet, "mind thy business! What art thou doing? make haste up!"

"Alas!" replied Jupiter, "one of the scholars has run away with the ladder."

Gringoire looked; it was even so. The communication with the stage was completely cut off. "The varlet!" murmured he. "And why did he take the ladder?"

"To go and see La Esmeralda," answered Jupiter, in a doleful tone. " 'Stay,' said he, 'here's a ladder that's of no use,'' and off he scampered with it.' "

This was the final blow. Gringoire received it with resignation.

"The devil fetch you!" said he to the performers. "If I am paid you shall be."

With downcast looks he then made his retreat, but not till the very last, like a general who has been soundly beaten. "A pretty pack of asses and boobies, these Parisians!" he muttered between his teeth, as he descended the winding staircase of the palace. "They come to hear a mystery, and will not listen to it. They will pay attention to everything and everybody—to Clopin Trouillefou, to the Cardinal, to Coppenole, to Quasimodo, to the devil! but on the Holy Virgin they have none to bestow. Had I

known, ye gaping ouphs, I should have given you Virgin
Maries, I warrant me! Turn your backs on such a piece!
Homer, it is true, begged his bread in the Greek towns;
and Naso died in exile among the Moscovites. But the
devil flay me if I comprehend what they mean by their La
Esmeralda. And what kind of word is it to begin with? It
must surely be Egyptian!"

7

Night comes early in the month of January. It was already dusk when Gringoire left the palace. To him the
nightfall was doubly welcome, as he proposed seeking
some obscure and sequestered street, where he might muse
unmolested, and where philosophy might apply the first
dressing to the poet's wounds. In fact, philosophy was his
only refuge; for he knew not where he should find a lodging. After the signal failure of his dramatic attempt, he
durst not return to that which he had occupied in the Rue
Grenier-sur-l'Eau, opposite to the Port au Foin, having
made sure that monsieur the provost would give him such
a remuneration for his labor as would enable him to pay
Master Guillaume Doulx-Sire, farmer of the customs on
beasts with cloven hoofs, for the six months' lodging
which he owed him; that is to say, twelve sols parisis—
twelve times the value of all that he possessed in the
world, including his hose, shirt, and doublet. Having considered for a moment, sheltering *ad interim* under the little
gateway of the prison of the treasurer of the Holy Chapel,
what quarters he should select for the night, having all the
pavements of Paris to choose among, he recollected having noticed, in the preceding week, a horsing-stone at the
door of a counselor of the parliament, in the Rue de la

Savaterie, and having said to himself that this stone would be, in case of emergency, an excellent pillow for a beggar or a poet. He thanked Providence for having sent this seasonable idea; but as he was preparing to cross the palace yard, for the purpose of entering the tortuous labyrinth of the city, with its ancient winding streets, such as those of La Barillerie, La Vielle-Draperie, La Savaterie, La Juiverie, and others, still standing, with their houses nine stories high, he saw the procession of the Pope of Fools coming out of the palace, and advancing across the court toward him, with loud shouts, the glare of numerous torches, and his own band of music. This sight tore open afresh the wounds of his self-love; he took to his heels. In the keen mortification of his dramatic miscarriage, everything that reminded him of the festival held that day touched him to the quick.

He resolved to make for the Pont St. Michel. Boys were running to and fro letting off squibs and crackers. "Curse the fireworks!" ejaculated Gringoire, and he bent his steps toward the Pont-au-Change. To the houses at the end of the bridge were attached three large pieces of canvas with likenesses of the king, the Dauphin, and Margaret of Flanders; and six smaller, on which were portrayed the Duke of Austria, and the Cardinal of Bourbon, and Monsieur de Beaujeu, and Madame Jeanne of France, and Monsieur the Bastard of Bourbon, and I know not whom besides—the whole lighted by torches. A crowd of spectators was admiring these performances.

"Happy painter, Jehan Fourbault!" said Gringoire, with a deep sigh, as he turned his back on the productions of that artist. There was a street just before him; it appeared to be so dark and so deserted that he hoped there to be out of hearing as well as out of sight of all the festivities; he entered it. Presently his foot struck against some obstacle; he stumbled and fell. It was the pole of the May-tree, which the clerks of the Bazoche had placed in the morning at the door of the president of the parliament, in honor of the day. Gringoire bore with fortitude this new misfortune;

he picked himself up, and pursued his way across the river. Leaving behind him the civil and criminal court of the parliament, and pursuing his way along the high wall of the king's gardens, upon the unpaved strand, where he was ankle-deep in mud, he arrived at the western point of the city, and surveyed for some time the islet of the cattle-ferry, which has since given place to the Pont Neuf with its bronze horse. The islet appeared to him in the dark like a black mass, beyond the white narrow strip of water, which separated him from it. By the glimmer of a faint light might be indistinctly discerned the kind of cabin in the shape of a bee-hive which afforded shelter to the ferryman during the night.

"Happy ferryman!" thought Gringoire—"thou dreamest not of glory, thou writest no epithalamiums! what to thee are the marriages of kings and duchesses of Burgundy!—while I, a poet, am hooted, and shiver with cold, and owe twelve sous, and the sole of my shoe is so thin that it might serve for the horn of a lantern. Thanks to thee, ferryman! thy cabin refreshes the eye and causes me to forget Paris."

He was awakened from his almost lyric ecstasy by the explosion of a double petard, suddenly fired from the happy cabin. It was the ferryman taking his share in the rejoicings of the day. The report made Gringoire shudder.

"Accursed festival!" cried he, "wilt thou pursue me whithersoever I go, even to the cabin of the ferryman?" He then looked at the Seine flowing at his feet, and a horrible temptation came over him. "Ah!" said he, "how gladly would I drown myself, only the water is so cold!"

He then formed a desperate resolution. Since he found it impossible to escape the Pope of Fools, the paintings of Jehan Fourbault, the May-trees, the squibs, and the petards, he determined to proceed to the Place de Greve, and to penetrate boldly into the very heart of the rejoicings. "At any rate," thought he, "I shall be able to get a warm at the bonfire, and perhaps a supper on some of the fragments of the collation provided at the public larder of the city."

8

Today little remains of the Place de Grève as it formerly existed. That last vestige is a turret in the northern corner of the square. The turret, once charming, is now covered by an unsightly whitewash which obscures the delicate lines of its carvings. Likely the whole turret will soon disappear, submerged by that flood of new houses which so rapidly overtakes all the old façades in Paris.

Those who, like ourselves, never pass over the Place de Grève without looking piteously and sympathetically at this poor turret, squeezed as it is between two paltry houses of the period of Louis XV, can easily reconstruct in imagination the assemblage of edifices to which it belonged, and thus imagine themselves in that fifteenth-century Gothic square.

It was then, as now, an irregular trapezium, bounded on one side by the quay, and on the other three by a series of high, narrow, gloomy houses. During the daytime, one could admire the variety of these buildings, all sculptured in stone or wood, and offering perfect examples of the various kinds of domestic architecture of the Middle Ages, going back from the fifteenth to the eleventh century, from the square window which then was beginning to supersede the pointed arch, back to the semicircular Roman arch, which had been supplanted by the pointed arch and which still occupied the first story of that ancient house of the Tower of Roland, at the corner of the square next to the Seine, on the same side as the Rue de la Tannerie. By night, nothing was distinguishable of that mass of buildings except the black jagged outline of the roofs encircling the square with their chain of pointed gables. One of the essential differences between the town as it was then and as it is today is that now the fronts of the houses face the squares and streets, but then it was the backs. For two centuries past, the houses have been turned around.

In the center, but toward the eastern side of the square, rose a heavy hybrid pile formed by three masses of houses in juxtaposition. It was called by three names which explain its history, its purpose, and its architecture: the Dauphin's House, because Charles V, when dauphin, had lived in it; the Marchandise, because it served as the Hotel de Ville; and the Pillar House, on account of a series of heavy pillars which supported its three stories. The town had there all that a good town like Paris needs: a chapel to pray in, a courtroom for holding magisterial sittings and on occasion for reprimanding the king's officers, and in the lofts, an arsenal stocked with artillery. For the good people of Paris, well knowing that it is not sufficient in every emergency, to plead and pray for the franchises of the City, have always in reserve, in the attics of the Hotel de Ville, a few good rusty harquebuses.

The Place de Grève then had that sinister aspect which it retains today, owing to the unpleasant ideas which it excites, and owing to the gloomy Hotel de Ville of Dominique Bocador which has replaced the Pillar House. It must be observed that a permanent gibbet and pillory—a *justice* and a *ladder*, as they were then called—erected side by side in the middle of the pavement, contributed not a little to make the passerby avert his eyes from this fatal spot, where so many human beings full of life and health suffered their last agony. It was this gibbet that fifty years later was to give birth to that St. Vallier fever, as it was called, that terror of the scaffold, the most monstrous of all sicknesses, because it is inflicted not by the hand of God, but by man.

It is a consolation, let it be said in passing, to reflect

that the death penalty, which, three hundred years ago, then encumbered with its iron wheels, with its stone gibbets, with all its apparatus for execution permanently fixed in the ground, the Place de Grève, Les Halles, the Place Dauphine, the Croix-du-Trahoir, the Marché-aux-Pourceaux, the hideous Montfaucon, the Barrière des Sergents, the Place-aux-Chats, the Porte Saint-Denis, Champeaux, the Porte Baudets, the Porte Saint-Jacques, not to mention the innumerable "ladders" of the provosts, the bishop, the chapters, the abbots, the priors, not to mention the judicial drownings in the river Seine; I repeat it is consoling to reflect that now, after losing, one by one, all those pieces of her panoply—her profusion of executions, her refined and fanciful torments, her torture, for applying which she made afresh every five years a bed of leather, in the Grand-Châtelet—this old queen of feudal society had nearly been thrust out of our laws and our towns, tracked from code to code, driven from place to place, so that she now possesses, in our vast metropolis of Paris, but one dishonored corner of the Place de Grève, only one miserable guillotine, stealthy, anxious, ashamed, which seems always afraid of being taken red-handed, so quickly does it vanish after dealing its fatal blow!

9

When Pierre Gringoire reached the Place de Greve he was quite benumbed with cold. He had gone over the Pont-aux-Meuniers, to avoid the crowd at the Pont-au-Change and the flags of Jehan Fourbault; but the wheels of all the bishop's mills had splashed him so unmercifully as he passed that his frock was drenched; it seemed, moreover, as if the failure of his play had rendered him still more chilly than ever. Accordingly, he hastened toward the bonfire which blazed magnificently in the middle of the Place. A large assemblage of people formed a circle round it.

"Cursed Parisians!" said he to himself; for Gringoire, like a genuine dramatic poet, was addicted to soliloquies; "there they are, shutting me out from the fire! And yet I am in great need of a comfortable chimney-corner. My shoes leak, and all those infernal mills showering upon me into the bargain! The devil fetch the Bishop of Paris and his mills! I would fain know what a bishop has to do with a mill! Does he expect to be obliged to turn miller some day or other? If he needs nothing but my malison for that, I give it to him, and to his cathedral, and to his mills, with all my heart. Stop a moment, let's see if these boobies will sheer off presently. But what are they doing there, I want to know? Warming themselves—fine amusement! Gaping at the bonfire—pretty sight, forsooth!"

On looking more closely he perceived that the circle was much larger than it needed to have been, had the persons composing it been desirous of warming themselves at the king's fire; and that the assemblage of spectators was not drawn together solely by the beauty of the hundred blazing fagots. In an extensive space left open between the crowd and the fire there was a young female dancing.

Whether this young female was a human being, or a fairy, or an angel, Gringoire, skeptical philosopher and satirical poet as he was, could not at the first moment decide, so completely was he fascinated by the dazzling vision. She was not tall, thought she appeared to be so from the slenderness and elegance of her shape. Her complexion was dark, but it was easy to divine that by daylight her skin must have the beautiful golden tint of the Roman and Andalusian woman. Her small foot, too, was Andalusian. She danced, whirled, turned round, on an old Persian carpet, carelessly spread on the pavement; and every time her radiant face passed before you as she turned, her large black eyes flashed lightning.

Every eye was fixed upon her, every mouth open; and in truth, while she was thus dancing, what with the sound of the tambourine, which her two plump exquisitely shaped arms held above her head, her bodice of gold without folds, her spotted robe which swelled with the rapidity of her motions, her bare shoulders, her finely turned legs which her petticoat now and then discovered, her black hair, her eyes of flame, she was a supernatural creature.

"Verily," thought Gringoire, "it is a salamander, a nymph, a goddess, a bacchanal of Mount Menalæus!"

At that moment one of the tresses of the salamander's hair got loose, and a piece of brass which had been fastened to it dropped to the ground. "Ha! no," said he, " 'tis a gypsy!" The illusion was at an end.

She began dancing again. She picked up from the ground two swords, which she balanced on their points upon her forehead, and made them turn round one way, while she turned the other. She was in fact a gypsy, neither more nor less. But though the spell was dissolved still the whole scene was not without fascination and charm for Gringoire; the bonfire threw a crude, red, trembling light on the wide circle of faces and on the tawny brow of the girl, and at the extremity of the Place, cast a faint tinge, mingled with their wavering shadows, upon the ancient, black, and furrowed facade of the Maison-aux-Piliers on the one hand, and upon the stone arms of the gibbet on the other.

Among the thousand faces to which this light communicated a scarlet hue, there was one which seemed to be more deeply absorbed in the contemplation of the dancer than any of the others. It was the face of a man, austere, calm, and somber. This man, whose dress was concealed by the surrounding crowd, appeared to be no more than thirty-five years of age; he was, nevertheless, bald, and had merely at his temples a few tufts of thin and already gray hair. His ample and lofty brow began to be furrowed with wrinkles; but in his deep-sunk eyes there was an expression of extraordinary youth, ardent life, and profound passion. He kept them intently fixed on the Bohemian; and while the lively girl of sixteen was delighting all the other spectators by her dancing and her capers, his reverie seemed to become more and more gloomy. At times a smile and a sigh would meet upon his lips, but the smile was by far the sadder of the two. The girl at length paused, panting with her exertions, and the people applauded with enthusiasm.

"Djali!" said the Bohemian, and up started a pretty little white goat, a nimble, lively, glossy creature, with gilt horns, gilt hoofs, and a gilt collar, which Gringoire had not yet perceived and which had till then been lying at the corner of the carpet watching her mistress dance. "Djali," said the girl, "it is your turn now"; and seating herself, she gracefully held the tambourine before the animal. "Djali," continued she, "what month are we in?" The goat raised her foreleg and struck one stroke upon the tambourine. It was actually the first month. The crowd applauded. "Djali," said the girl, turning the tambourine a different way, "what day of the month is this?" Djali again raised her little gilt hoof and struck six blows upon the instrument. "Djali," continued the Egyptian, again changing the position of the tambourine, "what o'clock is it?" Djali gave seven blows. At that moment the clock of the Maison-aux-Piliers struck seven. The people were astounded.

"There is sorcery at the bottom of this!" said a sinister voice in the crowd. It was that of the bald man, who never took his eyes off the Bohemian. She shuddered and turned away; and thunders of applause burst forth and drowned the morose exclamation. They had the effect of effacing it so completely from her mind that she continued to question her goat.

"Djali, show me how Master Guichard Grand Remy, captain of the city pistoleers, does in the Candlemas procession." Djali raised herself on her hindlegs, and began bleating and walking with such comic gravity, that the whole circle of spectators roared with laughter at this parody upon the interested devotion of the captain of the pistoleers.

"Djali," resumed the girl, emboldened by the increasing applause, "show me how Master Jacques Charmolue, the king's attorney in the ecclesiastical court, preaches." The goat sat down on her rump, and began bleating and shaking her forepaws in such a strange way, that, in gesture, accent, attitude, everything excepting bad French and worse Latin, it was Jacques Charmolue to the life. The crowd applauded more loudly than ever.

"Sacrilege! profanation!" ejaculated the bald man. The gypsy turned round once more. "Ah!" said she, "it is that odious man!" then lengthening her lower lip beyond the upper, she gave a pout that seemed to be habitual to her, turned upon her heel, and began to collect the donations of the multitude in her tambourine. Silver and copper coins of all sorts and sizes were showered into it. She came to Gringoire, who so readily thrust his hand into his pocket that she stopped. "The devil!" muttered the poet, fumbling in his pocket and finding the reality, that is nothing. The graceful girl stood still before him, looking at him with her large eyes, and holding out her tambourine. Big drops of perspiration started from Gringoire's brow. If he had had Peru in his pocket, he would certainly have given it to the dancer; but Gringoire had no Peru there, and besides, America was not yet discovered. An unexpected incident luckily relieved him.

"Wilt thou begone, Egyptian grasshopper?" cried a sharp voice issuing from the darkest corner of the Place. The young girl turned about in alarm. It was not the voice of the bald man; it was the voice of a female, a devout and spiteful voice. This exclamation, which frightened the gypsy, excited the merriment of a troop of boys who were strolling near the spot. " 'Tis the crazy woman in Roland's Tower," cried they with shouts of laughter; " 'tis Sacky who is scolding. Perhaps she has had no supper. Let us run to the city larder and see if we can get something for her!" And away they scampered to the Maison-aux-Piliers.

Meanwhile Gringoire had taken advantage of the girl's
agitation to sneak off. The shouts of the boys reminded
him that he had not supped either. He thought that he, too,
might as well try his luck at the larder. But the young
rouges ran too fast for him; when he arrived everything
was cleared away; there was not a scrap of any kind left.

It is not pleasant to be obliged to go to bed without supper, and still less agreeable to have no bed to go to as well
as no supper to eat. Such was Gringoire's predicament. He
found himself closely pressed on all sides by necessity,
and he thought necessity unnecessarily harsh. He had long
since discovered this truth, that Jupiter created man in a fit
of misanthropy, and that throughout the whole life of the
philosopher, his destiny keeps his philosophy in a state of
siege. For his own part he had never seen the blockade so
complete; he heard his stomach beat a parley; and he declared it a scurvy trick of malicious destiny to take his philosophy by famine.

In this melancholy reverie he became more and more
absorbed, when a strange kind of song, but remarkably
sweet, suddenly roused him from it. It was the Egyptian
girl who was singing. Her voice, like her dancing and her
beauty, was indefinable, something pure, sonorous, aerial,
winged, as it were. There were continual gushes of mel-
ody, unexpected cadences, then simple phrases interspersed with harsh and hissing ones; now leaps which
would have confused a nightingale, but in which harmony
was nevertheless preserved; and presently soft undulations
of octaves, which rose and fell like the bosom of the
young singer. Her fine face followed with extraordinary
versatility all the caprices of her song, from the wildest in-
spiration to the chastest dignity. You would have taken her
at one time for a maniac, at another for a queen.

The words which she sang were of a language unknown
to Gringoire, and apparently unknown to herself, so little
did the expression thrown into the singing accord with the
signification of those words. Thus these four lines were in
the highest strain of mirth:

> "Un coffre de gran requeza
> Hallaron dentro un pilar,
> Dentro del, nuevas banderas,
> Con figuras de espantar."

A moment afterward the tone which she infused into this stanza:

> "Alarabes de cavallo
> Sin poderse menear,
> Con espados, y los cuellos,
> Ballestas de buen echar,"

drew tears into the eyes of Gringoire. Mirth, however, was the predominant spirit of her lays, and she seemed to sing like the bird for sheer serenity and carelessness.

The song of the gypsy had disturbed Gringoire's reverie, but as the swan disturbs the water; he listened with a kind of rapture and forgetfulness of everything. It was the first respite from suffering that he had enjoyed for several hours. That respite was a short one. The same female voice which had interrupted the dancing of the gypsy was now raised to interrupt her singing. "Cease thy chirping, cricket of hell!" it cried, still issuing from the darkest corner of the Place. The poor cricket stopped short. "Curse thy screeching, thou bird of foul omen!" exclaimed Gringoire, clapping his hands to his ears. The other spectators also began to murmur. "The devil take the hag!" cried more than one, and the invisible trouble-feast might have had to rule her aggressions against the Bohemian, had not their attention been at that moment diverted by the procession of the Pope of Fools, which, after parading through the principal streets, was now entering the Place de Greve with all its torches and its clamor.

This procession, which set out, as the reader has seen, from the palace, was joined in its progress by all the idle ragamuffins, thieves, and vagabonds in Paris; accordingly

it exhibited a most respectable appearance when it reached
the Greve.

Egypt marched first, headed by the duke on horseback,
with his counts on foot, holding his bridle and stirrups.
They were followed by the Egyptians of both sexes, pell-
mell, with their young children crying at their backs; all of
them, duke, counts, and commons, in rags and tatters.
Next came the kingdom of Slang, that is to say, all the
rogues and thieves in France, drawn up according to their
respective dignities, the lowest walking first. Thus they
moved on, four by four, with the different insignia of their
degrees in this strange faculty, most of them cripples,
some having lost legs, others arms. Amid the conclave of
grand dignitaries, it was difficult to distinguish the king of
these ruffians, crouched in a little car drawn by two huge
dogs. After the kingdom of Slang came the empire of Galilee. The emperor, Guillaume Rousseau, marched
majestically in his purple robe stained with wine, preceded
by dancers performing military dances and scuffling together, and surrounded by his mace-bearers and subordi-
nate officers. Lastly came the Bazoche, the company of
lawyers' clerks, with their May-tree garlanded with flowers, in their black gowns, with music worthy of the Sabbath, and large candles of yellow wax. In the center of this
multitude, the officers of the fraternity of Fools bore upon
their shoulders a handbarrow, more profusely beset with
tapers than the shrine of St. Genevieve in time of pestilence; and on his throne glittered, with crosier, cope, and
mitre, the new Pope of Fools, the Notre Dame Quasimodo,
the hunchback.

Each of the divisions of this grotesque procession had
its particular band of music. The Egyptians played upon
their African balfoes and tambourines. The men of Slang,
a race by no means musical, had advanced no further than
the viol, the goat's horn, and the Gothic rebec of the
twelfth century. The empire of Galilee was but little before
them; the highest stretch of its music was some wretched
air of the infancy of the art, still imprisoned in the *re-*

la-mi. It was around the Pope of Fools that all the musical excellences of the age were commingled in one magnificent cacophony. It consisted only of viols, treble, alt, and tenor, besides flutes and instruments of brass. Our readers may not recollect that this was poor Gringoire's orchestra.

It is impossible to convey any idea of the look of pride and self-complacency which had overspread Quasimodo's dull and hideous countenance during this triumphal procession from the palace to the Greve. It was the first gratification of self-love that he had ever experienced. Hitherto he had met with nothing but humiliation, contempt for his condition, disgust of his person. Thus, deaf as he was, he enjoyed like a real pope the acclamations of that crowd which he hated because he knew he was hated by it. It mattered not to him that his subjects were a mob of cripples, mendicants, thieves, ruffians—still they were subjects, and he was a sovereign. He took in earnest all those ironical plaudits, all that mock reverence and respect, with which, we must however observe, there was mingled on the part of the crowd a certain degree of real fear; for the hunchback was strong, the bandy-legged dwarf was active, the deaf bell-ringer was spiteful, three qualities which tend to temper ridicule.

It was, therefore, not without surprise and alarm that, at the moment when Quasimodo, in this state of half-intoxication, was borne triumphantly past the Maison-aux-Piliers, his attendants beheld a man suddenly dart from among the crowd, and with an angry gesture snatch from his hands his crosier of gilt wood, the mark of his newly conferred dignity. This rash man was the bald-headed personage who, mingled in the group of spectators, had thrilled the poor gypsy girl by his exclamations of menace and abhorrence. He was attired in the ecclesiastical habit. At the moment when he issued from among the crowd, Gringoire, who had not before noticed him, recognized in him an old acquaintance. "Hold!" said he, with a cry of astonishment. "Sure enough it is my master in Hermes,

Dom Claude Frollo, the archdeacon! What the devil would
he be at with that one-eyed monster? He will eat him up."

Shrieks of terror burst from the crowd, as the formidable Quasimodo leaped from the litter to the ground; and
the women turned away their faces, that they might not see
the archdeacon torn in pieces. With one bound he was before the priest; he looked at him, and dropped upon his
knees. The priest pulled off his tiara, broke his crosier, and
tore his cope of tinsel. Quasimodo remained kneeling,
bowed his head, and clasped his hands. Then ensued between them a strange dialogue of signs and gestures, for
neither of them spoke; the priest, erect, irritated, threatening, imperious—Quasimodo at his feet, humble, submissive, suppliant. And yet, it is certain that Quasimodo could
have crushed the priest with his thumb.

At length the archdeacon, shaking the brawny shoulder
of Quasimodo, motioned him to rise and follow him. Quasimodo rose. The fraternity of Fools, their first stupor over,
were for defending their pope, who had been so unceremo-
niously dethroned. The Egyptians, the beggars, and the
lawyers' clerks, crowded yelping around the priest. Quasimodo, stepping before the priest, clenched his athletic
fists; and as he eyed the assailants, he gnashed his teeth
like an angry tiger. The priest resumed his somber gravity,
made a sign to Quasimodo, and withdrew in silence. Quasimodo went before, opening a passage for him through
the crowd.

When they were clear of the populace, a number of curious and idle persons began to follow them. Quasimodo
then fell into the rear; and facing the enemy walked backward after the archdeacon, square, massive, bristly, picking
up his limbs, licking his tusk, growling like a wild beast,
and producing immense oscillations in the crowd with a
gesture or a look. They pursued their way down a dark and
narrow street, into which no one durst venture to follow
them; the formidable figure of Quasimodo securing an unmolested retreat.

" 'Tis wonderful, by my faith!" exclaimed Gringoire; "but where the devil shall I find a supper?"

10

Gringoire took it into his head to follow the gypsy girl at all hazards. He saw her with her goat turn into the Rue de Coutellerie, and to the same street he directed his course. "Why not?" said he to himself by the way.

Nothing tends so much to produce a disposition to follow passengers, and especially those of the fair sex, in the streets, as the circumstances of having neither home nor harbor. Gringoire, therefore, walked pensively on after the girl, who quickened her pace and made her pretty little goat trot along by her side, when she saw the shopkeepers retiring to their houses, and the tavern-keepers, who had alone kept open on that day, shutting up for the night. "After all," this was what he thought, or something very much like it, "she must lodge somewhere. The gipsies are very good-natured. Who knows—" And the suspensive points, with which in his mind he cut short the sentence, involved certain ideas that tickled him mightily.

The streets, meanwhile, became every moment darker and more deserted. The curfew had long since rung and it was only at rare intervals that a passenger was met on the pavement, or a light seen at the windows. Gringoire, in following the Egyptian, had involved himself in that inextricable labyrinth of lanes and alleys and crossways, surrounding the ancient sepulcher of the Holy Innocents, and which resembled a skein of thread entangled by a playful cat. "Here are streets which have very little logic!" said Gringoire, lost in their thousand meanders, through which, however, the girl proceeded as along a way that was well-

known to her, and at a more and more rapid pace. For his
part, he should not have had the remotest conception of
where he was, had he not perceived, on turning a corner,
the octagon mass of the pillory of the Halles, the black
open-work top of which was distinctly defined against a
window still lighted in the Rue Verdelet.

He had, by this time, begun to attract the notice of the
young girl; she had more than once turned her head and
looked at him with some uneasiness; nay, she had stopped
short and taken advantage of a ray of light issuing from
the half-open door of a bakehouse, to scrutinize him attentively from head to foot. Gringoire had seen her, after this
survey, pout her lip as she had done before, and then she
passed on.

This pretty grimace set Gringoire about inquiring what
it might denote. It certainly conveyed an expression of disdain and dislike. He began, in consequence, to hang his
head, as if to count the stones of the pavement, and to
drop farther behind, when, on reaching the corner of a
street in which she had turned, he was startled by a piercing shriek. The street was extremely dark; a wick steeped
in oil, burning in an iron cage at the foot of the Blessed
Virgin, at the angle of the street, nevertheless enabled
Gringoire to distinguish the Bohemian struggling in the
grasp of two men, who were striving to stifle her cries.
The poor little goat, terrified at this attack, drooped her
head, presented her horns, and bleated.

"Watch! watch!" shouted Gringoire, boldly advancing.
One of the men who held the girl turned upon him. It was
the formidable visage of Quasimodo. Gringoire did not run
away, neither did he advance another step. Quasimodo
went up to him, and dealt him a backhanded blow that sent
him reeling three or four yards and stretched him sprawl-
ing upon the pavement; then, darting back, he caught up
the young girl, and bore her off across one of his arms like
a silken scarf. His companion followed, and the poor goat
ran after the three, bleating in a most plaintive manner.

"Murder! murder!" cried the unfortunate gypsy girl.

"Halt, scoundrels, and let the wench go!" suddenly roared, in a voice of thunder, a horseman who came dashing along out of the next street. It was the captain of the archers of the king's ordnance, armed cap-a-pie, and his drawn sword in his hand. He snatched the Bohemian out of the grasp of the stupefied Quasimodo, laid her across his saddle, and at the moment when the formidable hunchback, recovering from his surprise, would have rushed upon him to regain his prey, fifteen or sixteen archers, who followed close at the heels of their captain, came up armed with quarter-staves. It was part of a company of the king's ordnance, which did the duty of counterwatch, by the order of Messire Robert d'Estouteville, keeper of the provosty of Paris.

Quasimodo was surrounded, seized, and bound. He bellowed, he foamed, he kicked, he bit; and had it been daylight no doubt his face alone rendered doubly hideous by rage, would have sufficed to scare away the whole detachment; but night disarmed him of his most formidable weapon, his ugliness. His companion had disappeared during the struggle.

The Bohemian gracefully raised herself upon the officer's saddle. Clapping her two hands upon his shoulders, she looked at him intently for a few moments, as if charmed with his handsome face, and grateful for the seasonable succor which he had afforded her. Then, giving a sweeter tone than usual to her sweet voice, she inquired, "What is your name, sir?"

"Captain Phœbus de Chateauers, at your service, my dear," replied the officer, drawing himself up to his full height.

"Thank you," said she; and while the captain was turning up his whiskers *a la bourguignonne*, she slid down the horse's side to the ground, and vanished with the swiftness of lightning.

11

Gringoire, stunned by his fall, was extended on the pavement before the good Virgin at the corner of the street. By degrees he came to himself. At first he was floating for some minutes in a kind of dreamy reverie, which was rather soothing, though the aerial figures of the Bohemian and her goat were coupled with the weight of the ungentle fist of Quasimodo. This state was of short duration. A painful sensation of cold in that part of his body which was in contact with the pavement suddenly awoke him and recalled his mind to the surface. "Whence comes this cold?" said he, sharply, to himself. He then perceived that he was nearly in the middle of the kennel.

"Devil of a hunchback Cyclop!" muttered he, and attempted to rise but he was so stunned and bruised, that he was forced to remain where he was. His hand, however, was at liberty. He held his nose and resigned himself to his fate.

The mud of Paris, thought he—for he had decidedly made up his mind to it that the kennel would be his bed—the mud of Paris is particularly offensive; it must contain a great deal of volatile and nitrous salt. Besides, it is the opinion of Nicolas Flamel and of the alchemists——

The word alchemists suggested to his mind the idea of the archdeacon Claude Frollo. He bethought himself of the violent scene which he had just witnessed; he recollected that the Bohemian was struggling between the two men, that Quasimodo had a companion; and the stately and morose figure of the archdeacon passed confusedly before his imagination. That would be extraordinary! thought he. And with this datum and upon this foundation he began to erect the fantastic edifice of hypotheses, that card-house of philosophers. Then, suddenly recalled once more to reality, "Egad!" cried he, "I am freezing!"

The place, in fact, was becoming less and less tenable. Each particle of the water in the kennel carried off a particle of radiating caloric from the loins of Gringoire; and the equilibrium between the temperature of his body and the temperature of the kennel began to be established in a way that was far from agreeable. All at once he was assailed by an annoyance of a totally different kind.

A party of boys, of those little bare-legged savages, who have in all ages padded the pavement of Paris by the name of gamins, and who when we were boys, too, threw stones at us in the evening as we left school, because our trousers were not in tatters like their own; a party of these ragged urchins ran toward the spot where Gringoire lay, laughing, and whooping, and hallooing, and caring very little whether they disturbed the neighborhood or not. They were dragging after them something like an enormous bag; and the mere clattering of their wooden shoes would have been enough to wake the dead. Gringoire, who was not absolutely dead, propped himself up a little to see what was the matter.

"Halloo, Hennequin Dandeche! halloo, Jehan Pincebourde," they bawled at the top of their voices, "old Eustacche Moubon, the ironmonger at the corner, is just dead. We have got his paillasse and are going to make a bonfire of it!"

So saying, they threw down the paillasse precisely upon Gringoire, close to whom they had stopped without seeing him. At the same time, one of them took a handful of straw, and went to light it at the Virgin's lamp.

" 'Sdeath!" grumbled Gringoire, "I am likely to be hot enough presently!"

Between fire and water he was certainly in a critical situation. He made a supernatural effort, the effort of a coiner who is going to be boiled and strives to escape. He raised himself upon his feet, threw back the paillasse upon the urchins, and hobbled away as fast as he was able.

"Holy Virgin!" cried the boys, " 'tis the ironmonger's ghost!" and off they scampered in their turn.

The paillasse was left in possession of the field of battle. Belleforet, Father Le Juge, and Corrozet, relate that on the following day it was picked up with great pomp by the clergy of that quarter, and carried to the treasure-house of the church of St. Opportune, where the sacristan, down to the year 1789, made a very handsome income with the grand miracle performed by the statue of the Virgin at the corner of the Rue Muconseil, which had by its mere presence in the memorable night between the 6th and the 7th of January, 1482, exorcised the spirit of Jehan Moubon, which to play the devil a trick, had when he died maliciously hid itself in his paillasse.

12

After running for some time as fast as his legs would carry him, without knowing whither, knocking his head against many a corner of a street, plunging into many a kennel, dashing through many a lane, turning into many a blind alley, seeking a passage through all the meanders of the old pavement of the Halles, exploring in his panic, what is termed in the exquisite Latin of the charters *tota via, cheminum et viaria,* our poet stopped short, in the first place for want of breath, and in the next collared, as it were, by a dilemma, which just occured to his mind. "It seemeth to me, Master Pierre Gringoire," said he, to himself, clapping his finger to the side of his nose, "that you are running about like a blockhead. The young rogues were not a whit less afraid of you than you of them. It seemeth to me, I tell you, that you heard their wooden shoes clattering off to the south, while you are scudding away to the north. Now, either they have run away, and then the paillasse, which they have no doubt left behind in their fright is precisely the hospitable bed for which you have been running about ever since morning, and which the Virgin, blessed be her name, miraculously sends to reward you for having composed in honor of her a morality accompanied by triumphs and mummeries; or the boys have not run away; in that case they have set fire to the paillasse; and a good fire is the very thing you want to warm, to dry, and to cheer you. In either case, a good fire, or a good bed, the paillasse is a gift of Heaven."

He turned, and with eyes and ears on the alert, strove to steer his way back to the lucky paillasse, but in vain. His course was incessantly checked by intersections of houses, blind alleys, spots where several streets terminated, and where he was forced to pause in doubt and hesitation, more perplexed and more entangled in the intricacies of those dark narrow lanes and courts than he would have been in the maze of the Hotel de Tournelles itself. At length, losing all patience, he solemnly ejaculated, "Curse these branching streets! The devil must have made them in the image of his fork."

This exclamation relieved him a little, and a kind of reddish light which he perceived at the extremity of a long, narrow lane helped to cheer his spirits. "God be praised!" said he, "yonder it is. Yonder is my paillasse burning!" And comparing himself with the mariner who is wrecked in the night, *"Salve,"* he piously ejaculated, *"Salve maris stella!"*

Whether this fragment of the seaman's hymn was addressed to the Blessed Virgin or to the paillasse is more than we can take it upon us to decide.

Before he had proceeded many steps down the long lane, which was sloping and unpaved, and which became more and more muddy the farther he went, he perceived something that had a most extraordinary appearance. Here and there all the way along it, crawled a number of indistinct and shapeless masses, proceeding toward the light at the bottom of the lane.

Nothing makes a man so adventurous as an empty pocket. Gringoire continued to advance, and soon came up with the hindmost of these strange figures, which was leisurely wriggling itself along after the others. On a near approach, he perceived that it was only a wretched cripple in a bowl, who was hopping along upon both hands. At the moment when he was passing this species of spider with human face, it accosted him in a lamentable tone:

"La buona mancia, signor! la buona mancia!"

"The devil fetch thee," said Gringoire, "and me along with thee, if I know what thou meanest!" And he walked on.

He overtook another of those moving masses. This was a cripple too—a man who had suffered such mutilation in legs and arms that the complicated system of crutches and wooden legs by which he was supported gave him the appearance of a walking scaffold. Gringoire, who was fond of lofty and classic comparisons likened him in imagination to the living tripod of Vulcan.

This living tripod took off his hat to him as he passed, but held it up under Gringoire's chin, like a barber's basin, at the same time bawling in his ear, *"Señor caballero, para comprar un pedaso de pan!"*

"This fellow," said Gringoire, "seems to be talking too; but 'tis an odd language, and he must be cleverer than I am if he understands it."

He would have quickened his pace, but for the third time, something obstructed the way. This something, or rather this somebody, was a little blind man, with Jewish face and long beard, who, rowing on in the space around him with a stick, and towed by a great dog, sang out with nasal twang and Hungarian accent, *"Facitote caritatem."*

"Come," said Pierre Gringoire, "here is one at last who speaks a Christian language. I must have a most benevolent look for people to ask charity of me, in this manner, in the present meager state of my purse. My friend," continued he, turning toward the blind man, "it is not a week since I sold my last shirt, or as you understand no language but Cicero's, *Vendidi hebdomade nuper transita mean ultimam chemisam.*"

This said, he turned his back on the blind man, and pursued his way. At the same time, however, the blind man quickened his pace, and in a trice, up came the two cripples, in great haste, with a tremendous clatter of bowl and crutches upon the pavement. All three, jostling each other at the heels of poor Gringoire, opened upon him at once.

"Caritatem!" sang the blind man.

"La buona mancia!" sang the man of the bowl.

The other cripple joined in the concert with *"Un pedaso de pan!"*

Gringoire stopped his ears. "Oh, tower of Babel!" exclaimed he.

He began to run for it. The blind man ran. The man of the bowl ran. The man with the wooden leg ran. Presently he was surrounded by halt, and lame, and blind, by one-armed and one-eyed, and lepers with their hideous sores, some issuing from houses, others from the adjoining courts, and others from cellars, howling, bellowing, yelping, hobbling, rushing toward the light, and bedraggled with mire, like snails after a shower.

Gringoire, still followed by his three persecutors, and not knowing what to think of the matter, walked on in some alarm amid the others, and turning aside, and passing the cripples on crutches, stepping over the heads of those in bowls, and entangled in this crowd of limping, shuffling wretches, like the English captain who found himself suddenly surrounded by a prodigious host of land-crabs.

The idea occurred to him, to try to return. But it was too late. The whole legion had closed behind him, and his three mendicants stuck to him like bird-lime. He proceeded, therefore, propelled at once by this irresistible tide, by fear, and by dizziness which made the whole scene appear to him like a horrible dream.

At length he reached the extremity of the lane. It opened into a spacious place, where a thousand scattered lights flickered in the confused haze of night. Gringoire pursued his way into it, hoping by the lightness of his heels to escape from the three infirm specters who stuck so closely to him.

"Onde vas hombre?" cried the cripple upon crutches, throwing them down, and running after him on two as goodly legs as ever stepped upon the pavement of Paris. At the same moment the other cripple, standing bolt upright upon his feet, clapped his heavy bowl cased with iron upon Gringoire's head, by way of cap, and the blind man stared him in the face with a pair of flaming eyes.

"Where am I?" cried the affrighted poet.

"In the Cour des Miracles," replied a fourth specter, who had joined them.

"Miracles, upon my soul!" rejoined Gringoire, "for here are blind who see, and lame who run."

A sinister laugh was their only answer.

The poor poet cast his eyes around him. He was actually in that dreaded Cour des Miracles, into which no honest man had ever penetrated at such an hour, a magic circle, in which the officers of the Catelet and the sergeants of the provost, who ventured within it, were disposed of in a trice; the haunt of thieves; a hideous wen on the face of Paris; a sewer disgorging every morning and receiving every night that fetid torrent of vice, mendicity, and roguery which always overflows the streets of great capitals; a monstrous hive, to which all the drones of the social order retired at night with their booty; the hospital of imposture, where the gypsy, the unfrocked monk, the ruined scholar, the blackguards of all nations, Spaniards, Italians, Germans, of all religions, Jews, Christians, Mahometans, idolaters, covered with painted wounds, beggars by day, transmogrified themselves into banditti at night; immense robing-room in short, whither all the actors of that eternal comedy which theft, prostitution, and murder are performing in the streets of Paris, resorted at that period to dress and to undress.

The faint and flickering light of the fires enabled Gringoire to distinguish, in spite of his agitation, all round the immense place a hideous circumference of old houses, the decayed, worm-eaten, ruinous fronts of which, each perforated by one or two small lighted windows, appeared to him in the dark like enormous heads of old hags ranged in a circle, watching the witches' sabbath rites and winking their eyes. It was like a new world, unknown, unheard of, deformed, creeping, crawling, fantastic.

Gringoire—more and more terrified; held by the three mendicants as by three vices; deafened by a crowd of other faces bleating and barking around him—the unlucky Gringoire strove to rally his presence of mind, and to recollect whether it was Saturday or not. But his efforts were vain; the thread of his memory and of his thoughts was broken, and doubting everything, floating between what he saw and what he felt, he asked himself this puzzling question: "If I am, can this be? if this is, can I be?"

At this moment a distinct shout arose from amid the buzzing crowd by which he was surrounded, "Lead him to the king! lead him to the king!"

"Holy Virgin!" muttered Gringoire—"the king of this place! why, he can be nothing but a goat."

"To the king! to the king!" repeated every voice.

He was hurried away. The rabble rushed to lay hands on him, but the three mendicants held him fast in their grip, tearing him away from the others, and bawling, "He is ours!" The poet's doublet, previously in wretched plight, was utterly ruined in this struggle.

The sight which presented itself when his ragged escort had at length brought him to the place of his destination, was not calculated to carry him back to poetry, were it even the poetry of hell. It was more than ever the prosaic and brutal reality of the tavern. If our history did not pertain to the fifteenth century, we should say that Gringoire had descended from Michael Angelo to Callot.

Around a great fire which burned upon a large circular hearth, and the flames of which rose among the red-hot bars of a trevet unoccupied at the moment, sundry crazy tables were placed here and there at random; for the waiter had not deigned to study geometrical symmetry in their arrangement, or to take care at least that they should not intersect each other at too unusual angles. On these tables shone pots flowing with wine and beer, and round these pots were grouped a great many jolly faces, empurpled by the fire and by drink. Here a man, with huge paunch and jovial phiz, was whistling the while he took off the bandages from a false wound, and removed the wrappers from a sound and vigorous knee, which had been swathed ever since morning in a dozen ligatures. At the back of him was a shriveled wretch, preparing with suet and bullock's blood his black pudding for the ensuing day. Two tables off, a sharper, in the complete dress of a pilgrim, was twanging a stave of a religious hymn. In another place a young rogue was taking a lesson in epilepsy from an old cadger, who was also teaching him the art of foaming at the mouth by chewing a bit of soap. By the side of these a dropsical man was ridding himself of his protuberance, while four or five canters of the other sex were quarreling about a child they had stolen in the course of the evening. Circumstances these, which two centuries later, "appeared so ridiculous to the court," as Sauval tells us, "that they furnished pastime for the king, and were introduced into the royal ballet, called 'Night,' divided into four parts, and performed upon the stage of the Petit-Bourbon."

"Never," adds a spectator of this performance, "were the sudden metamorphoses of the Cour des Miracles more successfully represented."

A large dog was seated on his rump, looking at the fire. Young children were present at these orgies. The stolen boy was crying bitterly. Another, a stout fellow about four years old, was sitting on a high bench, dangling his legs at the table, which reached up to his chin, and saying not a word. A third was gravely spreading with his finger the melted tallow which ran from a candle upon the table. The last, a little urchin, crouching in the dirt, was almost lost in a kettle, which he was scraping with a tile, and from which he was extracting sounds that would have thrown Stradivarius into a swoon.

Near the fire stood a hogshead, and upon this hogshead was seated a mendicant. This was the king upon his throne. The three vagabonds who held Gringoire led him before the hogshead, and for a moment the whole motley assemblage was silent, excepting the kettle inhabited by the boy. Gringoire durst not breathe or raise his eyes.

"Hombre, quita tu sombrero," said one of the three fellows in whose clutches he was, and before he knew what was meant, one of the others took off his hat—a shabby covering, it is true, but still useful either against sun or rain. Gringoire sighed.

"What varlet have we here?" asked the king. Gringoire shuddered. This voice, though it now had a tone of menace, reminded him of another which had that very morning given the first blow to his mystery, by drawling out amid the audience, "Charity, if you please?" He raised his eyes. It was Clopin Trouillefou himself.

Clopin Trouillefou, invested with the insignia of royalty, had not a rag more or a rag less than usual. The sore on his arm had disappeared. He held in his hand one of the whips composed of thongs of white leather, which were used by the vergers in those days to keep back the crowd. On his head he wore a cap of such peculiar form that it was difficult to tell whether it was a child's biggin or a king's crown—so much are the two things alike. Gringoire, however, had regained some hope, though without knowing why, on recognizing in the king of the Cour des Miracles the provoking beggar of the great hall.

"Master," he stammered forth, "my lord—sire—what ought I to call you?" he at length asked, having arrived at the culminating point of his crescendo, and not knowing how to get higher or to descend again.

"Call me your majesty, or comrade, or what thou wilt. But make haste. What hast thou to say in thy defense?"

"In thy defense!" thought Gringoire, "I don't half like that. It was I—I—I——" he resumed, with same hesitation as before, "who this morning——"

"By the devil's hoofs!" cried Clopin, interrupting him, "thy name, knave, and nothing more. Mark me. Thou art in the presence of three mighty sovereigns, myself, Clopin Trouillefou, King of Thunes, and supreme ruler of the realm of Slang; Mathias Hunyadi Spicali, Duke of Egypt and Bohemia, that sallow old crone whom thou seest yonder, with a clout round his head; and Guillaume Rousseau, Emperor of Galilee, the porpoise who is too busy with that trull to attend to us. We are thy judges. Thou hast entered our territories without being one of our subjects; thou has violated the privileges of our city. Thou must be punished, unless thou art a prig, a cadger, or a stroller—or to use the gibberish of those who call themselves honest people, a thief, a beggar, or a vagrant. Art thou any of these? justify thyself; state thy qualities."

"Alas!" sighed Gringoire, "I have not that honor. I am an author——"

"Enough!" exclaimed Trouillefou, without suffering him to proceed. "Thou shalt be hanged. And quite right, too, messieurs honest citizens! As you deal by our people among you, so we will deal by yours among us. The law which you make for the vagabonds, the vagabonds will enforce with you. 'Tis your fault if it is a harsh one. It is but proper that an honest man should now and then be seen grinning through a hempen collar—that makes the thing honorable. Come, my friend, divide thy rags with a good grace among these wenches. I will have thee hanged to amuse the vagabonds, and thou shalt give them thy purse to drink. If thou hast any mummery to make, go down to the cellar; there is a capital crucifix in stone, which we picked up at St. Pierre-aux-oeufs. Thou hast four minutes to settle the affairs of thy soul."

This was an alarming announcement.

"Well said, upon my life! Clopin Trouillefou preaches like his holiness the pope," cried the Emperor of Galilee, breaking his pot to prop up his table.

"Most puissant emperors and kings," said Gringoire, quite coolly—I never could make out how he recovered sufficient firmness to talk so resolutely—"you cannot mean what you say. My name is Pierre Gringoire; I am the poet, whose morality was represented this morning in the great hall of the palace."

"Oho! master!" said Clopin. "I was there too. But, comrade, because we were annoyed by thee in the morning, is that any reason why thou shouldst not be hung to-night?"

"I shall be puzzled to get myself out of this scrape," thought Gringoire. He made nevertheless another effort.

"I do not see," said he, "why poets should not be classed among the vagabonds. Æsop was a vagabond, Homer a beggar, Mercury a thief."

Clopin interrupted him. "I verily believe thou thinkest to bamboozle us with thy palver. 'Sdeath! as thou must be hanged, make no more ado."

"Pardon me, most illustrious king of Thunes," replied Gringoire, disputing the ground inch by inch; "is it worth while—only one moment—you will not condemn me unheard——"

Clopin Trouillefou appeared to be conferring for a moment with the Duke of Egypt, and the Emperor of Galilee, who was quite drunk. He then cried out, sharply, "Silence, there!" and as the kettle and the frying-pan paid no attention to him, but continued their duet, he leaped from his hogshead, gave one kick to the kettle, which rolled away with the boy to the distance of ten paces, and another to the frying-pan, which upset all the fat into the fire. He then gravely reascended his throne, caring no more for the smothered crying of the child than for the grumbling of the hag, whose supper had gone off in a blaze.

"Fellow," said he to Gringoire, stroking his deformed chin with his horny hand, "I see no reason why thou shouldst not be hanged. Thou seemest indeed to have a dislike to it, but that is natural enough; you citizens are not used to it. You have too frightful an idea of the thing. After all we mean thee no harm. There is one way to get out of the scrape for the moment. Wilt thou be one of us?"

The reader may conceive what effect this proposition must have produced upon Gringoire, who saw that he had no chance of saving his life, and began to make up his mind to the worst. He caught eagerly at the proposed alternative.

"Certainly, most assuredly I will," said he.

"Thou consentest," rejoined Clopin, "to enroll thyself among the men of Slang?"

"The men of Slang, decidedly so," answered Gringoire.

"Thou acknowledges thyself one of the crew?" proceeded the King of Thunes.

"One of the crew."

"A subject of the kingdom of Cant?"

"Of the kingdom of Cant."

"A vagabond?"

"A vagabond."

"With all thy soul?"

"With all my soul."

"Take notice," said the king, "thou shalt nevertheless be hanged."

"The devil!" ejaculated the poet.

"Only," continued Clopin, with imperturbable gravity, "thou shalt be hanged not quite so soon and with more ceremony, at the cost of the good city of Paris, on a fair stone gibbet, and by the hands of honest men. That is some consolation."

"As you say," replied Gringoire.

"There are some other advantages which thou wilt enjoy. As one of the crew, thou wilt not have to pay rates, either for lamp, scavenger, or poor, to which the honest burgesses of Paris are liable."

"Be it so!" said the poet. "I am a vagabond, a subject of the kingdom of Cant, one of the crew, a man of Slang, anything you please; nay, I was all these before, august king of Thunes, for I am a philosopher; *et omnia in philosophia, omnes in philosopho continentur,* you know."

The august king of Thunes knitted his brows. "What do you take me for, my friend? What Hungary Jew gibberish are you talking now? I know nothing of Hebrew. One may be a ruffian without being a Jew."

Gringoire strove to slip in an excuse between these brief sentences cut short by anger. "I beg your majesty's pardon; it is not Hebrew, but Latin."

"I tell thee," rejoined Clopin, furiously, "I am not a Jew, and I will have thee hanged, varlet; ay, and that little Jew peddler there beside thee, whom I hope some day to see nailed to a counter, like a piece of base coin as he is."

As he thus spoke, he pointed to the little bearded Hungarian Jew, who, acquainted with no other language but that in which he had accosted Gringoire, was surprised at the ill-humor which the King of Thunes appeared to be venting upon him.

At length King Clopin became somewhat more calm. "Knave," said he to our poet, "thou hast a mind then to be a vagabond?"

"Undoubtedly," replied Gringoire.

"'Tis not enough to have a mind," said his surly majesty; "goodwill puts not one more onion into the soup. To be admitted into our brotherhood, thou must prove that thou are fit for something. Show us thy skill at picking a pocket."

"Anything you please," said the poet.

Clopin made a sign. Several of the vagabonds left the circle, and presently returned. They brought two poles, each having a flat horizontal piece of wood fastened at the lower extremity, upon which it stood upright on the ground. Into the upper ends of these poles the bearers fitted a crossbar, and the whole then formed a very handy portable gibbet, which Gringoire had the satisfaction to see set up before his face in a trice. Nothing was wanting, not even the cord, which dangled gracefully from the crossbar.

"What are they about now?" said Gringoire to himself,

while his heart sunk within him. A tinkling of small bells put an end to his anxiety. It was the figure of a man, a kind of scarecrow, in a red dress, so profusely bestudded with little bells that they would have sufficed for the comparison of thirty Castilian mules, which the vagabonds were suspending by the neck from the rope. The clatter of these thousand bells, occasioned by the swinging of the rope, gradually subsided, and at length ceased entirely with the motion of the effigy.

Clopin pointed to a crazy stool placed under the figure. "Get upon that," said he to Gringoire.

" 'Sdeath!" rejoined the poet, "I shall break my neck. Your stool halts like a distich of Martial's; it has one hexameter and one pentameter foot."

"Get up, knave!" repeated Clopin.

Gringoire mounted the stool, and after some oscillations of head and arms, recovered his center of gravity.

"Now," continued the King of Thunes, "cross thy right leg over the left and stand on tiptoe."

"Morbleu!" cried Gringoire, "then you absolutely insist on it that I shall break some of my limbs?"

Clopin shook his head. "Hark ye, my friend, thou talkest too much for me. In two words this is what thou hast to do. Thou must stand on tiptoe as I tell thee, so as to reach the pocket of the figure. Thou must take out a purse that is in it, and if thou canst do this without making any of the bells speak, 'tis well; thou shalt be a vagabond. We shall then have nothing to do but to beat thee soundly for a week or so."

"Ventre Dieu!" exclaimed Gringoire. "And if the bells should give mouth in spite of me?"

"Why, then thou shalt be hanged; dost thou comprehend me?"

"Not at all," answered Gringoire.

"Well then, I tell thee once more. Thou must pick the pocket of that figure of a purse, and if a single bell stirs, while thou are about it, thou shalt be hanged. Dost thou understand that?"

"I do," said Gringoire. "And then?"

"If thou art clever enough to prig the purse without setting the bells a-chattering, thou art a Canter, and shalt be soundly thrashed every now and then for a week. Thou understandest that, no doubt?"

"But what better shall I be? Hanged in one case, beaten in the other?"

"And a Canter!" rejoined Clopin, "a Canter! Is that nothing? It is for thy own benefit that we shall beat thee, to inure thee to blows."

"Many thanks to you!" replied the poet.

"Come, bear a hand!" said the king, stamping upon his hogshead, which sounded like a big drum. "To thy task, knave. And recollect, if I hear but a single bell, thou shalt change places with that figure."

The crew applauded Clopin's words, and ranged themselves in a circle round the gallows, with so pitiless a laugh that Gringoire saw he amused them too much not to have to fear the worst from them. The only hope he had left was the most precarious chance of succeeding in the ticklish task imposed upon him. Before he set about it, he addressed a fervent prayer to the effigy which he was going to rob, and which he would have softened as easily as the vagabonds. The myriad of bells, with their little copper tongues, seemed to him so many gaping jaws of serpents, ready to bite and to hiss.

"Oh," said he aside, "is it possible that my life depends on the slightest vibration of the smallest of these bells?" He tried the effect of a last effort on Trouillefou. "And if there should come a gust of wind?"

"Thou shalt be hanged," replied the King of Thunes, without hesitation.

Finding that there was neither respite nor reprieve, nor any possible evasion for him, he went resolutely to work. Crossing his right leg over the left, and raising himself on tiptoe, he stretched out his arm; but at the moment when he touched the effigy, he found himself tottering upon the stool, which had but three legs; he lost his balance, mechanically caught at the figure, and fell plump on the ground, stunned by the fatal jingle of the thousand bells of the figure, which yielding to the impulsion of his hand, at first turned round upon itself, and then swung majestically between the two poles.

"Sacre!" cried he, as he fell, and he lay like one dead, with his face toward the ground. He heard, however, the horrid chime above his head, the diabolical laugh of the Canters, and the voice of Trouillefou, who said, "Pick up the varlet, and hang him out of hand."

He rose. They had already taken down the effigy to make room for him. The vagabonds made him once more mount the stool. Clopin stepped up to him, put the rope about his neck, and patting him on the shoulder, "Farewell, my friend!" said he. "Thou canst not escape now, even with the devil's luck and thine own."

The word mercy died away on the lips of Gringoire. He glanced around him, but there was no hope; they were all laughing.

"Bellevigne de l'Etoile," said the King of Thunes, to a porpoise of a fellow, who stepped forth from the ranks, "scramble up to that crossbar." The monster mounted with an agility for which no one would have given him credit, and Gringoire, raising his eyes, beheld him with terror crouching on the crossbeam over his head.

"Now," resumed Clopin, "the moment I clap my hands, thou Andry the Red, kick away the stool; thou Francois Chanteprune pull the varlet's legs; and thou, Bellevigne, spring upon his shoulders—all three at once, d'ye hear?"

Gringoire shuddered.

"Are ye there?" said Clopin Trouillefou to the three ruffians ready to rush upon the unfortunate poet. The wretched man passed a moment of horrid suspense, while Clopin carelessly kicked into the fire a few twigs which the flames had not consumed. "Are ye there?" he repeated, opening his hands for the decisive clap.

He stopped short, as if a sudden thought had occurred to him. "Wait a moment!" said he, "I forgot. It is customary with us not to hang a blade till the women have been asked whether any of them will have him. Comrade, this is thy last chance."

Gringoire breathed once more. It was the second time that he had come to life within the last half-hour. He durst not, therefore, place much reliance upon this reprieve.

Clopin again mounted his hogshead. "This way, gentle folks!" cried he. "Is there any strumpet among you who will have this knave? Come forward and see! A husband for nothing! Who wants one?"

Gringoire, in this wretched plight, looked far from tempting. The female mumpers showed no eagerness to accept the offer. The unhappy man heard them answer one after another, "No, no, hang him, and that will be a pleasure for us all."

Three of them, however, stepped forward from among the crowd to take a look at him. The first was a strapping broad-faced wench. She closely examined the deplorable doublet and the threadbare frock of the philosopher. She shrugged her shoulders. "Queer toggery!" grumbled she. Then turning to Gringoire:

"Where is thy cloak?"

"I have lost it," answered he.

"Thy hat?"

"They have taken it from me."

"Thy shoes?"

"They are nearly worn out."

"Thy purse?"

"Alas!" stammered Gringoire, "I have not a denier left."

"Hang then, and be thankful!" replied the wench, turning on her heel and striding away.

The second, an old wrinkled hag, dark and hideously ugly, walked round Gringoire. He almost trembled lest she should take a fancy to him. At length she muttered to herself, "He is lean as a carrion," and away she went.

The third was young, fresh-looking, and not ill-favored. "Save me!" said the poor devil to her in a low tone. She surveyed him for a moment with a look of pity, cast down her eyes, twitched her petticoat, and stood for a moment undecided. He narrowly watched all her motions. It was the last glimmer of hope. "No," said she, at last; "no; Guillaume Longjoue would beat me," and she rejoined the crowd.

"Comrade," said Clopin, "thou art unlucky."

Then standing upon his hogshead, "Will nobody bid?" cried he, imitating the manner of an auctioneer, to the high diversion of the crew. "Will nobody bid? once, twice, three times!" and then turning to the gallows, with a nod of the head, "Gone!"

Bellevigne de l'Etoile, Andry the Red and Francois Chanteprune again surrounded the gibbet. At that moment cries of "La Esmeralda! La Esmeralda!" arose among the vagabonds. Gringoire shuddered, and turned the way from which the clamor proceeded. The crowd opened and made way for a bright and dazzling figure. It was the gypsy girl.

"La Esmeralda!" ejaculated Gringoire, struck, amid his agitation, at the sudden manner in which that magic name connected his scattered recollections of the events of the day. This extraordinary creature appeared by her fascination and beauty to exercise sovereign sway over the Cour des Miracles itself. Its inmates of both sexes respectfully drew back for her to pass, and at sight of her their brutal faces assumed a softer expression. With light step she approached the sufferer. Her pretty Djali followed at her heels. Gringoire was more dead than alive. She eyed him for a moment in silence.

"Are you going to hang this man?" said she, gravely, to Clopin.

"Yes, sister," replied the King of Thunes, "unless thou wilt take him for thy husband."

Her lower lip was protruded into the pretty pout already described.

"I will take him," said she.

Gringoire was now thoroughly convinced that he had been in a dream ever since morning, and that this was but a continuation of it. The shock, though agreeable, was violent. The noose was removed, the poet was dismounted from the stool, on which he was obliged to sit down, so vehement was his agitation.

The Duke of Egypt, without uttering a word, brought an earthenware jug. The gypsy girl handed it to Gringoire. "Drop it on the ground," said she to him. The jug broke into four pieces.

"Brother," said the Duke of Egypt, placing a hand upon the head of each, "she is thy wife. Sister, he is thy husband. For four years. Go."

13

In a few moments our poet found himself in a small room, with coved ceiling, very snug and very warm, seated at a table, which appeared to desire nothing better than to draw a few loans from a cupboard suspended close by, having a prospect of a good bed, and a *tête-à-tête* with a handsome girl. The adventure was like absolute enchantment. He began seriously to take himself for the hero of some fairy tale, and looked round from time to time to see whether the chariot of fire drawn by griffins, which could alone have conveyed him with such rapidity from Tartarus to Paradise, was still there. Now and then, too, he would fix his eyes on the holes in his doublet, as if to satisfy himself of his identity. His reason, tossed to and fro in imaginary space, had only this thread to hold by.

The girl appeared to take no notice of him; she moved backward and forward, setting things to rights, talking to her goat, and now and then pouting her lip. At length she sat down near the table, and Gringoire had a good opportunity to scrutinize her.

You have been a child, reader, and may perhaps have

the good fortune to be so still. I dare say you have often
(I know I have for whole days together, ay, and some of
the best days of my life) followed from bush to bush on
the bank of a stream, on a fine sunshiny day, some beautiful green and blue dragonfly, darting off every moment at
acute angle, and brushing the ends of all the branches.

You remember with what amorous curiosity your attention and your eyes were fixed on those fluttering wings of
purple and azure, amidst which floated a form rendered indistinct by the very rapidity of its motion.

He became more and more absorbed in his reverie. This
then, thought he, while his eyes vaguely followed her motions, is La Esmeralda! a celestial creature! a street-
dancer! So much and so little. It was she who gave the
finishing stroke to my mystery this afternoon, and it is she
who saves my life tonight. My evil genius! my good angel! A sweet girl, upon my word! and who must love me
to distraction, to have taken me in this manner. For, said
he, rising all at once with that candor which formed the
groundwork of his character and of his philosophy, I know
not exactly how it has come to pass, but I am her husband.

With this idea in his head and in his eyes, he approached the girl with such ardent impetuosity that she
drew back. "What do you want with me?" inquired she.

"Can you ask such a question, adorable Esmeralda?" rejoined Gringoire, in so impassioned a tone that he was astonished at himself.

The Egyptian opened her large eyes. "I know not what
you mean," said she.

"What!" replied Gringoire, warming more and more,
and thinking that after all it was but a virtue of the Cour
des Miracles that he had to do with; "am I not thine, my
sweet friend? art thou not mine?" With these words he
fondly threw his arm round her waist.

The drapery of the Bohemian glided through his hands
like the skin of an eel. Bounding from one end of the cell
to the other, she stooped, and raised herself again with a
little dagger in her hand, before Gringoire could see

whence it came, with swollen lip, distended nostril, cheeks as red as an apricot, and eyes flashing lightning. At the same moment the little white goat placed itself before her in the attitude of attack, presenting to Gringoire two very pretty but very sharp gilt horns. All this was done in a twinkling.

Our philosopher stood petrified, alternately eyeing the goat and her mistress. "Holy Virgin!" he at length ejaculated, when surprise allowed him to speak, "what a couple of vixens!"

"And you," said the Bohemian, breaking silence on her part, "must be a very impudent fellow."

"Pardon me," replied Gringoire, smiling. "But why did you take me for your husband?"

"Ought I to have let you be hanged?"

"Then," rejoined the poet, somewhat disappointed in his amorous hopes, "you had no other intention in marrying me but to save me from the gallows?"

"And what other intention do you suppose I could have had?"

Gringoire bit his lips. "Go to," said he, to himself, "I am not so triumphant in love affairs as I imagined. But then, of what use was it to break the poor jug?"

Meanwhile Esmeralda's dagger and the horns of her goat were still upon the defensive.

"Mademoiselle Esmeralda," said the poet, "let us capitulate. I am not a clerk to the Chatelet, and shall not provoke you thus to carry a dagger in Paris, in the teeth of the provost's ordinances and prohibitions. You must, nevertheless, be aware that Noel Lescrivain was sentenced a week ago to pay a fine of ten sous parisis for having carried a short sword. But that is no business of mine, so to return to the point—I swear to you by my hopes of Paradise not to approach you without your permission and consent; but for heaven's sake, give me some supper."

In reality Gringoire, like Despreaux, was not of a very amorous temperament. He belonged not to that chivalric and military class who take young damsels by assault. In love, as in all other affairs, he was for temporizing and pursuing middle courses; and to him a good supper, with an agreeable companion, appeared, especially when he was hungry, an excellent interlude between the prologue and the winding-up of a love adventure.

The Egyptian made no reply. She gave her disdainful pout, erected her head like a bird, and burst into a loud laugh; the pretty little dagger vanished as it had come, so that Gringoire could not discover where the bee concealed its sting.

In a moment a loaf of rye-bread, a slice of bacon, some wrinkled apples, and a jug of beer, were set out upon the table. Gringoire fell to with such avidity, as if all his love had been changed into appetite. His hostess, seated before him, looked on in silence, visibly engaged with some other thought, at which she smiled from time to time, while her soft hand stroked the head of the intelligent goat, closely pressed between her knees. A candle of yellow wax lighted this scene of voracity and reverie.

The first cravings of his stomach being appeased, Gringoire felt a degree of false shame on perceiving that there was only one apple left. "Do you not eat something, Mademoiselle Esmeralda?" said he. She replied in the negative by a shake of the head, and her pensive looks were fixed on the vaulted ceiling of the cell.

"What the devil does she be thinking of?" said Gringoire to himself, turning his eyes in the same direction as hers. "It is impossible that yon ugly head carved on the groining can thus engross her attention. Surely I may stand a comparison with that."

"Mademoiselle," said he, raising his voice. She appeared not to hear him. "Mademoiselle Esmeralda," he again began in a still louder tone, to just as little purpose. The spirit of the damsel was elsewhere, and the voice of Gringoire had not the power to recall it. Luckily for him the goat interfered, and began to pull her mistress gently by the sleeve. "What do you want, Djali?" said the Egyptian, sharply, starting like one awakened out of a sound sleep.

"She is hungry," said Gringoire, delighted at the opportnity of opening the conversation.

La Esmeralda began crumbling some bread, which Djali gracefully ate out of the hollow of her hand. Gringoire, without giving her time to resume her reverie, ventured upon a delicate question. "Then you will not have me for your husband?" said he.

The damsel looked at him intently for a moment, and replied, "No."

"For your lover?" asked Gringoire.

She pouted her lip, and again replied, "No."

"For your friend?" continued Gringoire.

She again fixed her eyes steadfastly upon him. "Perhaps," said she, after a moment's reflection.

This perhaps, so dear to philosophers, emboldened Gringoire. "Do you know what friendship is?" he inquired.

"Yes," replied the Egyptian; "it is to be as brother and sister, two souls which touch each other without uniting, like two fingers of the same hand."

"And love?" proceeded Gringoire.

"Oh, love!" said she, and her voice trembled, and her eyes sparkled. "It is to be two and yet but one—it is a man and a woman blending into an angel—it is heaven itself."

The street-dancer, as she uttered these words, appeared invested with a beauty which powerfully struck Gringoire, and seemed in perfect unison with the almost oriental exaggeration of her language. A faint smile played upon her pure and rosy lips; her bright and serene brow was now and then clouded for a moment, according to the turn of her thoughts, as a mirror is by the breath; and from her long, dark, downcast eyelashes emanated a sort of ineffable light, which imparted to her profile that ideal suavity which Raphael subsequently found at the mystic point of intersection of virginity, maternity, and divinity.

Gringoire nevertheless proceeded. "And what should one be," said he, "to please you?"

"A man."

"What am I, then?"

"A man has a helmet upon his head, a sword in his fist, and gold spurs at his heels."

"So then," rejoined Gringoire, "without a horse one cannot be a man. Do you love anyone?"

She remained pensive for a moment, and then said, with a peculiar kind of expression: "I shall soon know that."

"Why not tonight?" replied the poet, tenderly. "Why not me?"

She eyed him with a serious look. "Never can I love any man but one who is able to protect me."

Gringoire blushed, and made sure that this stroke was aimed at him. It was evident that the girl was alluding to the little assistance he had afforded her in the critical situation in which she had found herself two hours before. At the recollection of this circumstance, which his own subsequent adventures had banished from his mind, he struck his forehead.

"Indeed," said he, "I ought to have begun with that subject. Forgive the confusion of my ideas. How did you contrive to escape from Quasimodo's clutches?"

This question made the gypsy girl shudder.

"Oh, the horrid hunchback!" she exclaimed, covering her face with her hands, and she shivered as from the effect of intense cold.

"Horrid, indeed!" said Gringoire, without relinquishing his idea; "but how did you get away from him?"

La Esmeralda smiled, sighed, and made no reply.

"Do you know why he followed you?" resumed Gringoire, seeking to return to his question by a roundabout way.

"I do not," said the girl. "But," added she, sharply, "you followed me, too; why did you follow me?"

"In good sooth," replied Gringoire, "I do not know either."

Both were then silent. Gringoire took up his knife and began to cut the table. The damsel smiled and seemed to be looking at something through the wall. All at once she commenced singing in a voice scarcely articulate:

> "Quando las pantidas aves
> Mudas estan, y la tierra."

She then abruptly broke off and began to caress her Djali.

"That is a pretty creature of yours," observed Gringoire.

" 'Tis my sister," replied she.

"Why are you called La Esmeralda?" inquired the poet.

"I can't tell."

"No, sure!"

She drew from her bosom a small oblong bag, attached to a necklace of small red seeds, and emitting a very strong scent of camphor. The outside was green silk, and in the middle of it there was a large bead of green glass in imitation of emerald.

"Perhaps it is on account of this," said she.

Gringoire extended his hand to lay hold of the bag, but she started back. "Don't touch it," said she; " 'tis an amulet. You might do an injury to the charm, or the charm to you."

The curiosity of the poet was more and more excited. "Who gave you that?" he asked.

She laid her finger upon her lips, and replaced the amulet in her bosom. He ventured upon further questions, but could scarcely obtain answers to them.

"What is the meaning of La Esmeralda?"

"I know not," said she.

"To what language does the word belong?"

"It is Egyptian, I believe."

"I thought so," said Gringoire. "You are not a native of France?"

"I don't know."

"Are your parents living?"

She began singing to the tune of an old song:

> "My father's a bird,
> And my mother's his mate;
> I pass the broad waters
> Without boat or bait."

"How old were you when you came to France?"

"I was quite a child."

"And to Paris?"

"Last year. At the moment we were entering the papal gate, I saw the yellow-hammers flying in a line over our heads. It was then the end of August, and I said, 'We shall have a sharp winter.' "

"And so we have," said Gringoire, delighted with this commencement of conversation; "I have done nothing but blow my fingers since it set in. Why, then, you possess the gift of prophecy?"

"No," replied she, relapsing into her laconic manner.

"The man whom you call the Duke of Egypt is the chief of your tribe, I presume?"

"Yes."

"And yet it was he who married us," timidly observed the poet.

Her lip exhibited the accustomed pout. "I don't even know your name," said she.

"My name, if you wish to know it, is Pierre Gringoire."

"I know a much finer," said she.

"How unkind!" replied the poet. "Never mind; you shall not make me angry. You will, perhaps, love me when you are better acquainted with me; and you have related your history to me with such candor that I cannot withhold mine from you.

"You must know, then, that my name is Pierre Gringoire, and that my father held the situation of notary at Gonesse. He was hanged by the Burgundians, and my mother was murdered by the Picards, at the siege of Paris twenty years ago; so, at six years old I was left an orphan, with no other sole to my foot but the pavement of Paris. I know not how I passed the interval between six and sixteen. Here, a fruit-woman gave me an apple or a plum; there a baker tossed me a crust of bread; at night I threw myself in the way of the watch, who picked me up and put me in prison, where I found at last a bundle of straw. In spite of this kind of life I grew tall and slim, as you see. In winter I warmed myself in the sunshine, under the porch of the hotel of Sens, and I thought it very absurd that the bonfires of St. John should be deferred nearly to the dogdays. At sixteen I began to think of adopting a profession, and successively tried my hand at everything. I turned soldier, but was not brave enough; I became a monk, but was not devout enough, and besides, I could not drink hard enough. In despair I apprenticed myself to a carpenter, but was not strong enough. I had a much greater fancy to be a schoolmaster; true, I had not learned to read, but what of that? After some time I discovered that, owing to some deficiency or other, I was fit for nothing, and therefore set up for a poet. This is a profession to which a man who is a vagabond may always betake himself, and it is better than to thieve, as some young rogues of my acquaintance advised me to do. One day, as good luck would have it, I met with Dom Claude Frollo, the reverend archdeacon of Notre Dame, who took a liking to me, and to him I owe it that I am this day a learned man, not unpracticed either in scholastics, poetics, or rhythmics, or even in hermetics, that a sophia of all sophias. I am the author of the mystery that was performed today before a prodigious concourse of people, with immense applause, in the great hall of the Palace of Justice. I am wholly at your service, damsel, my body and soul, my science and my learning, ready to live with you in any way you please, chastely or jovially, as husband and wife, if you think proper, as brother and sister, if you like better."

Gringoire paused, waiting the effect of his address on his hearer. Her eyes were fixed on the ground.

"Phœ," said she, in an undertone, and then turning to the poet—"Phœbus, what does that mean?"

Gringoire, though unable to discover what connection

there could be between the subject of his speech and this question, was not displeased to have an opportunity of displaying his erudition. "It is a Latin word," said he, "and means the sun."

"The sun!" she exclaimed.

"It is the name of a certain handsome archer, who was a god," added Gringoire.

"A god!" repeated the Egyptian, and there was in her tone something pensive and impassioned.

At this moment one of her two bracelets, having accidentally become loose, fell to the ground. Gringoire instantly stooped to pick it up; when he raised himself the damsel and the goat were gone. He heard the sound of a bolt upon a door communicating no doubt with an adjoining cell which fastened on the inside.

"No matter, so she has left me a bed!" said our philosopher. He explored the cell. It contained not a piece of furniture fit to lie down upon, excepting a long coffer, and the lid of this was carved in such a manner as to communicate to Gringoire, when he stretched himself upon it, a sensation similar to that experienced by Micromegas when he lay at his full length upon the Alps.

"Well," said he, accommodating himself to this uncomfortable couch as well as he could, " 'tis of no use to grumble. But at any rate this is a strange wedding night!"

14

Even today, the edifice of the Cathedral of Notre Dame remains majestic and sublime. Although time and man have caused much damage and mutilation to this noble building, it remains a venerable monument. But one cannot ignore the changes made, even between the time that the first stone was laid by CharleMagne and the last by Philip-Augustus.

On the face of this old queen of French cathedrals, beside each wrinkle you always find a scar. *Tempus edox, homo edacior,** which I would translate: Time is blind, but man is stupid.

If we had time to examine with the reader, one by one, the many traces of destruction stamped on this ancient church, the ravages of time would be found to have done the least; the worst destruction has been perpetrated by men, especially by men of art. We must say "men of art," because there have been men in France who, in the last two centuries, have assumed the character of architects.

First of all, to cite only a few outstanding examples, there are without any question few finer architectural examples than that facade of the Parisian cathedral, in which, successively and at once, you see three deep Gothic doors; the decorated and indented band of twenty-eight royal niches; the immense central rose-window, flanked by two lateral ones, like the priest flanked by the deacon and sub-deacon; the lofty and fragile gallery of trifoliated arcades, supporting a heavy platform upon its delicate columns; finally the two dark and massive towers, with their eaves of slate, harmonious parts of one magnificent whole, rising one above the other in five gigantic stories, unfold themselves to the eye. These towers are grouped, yet unconfused, even with their innumerable details of statuary, sculpture, and carving; they are more powerfully wedded to the tranquil grandeur of the whole. The cathedral is a vast symphony in stone, so to speak, the colossal work of a man and of a nation, a unified complex ensemble, like the Iliads and the Romanceros, to which it is a sister production. Notre-Dame's facade is the prodigious result of the combination of all the resources of an age, in which, upon every stone, is seen displayed in a hundred forms the

*"Time gnaws, man gnaws more."

imagination of the craftsman disciplined by the genius of the artist. Here is a sort of human creation; in short, mighty and fertile like the divine creation, from which this cathedral seems to have borrowed the double character of variety and eternity.

And what we have here said of the facade must be said of the church as a whole; and what we say of the cathedral of Paris must be said of all the churches in Christendom during the Middle Ages. Everything has its place in that self-created, logical, well-proportioned art. By measuring the toe, we estimate the giant.

But let us return to the facade of Notre-Dame as we find it today. We gaze in reverent admiration upon this solemn and mighty cathedral, awesome, as its chroniclers express it: *Quae mole sua terrorem incutit spectantibus.**

Three things of importance are now missing from that facade. First, the flight of eleven steps by which it formerly rose above the level of the ground; secondly, the lower row of statues, which once occupied the niches of the three portals; and finally, the upper series of statues of the twenty-eight or more ancient kings of France, which filled the gallery on the first story, beginning with Childebert and ending with Philip-Augustus, each king holding in his hand "the imperial globe."

Time is responsible for the loss of the eleven steps, since time relentlessly raised the ground level of the city. But while so doing, time added to the cathedral more than it took away. Time spread over her face that dark gray patina which gives to very old monuments their season of beauty.

But who knocked down those two rows of statues? Who left the niches empty? Who chiseled into the very middle of the central portal that new and bastard pointed arch? Who dared to frame it in that heavy, tasteless wooden door carved in the style of Louis XV, beside the arabesque of Biscornette? Men, architects, the artists of our time!

*"Which by its mass inspires terror in the spectators."

And, if we enter the interior of the edifice, who overturned that colossal Saint Christopher, proverbial among statues for its magnitude as the Great Hall of the Palace was among halls, as the spire of Strasburg was among steeples? And those myriads of statues which thronged all the intercolumniations of the nave and the choir, kneeling, standing on horseback, men, women, children, kings, bishops, warriors, in stone, marble, gold, silver, brass, and even wax; who brutally swept them away? It was not time certainly.

And who substituted for the old Gothic altar, splendidly encumbered with shrines and reliquaries, that clumsy sarcophagus of marble, with angels' heads and clouds, which looks like an unmatched specimen from the Val-de-Grâce or the Invalides? Whose stupidity set that heavy anachronism of stone in the Carolingian pavement of Hercandus? Was it not Louis XIV fulfilling the vow of Louis XIII?

And who put cold white glass in place of those deeply tinted panes which made the wondering eyes of our forefathers hesitate between the rose-window over the grand doorway and the arched ones of the chancel? And what would a subchorister of the sixteenth century say could he see that beautiful yellow washing with which the vandal archbishops besmeared the stone of their cathedral? He would remember that it was the color which the hangman brushed over buildings of ill repute; he would recall the Hotel du Petit-Bourbon, which had thus been washed all over with yellow because of the constable's treason— "Yellow, after all, so well mixed," writes Sauval, "and so well applied, that the lapse of a century or more has not yet dulled its color." He would think that the holy place had become infamous, and would flee from it.

And then if we ascend the cathedral, without stopping to examine a thousand other barbarisms of every kind, what did they do with that charming miniature steeple which rose from the intersection of the transept and which, no less bold and fragile than its neighbor, the spire (also destroyed) of the Sainte-Chapelle, pierced the sky, yet farther than the towers—slender, sharp, airy, sonorous? An architect of good taste amputated it in 1787, and thought it was enough to hide the wound with that great plaster of lead which resembles the lid of a soup pot.

Thus it is that the magnificent art of the Middle Ages was ill-treated in almost every country, but especially in France. Three distinguishable agents caused Notre-Dame's mutilations. Each made disfigurements of different intensity. First, time, which gradually made inroads here and there, and gnawed over the church's whole surface; then religious and political revolutions, which, blind and angry by nature, rushed tumultuously upon it, and tore its rich garment of sculpture and carving, smashed its rose-shaped windows, broke its necklaces of arabesques and miniature figures, tore down its statues, here for their miter, there for their crown; and lastly, changes of fashion which, growing more and more grotesque and stupid ever since the anarchical yet splendid deviations of the Renaissance, succeeded one another in the necessary decline of architecture. Fashion has done more harm than revolutions. It has cut to the quick; it has attacked the very bone and framework of art. It has mangled, hacked, killed the edifice, in its form as well as in its meaning, in its logic as well as in its beauty. And then, it has remade, which, at least, neither time nor revolutions had pretended to do. In the name of "good taste," fashion has clapped on the wounds of Gothic architecture the wretched gewgaws of the day: marble ribands, metal pompons, a veritable leprosy of ovoli, volutes, scallops, draperies, garlands, fringes, stone flames, brazen clouds, fleshy cupids, and chubby cherubim. All these embellishments began to eat away at art in the oratory of Catherine de Medicis, and made it expire two centuries later, tortured and convulsed, in the boudoir of Madame Du Barry.

Thus to sum up the remarks we have made, three kinds of ravages now disfigure Gothic architecture. Wrinkles and warts have appeared on the surface—these are the work of time. Acts of violence, brutalities, contusions, fractures—

these are the work of revolutions, from Luther down to Mirabeau. Mutilations, amputations, dislocation of members, restorations—these are Grecian, Roman, and barbaric labors of the professors according to Vitruvius and Vignola. That magnificent art which the Vandals had produced, the academies murdered. To the work of time and of revolutions, which, at least, devastated with impartiality and magnitude, was added that of a swarm of school-trained architects, licensed, privileged, and patented. They degraded with all the discernment and selection of bad taste, substituting, for instance, the *chicorées* of Louis XV for the Gothic lacework to the greater glory of the Parthenon. This is the kick of the ass at the expiring lion. This is the old oak which, having begun to wither at the top, is stung, gnawed, and cut to pieces by caterpillars.

How vastly different is all this from the time when Robert Cenalis, comparing Notre-Dame in Paris to the famous temple of Diana at Ephesus, "so much vaunted by the ancient pagans," which immortalized Erostratus, thought the Gaulish cathedral "more excellent in length, breadth, height, and structure."

Notre-Dame, however, as an architectural monument, is not one of those which can be called complete, finished, belonging to a definite class. It is not a Romanesque church, nor is it a Gothic church. It is not typical of any individual style. Notre-Dame has not, like the abbey of Tournus, the massive solemn squareness, the round broad vault, the icy bareness, the majestic simplicity of the edifices which have been based upon the circular arch. Nor is it, like the Cathedral of Bourges, the magnificent, airy, multiform, tufted, pinnacled, florid production of the pointed arch. It cannot be ranked among that antique family of churches—gloomy, mysterious, low, and crushed, as it were, by the weight of the circular arch; almost Egyptian, even to their ceilings; hieroglyphic, sacerdotal, symbolical; more abounding in their ornamentations with lozenges and zigzags than with flowers, with flowers than with animals, with animals than with human figures; these,

the work not so much of an architect as of a bishop; the
first transformation of the art, all stamped with theocratic
and military discipline, which took root in the Lower Empire, and stopped at the time of William the Conqueror.
Nor can this cathedral be ranked with that other family of
churches—lofty, airy, rich in sculpture and stained-glass
windows; with sharp forms and bold outlines; communal
and middle-class as political symbols, free, capricious, licentious, as works of art. This is the second transformation
of architecture, no longer hieroglyphic, immutable, and
sacerdotal, but artistic, progressive, and popular, beginning
with the return from the Crusades and ending with Louis
XI. Notre-Dame, then, is not of purely Romanesque origin
like the first group, nor of purely Arabic origin like the
second group.

Notre-Dame is a structure of transition. The Saxon architect was just finishing the first pillars of the nave, when
the pointed arch, arriving from the Crusades, came and
seated itself like a conqueror upon the broad Romanesque
capitals which had been designed to support only circular
arches. The pointed arch, thenceforth master of the field,
determined the construction of the remainder of the
church. However, though inexperienced and timid at its
beginnings, we find the pointed arch widening its compass, and, as it were, restraining itself, as though not yet
daring to spring up into slender spires and lancets, as it afterward did in so many wonderful cathedrals. This arch
might be said to have been affected by the neighboring
heavy, Romanesque pillars.

Besides, these edifices, built during the transition from
the Romanesque to the Gothic period, are no less valuable
for study than the pure examples. They express a nuance
of the architectural art which would be lost without them.
They illustrate how the pointed style was grafted upon the
circular.

Notre-Dame, in particular, is a curious example of this
variation. Each face, each stone of this venerable monument is not only a page of the history of the country, but

of the history of science and art. Thus, to point out here
only some of the principal details: while the small Porte-
Rouge attains almost to the limit the Gothic delicacy of the
fifteenth century, the pillars of the nave, in their amplitude
and solemnity, go back almost as far as the Carolingian
abbey of Saint-Germain-des-Prés. One would think there
were six centuries between that door and those pillars. Not
even the hermetics fail to find, in the emblematical devices
of the great portal, a satisfactory compendium of their
science, of which the church of Saint-Jacques-de-la-
Boucherie was so complete a hieroglyphic. Thus the Romanesque abbey, the philosophical church, Gothic art,
Saxon art, the heavy round pillar which reminds us of
Gregory VII, the hermetical symbolism by which Nicolas
Flamel anticipated Luther, papal unity, the schism, Saint-
Germain-des-Prés, and Saint-Jacques-de-la-Boucherie—all
are mingled, combined, and amalgamated in Notre-Dame.
This central mother-church is a sort of chimera among the
other old churches of Paris; it has the head of one, the
limbs of another, the back of a third—something from ev-
ery one.

We repeat: these hybrid structures are none the less interesting to the artist, the antiquarian, and the historian.
They make us feel in how great a degree architecture is a
primitive art, inasmuch as they also demonstrate the Cyclopean remains, the Egyptian pyramids, and the gigantic
Hindu pagodas; and they demonstrate that the greatest productions of architecture are not so much the work of indi-
viduals as of society—the offspring rather of national
efforts than the outcome of a particular genius; a legacy
left by the whole people, the accumulation of ages, the res-
idue of successive evaporations of human society; in short,
a species of formations. Each wave of time leaves its allu-
vium, each race leaves a deposit upon the monument, each
individual lays his stone. Such is the process of beavers,
such that of bees, such that of men. The great symbol of
architecture, Babel, is a hive.

Great edifices, like great mountains, are the work of the

ages. Often art undergoes a transformation while they are
yet in progress—*pendent opera interrupta**—they go on
again quietly, in accordance with the change in art. The
new art form takes the structure as it finds it, encrusts itself upon it, assimilates it, develops it after its own fashion, and finishes it if possible. The whole process is
accomplished without effort, without reaction, without disturbance, according to a natural and tranquil law. A shoot
is grafted on, it grows, the sap circulates; vegetation is in
progress. Certainly there is a volume of material, even a
history of all human nature, in those successive engraft-
ings of several styles at different heights upon the same
structure. The man, the artist, the individual is lost under
those great masses without an author's name. Human intelligence can be traced there only in its aggregate. Time is
the architect, the nation is the builder.

Let us consider here only the architecture of Christian
Europe—that younger sister of the great masonries of the
East—which appears as an immense formation, divided
into three clearly defined superimposed zones: The Romanesque zone, the Gothic zone, and the zone of the Renaissance, which we would prefer to call Greco-Roman.
The Romanesque stratum, the most ancient and the lowest,
is occupied by the circular arch, which reappears supported by the Grecian column in the modern and upper
stratum of the Renaissance. The pointed arch is somewhere between the two. The edifices which belong to one
or the other of these extra strata exclusively are perfectly
distinct, uniform, and complete. Such is the Abbey of
Jumièges, the Cathedral of Rheims, the Church of Saint-
Croix in Orleans. But the three zones mingle, combine,
overlap like the colors of a prism. And hence, these complex edifices, these structures of transition: one is Romanesque at the foot, Gothic in the middle, and Greco-Roman
in the head. This happened when six hundred years were
required to build it. This variety is rare: the dungeon tower

---

*"Works, once interrupted, remain suspended."

of Estampes is an example. But the edifices of two formations are more frequent. Such is Notre-Dame de Paris, an edifice of the pointed arch, the first pillars of which belong to the Romanesque zone like the portal of Saint-Denis and the nave of Saint-Germain-des-Prés. Such is the charming semi-Gothic chapter house of Bocherville, in which the Romanesque layer rises halfway up. Such is the Cathedral of Rouen, which would have been entirely Gothic, had not the extremity of its central spire pierced into the zone of the Renaissance.

However, all these gradations, all these differences affect only the surface of the structures. It is only art that has changed its skin. The constitution of the Christian church itself has remained untouched. It has ever the same internal framework, the same logical disposition of its parts. Whatever may be the sculptured and decorated outside of a cathedral, we constantly find underneath it at least the rudiments of the Roman basilica. It eternally develops itself upon the ground according to the same law. There are invariably two naves crossing each other at right angles, the upper extremity of which cross is rounded into a chancel; there are always two low sides for the internal processions and for the chapels—a sort of lateral ambulatory communicating with the principal nave by the intercolumniations. This being once laid down, the number of chapels, of doorways, of steeples, of spires is variable to infinity, according to the caprice of the age, of the nation, of art. The performance of worship being once provided for and insured, architecture is at liberty to do what it pleases. Statues, stained glass, rose-shaped windows, arabesques, indentations, capitals, and bas-reliefs—all these as best suit it. Hence the prodigious external variety of these edifices; in the main structure of each there dwells much order and uniformity. The trunk of the tree is unchanging, the vegetation is capricious.

15

The preceding chapter attempts to portray the venerable Cathedral of Notre Dame. The reader has learned of the remarkable beauty the building possessed during the fifteenth century, and that some of the beauty no longer remains. Not included was the church's greatest beauty—its view of Paris, as seen from the top of its towers.

It was indeed when, after groping your way up the long dark spiral staircase that climbs between the thick walls of the steeple, you at last emerged on one of the two lofty platforms, flooded with light and air, that a breathtaking picture opened before you on every side—a spectacle *sui generis*. Some idea of this may easily be had by such of our readers as have had the good fortune to see one of the few Gothic towns still left entire, complete, homogeneous; such as Nuremberg in Bavaria, Vittoria in Spain, or even smaller specimens, provided they be in good preservation, as Vitré in Brittany, and Nordhausen in Prussia.

The Paris of three hundred and fifty years ago, the Paris of the fifteenth century, was already a giant city. We Parisians, generally speaking, are mistaken as to the ground which we think it has gained. Paris, since the time of Louis XI, has not grown territorially by much more than a third, and certainly it has lost much more in beauty than it has gained in size.

Paris was born, as everyone knows, on that ancient island of the Cité, or City, which is in the shape of a cradle. The shores of that island were its first walls, the Seine was its first moat. For several centuries Paris remained only on this island. She had two bridges, one on the north, the other on the south. The two bridgeheads, the Grand-Châtelet on the right bank and the Petit-Châtelet on the left, were at once its gates and its fortresses. Then, under the first kings, being too much confined within the limits of its island, and unable to turn itself about, Paris crossed the river. So, on each side, beyond either Châtelet, the first line of walls and towers began to encroach upon the countryside on both sides of the Seine. Of this ancient enclosure, some vestiges still remained as late as the last century; today nothing remains but the memory, and here and there a landmark, such as the Baudets Gate, or Baudoyer—*Porta Bagauda.*

Gradually, the flood of houses, constantly impelled from the heart of the town to the exterior, overflowed, wore away, and erased this enclosure. Philip-Augustus constructed a new wall. He imprisoned Paris within a circular chain of tall, solid, massive towers. For more than a century the houses crowded each other, accumulated, and rose higher in this basin, like water in a reservoir. Story was piled upon story; they climbed, so to speak, one on the other. They shot up like compressed sap, and strove each to lift its head above its neighbors, in order to get a breath of air. The streets became deeper and narrower, as every open space was covered. Finally, the houses leaped over Philip-Augustus' wall, and merrily scattered themselves helter-skelter, like escapees, without plan or order. There they squatted at their ease, and the people carved themselves gardens out of the fields.

By 1367, the suburbs were so extensive that a new enclosure was needed, especially on the right bank, and one was built by Charles V.

But a town like Paris is constantly growing. It is only such towns that become capital cities. They are like funnels into which are poured all the geographical, political, and moral drains of a country, all the natural tendencies of a people; they become the cisterns of civilization, so to speak. Also, they are the sinks, into which commerce, industry, intelligence, population, all the vital juices, all that is life, all that is soul in a nation filters and collects, drop by drop, century by century. The enclosure of Charles V had therefore the same fate as the wall of Philip-Augustus. By the end of the fifteenth century, it too was overtaken and passed, and new suburbs grew. In the sixteenth century, this enclosure seemed visibly to recede and to become buried deeper and deeper in the old town, so dense was the new growth outside of it. Thus, in the fifteenth century—to stop there—Paris had already worn away three concentric circles of walls. At the time of Julian the Apostate Paris was in embryo, so to speak, inside the Grand-Châtelet and the Petite-Châtelet. Then the mighty city successively burst its four wall-belts, like a growing child who can no longer wear the clothing of a year ago. Under Louis XI, one could see rising here and there, in that sea of houses, clusters of ruined towers belonging to the ancient bulwarks, like the tops of hills after an inundation, like archipelagoes of the old Paris submerged by the new.

Since then, Paris has, unfortunately for us, optically undergone yet another change; but it has jumped only one more enclosure; namely, the wall of Louis XV, that miserable wall of mud and rubbish, worthy of the king who constructed it and the man who sang of it:

Le mur murant Paris rend Paris murmurant. *

In the fifteenth century, Paris was still divided into three totally distinct and separate cities, each having its own physiognomy, manners, customs, privileges, and history: the City, the University, and the Town. The City, which occupied the island, was the oldest, the smallest, and the mother of the other two, squeezed between them like (excuse the comparison) a little old woman between two tall beautiful daughters. The University covered the left bank of the Seine, from the Tournelle to the Tower of Nesle,

*"The wall surrounding Paris makes Paris murmur."

points corresponding, in the Paris of today, one to the Halles-aux-Vins, and the other to the Mint. Its circular wall encroached upon a rather large plain where Julian had built his baths. It included the Hill of Sainte-Geneviève. The culminating point of this curve of walls was the Porte-Papale, that is to say, very nearly, the site of the present Pantheon. The Town, which was the largest of the three portions of Paris, occupied the right bank. Its quay, interrupted at several points, stretched along the Seine, from the Tower of Billy to the Tower du Bois; that is to say, from the spot where the Grenier d'Abondance now stands, to the spot now occupied by the Tuileries. These four points where the Seine intersected the enclosure of the capital, the Tournelle, and the Tower of Nesle on the left, the Tower of Billy and the Tower du Bois on the right, were called "the four towers of Paris." The Town penetrated still farther into the country than did the University. The culminating point of the Town's enclosure (the one constructed by Charles V) was at the gates of Saint-Denis and Saint-Martin, the sites of which have not changed to this day.

As we have just remarked, each of these three large divisions of Paris was a town, but each town was too specialized to be complete in itself. None could do without the other two. Thus they had three different aspects. In the City, churches were abundant; in the Town, palaces; in the University, schools. Leaving aside for the moment the secondary jurisdictions of the old Paris and the capricious intricacies of the right of way, and noting only the great masses in the chaos of communal jurisdictions, we may say in general that the island was controlled by the bishop; the right bank, by the provost of merchants; the left bank, by the rector of the University. The provost of Paris, a royal and not a municipal officer, was in charge of all. The City had Notre-Dame; the Town had the Louvre and the Hotel de Ville; the University had the Sorbonne. The Town also had Les Halles; the City, the Hotel-Dieu; the University, the Pré-aux-Clercs. For crimes committed by the students on the left bank, in their Pré-aux-Clercs, there were trials at the Palace of Justice on the island, and punishment was meted out on the right bank at Montfaucon, unless the rector, feeling the University to be strong and the king weak, intervened; for it was a privilege of the scholars to be hung in their own district.

Most of these privileges, to note in passing, and some of them were more valuable than the one just mentioned, had been extorted from the kings by revolts and mutinies. It is the time-honored way. The king only yields what the people take. There is an old French charter which defines loyalty quite simply: *Civibus fidelitas in reges, quae tamen aliquoties seditionibus interrupta, multa peperit privilegia.**

In the fifteenth century, five islands of the Seine were embraced within the circuit of Paris: the Ile Louviers, on which there were then trees, though there is now only wood; the Ile-aux-Vaches, the Ile Notre-Dame, both uninhabited (except for one sorry hovel), both fiefs of the bishop. In the seventeenth century these two islands were converted into one, which we call today Ile Saint-Louis. Lastly the City, having at its western extremity the islet of the Passeur-aux-Vaches, now buried under the foundations of the Pont-Neuf, had at that time five bridges: three on the right (the Pont Notre-Dame and the Pont-au-Change, both made of stone, and the Pont-aux-Meuniers, which was made of wood) and two on the left (the Petit-Pont, made of stone, and the Pont Saint-Michel, made of wood). All the bridges were lined with houses.

The University had six gates, all built by Philip-Augustus. Starting from the Tournelle, they were: the Porte Saint-Victor, the Port Bordelle, the Port-Papale, the Porte Saint-Jacques, the Porte Saint-Michel, and the Porte Saint-Germain.

The Town likewise had six gates, all built by Charles V.

*"Loyalty to kings, interrupted however by several revolts, has procured many privileges for the citizens."

Setting from the Tower of Billy, they were: the Porte Saint-Antoine, the Porte du Temple, the Porte Saint-Martin, the Porte Saint-Denis, the Porte Montmartre, and the Porte Saint-Honoré. All these gates were strong, and handsome, too, which latter attribute is by no means incompatible with strength. In a wide, deep trench, with a swift current during the winter floods, ran the Seine, washing the base of the walls all around Paris. At night the gates were closed; a heavy iron chain was fastened across the river at each of the two extremities of the town; and Paris slept quietly.

Seen from a bird's-eye view, these three boroughs—the City, the University, the Town—each appeared like an inextricable tangle of weirdly jumbled streets. However, at first glance, you recognized that these three fragments of a city formed a single whole. You immediately distinguished two long parallel streets, running without interruption or deviation, almost in a straight line, through all three sections of Paris, from one extremity to the other, from south to north, at right angles to the Seine. These connecting strands drew the divisions together, and the people ever passing from one precinct to another made the three one. One of these two long streets ran from the Porte Saint-Jacques to the Porte Saint-Martin, and was called in the University, Rue Saint-Jacques; in the City, Rue de la Juiverie; and in the Town, Rue Saint-Martin. It crossed the river twice, under the names of the Petit-Pont and the Pont Notre-Dame. The other street—which was called on the left bank, Rue de la Harpe; on the island, Rue de la Barillerie; on the right bank, Rue Saint-Denis—on one side of the Seine, Pont Saint-Michel, and on the other, Pont-au-Change—ran from the Porte Saint-Michel in the University to the Porte Saint-Denis in the Town. Although there were various names according to the sections they traversed, these still were in fact only two streets, the long mother streets, the two arteries of Paris, which fed all the other veins of the triple city, or into which they flowed.

Independent of these two principal streets, running

straight across all Paris, and common to the entire capital, the Town and the University had each its own great street, running parallel to the Seine, and intersecting the two arterial streets at right angles. Thus, in the Town, you descended in a straight line from the Porte Saint-Antoine to the Porte Saint-Honoré; in the University, from the Porte Saint-Victor to the Porte Saint-Germain. These two large roads, crossing the first two arteries mentioned above, formed with them the framework upon which was laid, knotted, and drawn in every direction the tangled network of the streets of Paris. In this tangle, you might, however, also discover, upon attentive observation, two bunches of wide streets, one in the University and one in the Town, which ran from the bridges to the gates. Something of this same geometrical plan still exists in Paris today.

Now, what else, besides this confusion of streets, could you see from the towers of Notre-Dame in 1482? That is what we shall try to describe.

The spectator, on arriving, out of breath, upon this summit, was at first dazzled by the confusion of roofs, chimneys, streets, bridges, squares, spires, steeples. Everything struck the eye at once: the carved gable, the sharp roofing, the hanging turret at the corner of the walls, the stone pyramid of the eleventh century, the slate obelisk of the fifteenth, the round, naked tower of the castle turret, the square and decorated tower of the church, the large and small, the massive and the light. The gaze for some time was utterly bewildered by this labyrinth, in which everything had its particular originality, its reason, its genius, its beauty, everything had proceeded from art, from the most inconsiderable carved and painted house-front, with external timbers, low doorway, and stories projecting each above the other, to the royal Louvre itself, which, at that time, had a colonnade of towers. But here are the principal masses which were distinguished once the eye became accustomed to this tumult of structures.

First of all, the City. The island of the City, as is observed by Sauval, the most laborious of the old explorers

of Parisian antiquity, who among all his incongruities has
an occasional good idea; namely, "The island of the City
is shaped like a great ship, sunk in the mud, lengthwise in
the stream, in about the middle of the Seine." We have already shown that, in the fifteenth century, the ship was
moored to the two banks of the river by five bridges. This
idea of the hull of a vessel had also struck the heraldic
scribes, for, from this circumstance, according to Favyn
and Pasquier, and not from the siege by the Normans,
came the ship emblazoned upon the old escutcheon of
Paris. To him who can decipher it, heraldry is an emblematic language. The whole history of the latter half of the
Middle Ages is written in heraldry, as that of the former
half is in the symbolism of the Romanesque churches.
Thus do the hieroglyphics of feudalism succeed those of
theocracy.

The City, then, first presented itself to the viewer with
its stern to the east and its prow to the west. Facing the
prow, you saw an innumerable congregation of old roofs,
with the lead-covered apse of the Sainte-Chapelle rising
above them, broad and round, like an elephant's back with
a tower upon it. Only, here, that tower was the boldest, airi-
est, most notched and ornamented spire that ever showed
the sky through its lacework cone. Directly in front of
Notre-Dame three streets terminated in an open space, a
fine square of old houses. The southern side of this square
was overhung by the furrowed and rugged front of the
Hotel-Dieu, whose roof looks as if it were covered with
pimples and warts. And then, right and left, east and west,
within that narrow circuit of the City, rose the steeples of
its twenty-one churches, of all dates, shapes, and sizes,
from the low and decayed Romanesque companile of
Saint-Denys-du-Pas, to the delicate spires of Saint-Pierre-
aux-Boeufs and Saint-Landry. Behind Notre-Dame extended, northward, the cloister with its Gothic galleries;
southward, the semi-Romanesque palace of the bishop;
and eastward, the uninhabited point of the island, called
the Terrain. Amid that mass of houses, the eye could also

distinguish, by the high perforated miters of stone which, at that period, placed aloft upon the roof, crowned even the highest windows of palaces, the mansion given by the Parisians, in the reign of Charles VI, to Juvénal des Ursins; a little farther on, the black, pitch-covered sheds of the market of Palus, and in another direction, the new chancel of Saint-Germain-le-Vieux, lengthened in 1458 by an encroachment upon one end of the Rue-aux-Febves; and also here and there were to be seen some crossways crowded with people; a pillory erected at the corner of a street; some fine pieces of the pavement of Philip-Augustus (magnificent flagstone grooved for horses' hooves in the middle of the street, and so ill-replaced in the sixteenth century by wretched pebbling called *pavé de la Ligue*); a deserted backyard, with one of those transparent staircase turrets which they used to build in the fifteenth century, one of which is still to be seen in the Rue des Bourdonnais. Lastly, to the right of the Saint-Chapelle, toward the west, the Palace of Justice lifted its group of towers above the water's brink. The groves of the royal gardens, which occupied the western sector of the island, hid from view the islet of the Passeur. As for the river itself, it was hardly visible on either side of the City from the towers of Notre-Dame, because of the Seine's disappearing under the bridges, and the bridges' hiding under the houses.

And when you looked beyond those bridges, whose roofs were tinged with green, having contracted untimely moldiness from the mist which rose from the water, if you cast your eye to the left, toward the University, the first edifice that drew your attention was a large, low cluster of towers, the Petit-Châtelet, the gaping porch of which seemed to devour the extremity of the Petit-Pont. Then, if your view ranged along the shore from east to west, from the Tournelle to the Tower of Nesle, you beheld a long line of houses exhibiting sculptured beams, colored window glass, each story overhanging the one beneath it—an interminable zigzag of ordinary houses, cut off at frequent intervals by the end of some street, and now and then also by the front or the corner of some huge stone mansion, which seemed to stand unconcerned, with its courtyards and gardens, its wings and its compartments, among that rabble of houses crowding and pinching one another, like a great lord among a mob of rustics. There were five or six of these mansions upon the quay, from the Logis de Lorraine, which shared with the house of Bernardines the great neighboring enclosure of the Tournelle, to the Hotel de Nesle, whose principal tower marked the limits of Paris on that side, and whose pointed roofs cut with their dark triangles, during three months of the year, the scarlet disk of the setting sun.

That side of the Seine was, however, the less mercantile of the two; there was more noise from crowds of scholars than from artisans, and there was not, properly speaking, any quay, except from the Pont Saint-Michel to the Tower of Nesle. The rest of the bank of the Seine was either a bare strand, as was the case beyond the Bernardines, or a close row of houses with water at their foundations, as between the two bridges. There was a great clamor of washerwomen along the waterside, talking, shouting, singing, from morning till night, and beating away at their linens—as they do today, contributing their full share to the gaiety of Paris.

The University brought the eye to a full stop. From one end to the other, it was a compact, homogeneous whole. Those thousand thickset angular roofs, clinging together, nearly all composed of the same geometrical element, when seen from above, looked almost like the crystallization of a single substance. The capricious fissures formed by the streets did not cut this conglomeration of houses into slices too disproportionate. The forty-two colleges were distributed among them very equally, and were to be seen in every quarter. The amusingly varied pinnacles of those beautiful buildings were a product of the same art as the ordinary roofs which they overtopped, being nothing more than the square or the cube of the same geometrical

figure. Thus they complicated the whole without confusing
it, completed without overloading it. Geometry is a kind of
harmony. Several fine mansions, too, lifted their heads
proudly here and there above the picturesque attic stories
of the left bank; for example, the Logis de Nevers, the
Logis de Rome, the Logis de Reims—which have disappeared—and the Hotel de Cluny, which still exists for the
artist's consolation, but whose tower was so stupidly un-
crowned a few years ago. Near the Hotel de Cluny was
that Roman palace, with its fine semicircular arches, once
the Baths of Julian. There were also a number of abbeys,
of a beauty more religious, of a grandeur more solemn,
than the secular mansions, but neither less handsome nor
less spacious. Those which first attracted attention were
the abbeys of the Bernardines, with their three steeples;
second, that of Sainte-Geneviève, whose square tower,
which still exists, makes us so much regret the disappearance of the rest; then the Sorbonne, half college, half monastery, whose admirable nave yet survives; also, the fine
quadrilateral Cloister of the Mathurins; and, adjacent to it,
the Cloister of Saint-Benedict; the house of the Cordeliers,
with its three enormous and contiguous gables; that of the
Augustines, whose graceful spire formed, after the Tower
of Nesle, the second indentation on that side of Paris,
starting from the west. The colleges, which are, in fact, the
intermediate link between the cloister and the world, balanced the architecture between the abbeys and the great
mansions, exhibiting a severe elegance, a sculpture less
airy than that of the palaces, an architecture less stern than
that of the convents. Unfortunately, scarcely anything remains of these structures, in which Gothic art kept so fine
a balance between richness and economy. The churches—
which were numerous and splendid in the University, and
which represented every architectural era, from the round
arches of Saint-Julian to the Gothic ones of Saint-
Severin—rose above all; and, as one harmony more in that
harmonious mass, they accented in close succession the indented outline of the roofs, with their boldly cut spires,

with their perforated steeples, and their slender needles, the lines of which were themselves but a magnificent exaggeration of the acute angle of the roofs.

The terrain of the University was hilly. The Hill of Sainte-Geneviève, to the southeast, formed an enormous swelling, and it was curious to see, from the top of Notre-Dame, that multitude of narrow, winding streets, now called the Latin Quarter, those clusters of houses which scattered in every direction from the summit of that eminence, and spread themselves in disorder, almost precipitously, down its sides to the water's edge, some looking as if they were falling, others as if they were climbing up, and all as if clinging to one another, while the continual motion of a thousand dark objects crossing one another upon the pavement gave the whole an appearance of life. These were people on the streets, as beheld thus from on high and at a distance.

Then, in the spaces between those roofs, those spires, those numberless odd buildings, which bent, twisted, and indented the highest outline of the University in so fantastic a manner, were to be seen, here and there, a great patch of moss-covered wall, a solid round tower, an embattled, fortresslike town-gate. This marked the enclosure of Philip-Augustus. Green meadows were spread beyond, across which roads diverged. Along their sides were a few straggling houses, growing fewer as the distance from the protecting wall increased. However, some drew together into suburbs of considerable size. Leaving the Tournelle, first was the village of Saint-Victor, with its bridge of one arch over the Bièvre, its abbey, where the epitaph of King Louis the Fat could be read, and its church, with an octagonal steeple flanked by four belfries of the eleventh century (such a one can still be seen at Estampes). Then there was Saint-Marceau, which already had three churches and a convent. Next, leaving on the left the mill of Gobelins with its four white walls, came the village of Saint-Jacques, with its elegant sculptured cross at the crossroads. This place contained several churches: the church of Saint-

Jacques-du-Haut-Pas, at that time a charming Gothic structure; Saint-Magloire, with its beautiful nave of the fourteenth century, which Napoleon turned into a hay shed; Notre-Dame-des-Champs, where were to be seen Byzantine mosaics. Lastly, after leaving the open country where stood the monastery of the Carthusians, a rich structure belonging to the same period as the Palace of Justice, with its little compartmentalized gardens, and the haunted ruins of Vauvert, the eye fell, to the west, upon the three Romanesque spires of Saint-Germain-des-Prés. The village of Saint-Germain, already a large commune, contained fifteen or twenty streets. The sharp steeple of Saint-Sulpice marked one of the corners of the village. Close by it was to be distinguished the quadrilateral enclosure of the fair of Saint-Germain, where there is today a marketplace. Then came the abbey's pillory, a pretty little round tower, capped by a lead cone; farther on were the tile factories and the Rue du Four, leading to the manorial bake-house, and the mill perched upon its mound, and the hospital for lepers, a small, isolated building, difficult to see.

But what particularly caught the eye, and kept it fixed for a long time in this direction, was the abbey itself. It is certain that that monastery, which had an air of importance both as a church and as a lordly residence, that abbatial palace, where the bishops of Paris deemed themselves fortunate to sleep a single night, that refectory, to which the architect had given the air, the beauty, and the splendid rose-window of a cathedral, that elegant chapel of the Virgin, that monumental dormitory, those spacious gardens, that portcullis, that drawbridge, that belt of crenelated wall which notched the outline of the verdure of the surrounding meadow, those courts where the mail of the men-at-arms gleamed among the golden copes—the whole, grouped around three round-arched spires firmly seated upon a Gothic chancel, made a magnificent outline on the horizon.

When finally, after having contemplated the University at length, you turned toward the right bank, toward the

Town, the character of the scene suddenly changed. The
Town, in fact, was not only much larger than the University,
but also less homogeneous. At first glance it appeared
to be divided into several masses, singularly distinct from
one another. First of all, to the east, in that sector of the
Town which still takes its name from the marsh in which
Camulogenes lured Caesar, there was a collection of palaces,
which extended to the waterside. Four great, almost
contiguous mansions—the hotels of Jouy, Sens, Barbeau,
and the Queen's House—cast upon the Seine the reflection
of their slated roofs intersected by slender turrets. These
four edifices occupied the space from the Rue des Nonaindières
to the abbey of the Celestines. The small spire of
this abbey formed a graceful relief to the mansions' line of
gables and battlements. Some greenish hovels overhanging
the water in front of these elaborate buildings did not conceal
from view the beautifully ornamented corners of their
facades, their large square windows with stone casements,
their Gothic porticoes heavy with statuary, the bold,
clearcut parapets of their walls, and all those charming
oddities of architecture which made Gothic art seem as if
it were resorting to new combinations with each new
structure. Behind those palaces ran in every direction,
sometimes divided, palisaded and embattled like a citadel,
sometimes shaded by huge trees like a Carthusian monastery,
the immense and multiform enclosure of that miraculous
Hotel de Saint-Pol. Here the King of France had
room to lodge superbly twenty-two princes equal in rank
to the dauphin and the Duke of Burgundy, with their servants
and retinues, not to mention the great barons, and
the emperor when he came to visit Paris. Even their lions
had a hotel to themselves in the royal palace. Let it here
be noted that lodgings for a prince then consisted of not
less than eleven apartments, from the audience room to the
oratory, besides galleries, baths, steam-bath rooms, and
other "superfluous places" with which each apartment was
provided; not to mention a private garden for each one of
the king's guests; not to mention the kitchens, cellars, pan-

tries, and general refectories for the household. Moreover the hotel contained inner courts where there were twenty-two general laboratories from the bakehouse to the royal wine cellar; grounds for every sort of game (mall, tennis, the ring), aviaries, fish ponds, menageries, and stables; libraries, arsenals, and foundries. Such was then the palace of a king, a Louvre, a Hotel de Saint-Pol. It was a city within a city.

From the Notre-Dame tower, the Hotel de Saint-Pol, though almost hidden by the four great mansions of which we have already spoken, was, nevertheless, tremendous and a wonderful sight to see.

The three mansions which Charles V absorbed into his palace, though skillfully connected to the main building by long galleries with windows and small pillars, could be clearly distinguished. These were the Hotel du Petit-Muce, with the lacy balustrade that gracefully bordered its roof; the Hotel of the Abbot of Saint-Maur, having the appearance of a fortress, with its massive tower, its machicolations, shot-holes, iron bulwarks, and on its huge Saxon gate, the abbot's escutcheon between the two notches for the drawbridge; and the Hotel of the Count d'Estampes, the turret of which, in ruin at the top, appeared jagged and notched like the comb of a cock. Here and there were three or four old oaks, grouped together in one large bushy clump, like enormous cauliflowers; swans floated in the clear water of the fish-ponds, all streaked with light and shade. The mansion for the lions, with its low pointed arches supported by short Saxon pillars and its iron bars, roared continuously. Shooting up above the group of buildings, the scaly spire of the Ave-Maria; on the left the residence of the provost of Paris was flanked by four finely wrought turrets. In the middle, in the heart of it all, stood Hotel de Saint-Pol itself, with its multiplicity of facades, its successive embellishments since the time of Charles V, the hybrid excrescences with which the whims of architects had heaped it during two centuries, with all the chancels of its chapels, all the gables of its galleries, its thousand weathercocks, and its two lofty contiguous towers whose conical roofs, surrounded at their base with battlements, looked like pointed hats with the brims turned up.

Let the eye continue to mount the steps of that amphitheater of palaces, and cross a deep fissure in the roofs of the Town, which marks the course of the Rue Saint-Antoine. Soon you would notice the Logis d' Angoulème, an immense structure of several periods, parts of which were quite new and white, harmonizing with the rest hardly better than a red patch on a blue doublet. However, the singularly sharp and elevated roof of the modern palace, bristling with carved spout ends, and covered with sheets of lead, over which ran sparkling encrustations of gilded copper in a thousand fantastic arabesques—that roof so curiously ornamented rose gracefully from the brown ruins of the ancient edifice, whose old massive towers were bellying casklike with age, their height shrunk with decrepitude, and bursting from top to bottom. Behind, rose a forest of needlelike spires on the Palais des Tournelles. There was not a view in the world, not even at Chambord nor at the Alhambra, more magical, more aerial, more captivating, than that grove of spires, belfries, chimneys, weathercocks, spirals, airy lanterns, pavilions, spindle-shaped turrets—all differing in height and position. You could have taken the whole for an immense stone chessboard.

To the right of the Tournelles, that cluster of enormous black towers, black as ink, running one into another, and bound together, as it were, by a circular ditch, that dungeon pierced through with more shot-holes than with windows, that drawbridge always raised, that portcullis always down, that is the Bastille. Those black beaks projecting from the battlements, and which at a distance you mistake for rain spouts, are cannons.

Within their range, at the foot of the formidable structure, is the Porte Saint-Antoine, crouching between its two towers.

Beyond the Tournelles, as far as the wall of Charles V, stretched in rich diversity of verdure and flowers a velvet carpet of gardens and royal parks, in the center of which might be recognized, by its maze of groves and walks, the famous Daedalus garden which Louis XI had given to Coictier. The doctor's observatory rose above the labyrinth like a great isolated column, having a small house for its capital. In that laboratory some terrible astrological crimes were practiced.

Today it is the site of the Palace Royale.

As we have already stated, the palace quarter, of which we have endeavored to give the reader some idea, however sketchily, by detailing only its most important places, filled the corner which Charles V's wall made with the Seine to the east. The center of the Town was occupied by a heap of ordinary houses. In fact it was there that the three bridges of the City on the right bank disgorged their masses of people; and bridges led to houses before palaces. This mass of ordinary dwellings, pressed against each other like the cells in a hive, was not without charm.

And in the waves of the sea, so in the roofs of a great city there is something grand. First of all, the streets, crossing and intertwining, formed a hundred amusing figures. Around Les Halles, it was like a star with a thousand rays. The streets Saint-Denis and Saint-Martin, with their numberless ramifications, ran along beside each other, like two tall trees intertwining their branches. And then there were those tortuous streets, Rue de la Plâtrerie, Rue de la Verrerie, Rue de la Tixeranderie, etc., which snaked through the whole. There were also some handsome edifices which rose above the petrified undulations of this sea of gables. First, at the entrance of the Pont-aux-Changeurs, where the Seine could be seen foaming under the mill wheels at the Pont-aux-Meuniers, was the Châtelet, no longer a Roman tower as under Emperor Julian, but a feudal tower of the thirteenth century, built of stone so hard that three hours' digging with a pick could not remove more than a piece the size of a man's fist. Then there was the rich square belfry tower of Saint-Jacques-de-la-Boucherie, its corners all rounded with statuary, already worthy of admiration, though it was not finished in the fifteenth century. It lacked in particular those four gargoyles which, even to this day, perched at the four corners of its roof, look like so many sphinxes giving to modern Paris an ancient enigma to solve. Rault, the sculptor, placed them there only in 1516, and got twenty francs for his trouble. Also, there was the Maison-aux-Piliers, overlooking that Place de Grève which we have already described. There was the church of Saint-Gervais, that a doorway "in good taste" has since spoiled, the church of Saint-Méry, whose old pointed arches were almost semicircular; and the church of Saint-Jean, whose magnificent spire was proverbial; besides twenty other structures which did not disdain to bury their attractions in that chaos of deep, dark, and narrow streets. Add to these the carved stone crosses, even more frequently seen at crossroads than gibbets themselves; the wall surrounding the cemetery of the Innocents, which could be seen at a distance; the top of Les Halles' pillory, which was visible between the chimneys of the Rue de la Cossonnerie; the gibbet of the Crois-du-Trahoir stood at the corner of a very busy thoroughfare; the circular hovels of the Halle-au-Blé; and broken sections of Philip-Augustus' old wall were distinguishable here and there, buried among houses, ivy-mantled towers, fallen gateways, crumbling and shapeless pieces of wall. Then on the riverbank was the quay with its thousand shops and its bloody skinning yards. Now you come to the Seine itself, covered with boats from the Port-au-Foin to the For-l'Evêque. Thus you have a general idea of the central trapezium of the Town in 1482.

Besides these two quarters—the one of palaces, the other of houses—the Town contributed a third element to the view: that of a long belt of abbeys which bordered almost its whole circumference, from east to west, and, behind the line of fortifications by which Paris was shut in, formed a second internal wall, consisting of convents and

chapels. Thus, close to the park of the Tournelles, between
the Rue Saint-Antoine and the old Rue du Temple, there
was Sainte-Catherine's, with its immense grounds,
bounded only by the wall of Paris. Between the old and
the new Rue du Temple there was the Temple itself, a
frowning bundle of towers, lofty, erect, and isolated in
the midst of an extensive embattled enclosure. Between
the Rue Neuve-du-Temple and the Rue Saint-Martin,
in the midst of its gardens, stood Saint-Martin's, a superb
fortified church, whose girdle of towers, whose tiara of
steeples, were second in strength and splendor only to
Saint-Germain-des-Prés. Between the two streets, Saint-
Martin and Saint-Denis, was the enclosure of the Trinity.
And, finally, between the Rue Saint-Denis and the Rue
Montorgueil was that of the Filles-Dieu. Close by the latter were to be distinguished the decayed roofs and unpaved enclosure of the Court of Miracles, the only profane
link that obtruded itself into that chain of religious houses.

Finally, the fourth compartment which rose distinctly in
the conglomeration of roofs upon the right bank, occupy-
ing the western corner of the great enclosure, down to the
river's edge, was another group of palaces and great mansions crowding against the Louvre. The old Louvre of
Philip-Augustus, an immense structure, whose great tower
mustered around it twenty-three principal towers, besides
all the smaller ones, seemed at a distance to be framed, as
it were, within the Gothic summits of the Hotel
d' Alençon and the Petit-Bourbon. This hydra of towers, this
giant guardian of Paris, with its twenty-four upraised
heads and with monstrous ridges on its back, sheathed in
lead or scaled with slates, and all variegated with glittering
metallic streaks, marked in a surprising manner the western boundary of the Town.

Thus, you saw an immense mass, what the Romans
called an "island," of ordinary dwellings, flanked on both
sides by two great clusters of palaces, topped on one side
by the Louvre and on the other by the Tournelles, and bordered on the north by a long belt of abbeys and walled

gardens—the whole combined and blended to the sight. Over those thousands of buildings, whose tiled and slated roofs ran in so many fantastic chains, were the engraved, embroidered, and inlaid steeples of the forty-four churches on the right bank. Among them were the myriads of cross streets. The boundary on one side was a line of lofty walls with square towers (that of the University wall being round), and on the other, the Seine, crossed by bridges and crowded with countless boats. Such was Paris in the fifteenth century.

Beyond the walls were the suburbs, huddled against the gates, but less numerous and more scattered than those on the University side. Thus, behind the Bastille, there squatted a score of hovels, clustered around the Cross of Faubin, with its curious sculptures, and the abbey of Saint-Antoine-des-Champs, with its flying buttresses. Also there was then Popincourt, lost amid the cornfields; then La Courtille, a merry village of taverns; the village of Saint-Laurent, with its church, whose belfry from a distance seemed to be a part of the pointed towers of the Porte Saint-Martin; the suburb of Saint-Denis, with the extensive enclosure of Saint-Ladre; outside the Porte Montmartre, the Grange-Batelière encircled with white walls; and behind it the chalky slopes of Montmartre itself. Montmartre then had almost as many churches as windmills, but has retained only the windmills, since society now seeks only bread for the body. And beyond the Louvre, you saw, stretching into the meadows, the suburb of Saint-Honoré, even then of considerable size; green La Petite-Bretagne; and, spreading itself out, the Marché-aux-Pourceaux, in the center of which stood the horrible boiler used for executing those convicted of counterfeiting. Between La Courtille and Saint-Laurent your eye had already remarked, on the summit of a little hill that rose in a lonely plain, a structure which looked from a distance like a ruined colonnade standing over a basement with its foundation exposed. This, however, was neither a Parthenon nor a Temple of the Olympian Jupiter; it was Montfaucon.

Now, if the enumeration of so many edifices, brief as we have tried to be, has not shattered in the reader's mind the general image of old Paris as fast as we have endeavored to construct it, we will recapitulate it in a few words. In the center was the island of the City, resembling in its form an enormous tortoise, extending on either side its bridges all scaly with tiles, like so many feet, from under its gray shell of roofs. On the left, the close, dense, bristling, and homogeneous quadrangle of the University, and on the right the vast semicircle of the Town, much more interspersed with gardens and great edifices. The three masses—City, Town, and University—are veined with innumerable streets. Through the whole runs the Seine, the "life-giving Seine," as Father Du Breul calls it, dotted with islands, crossed by bridges, and boats. All around is an immense plain, checkered with fields, planted with a thousand different sorts of vegetation, and strewn with beautiful villages—on the left, Issy, Vanves, Vaugirard, Montrogue, Gentilly, with its round tower and its square tower, etc.; and on the right twenty others, from Conflans to Vile-l'Evêque. On the horizon a circle of hills formed, as it were, the rim of this vast basin. Finally, in the distance on the east, was Vincennes, with its seven quadrangular towers; on the south, Bicêtre with its pointed turrets; on the north, Saint-Denis and its spire; and on the west, Saint-Cloud and its castle-keep. Such was the Paris viewed from the towers of Notre-Dame by the ravens who lived in 1482.

And yet it is of this city that Voltaire said, "Before the time of Louis XIV, it possessed only four fine pieces of architecture"; that is to say, the dome of the Sorbonne, the Val-de-Grâce, the modern Louvre, and I have forgotten the fourth; perhaps it was the Luxembourg. Fortunately, Voltaire was nonetheless the author of "Candide"; as such, and for having made this observation, he proved himself not the least sardonic of the many men who succeeded him. This proves, besides, that one may be a genius, and yet understand nothing of an art which he has not yet studied. Didn't Molière think he was doing a great honor to Raphael and Michelangelo when he called them "those Mignards of their age"?

But to return to fifteenth-century Paris.

It was then not only a beautiful city, but a homogeneous one, an architectural and historical product of the Middle Ages—a chronicle in stone. It was a city composed of two architectural strata only, the Romanesque and the Gothic, for the Roman layer had disappeared long ago except in the Baths of Julian, where it still pierced through the thick incrustation of the Middle Ages. As for the Celtic stratum, specimens could no longer be found, even when digging a well.

Fifty years later, when the Renaissance came to blend with this severe yet diversified unity the dazzling profuseness of its own systems and its fantasies that rioted among Roman arches, Grecian columns, and Gothic vaults, its delicate and lifelike sculpture, its own peculiar taste for arabesques and foliage, its architectural paganism contemporary with Luther, Paris was perhaps more beautiful still, though less harmonious to the eye and to the mind. But that glorious period was of short duration. The Renaissance was not impartial. Not content with erecting, it thought proper to pull down; it must be acknowledged, too, that it needed room. So the Gothic Paris was complete but for a moment. Scarcely was the tower of Saint-Jacques-de-la-Boucherie completed before the demolition of the old Louvre was begun.

Since that time, this great city has been daily lapsing into deformity. The Gothic Paris, under which the Romanesque Paris disappeared, passed away in its turn. But what name shall we give to the Paris that has taken its place?

There is the Paris of Catherine de Medicis at the Tuileries, the Paris of Henri II at the Hotel de Ville—two edifices which are still in fine taste; the Paris of Henry IV at the Place Royale—a brick front, faced with stone, and roofed with slate, tri-colored houses; the Paris of Louis XIII at the Val-de-Grâce—a squat, clumsy style, with basket-handle vaults, big-bellied columns, and a hunch-backed dome; the Paris of Louis XIV at the Invalides—great, rich, gilded, and cold; the Paris of Louis XV at Saint-Sulpice—with volutes, knots of ribbons, clouds, ver-micelli, and chicory, all in stone; the Paris of Louis XVI at the Pantheon—a wretched copy of St. Peter's in Rome (the building has settled awkwardly, which has by no means rectified its lines); the Paris of the Republic at the School of Medicine, a poor Greek and Roman style, just as much to be compared to the Colosseum or the Parthenon as the constitution of the year III is to the laws of Minos—which style in architecture is called the "Messidor"; the Paris of Napoleon at the Place Vendôme—something sub-lime, a brazen column composed of melted cannon; the Paris of the Restoration at the Bourse—a very white col-onnade, supporting a very smooth frieze; the whole is square and cost twenty million francs.

To each of these characteristic structures is allied, by similarity of style, manner, and arrangement, a certain number of houses scattered over the different quarters of the Town, which the eye of the connoisseur easily distin-guishes and assigns to their respective dates. When a man understands the art of seeing, he can trace the spirit of an age and the features of a king even in the knocker on a door.

Contemporary Paris has therefore no general physiog-nomy. It is a collection of parts from several different ages, and the finest of all have disappeared. This capital is increasing in houses only, and what houses! If it goes on as it is going now, Paris will be rebuilt every fifty years. So also the historical meaning of its architecture is daily wearing away. Its great structures are becoming fewer and fewer, seeming to be swallowed up one after the other by this flood of houses. Our fathers had a Paris of stone, our children will have a Paris of plaster.

As for the modern structures of the new Paris, we shall gladly decline from enlarging upon them. Not, indeed, that we do not pay them all proper admiration. Soufflot's

Sainte-Geneviève is certainly the finest Savoy cake that
was ever made of stone. The Palace of the Legion of
Honor is also a very distinguished piece of pastry. The
dome of the Halle-au-Blé is an English jockey-cap on a
magnificent scale. The towers of Saint-Sulpice are two
great clarinets; now, nobody can deny that a clarinet shape
is a shape, and then the telegraph, crooked and grinning,
makes an admirable diversity upon the roof. The church of
Saint-Roch has a doorway with whose magnificence only
that of Saint-Thomas Aquinas can compare; it also has a
high-relief Calvary down in the cellar, and a sun of gilded
wood. These things, it must be owned, are positively marvelous. The lantern of the labyrinth at the Garden of
Plants, too, is vastly ingenious. As for the Palais de la
Bourse, which is Grecian in its colonnade, Roman in the
circular arches of its doors and windows, and of the Renaissance in its great vaulted ceiling, it doubtless is a structure of great correctness and purity of taste, one proof of
which is that it is crowned by an attic story such as was
never seen in Athens, a fine straight line gracefully intersected here and there by stove pipes. Let us here add that
if it be a rule that the architecture of a building should be
so adapted to the purpose of the building, that the aspect
of the edifice should at once declare that purpose, we cannot too much admire a structure which from its appearance
might be either a royal palace, a chamber of deputies, a
town hall, a college, a riding house, an academy, a repos-
itory, a court of justice, a museum, a barracks, a mauso-
leum, a temple, or a theater, but which is all the while the
Bourse. A building ought moreover to be adapted to the
climate. This one has evidently been built expressly for a
cold and rainy sky. Its roof is almost flat, as in the East;
and consequently in winter, when there is snow, the roof
has to be swept. And does anyone doubt that roofs are intended to be swept? As for the purpose of which we have
just now been speaking, the building fulfills it admirably.
It is the Bourse in France, as it would have been a temple
in Greece. True it is that the architect had much ado to

conceal the dial of the clock, which would have destroyed the purity of the noble lines of the facade; but to make amends we have that colonnade around the whole structure, under which, on important days of religious solemnity, may be magnificently developed the schemes of money-brokers and stock-jobbers.

These, doubtless, are very superb structures. Add to these many a pretty street, amusing and diversified, like the Rue de Rivoli, and we need not despair that Paris shall one day present, when seen from a balloon, that richness of outline and opulence of detail, that peculiar diversity of aspect, that something surpassingly grand in the simple and striking in the beautiful, which distinguishes a draftboard.

However, admirable as you may think the present Paris, reconstruct in your imagination the Paris of the fifteenth century; look at the sky through that surprising forest of spires, towers, and steeples; pour forth through the midst of the vast city, tear upon the tips of the islands, bend under the arches of the bridges of the Seine with her large patches of green and yellow, more changeable than a serpent's skin; project distinctly upon an azure horizon the Gothic profile of that old Paris; make its outline float in a wintry mist clinging to its innumerable chimneys; plunge it into deep night, and observe the fantastic display of the lights against the darkness of that gloomy labyrinth of buildings; cast upon it a ray of moonlight, showing the city in glimmering vagueness, with its towers lifting their great heads from that foggy sea; or revert again to that dark silhouette, reanimate with shadow the thousand sharp angles of its spires and gables and make it stand out, more jagged than a shark's jaw, against the copper-colored sky of the setting sun.

Now compare.

And if you would receive from the old city an impression which the modern one is quite incapable of giving, ascend, on the morning of some great holiday, at sunrise, on Easter or on Pentecost Sunday, to some elevated point from which your eye can command the whole capital, and attend the awakening of the chimes. Behold, at a signal from heaven—for it is the sun that gives it—those thousand churches starting from their sleep. At first you hear only scattered tinklings from church to church, as when musicians are giving one another notice to begin. Then, all of a sudden, behold—for there are moments when the ear itself seems to see—behold, ascending at the same moment from every steeple a column of sound, as it were, a cloud of harmony. At first, the vibration of each bell mounts direct, clear, and, as it were, isolated from the rest into the splendid morning sky. Then by degrees, as they expand, they mingle, unite, and are lost in one another. All are confounded in one magnificent concert. They become a mass of sonorous vibrations, endlessly sent forth from the innumerable steeples—floating, undulating, bounding, and eddying over the town, and extending far beyond the horizon the deafening circle of its oscillations. Yet that sea of harmony is no chaos. Wide and deep as it is, it has not lost its transparency: you perceive the winding of each group of notes that escapes from the several chimes; you can follow the dialogue by turns grave and clamorous, of the *crescelle* and the *bourdon*; you perceive the octaves leaping from steeple to steeple; you observe them springing aloft, winged, light, and whistling from the silver bell, falling broken and limping from the wooden bell. You admire among them the seven bells of Saint-Eustache, whose peals incessantly descend and ascend. And you see clear and rapid notes running across, as it were, in three or four luminous zigzags, and vanishing like flashes of lightning. Down there in Saint-Martin's Abbey is a shrill and broken-voiced songstress; nearer is the sinister and sullen voice of the Bastille; and farther away is the great tower of the Louvre, with its counter tenor. The royal carillon of the Palace unceasingly casts on every side resplendent trillings, upon which fall at regular intervals the heavy stroke from the great bell of Notre Dame, making sparkles of sound as a hammer upon an anvil. Frequently, many tones

come from the triple peal of Saint-Germain-des-Prés.
Then, again, from time to time that mass of sublime noise
half opens, and gives passage to the finale of the Ave-
Maria, which glitters like a cluster of stars. Below, in the
deeps of the concert, you distinguish the confused, internal
voices of the churches, exhaled through the vibrating pores
of their vaulted roofs. Here, certainly, is an opera worth
hearing. Ordinarily, the murmur that escapes from Paris in
the daytime is the city talking; in the night, it is the city
breathing, but here, it is the city singing. Listen then to
this ensemble of the steeples; diffuse over it the murmur of
half a million people, the everlasting plaint of the river, the
boundless breathings of the wind, the grave and distant
quartet of the four forests placed upon the hills in the distance like so many vast organs, immersing in them, as in
a demitint, all in the central concert that would otherwise
be too raucous or too sharp, and then say whether you
know of anything in the world more rich, more joyous,
more golden, more dazzling than this tumult of bells and
chimes, this furnace of music, these ten thousand voices of
brass, all singing together in flutes of stone three hundred
feet high—than this city which is no longer anything but
an orchestra—than this symphony as loud as a tempest.

16

Sixteen years before the period of the events recorded in
this history, one fine morning—it happened to be Quasimodo Sunday—a living creature was laid after mass in
the church of Notre Dame in the wooden bed walled into
the porch on the left hand, opposite to that great image of
St. Christopher which faced the kneeling figure sculptured
in stone of Antoine des Essarts, knight, till 1413, when

both saint and sinner were thrown down. On this wooden bed it was customary to expose foundlings to the public charity. Anyone took them who felt so disposed. Before the wooden bed was a copper basin to receive the alms of the charitable.

The living creature which lay upon this hard couch on the morning of Quasimodo Sunday, in the year of our Lord 1467, appeared to excite a high degree of curiosity in the considerable concourse of persons who had collected around it. They consisted chiefly of the fair sex, being almost all of them old women.

In the front row, nearest to the bed, were four whom from their gray cassocks you would judge to belong to some religious sisterhood. I see no reason why history should not transmit to posterity the names of these four discreet and venerable matrons. They were Agnes la Herme, Jehanne de la Tarme, Henriette la Gaultiere, and Gauchere la Violete, all four widows, and sisters of the chapel of Etienne Haudry, who had left their house with the permission of their superior, and agreeably to the statutes of Pierre d'Ailly, for the purpose of attending divine service.

If, however, these good creatures were observing the statutes of Pierre d'Ally, they were certainly violating at the moment those of Michel de Brache and the Cardinal of Pisa, which most inhumanly imposed upon them the law of silence.

"What is that, sister?" said Agnes to Gauchere, looking intently at the little creature, yelping and writhing on the wooden couch, and terrified at the number of strange faces.

"What will the world come to," said Jehanne, "if that is the way they make children nowadays?"

"I don't pretend to know much about children," rejoined Agnes, "but it must be a sin to look at that thing."

" 'Tis not a child, Agnes—'tis a misshapen ape," observed Gauchere.

" 'Tis a miracle!" ejaculated La Gaultiere.

"Then," remarked Agnes, "this is the third since Lætare Sunday, for it is not a week since we had the miracle of the scoffer of the pilgrims punished by our Lady of Aubervillivers, and that was the second miracle of the month."

"This foundling, as they call it, is a real monster of abomination," resumed Jehanne.

"He bellows loud enough to deafen a chanter," continued Gaultiere.

"And to pretend that Monsieur de Remis could send this fright to Monsieur de Paris!" added La Gaultiere, clasping her hands.

"I cannot help thinking," said Agnes la Herme, "that it is some brute, something between a Jew and a beast—something in short that is not Christian, and ought to be drowned or burned."

"I do hope," resumed La Gaultiere, "that nobody will apply for it."

"Good God!" exclaimed Agnes, "how I pity the poor nurses at the foundling hospital in the lane yonder going down to the river, close by the Archbishop's, if this little monster should be carried to them to be suckled! Why, I declare I would rather suckle a vampire!"

"Poor la Herme! what a simpleton she is!" rejoined Jehanne. "Don't you see, sister, that this little monster is at least four years old, and that he would like a lump of meat a deal better than your breast?"

In fact, "this little monster"—we should be puzzled ourselves to call it anything else—was not a newborn infant. It was a little, shapeless, moving mass, tied up in a hempen bag, marked with the initials of Guillaume Chartier, the then Bishop of Paris, and leaving the head alone exposed. And that head was so deformed as to be absolutely hideous; nothing was to be seen upon it but a forest of red hair, one eye, a mouth, and teeth. The eye wept, the mouth cried, and the teeth seemed sadly in want of something to bite. The whole was struggling in the sack, to the no small wonderment of the crowd incessantly coming and going and increasing around it.

Dame Aloise de Gondelaurier, a noble and wealthy lady, who held by the hand a sweet little girl about six years old, and had a long veil hanging from the gold peak of her bonnet, stopped before the bed, and for a moment surveyed the unfortunate creature, while her charming little daughter Fleur-de-lys, dressed entirely in silk and velvet, pointing with her delicate finger to each letter of the permanent inscription attached to the wooden bed, spelt the words Enfans Trouves (Foundlings).

"I really thought," said the lady, turning away, with disgust, "that children only were exposed here."

As she turned her back, she threw into the basin a silver florin, which rang among the liards, and made the poor sisters of the chapel of Etienne Haudry lift their eyes in astonishment.

A moment afterward, the grave and learned Robert Mistricolle, the king's prothonotary, passed with an enormous missal under one arm, and his wife, Damoiselle Guillemette la Mairesse, under the other, thus having at his side two regulators, the one spiritual, the other temporal.

"A foundling!" he exclaimed, after intently examining the object—"found apparently on the banks of the Phlegeton."

"He seems to have but one eye," observed Damoiselle Guillemette; "and there is a great wart over the other."

" 'Tis no wart," replied Master Robert Miostricolle, "but an egg, which contains another demon exactly like this, with another little egg, containing a third devil, and so on."

"La! how know you that?" asked Guillemette.

"I know it pertinently," replied the prothonotary.

"Mr. Prothonotary," inquired Gauchere, "what prophesy you from this kind of foundling?"

"The greatest calamities," replied Miostricolle.

"Gracious Heaven!" exclaimed an old woman who stood by, "no wonder we had such a pestilence last year, and that the English, it is said, are going to land in force at Harefleu!"

"Perhaps that may not prevent the queen from coming to Paris in September," rejoined another; "trade is very flat already."

"I am of opinion," cried Jehanne de la Tarme, "that it would be better for the people of Paris if that little sorcerer were lying upon a fagot than upon a plank."

"Ay—a bonny blazing one!" added the old dame.

"That might be more prudent," observed Miostricolle.

For some moments, a young priest had been listening to the comments of the women and the prothonotary. He was a man of an austere countenance, with an ample brow and piercing eye. Pushing aside the crowd without speaking, he examined "the little sorcerer," and extended his hand over him. It was high time, for all the pious bystanders were agog for the "bonny blazing fagot."

"I adopt this child," said the priest.

He wrapped him in his cassock and carried him away. The bystanders looked after him with horror, till he had passed the Porte-Rouge which then led from the church to the cloisters, and was out of sight.

When they had recovered from their first astonishment, Jehanne de la Tarme, stooping till her lips were near the ear of La Gaultiere, "Sister," whispered she, "did I not tell you that yon young clerk, Monsieur Claude Frollo, is a sorcerer?"

17

Claude Frollo was, in fact, no ordinary personage. He belonged to one of those families who, in the impertinent language of the last century, were called indiscriminately *haute bourgeoisie* or *petite noblesse*. This family had inherited from the Paclets the fief of Tirechappe, which was held under the Bishop of Paris, and the twenty-one houses of which had been in the thirteenth century the subject of so many pleadings before the official. Claude Frollo, as possessor of this fief, was one of the one hundred and forty-one seigneurs who claimed manorial rights in Paris and its suburbs; and as such his name was long to be seen registered between the Hotel de Tancarville, belonging to Master Francois de Rez, and the College de Tours, in the cartulary preserved in the church of St. Martin-des-Champs.

Claude Frollo had from his childhood been destined by his parents for the church. He was taught to read Latin, to cast down his eyes, and to speak low. While quite a boy, his father had placed him in the College of Torchi in the University; and there he had grown up on the missal and the lexicon.

Having passed through theology, he had fallen upon the capitularies of Charlemagne, and, with his keen appetite for knowledge, had devoured decretals after decretals, those of Theodore Bishop of Hispala, of Bouchard Bishop of Worms, of Yves Bishop of Chartres; then the decree of Gratian, which succeeded the capitularies of Charlemagne; then the collection of Gregory IX; then Honorius the Third's epistle *Super Specula*; till he had made himself perfectly familiar with that long and tumultuous period, in which the canon law and the civil law were struggling and laboring amid the chaos of the middle ages—a period opening with Theodore in 618, and closing with Pope Gregory in 1227.

It was about this time that the intense heat of the summer of 1466 generated that destructive pestilence which swept away more than forty thousand human beings in the vicinity of Paris, and among others, saith Jean de Trooyes, "Master Arnoul, the king's astrologer, a right honest, wise, and agreeable man."

A rumor reached the University that the Rue Tirechappe

in particular was afflicted with this malady. There, in the midst of their fief, dwelt the parents of Claude. The young scholar hastened in great alarm to the paternal residence. On reaching it, he learned that his father and mother had died the preceding night. An infant brother was still alive, and crying, abandoned in his cradle. This babe was the only member of Claude's family that was left to him; he took the child in his arms, and quitted the house absorbed in thought. Hitherto he had lived only in learning and science; he now began to live in life.

This catastrophe was a crisis in the existence of Claude. An orphan and head of a family at nineteen, he felt himself rudely roused from the reveries of the schools to the realities of the world. Moved with pity, he conceived a passionate fondness for his helpless infant brother—a strange and delightful thing, this human affection, to him who heretofore had loved nothing but books.

This affection developed itself to an extraordinary degree; in a soul so new to the feeling it was like a first love. Separated from childhood from his parents, whom he had scarcely known, cloistered and as it were spell-bound by his books, eager above all things to study and to learn, exclusively attentive till then to his understandings which expanded itself in science, to his imagination which grew up in letters, the young scholar had not yet had time to find out where his heart lay.

He gave himself up therefore to the love of his little Jehan, the passion of a character already ardent, energetic, and concentrated. This poor, frail, fair, delicate creature, this orphan without any protector, moved him to the bottom of his soul; and, grave thinker as he was, he began to muse upon Jehan with feelings of infinite compassion. He bestowed on him all possible care and attention, just as if he had been something exceedingly fragile and exceedingly valuable. He was more than a brother to the infant; he became a mother to him.

Little Jehan was still at the breast when he lost his mother; Claude put him out to nurse. Besides the fief of

Tirechappe he had inherited from his father a mill situated on a hill near the castle of Winchester, since corrupted to Bicetre. The miller's wife was just suckling a fine boy; it was not far from the University, and Claude carried little Jehan to her himself.

Thenceforth the thought of his little brother became not only a recreation but even the object of his studies. He resolved to devote himself entirely to the care of him, and never to have any other wife, or any other child, but the happiness and prosperity of his brother. He attached himself therefore more strongly than ever to his clerical vocation. His merit, his learning, his condition of immediate vassal of the Bishop of Paris, threw the doors of the church wide open to him. At the age of twenty, by a special dispensation of the Holy See, he was a priest, and as the youngest of the chaplains of Notre Dame he performed the service of the altar, called, on account of the lateness of the mass said there, *altare pigrorum.*

There, more than ever absorbed by his beloved books, which he never quitted but to run for an hour to the mill, this mixture of learning and austerity, so uncommon at his age, quickly gained him the admiration and the respect of the convent. From the cloister his reputation for learning spread among the people, and among some of them it even procured him the character of a sorcerer—a frequent circumstance in that superstitious age.

It was at the moment when he was returning on Quasimodo Sunday, from saying mass at "the altar of the lazy," which stood by the door of the choir on the right, near the image of the Blessed Virgin, that his attention was attracted by a group of old women cackling around the bed of the foundlings. He approached the unfortunate creature, so hated and so threatened. Its distress, its deformity, its destitution, the thought of his young brother, the idea which suddenly flashed across his mind, that if he were to die his poor little Jehan too might perhaps be mercilessly thrown upon the same spot, assailed his heart all at once; it melted with pity, and he carried away the boy.

He baptized his adopted child and named him Quasimodo, either to commemorate the day on which he had found him, or to express the incomplete and scarcely finished state of the poor little creature. In truth. Quasimodo, with one eye, hunchback, and crooked legs, was but an apology for a human being.

18

Now, by the year 1482, Quasimodo had grown up. He had been several years bell-ringer to the cathedral of Notre Dame, thanks to his foster father, Claude Frollo, who had become archdeacon of Josas, thanks to his diocesan, Messire Louis de Beaumont, who had been appointed Bishop of Paris in 1472, thanks to his patron Olivier le Daim, barber to Louis XI, by the grace of God, king, etc.

In process of time, the strongest attachment took place between the bell-ringer and the church. Cut off forever from society by the double fatality of his unknown parentage and his misshapen nature, imprisoned from childhood within these impassable boundaries, the unhappy wretch was accustomed to see no object in the world beyond the religious walls which had taken him under their protection. Notre Dame had been successively, to him, as he grew up and expanded, his egg, his nest, his home, his country, the universe.

A sort of mysterious and preexistent harmony had grown up between this creature and the edifice. While, still quite a child, he crawled about, twisting and hopping in the shade of its arches, he appeared with his human face and his limbs scarcely human, the native reptile of that dark damp pavement, among the grotesque shadows thrown down upon it by the capitals of the Roman pillars.

As he grew up, the first time that he mechanically grasped the rope in the tower, and, hanging to it, set the bell in motion, the effect upon his foster-father was like that produced upon a parent by the first articulate sounds uttered by his child.

Thus, by little and little, his spirit expanded in harmony with the cathedral; there he lived, there he slept; scarcely ever leaving it, and, being perpetually subject to its mysterious influence, he came at last to resemble it, to be incrusted with it, to form, as it were, an integral part of it. His salient angles dovetailed, if we may be allowed the expression, into the receding angles of the building, so that he seemed to be not merely its inhabitant, but to have taken its form and pressure. Between the ancient church and him there were an instinctive sympathy so profound, so many magnetic affinities, that they stuck to it in some measure as the tortoise to its shell.

It is scarcely necessary to say how familiar he had made himself with the whole cathedral in so long and so intimate a cohabitation. There was no depth that Quasimodo had not fathomed, no height that he had not scaled.

Not only did the person but also the mind of Quasimodo appear to be molded by the cathedral. It would be difficult to determine the state of that soul, what folds it had contracted, what form it had assumed, under its knotty covering, during this wild and savage life. Quasimodo was born one-eyed, humpbacked, lame. It was not without great difficulty and great patience that Claude Frollo had taught him to speak; but there was a fatality attached to the unhappy foundling. Having become ringer of the bells of Notre Dame at the age of fourteen, a fresh infirmity had come upon him; the volume of sound had broken the drum of his ear, and deafness was the consequence. Thus the only gate which Nature had left wide open between him and the world was suddenly closed, and forever. In closing, it shut out the only ray of light and joy that still reached his soul, which was now wrapped in profound darkness. The melancholy of the poor fellow became incurable and complete as his deformity. His deafness rendered him in some measure dumb also; for, the moment he lost his hearing, he resolved to avoid the ridicule of others by a silence which he never broke but when he was alone. He voluntarily tied up that tongue, which Claude Frollo had taken such pains to loosen; hence, when necessity forced him to speak, his tongue was benumbed, awkward, and like a door the hinges of which have grown rusty.

If then we were to attempt to penetrate through this thick and obdurate bark of the soul of Quasimodo; if we could sound the depths of this bungling piece of organization; if we were enabled to hold a torch behind these untransparent organs, to explore the gloomy interior of this opaque being, to illumine its obscure corners and its unmeaning cul-de-sacs, and to throw all at once a brilliant light upon the spirit enchained at the bottom of this den; we should doubtless find the wretch in some miserable attitude, stunted and rickety, like the prisoners under the leads of Venice, who grow old, doubled up in a box of stone, too low to stand up and too short to lie down in.

The first effect of this vicious organization was to confuse the view which he took of things. He received scarcely a single direct perception. The exterior world appeared to him at a greater distance than it does to us. The second result of his misfortune was that it rendered him mischievous. He was, in truth, mischievous because he was savage; he was savage because he was ugly. There was logic in his nature, as there is in ours. His strength, developed in a most extraordinary manner, was another cause of his propensity to mischief. *Malus puer robustus,* says Hobbes. We must nevertheless do him justice; malice was probably not innate in him. From his earliest intercourse with men he had felt, and afterward he had seen, himself despised, rejected, cast off. Human speech had never been to him aught but a jeer or a curse. As he grew up, he had found nothing but hatred about him. He had adopted it. He had acquired the general malignity. He had picked up the weapon with which he had been wounded.

After all, he turned toward mankhind with reluctance; his cathedral was enough for him. It was peopled with figures of marble, with kings, saints, bishops, who at least did not laugh in his face, and looked upon him only with an air of tranquility and benevolence. The other statues, those of monsters and demons, bore no malice against him. They were too like him for that. Their raillery was rather directed against other men. The saints were his friends, and blessed him; the monsters were his friends, and guarded him; he would therefore pass whole hours crouched before one of these statues, and holding solitary converse with it. If anyone came by, he would run off like a lover surprised in a serenade.

The cathedral was not only his society, but his world—in short, all nature to him. He thought of no other trees than the painted windows, which were always in blossom; of no other shades than the foliage of stone adorned with birds in the Saxon capitals; of no other mountains than the colossal towers of the church; of no other ocean than Paris which roared at their feet.

But that which he loved most of all in the maternal edifice, that which awakened his soul and caused it to spread its poor wings that otherwise remained so miserably folded up in its prison, that which even conferred at times a feeling of happiness, was the bells. He loved them, he caressed them, he talked to them, he understood them—from the chimes in the steeple of the transept to the great bell above the porch. The belfry of the transept and the two towers were like three immense cages, in which the birds that he had reared sang for him alone. It was these same birds, however, which had deafened him; but mothers are often fondest of the child which has caused them the greatest pain. It is true that theirs were the only voices he could still hear. On this account the great bell was his best beloved. He preferred her before all the other sisters of this noisy family, who fluttered about him on festival days.

This great bell he called Mary. She was placed in the southern tower, along with her sister Jacqueline, a bell of inferior size, enclosed in a cage of less magnitude by the side of her own. This Jacqueline was thus named after the wife of Jehan Montague, who gave her to the church; a gift which, however, did not prevent his figuring without his head at Montfaucon. In the second tower were six other bells; and, lastly, the six smallest dwelt in the steeple of the transept, with the wooden bell, which was only rung between noon on Holy Thursday and the morning of Easter Eve. Thus Quasimodo had fifteen bells in his seraglio, but big Mary was his favorite.

It is impossible to form a conception of his joy on the days of the great peals. The instant the archdeacon let him off, and said "Go," he ran up the winding staircase of the belfry quicker than another could have gone down. He hurried out of breath, into the aerial chamber of the great bell, looked at her attentively and lovingly for a moment; then began to talk kindly to her, and patted her with his hand, as you would do a good horse which you are going to put to his mettle. He would pity her for the labor she was about to undergo. After these first caresses, he shouted to his assistants in a lower story of the tower to begin. They seized the ropes, the windless creaked, and slowly and heavily the enormous cone of metal was set in motion. Quasimodo, with heaving bosom, watched the movement. The first shock of the clapper against the wall of brass shook the woodwork upon which it was hung. Quasimodo vibrated with the bell. "Vah?" he would cry, with a burst of idiot laughter.

The presence of this extraordinary being seemed to infuse the breath of life into the whole cathedral. A sort of mysterious emanation seemed—at least so the superstitious multitude imagined—to issue from him, to animate the stones of Notre Dame, and to make the very entrails of the old church heave and palpitate. When it was known that he was there, it was easy to fancy that the thousand statues in the galleries and over the porches moved and were instinct with life. In fact, the cathedral seemed to be a docile and obedient creature in his hands; waiting only his will to raise her mighty voice; being possessed and filled with Quasimodo as with a familiar genius. He might be said to make the immense building breathe. He was, in fact, everywhere; he multiplied himself at all the points of the edifice. At one time the spectator would be seized with affright, on beholding at the top of one of the towers an odd-looking dwarf, climbing, twining, crawling on all fours, descending externally into the abyss, leaping from one projecting point to another, and fumbling in the body of some sculptured Gorgon; it was Quasimodo unnesting the daws. At another, the visitor stumbled, in some dark corner of the church, upon a crouching, grim-faced creature, a sort of living chimera—it was Quasimodo musing. At another time might be seen under a belfry an enormous head and a bundle of ill-adjusted limbs furiously swinging at the end of a rope—it was Quasimodo ringing the vespers or the angelus. Frequently, at night, a hideous figure might be seen wandering on the delicate open-work balustrade which crowns the towers and runs round the apsis—it was still the hunchback of Notre Dame. At such times, according to the reports of the gossips of the neighborhood, the whole church assumed a fantastic, supernatural, frightful aspect; eyes and mouths opened here and there; the dogs, and the dragons, and the griffins of stone, which keep watch day and night with outstretched neck and open jaws, around the monstrous cathedral, were heard to bark and howl. At Christmas, while the great bell, which seemed to rattle in the throat, summoned the pious to the midnight mass, the gloomy facade of the cathedral wore such a strange and sinister air, that the grand porch seemed to swallow the multitude, while the rose-window above it looked on. All this proceeded from Quasimodo. Egypt would have taken him for the god of the temple; the middle age believed him to be its demon; he was the soul of it. To such a point was he so, that to those who knew that Quasimodo once existed Notre Dame now appears de-

serted, inanimate, dead. You feel that there is something
wanting. This immense body is void; it is a skeleton; the
spirit has departed; you see its place, and that is all. It is
like a skull; the sockets of the eyes are still there, but the
eyes themselves are gone.

19

There was, however, one human being whom Quasimodo excepted from his antipathy, and to whom he
was as much, nay, perhaps more strongly attached than to
his cathedral—that being was Claude Frollo.

The thing was perfectly natural. Claude Frollo had taken
pity on him, adopted him, supported him, brought him up.
It was between Claude Frollo's legs, that, when quite
small, he had been accustomed to seek refuge when teased
by boys or barked at by dogs. Claude Frollo had taught
him to speak, to read, to write. To crown all, Claude Frollo
had made him bell-ringer.

The gratitude of Quasimodo was in consequence profound, impassioned, unbounded; and though the countenance of his foster-father was frequently gloomy and
morose, though his way of speaking was habitually short,
harsh, and imperious, never had this gratitude ceased for a
moment to sway him. The archdeacon had in Quasimodo
the most submissive of slaves, the most docile of attendants, the most vigilant of warders. After the poor bell-
ringer had lost his hearing, Claude Frollo and he
conversed in a language of signs, mysterious and understood by themselves alone. Thus the archdeacon was the
only human creature with whom Quasimodo had kept up
communication. There were but two things in the world

which he still had intercourse—Notre Dame and Claude Frollo.

Nothing on earth can be compared with the empire of the archdeacon over the bell-ringer, and the attachment of the bell-ringer to the archdeacon. A sign from Claude, and the idea of giving him pleasure would have sufficed to make Quasimodo throw himself from the top of the towers of Notre Dame. It was truly extraordinary to see all that physical strength, which had attained such a surprising development in Quasimodo, placed implicitly by him at the disposal of another. It bespoke undoubtedly filial submission, domestic attachment; but it proceeded also from the fascination which mind exercises upon mind. It was an imperfect, distorted, defective organization, with head abased and supplicating eyes, before a superior, a lofty, a commanding intelligence; but, above all, it was gratitude—but gratitude so carried to its extreme limit that we know not what to compare it with. This virtue is not one of those of which the most striking examples are to be sought among men. We shall therefore say Quasimodo loved the archdeacon as never dog, never horse, never elephant loved his master.

In 1482 Quasimodo was about twenty, Claude Frollo about thirty-six. The one had grown up, the other began to grow old.

Claude Frollo was no longer the simple student of the college of Torchi, the tender protector of an orphan child, the young and thoughtful philosopher, so learned and yet so ignorant. He was an austere, grave, morose churchman, second chaplain to the bishop, archdeacon of Josas, having under him the two deaneries of Montlhery and Chateaufort, and one hundred and seventy-four parish priests. He was a somber and awe-inspiring personage, before whom trembled the singing boys in albs and long coats, the precentors, the brothers of St. Augustin, the clerk, who officiated in the morning services at Notre Dame, as he stalked slowly along beneath the lofty arches of the choir, majestic, pensive, with arms folded and head so bowed upon his bosom that no part of his face was to be seen but his bald and ample forehead.

Dom Claude Frollo, however, had not meanwhile abandoned either the sciences or the education of his young brother, those two occupations of his life; but time had dashed those fond pursuits with the bitterness of disappointment. Little Jehan Frollo, surnamed du Moulin, from the place where he had been nursed, had not as he grew up taken that which Claude was solicitous to give him. His brother had reckoned upon a pious, docile, and virtuous pupil; but the youth, like those young trees which, in spite of all the gardener's efforts, obstinately turn toward the quarter from which they receive air and sun, grew and flourished, and threw out luxuriant branches toward idleness, ignorance, and debauchery alone. Reckless of all restraint, he was a downright devil, who often made Dom Claude knit his brow, but full of shrewdness and drollery, which as often made him laugh. Claude had placed him in the same college of Torchi where he had passed his early years in study and retirement; and it was mortifying to him that this sanctuary, formerly edified by the name of Frollo, should now be scandalized by it. On this subject he frequently read Jehan very severe and very long lectures, to which the latter listened with exemplary composure. After all the young scapegrace had a good heart; when the lecture was over, he nevertheless returned quietly to his profligate courses. At one time it was a newcomer whom he worried into the payment of his footing—a precious tradition which has been carefully handed down to the present day; at another he had instigated a party of the students to make a classic attack upon some tavern, where, after beating the keeper with bludgeons, they merrily gutted the house, staving even the wine pipes in the cellar.

Grieved and thwarted by these circumstances in his human affections, Claude had thrown himself with so much the more ardor into the arms of Science, who at least does not laugh you in the face, and always repays you, though sometimes in rather hollow coin, for the attentions which you have bestowed on her. Thus he became more and more learned, and at the same time, by a natural consequence, more and more rigid as a priest, more and more gloomy as a man.

It is certain that the archdeacon frequently visited the churchyard of the Innocents, where, to be sure, his parents lay buried with the other victims of the pestilence of 1466; but then he appeared to take much less notice of the cross at the head of their grave than of the tomb erected close by it for Nicolas Flamel and Claude Pernelle.

It is certain, moreover, that the archdeacon was smitten, with a strange passion for the emblematic porch of Notre Dame, that page of conjuration written in stone by Bishop William, of Paris, who has no doubt been damned for having prefixed so infernal a frontispiece to the sacred poem everlastingly changed by the rest of the edifice. It was also believed that the archdeacon had discovered the hidden meaning of the colossal St. Christopher, and of the other tall enigmatical statue which then stood at the entrance of the Parvis, and which the people called in derision Monsieur Legris. But a circumstance which everybody might have remarked was his sitting hours without number on the parapet of the Parvis, contemplating the sculptures of the porch, sometimes examining the foolish virgins with their lamps reversed, sometimes the wise virgins with their lamps upright; at others calculating the angle of vision of the raven on the left-hand side of the porch, looking at some mysterious spot in the church, where the philosopher's stone is certainly concealed, if it is not in Nicolas Flamel's cellar.

Lastly, it is certain that the archdeacon had fitted up for himself in the tower nearest to the Greve, close to the belfry, a small and secret cell, which none, it was said, but the bishop durst enter without his permission. The cell had been made of old almost at the top of the tower, among the ravens' nests, by Bishop Hugo, of Besaaco, who had there practiced the black art in his time. None knew what that cell contained; but from the Terrain there had often been seen at night, through a small window at the back of the tower, a strange, red, intermitting light, appearing, disappearing, and reappearing at short and equal intervals, apparently governed by the blast of a bellows, and proceeding rather from the flame of a fire than that of a lamp or candle. In the dark this had a singular effect at that height, and the good-wives would say: "There's the archdeacon puffing away again; hell is cracking up yonder!"

These, after all, were no very strong proofs of sorcery; still there was sufficient smoke to authorize the conclusion that there must be some fire; at any rate the archdeacon had that formidable reputation. It is nevertheless but just to state that the sciences of Egypt, necromacy, magic, even the whitest and the most innocent, had not a more inveterate enemy, a more pitiless accuser, before the officials of Notre Dame. Whether this horror was sincere or merely the game played by the rogue who is the first to cry, "Stop thief!" it did not prevent his being considered by the learned heads of the chapter as a soul lost in the mazes of the Cabala, groping in the darkness of the occult sciences, and already in the vestibule of hell. The people held much the same opinion; all who possessed any sagacity regarded Quasimodo as the demon and Claude Frollo as the conjurer. It was evident that the bell-ringer had engaged to serve the archdeacon for a specific time, at the expiration of which he would be sure to carry off his soul by way of payment. Accordingly the archdeacon, in spite of the extreme austerity of his life, was in bad odor with all good Christians, and there was not a devout nose among them but could smell the magician.

These symptoms of a violet moral preoccupation had acquired an unusual degree of intensity at the period of the occurrences related in this history. More than one of the singing-boys had fled affrighted on meeting him alone in the church, so strange and alarming were his looks. More than once, during the service in the choir, the priest in the next stall to his had heard him mingle unintelligible parentheses with the responses. More than once the laundress of the Terrain, employed to wash for the chapter, had observed, not without horror, marks as if scratched by claws or fingernails upon the surplice of Monsieur the Archdeacon of Josas.

In other respects his austerity was redoubled, and never had he led a more exemplary life. From disposition as well as profession he had always kept aloof from women; he seemed now to dislike them more than ever. At the mere rustling of a silk petticoat his hood was over his eyes. On this point he was so strict that when the king's daughter, the lady of Beaujeu, came in the month of December, 1481, to see the cloisters of Notre Dame, he seriously opposed her admission, reminded the bishop of the statute of the black book, dated on the vigil of St. Bartholomew, 1334, which forbids access to the cloister to every woman "whatsoever, whether old or young, mistress or servant." Whereupon the bishop was forced to appeal to the ordinance of Otho the legate, which excepts "certain ladies of quality, who cannot be refused without scandal"—*aliquæ magnates mulieres quæae sine scandalo evitari non possunt.* Still the archdeacon protested, alleging that the ordinance of the legate, which dated from 1207, was anterior by one hundred and twenty-seven years to the black book, and consequently annulled in point of fact by the latter; and he actually refused to appear before the princess.

It was moreover remarked that his horror of the Egyptians and Zingari seemed to have become vehement for some time past. He had solicited from the bishop an edict expressly prohibiting the Bohemians to come and dance and play in the area of the Parvis; and he had recently taken the pains to search through the musty archives of the officials for cases of wizards and witches sentenced to the flames or the gallows for practicing the black art in association with cats, swine, or goats.

20

It has been mentioned earlier that Claude and Quasimodo were not well liked by the people who lived near the cathedral—neither by the members of the higher nor lower classes. When the archdeacon and the bellringer went out together, as they did frequently, they appeared always the same—the servant followed the master. While crossing the narrow, dark, cold streets in the neighborhood of Notre Dame, they heard many mean words, mocking laughs, and insults, except on the rare times when Claude Frollo walked proudly, with his head held high, showing a severe and nearly regal countenance to the surprised masses waiting to harrass them.

Both were known in the neighborhood as "the poets" of whom Régnier says:

> All kinds of people chase after poets,
> Like screech owls after linnets.

Sometimes some ill-natured marmot would risk his hide and bones just to have the ineffable pleasure of sticking a pin in Quasimodo's hump. Sometimes some pretty wench, with more sporting effrontery than was seemly, would brush against the priest's cassock, singing right in his face some naughty song:

> Hide, hide, the devil is taken.

Sometimes a group of squalid old women, crouching in the shadows on the steps of a porch, would heap abuses on the archdeacon and the bellringer as they passed by, or hurl after them with curses the flattering remark: "Hum! There goes one whose soul is like the other's body!" Or some band of schoolboys playing marbles or hopscotch would rise up in mass and salute them in classical manner, with some Latin greeting such as *"Eia! Eia! Claudius cum claudo!"** *

21

Dom Claude Frollo's name was known across the land. Because of his fame, near the time he refused to see Lady Beaujeau, he received visitors whom he was to remember for a long time.

It happened one evening, just as he had retired after the evening office to his canonical cell in the cloister of Notre-Dame. Except for a few glass phials that were stacked in a corner full of some powder, which looked very much like an explosive, the cell had nothing special or mysterious about it. Here and there were some inscriptions on the wall, but they were merely learned axioms or pious sayings from good authors. The archdeacon had just seated himself at a huge oak table covered with manuscripts, and had lighted a three-armed brass lamp. He had leaned his elbow on a wide open book by Honorius d'Autun, *De praedestinatione et libero arbitrio,* and, deep in thought, he was leafing through a printed folio, the sole product of a printing press which he had in his cell. While he was thus busy, there came a knock at the door.

"Who's there?" called the scholar in the friendly tone of a famished dog disturbed over a bone.

*"Hey, Claude with the cripple."

"Your friend Jacques Coictier," answered a voice from outside.

The priest went to open the door.

It was, indeed, the king's physician, a man about fifty years old, whose somber face was somewhat lighted by a look of great cunning. Another man was with him. Both wore long, slate-gray, squirrel-lined robes, fastened from top to bottom and belted around the waist, and hats of the same material. Their hands were hidden in their sleeves, their feet under their robes, and their eyes beneath their caps.

"God help me, messire!" said the archdeacon as he led them in. "I was not expecting such honorable visitors at this hour." And while he spoke thus courteously, he glanced suspiciously and curiously from the physician to his companion.

"The hour is never too late to visit with so distinguished a scholar as Dom Claude Frollo of Tirechappe," replied Doctor Coictier, whose Burgundian accent made all his sentences flow majestically like a trailing robe.

The physician and the archdeacon then began one of those congratulatory prologues which, at that period, customarily introduced every conversation between scholars and which did not prevent them from most cordially hating one another. Moreover, it is the same today; the mouth of every scholar who compliments another is a vessel full of honeyed gall.

The felicitations addressed by Claude Frollo to Jacques Coictier alluded chiefly to the numerous material advantages which the worthy physician had known how to extract, in the course of his much-envied career, from each illness of the king's—a better and more certain kind of alchemy than the pursuit of the philosophers' stone.

"Indeed, Doctor Coictier, I was most happy to learn of the promotion of your nephew, my reverend superior, Pierre Versé, to the bishopric. Isn't he now the Bishop of Amiens?"

"Yes, Monsieur the Archdeacon; it is a gracious and merciful gift of the Lord."

"You know, you looked very well on Christmas day at the head of your company of the Chamber of Accountants, Monsieur the President!"

"Vice-President, Dom Claude. Alas! Nothing more than that."

"And how is your superb mansion in the Rue Saint-André-des-Arts? Really, it's like the Louvre! I greatly admire the apricot tree sculptured on the door with that delightful play on words: *A l'Abri-Cotier*."

"Alas! Master Claude, all that masonry has cost me dearly. The more I do with the mansion, the more I am being ruined financially."

"Oh, don't you have revenue from the jail, and provostship of the Palace of Justice, and rents from all the houses, workshops, booths, and market-stalls all around Paris? That's milking a fine cow!"

"My estate at Poissy has brought me nothing this year."

"But your toll dues at Triel, Saint-James, and Saint-Germain-en-Laye are always sure?"

"Six times twenty pounds, not even parisis."

"But you have your position as counselor to the king. That warrants a fixed income."

"Yes, my confrère Claude, but that cursed manor of Poligny, which they make so much ado about, is not worth more to me than sixty gold crowns, in a good or bad year."

There was in these compliments which Claude addressed to Jacques Coictier a certain veiled, bitter, sardonic raillery, with that sad yet cruel smile of a superior but unfortunate man, who is enjoying a moment's distraction tilting with the gross vulgarity of a prosperous man. The other never even noticed it.

"Upon my soul!" said Claude at last, shaking his hand, "I am pleased to see you in such fine health."

"Thank you, Master Claude."

"Speaking of health," exclaimed Dom Claude, "how is your royal patient?"

"He doesn't pay his physician very well," answered the doctor with a side glance toward his companion.

"Don't you think so, Monsieur Coictier?" said his companion.

These words, uttered in a tone of surprise and reproach, recalled the archdeacon's attention to the stranger's presence, though to tell the truth, he had never, from the moment he crossed the threshold, quite turned away from the unknown guest. Indeed it required the thousand reasons Claude had for humoring the all-powerful physician of Louis XI to make him consent to receive him thus accompanied.

Therefore, his expression was not too friendly when Jacques Coictier said to him, "By the way, Dom Claude, I bring you a colleague, who wanted to meet you, having heard so much about you."

"Monsieur is a scholar?" asked the archdeacon, looking intently at Coictier's companion. From the stranger's eyes Dom Claude met a glance just as piercing and suspicious as his own.

He was, as far as one could make out by the dim lamplight, a man of about sixty, of average height, who seemed to be ill and distraught. His expression, although his features were quite common, indicated power and severity; and under his hat, pulled down almost to his nose, one surmised the broad forehead of a genius. Beneath this, his eyes shone like lights deep in some cave.

He took upon himself to answer the archdeacon's question.

"Reverend master," he said in a serious tone, "I have heard of your fame and I have wanted to consult with you. I am but a poor gentleman from the provinces who should take off is shoes before entering the dwelling of the learned. I must tell you my name. It is Compère Tourangeau."

"An odd name for a gentleman!" thought the archdeacon. However, he felt himself in the presence of someone strong and commanding. His own intelligence made him

suspect that here was an intelligence no less gifted beneath
the furry cap of Compère Tourangeau. So, as he studied
that grave countenance, the ironic sneer that the presence
of Jacques Coictier had engendered on his morose face
slowly vanished, like the sunset glow of an evening horizon.

Claude Frollo seated himself again, gloomy and silent in
his great armchair, his elbow resumed its accustomed
place on the table, his head rested on his hand. After a few
minutes of reflection, he made a sign to the two visitors to
be seated, and then spoke to Compère Tourangeau.

"You come to consult with me, sir, and about what?"

"Reverend," answered Compère Tourangeau, "I am
sick, very sick. They say you are another great Aescula-
pius, and I have come to you to ask for medical advice."

"Medical advice!" said the archdeacon, shaking his
head. He seemed to collect his thoughts a moment, and
then he said, "Compère Tourangeau, since that is your
name, turn around, and you will find my advice written
succinctly on the wall."

Tourangeau obeyed, and read, above his head, an inscription, "Medicine is the daughter of dreams—
Jamblichus."

Meanwhile, Doctor Jacques Coictier had listened to his
companion's question with a disdain that Dom Claude's
answer only served to increase. He leaned over and whispered in Tourangeau's ear, so low that the archdeacon
could not hear, "I told you that he was mad! But you
wanted to see him!"

"But, Doctor Coictier, it could very well be that he is
right, this mad fool!" replied his friend in the same whispered tone and smiling bitterly.

"As you please!" answered Coictier dryly. Then, turning
to the archdeacon, he continued, "You are very quick with
your answers, Dom Claude, and Hippocrates apparently
presents no more difficulties to you than a nut to a monkey. Medicine a dream! I doubt if the apothecaries and
doctors, were they here, would refrain from stoning you.

So you deny the effect of philters on the blood, of unguents on the skin! You deny that the eternal pharmacy of plants and metals which we call the World, created expressly for the eternal patient we call Man!"

"I deny," replied Dom Claude coldly, "neither pharmacy nor the patient. I deny the doctor."

"Therefore it isn't true," went on Coictier heatedly, "that gout is an internal eruption; that a gunshot wound can be cured by the application of a roasted mouse; that young blood, properly injected into the veins, will restore youth to the aged; it is not true then that two and two are four, and that emprosthotonos follows opisthotonos!"

The archdeacon replied calmly, "There are certain subjects about which I think in a certain way."

Coictier flushed with anger.

"Come, come, my good Coictier, let's not be angry," said Compère Tourangeau. "Monsieur the Archdeacon is our host."

Coictier calmed down, but muttered to himself, "Oh, he's a madman, anyway."

"*Pasquedieu!* Master Claude," resumed Tourangeau, after a moment of silence, "you upset me. I came to consult you on two points; one concerning my health, the other concerning my star."

"Monsieur," replied the archdeacon, "if that is what you want, you would have done better not to have wasted your breath mounting my staircase. I do not believe in medicine, and I don't believe in astrology."

"Is that so?" said Tourangeau, with a hint of surprise.

Coictier forced a laugh. "Can't you see that he's mad?" he whispered again in Tourangeau's ear. "He does not believe in astrology."

"How can anyone belive," continued Dom Claude, "that every ray of a star is a thread attached to a man's head?"

"And what are your beliefs then?" cried Tourangeau.

The archdeacon hesitated a moment, then, with a cold smile which seemed to put the lie to his words, *"Credo in Deum."*

*"Dominum nostrum,"** added Tourangeau, making the sign of the cross.

"Amen," said Coictier.

"Reverend master," resumed Tourangeau, "I am charmed deeply to see you so devout. But learned man that you are, have you reached the point of no longer believing in science?"

"No!" cried the archdeacon, grabbing Compère Tourangeau's arm, while enthusiasm shone in his eyes. "No, I do not deny science. I have not crawled so long on my belly with my nails dug in the earth through all the innumerable windings of that dark cave of science, without perceiving in the distance, at the end of the dim passage, a light, a flame, a something—the reflection, no doubt, from that dazzling central laboratory where the patient and the wise have encountered God."

"And now," interrupted Tourangeau, "what do you hold for true and certain?"

"Alchemy!"

Coictier exclaimed, "*Pardieu*, Dom Claude, no doubt there is much truth to be found in alchemy, but why blaspheme medicine and astrology?"

"Your science of man, your science of the heavens is nothing!" said the archdeacon imperiously.

"But that's dealing hardly with Epidaurus and Chaldea," replied the physician with a sneer.

"Listen, Messier Jacques. I say this to you honestly, I am not a king's doctor, and His Majesty did not give me a laboratory in which to observe the heavenly constellations. Now don't get angry; just listen to me. What truth have you extracted—I will not say from medicine—which is really too foolish—but from astrology? Cite for me the virtues of the vertical boustrophedon, or the treasures to be found in the number ziruph, or in the number zephirod."

"Will you deny," queried Coictier, "the sympathetic in-

*"I believe in God, Our lord."

fluence of the clavicle, or that it is the key to all cabalistic science?"

"Errors, Messire Jacques. None of your formulas have proved anything conclusive, but alchemy has. Will you contest these results: ice, buried underground for a thousand years, is converted into rock crystal. Lead is the origin of all metals. (For gold is not a metal; it is light.) Lead requires but four periods of two hundred years each to pass successively from the condition of lead to that of red arsenic, from red arsenic to tin, from tin to silver. Are these facts or not? But to believe in the clavicle, in the mystic significance of the junction of two lines, and in the stars is as ridiculous as to believe, like the inhabitants of Cathay, that the oriole changes into a mole, and grains of wheat into a kind of carp!"

"I have studied hermetics," exclaimed Coictier, "and I affirm . . ."

The archdeacon, raging, would not let him finish. "And I, I have studied medicine, astrology, and hermetics. Here alone is truth!"

And as he spoke, he took up one of those glass phials of which mention has been made, saying, "Here alone is knowledge! Hippocrates, a dream! Urania, a dream; Hermes, a phantasm! Gold is the sun, to make gold is to be God. That's the only science. I have sounded medicine and astrology to their depths! Nothing! Nothing I tell you. The human body, darkness; the stars, darkness!"

Almost regally, he relaxed in his chair. Tourangeau watched him in silence. Coictier forced a sneering grin, shrugged his shoulders slightly, and repeated under his breath, "A madman!"

"Well," expostulated Tourangeau suddenly, "what stupendous results? Have you produced something? Have you made any gold?"

"If I had," answered the archdeacon, articulating slowly as if in deep thought, "the King of France would be named Claude, not Louis."

Tourangeau arched his eyebrows.

"Oh, what am I saying?" resumed Dom Claude with a disdainful smile. "What would the throne of France mean to me since I could reconstruct the Empire of the East."

"Well said!" cried Tourangeau.

"Oh, the poor fool!" murmured Coictier.

"But no," went on the archdeacon, as if he were answering his own thoughts, "I am still crawling, I am still bloodying my face and knees on the stones of the subterranean passage. I can see, but not clearly. I cannot read; I can make out only a few letters!"

"And when you have learned to read," asked Tourangeau, "will you then be able to make gold?"

"Undoubtedly," replied the archdeacon.

"In that case, Our Lady knows that I am in dire need of money, and would gladly learn to read your book. Tell me, reverend master, isn't your science inimical or displeasing to Our Lady?"

To Tourangeau's question, Dom Claude answered simply, "Whose archdeacon am I?"

"That's true, master. Well, then, would it please you to initiate me? Let me learn to read with you."

Claude assumed a majestic, pontifical attitude like a Samuel, and said, "Old man, it would require more years than yet remain to you to complete the journey into all these mysteries. Your head is already gray. One emerges from the cave with white hair, but one must enter it with black. Science knows well enough how to furrow and shrivel up the face of man; she has no need that age should bring to her faces that are already lined. If, however, you greatly desire to study hard, even at your age, and to decipher the difficult alphabet of the wise men, well and good, come with me, and I will try to help you. I will not command you, poor old man, to visit the sepulchral chamber of the pyramids, of which the ancient Herodotus speaks, nor the brick tower of Babylon, nor the vast white marble sanctuary of the Indian Temple of Eklings. Even I have not seen the Chaldean walls built in accordance with the sacred formula of Sikra, nor the Temple of Solomon, which was destroyed, nor the stone doors of the sepulchers of the Israelite kings, which have crumbled to pieces. We shall content ourselves with the fragments of the Book of Hermes, which we have here. I will explain to you the statue of Saint Christopher, the symbol of the Sower, and that of the two angels sculptured on the door of the Sainte-Chapelle, one of whom has his hand in a vase, and the other in a cloud."

Here, Jacques Coictier, who had been quite overwhelmed by the learned mutterings of the archdeacon, recovered his composure and interrupted him with the triumphant tone of one wise man disputing another, "You err, friend Claude. The symbol is not a number. You mistake Orpheus for Hermes."

"It is you who are in error," retorted the archdeacon. "Daedalus is the foundation; Orpheus is the wall; Hermes is the whole structure. Come when you please," he continued, turning to Tourangeau. "I will show you the particles of gold left in the bottom of Nicolas Flamel's crucible which you can compare with the gold of Guillaume de Paris. I will teach you the strength of the Greek word *peristera*.* But above all, I shall have you read, one after another, the marble letters of the alphabet, the granite pages of the book. We shall go from the door of Bishop Guillaume and of Saint-Jean-le-Rond to the Sainte-Chapelle, then to the house of Nicolas Flamel, on Rue Marivaulx, to his tomb in the cemetery of the Holy Innocents, to his two hospices on Rue de Montmorency. I shall have you read the hieroglyphics with which the four heavy iron supports in the doorway of the Hospice of Saint-Gervais are covered. Together we shall spell out the facades of Saint-Côme, of Sainte-Geneviève-des-Ardents, of Saint-Martin, of Saint-Jacques-de-la-Boucherie . . ."

For some time past, Tourangeau, who looked so intelligent, did not seem to follow Dom Claude. He interrupted, "*Pasque-Dieu!* What are your books?"

---

*This word has a double meaning: 1) dove or pigeon: 2) verbena.

"Here is one," replied the archdeacon, opening the window of his cell; he pointed to the Cathedral of Notre-Dame, whose two black towers, stone walls, and huge roof were silhouetted against the starry vault of heaven, like a monstrous two-headed sphinx in the middle of the City.

For some time the archdeacon contemplated in silence this gigantic structure; then, with a sigh, pointing with his right hand to the printed book opened on the table, and with his left hand to Notre Dame, and casting a mournful glance from book to church, "Alas!" he said, "this will kill that."

Coictier, who had come over to the book eagerly, exclaimed, "Ha! but what is so remarkable about this: *Glossa in Epistolas D. Pauli, Norimbergae, Antoniue Koburger, 1474*. That is not new. The book is by Pierre Lombard, the Master of Sentences. Is it so powerful because it has been printed?"

"Yes," replied Claude, who seemed absorbed in profound meditation, standing with his finger on the folio which had come from the famous printing press of Nuremberg. Then he added ominous words, "Alas! the small thing shall bring down the great things; a tooth triumphs over a whole carcass. The rat of the Nile destroys the crocodile, the swordfish kills the whale; the book will kill the edifice."

The curfew of the cloister tolled just as Doctor Jacques was repeating in whispered tones to his companion his eternal refrain, "He is mad!" To which Tourangeau this time answered, "I do believe it."

This bell marked the hour when no stranger could longer remain in the cloister.

As the two visitors were leaving, Tourangeau said to the archdeacon, "Master, I like scholars and men of great intellect, and I do respect you. Come tomorrow to the Palace of Tournelles, and ask for the Abbot of Saint-Martin of Tours."

The archdeacon, dumbfounded, returned to his cell, now comprehending at last who the person calling himself

Compère Tourangeau really was, for he recalled this passage from the Charter of Saint-Martin of Tours.: *Abbas beati Martini,* SCILICET REX FRANCIAE, *est canonicus de conseutudine et habet parvam praebendam quam habet sanctus Venantius et debet sedere in sede thesaurarii.**

It has been said that dating from that visit the archdeacon had frequent conferences with Louis XI, whenever His Majesty came to Paris, and that the king's regard for Dom Claude quite overshadowed the renown of Olivier le Daim and Jacques Coictier; the latter, consequently, as was his custom, berated the king for it.

22

We must now beg pardon to spend a moment examining the archdeacon's puzzling statement that "the book will kill the edifice."

In our opinion, the thought had two meanings. First of all, it was the view of a priest. It was the fear of an ecclesiastic before a new force, the printing press. It was the frightened yet dazzled man of the sanctuary confronting the illuminating Gutenberg press. It was the pulpit and the manuscript, the spoken word and the written word, alarmed because of the printed word; something like a sparrow frozen at the sight of a legion of angels spreading their six million wings. It was the cry of the prophet who already hears the rumbling of emancipated humanity; who sees in the distant future intelligence sapping faith, opinion dethroning belief, the world shaking the foundations of

---

*"The Abbot of Saint-Martin, that is to say the King of France, is canon according to custom, and has the small benefice which Saint-Venantius had, and must sit in the seat of the treasurer."

Rome. It was the prognostication of a philosopher who sees human thought, volatized by the press, evaporating from the theocratic vessel. It was the terror of a soldier who examines the steel battering-ram and says, "The tower will crumble." It signified that one great power was following upon the heels of another great power. It meant: The printing press will destroy the Church.

But besides this first thought, there was, in our opinion, a second, the more obvious of the two, a more modern corollary to the former idea, less easily understood and more likely to be contested. This view is quite as philosophical, but it no longer belongs to the priest alone but to the scholar and to the artist as well. Here was a premonition that human thought had advanced, and, in changing, was about to change its mode of expression, that the important ideas of each new generation would be recorded in a new way, that the book of stone, so solid and so enduring, was about to be supplanted by the paper book, which would become more enduring still. In this respect, the vague formula of the archdeacon had a second meaning: That one art would dethrone another art. It meant: Printing will destroy architecture.

In fact, from the beginning of things to the fifteenth century of the Christian era inclusive, architecture was the great book of the human race, man's principal means of expressing the various stages of his development, physical and mental.

When the legends of primitive races became so numerous, and their reciting was so confused that the stories were about to be lost, people began to transcribe these memories in the most visible, the most lasting, and at the same time the most natural medium. Every tradition was sealed under a monument.

The first records were simply squares of rock "which had not been touched by iron," says Moses. Architecture began like writing. It was first an alphabet. A stone was planted upright to be a letter and each letter became a hieroglyph. And on every hieroglyph there rested a group of

ideas, like the capital of a column. Thus primitive races of
the same period "wrote" all over the world. One finds the
"upright stone" of the Celts in Siberia and on the pampas
of America.

Later they made words by superimposing stone upon
stone. They coupled those syllables of granite. The verb
tried various combinations. The Celtic dolmen and
comlech, the Etruscan tumulus, the Hebrew galgal are
words. Some, especially the tumulus, are proper nouns.
Sometimes, on a vast beach they joined these stone words
and wrote a sentence. The immense pile of Karnak is by
itself a complete formula.

Lastly, they made books. The traditions had given birth
to symbols, under which they disappeared like the trunk of
a tree under its foliage. All these symbols, in which humanity believed, grew, multiplied, and became more and
more complicated. The first simple stones no longer sufficed to contain them; they overflowed on all sides;
scarcely could one decipher the original traditions, which,
like the stones, simple and naked, had been planted in the
soil. The rock symbols had a need to expand into a structure.

Architecture, therefore, developed concomitantly with
human thought; it became a giant with a thousand heads
and arms, capable of holding in one visible, tangible, eternal form all this floating symbolism. While Daedalus, who
is strength, was measuring; while Orpheus, who is intelligence, was singing; the pillar, which is a letter; the arch,
which is a syllable; the pyramid, which is a word, set in
motion at once by geometric law and by the law of poetry,
began to group themselves together, to combine, to amal-
gamate, to sink, to rise, to stand side by side on the
ground, and to pile themselves up to the sky, until, at the
dictation of the prevailing ideas of the era, they had written those marvelous books, which were also marvelous
structures; to wit, the Pagoda of Eklinga, the pyramids of
Egypt, and the Temple of Solomon.

The germinal idea, the verb, was not only the basis of

these edifices, but dictated their form. The Temple of Solomon, for example, was not simply the cover of a sacred book, it was the sacred book itself. On every word of these concentric enclosures, the priests could read the Word translated and manifested visibly; they could thus follow its transformations from sanctuary to sanctuary, until at last they could seize upon it in its final tabernacle, under its most concrete form, which was yet architecture: the Ark. Thus the Word was enclosed in the edifice, but its image was on its outer covering, as the human figure is carved on the coffin of a mummy.

Not only the edifices, but also the location of them revealed the ideas they were to impart. If the thoughts to be expressed were gracious, Greece crowned her mountains with temples harmonious to the eye; if somber, India disemboweled her hills to chisel out those unharmonious, half-subterranean pagodas, which are supported by rows of gigantic granite elephants.

So, during the first six thousand years of the world's history, from the time of the pagoda of Hindustan to that of the cathedral of Cologne, architecture has recorded the great ideas of the human race. Not only every religious symbol, but every human thought has its page in that vast book.

Every civilization begins as a theocracy and ends as a democracy. This law of liberty succeeding unity is recorded in architecture. For, and let us emphasize this point, we must not suppose that architecture is capable only of erecting the temple, only of expressing the sacerdotal myth and symbolism, only of transcribing in hieroglyphics on its stone pages the mysterious tables of the law. If this were so, since there arrives in every human society a moment when the sacred symbol is worn out and is obliterated by free thought, when man divests himself of the priest, when the excrescences of the philosophies and systems eat away the face of religion, architecture would be powerless to reproduce this new phase of the human mind: its pages, written on one side, would be blank on the other side; its work would be cut off; the book would be incomplete. But no, such is not the case.

Let us take, for example, the Middle Ages, which we can understand because this time is nearer to us. During its first period, while theocracy was organizing Europe, while the Vatican was rallying and grouping around itself the elements of a Rome constructed of the Rome which lay in ruin about the capitol, while Christianity was setting out to seek among the ruins of an anterior civilization all the stages of society, and out of its remains rebuilt a new hierarchy of which the priesthood was the keystone, we heard a new architecture stirring faintly in the chaos. Then, gradually, using the breath of Christianity, emerging from the grip of the barbarians, rising out of the rubble of dead architecture, Greek and Roman, there arose that mysterious Romanesque architecture, sister of the theocratic masonry of Egypt and India, that unalterable emblem of pure Catholicism, the immutable hieroglyph of papal unity. All the though thought of that time is written in this somber Romanesque style. Everywhere we can sense its authority, its unity, the imperturbable, the absolute, Gregory VII; everywhere the priest, never the man, everywhere the caste, never the people.

Then came the Crusades, a great popular movement, and every great popular movement, whatever its cause and purposes, has as its final precipitate the spirit of liberty. Innovations tried to be born. Here began the stormy period of the Peasant Wars, the Revolt of the Burghers. Authority was topped; unity was split and the divisions went in two directions. Feudalism demanded a share with theocracy. But when "the people" arrived on the scene, they as always took the lion's share. *Quia nominor leo.** Hence we see how feudalism pierced through theocracy, and the people through feudalism. The face of Europe was changed. Well! The face of architecture changed too. Like civilization, it turned a page, and the new spirit of the times found

*"Because I am called lion."

her ready to write its new dictates. She returned from the Crusades bearing the pointed arch, as the nations came home with liberty. Henceforth, as Rome was gradually dismembered, Romanesque architecture began its death throes. The hieroglyph deserted the cathedral and went to assist heraldry in order to heighten the prestige of feudalism. The cathedral itself, that structure once so dogmatic, now invaded by the people, by the spirit of liberty, escaped from the priest and fell into the hands of the artist. The artist designed it as he saw fit. Farewell to mystery, to myth, to law. Now fantasy and caprice became the rule. Provided the priest be left his basilica and his altar, he had nothing to say. The artist now took over the four walls. The architectural book no longer belonged to the priest, to religion, to Rome; it belonged to imagination, to poetry, to the people. Henceforth came the rapid and innumerable transformations of an architecture that would last only three centuries, but which was striking after the six or seven centuries of the stagnant immobility of the Romanesque style.

Meanwhile art marches on with giant strides. Popular genius and originality do what formerly the bishops did. Each passing generation writes its line in the book; it erases the ancient Romanesque hieroglyphics from the frontispiece of the cathedral—so thoroughly that one can barely see here and there some old dogma glimmering faintly through the new symbol covering it. The religious bone structure is scarcely visible through this new drapery. One can hardly grasp the extent of the license taken at that time by the architects, even on the churches. Such are the shamelessly intertwined groups of monks and nuns on the capitals, as in the Salle des Chiminées of the Palace of Justice in Paris. Such is the episode from the Book of Noah, sculptured "to the letter" under the great portal of the Cathedral of Bourges. Such is the bacchic monk, with ears as large as an ass's, with a glass in his hand, smiling in the face of the whole community, on the lavabo of the Abbey of Bocherville. At that time, for the thought written in stone, there existed a privilege perfectly comparable to our present liberty of the press. It was the liberty of architecture.

This liberty went very far. Sometimes a door, a facade, an entire church presents a symbolical meaning, absolutely unconnected with the worship, even hostile to the teaching of the Church. In the thirteenth century Guillaume de Paris, and Nicolas Flamel in the fifteenth, wrote seditious pages. Saint-Jacques-de-la-Boucherie was a church full of oppositions.

Because architecture was the only free medium, it therefore found full expression in those books called edifices. Without them, new ideas would have been burned in the public square. But a thought written in stone on the door of a church would have assisted at the torture of a thought written in a book. Thus, having only this one outlet, architecture, thought rushed toward it at every opportunity. Hence the countless number of cathedrals spread all over Europe, a number so prodigious that it is unbelievable, even after you have counted them. All the material and intellectual forces of society converged on the same point—architecture. In this manner, under the pretext of erecting churches to God, art developed to a high degree.

In those days, he who was born a poet became an architect. Genius spread among the masses, and, crushed down on all sides under feudalism, as under a *testudo* of brass bucklers, and finding no outlet but architecture, escaped by way of that art, and its epics took the form of cathedrals. All the other arts obeyed, and put themselves under the tutelage of architecture. They were the artisans for great work. The architect, the poet, the master, summed up in his own person sculpture, which carved his facade; painting, which colored his stained-glass windows; music, which set his bells in motion and pumped air into his organs. Even poor poetry—properly so called, which still persisted in eking out a scanty existence in manuscripts—was obliged, if she was to be recognized at all, to enroll herself in the service of the edifice, either as a hymn or prosody; it was the same role, after all, played by the tragedies of Aeschylus in the priestly rites of Greece, and by the Book of Genesis in the Temple of Solomon.

Thus, till Gutenberg's time, architecture was the principal, universal form of writing. This gigantic book in stone, begun by the East, continued by ancient Greece and Rome, in the Middle Ages wrote its last page. Moreover, this phenomenon of a people's architecture succeeding an architecture belonging to a caste, which we have just observed in the Middle Ages, occurs in precisely analogous stages in human intelligence during other great epochs of history. Thus, to sum up here a law which would really require volumes: in the Far East, the cradle of primitive history, after Hindu architecture came the Phoenician, that fruitful mother of Arabian architecture; in antiquity, Egyptian architecture, of which the Etruscan style and the Cyclopean monuments are but a variety, was succeeded by the Greek, of which the Roman is merely a prolongation burdened with the Carthaginian dome; then, in modern times, after Romanesque architecture, came the Gothic. If we separate each of these three divisions, we shall find that the three elder sisters—Hindu, Egyptian, and Romanesque architecture—have the same symbol; namely, theocracy, the caste system, unity, dogma, myth, God; and that the three younger sisters—Phoenician, Greek, Gothic architecture—whatever diversity of form is inherent in their nature—have the same significance also: liberty, the people, man.

Let him be called Brahmin, magus, or pope, in Hindu, Egyptian, or Romanesque architecture, we always feel the presence of the priest, and nothing but the priest. It is not the same with an architecture of the people. Their architecture is richer and less saintly. In Phoenician architecture, we feel the impact of the merchant; in the Greek, of the republican; in the Gothic, of the bourgeoisie.

The general characteristics of every theocratic architecture are immutability, horror of progress, preservation of traditional lines, consecration of primitive types, the constant adaptation of every aspect of man and nature to the incomprehensible caprices of the symbol. These are dark, foreboding books which only the initiated can decipher. Furthermore, every form, even every deformity in them has a meaning which renders it inviolable. Don't ask Hindu, Egyptian, or Romanesque architects to reform their designs or to perfect their statuary. Every improvement, to them, is an impiety. Here, it seems that the rigidity of dogma is spread over the stone like a second layer of petrifaction.

On the other hand, the general characteristics of popular architectures are variety, progress, originality, opulence, perpetual movement. They are already sufficiently detached from religion to dream of beauty, to nurture it, to alter without ceasing their ornament of statues and arabesques. They suit the times. They have something human about them which they constantly mix with a divine symbolism, under which they still occur. Hence, structures are accessible to every soul, to every intelligence, to every imagination; though symbolic, they are easily comprehensible, like nature herself. Between theocratic architecture and this style, there is the same difference as between the sacred and vulgar language, as between hieroglyphics and art, as between Solomon and Phidias.

If we summarize what we have here very sketchily pointed out, disregarding a thousand detailed proofs and objections, we are led to conclude: that up to the fifteenth century, architecture was the chief recorder for the human race. During this interval of time every thought, no matter how complicated, was embodied in some structure; every idea that rose from the people, every religious law, had its counterpart in monuments; finally, every important thought of the human race was recorded in stone. And why? Because every thought, be it religious or philosophic, wants to be perpetuated; because an idea which has motivated one generation wants to motivate another, and to leave its trace. But how precarious is the immortality of the manuscript! How far more solid, lasting, and resistant is the edifice, the book in stone! To destroy the written word, you need only a torch and a Turk. To demolish the constructed word, you need a social revolution or an earthquake. Barbarism swept over the Colosseum; a deluge, perhaps, over the pyramids.

In the fifteenth century everything changed.

Human intelligence discovered a way of perpetuating itself, one not only more durable and more resistant than architecture, but also simpler and easier. Architecture was dethroned. The stone letters of the Orpheus gave way to the lead letters of Gutenberg.

The book will kill the edifice.

The invention of printing was the greatest event in history. It was the parent revolution; it was the fundamental change in mankind's mode of expression, it was human thought doffing one garment to clothe itself in another; it was the complete and definitive sloughing off of the skin of a serpent, which, since the time of Adam, has symbolized intelligence.

When put into print, thought is more imperishable than ever; it is volatile, intangible, indestructible; it mingles with the air. In the time of architecture, it became a mountain, and made itself master of a century and a region. Now it has been transformed into a flock of birds, scattering to the four winds and filling all air and space.

We repeat: who does not see that in this form thought is more indelible? Instead of being solid it has become long-lived. It has exchanged durability for immortality. We can demolish a substance, but who can extirpate ubiquity? Let a deluge come, birds will still be flying over the mountain long after that mountain has disappeared; and let but a single ark float upon the surface of the cataclysm, and they will seek safety upon it and there await the subsiding of the waters. The new world arising out of this chaos will see, when it awakens, hovering over it, winged and alive, the thought of the world that has been swallowed up.

And when one observes that this mode of expression is not only the most enduring, but also the simplest, the most convenient, the most practicable, when one considers that it is not encumbered and does not need an excess of tools; when one thinks how thought, in order to translate itself into an edifice, is forced to call to its assistance four or five other arts and tons of gold, to collect a mountain of stones, a forest of wood, a nation of workmen—when one compares this with the thought that only needs a little bit of paper, a little ink, a pen, and a press, in order to become a book, is it any wonder that human intelligence quitted architecture for printing? If you can abruptly cut off the pristine bed of a river by means of a canal dug upstream from it, the river will abandon its bed.

Then observe, too, how, after the discovery of printing, architecture gradually became dry, withered, naked; how the spring visibly sank, sap ceased to rise, the thought of the times and of the people deserted it. This cooling off is hardly perceptible in the fifteenth century; the press is still too feeble, and what little it does abstract from all-powerful architecture is but the superabundance of its strength. But in the sixteenth century the sickness is quite patent. Already architecture is no longer the essential expression of society; it miserably degenerates into classic art. From being Gallic, European, indigenous, it becomes Greek and Roman; from the genuine and modern, it becomes pseudo-antique. It is this decadence that we call the Renaissance. A magnificent decadence, we might add, for the old Gothic genius, that sun which is now setting behind the gigantic printing press of Mayence, for a little while still sends its last rays over this hybrid mass of Latin arches and Corinthian colonnades.

It is to this setting sun that we look for a new dawn.

However, from the moment that architecture is only an art like any other, it is no longer the master, the sovereign, the tyrant; it becomes incapable of retaining the services of the other arts. They emancipate themselves, cast off the yoke of the architect, and go their separate ways. Each of these other arts gains by this divorce. Isolation magnifies everything. Sculpture becomes statuary, imagery becomes painting, chanting becomes music. One would say that a whole empire crumbles on the death of its Alexander, and that each of its provinces becomes a kingdom.

Now we are in the time of Raphael, Michelangelo, Jean Goujon, Palestrina—those splendors of the dazzling sixteenth century.

With the emancipation of the arts, thought, too, is everywhere set free. The freethinkers of the Middle Ages had already made gaping wounds in the side of Catholicism. The sixteenth century ripped asunder religious unity. Before the printing press, the Reformation would have been but a schism; printing made it a revolution. Take away the press and heresy is paralyzed. Be it fatal or providential, Gutenberg is the precursor of Luther.

However, when the sun of the Middle Ages has completely set, when the light of the Gothic genius has gone out forever over the horizon of art, architecture, too, becomes more and more pale, colorless, and lifeless. The printed book, that gnawing worm in the structure, sucks its blood and eventually devours it. It droops, withers, wastes away before your very eye. It becomes shabby, poor, of no account. It no longer expresses anything, not even the art of another time. Architecture left to itself, abandoned by the other arts, because human thought has deserted it, must employ the artisan in default of the artist. Plain glass replaces stained glass; the stone mason, the sculptor. Farewell to the vital juices, to originality, to life, and to intelligence. Like a lamentable beggar of the studios, it drags itself from copy to copy. Michelangelo, doubtless aware of its demise in the sixteenth century, made one last despairing attempt to save it. That titan of the world of art piled the Pantheon on the Parthenon, and so made Saint Peter's of Rome, a gigantic work that deserved to remain unique, the last expression of architectural originality, the signature of a great artist at the bottom of a colossal register in stone thus closed. But when Michelangelo was dead, what then did this wretched architecture do, this architecture which only survived as a specter, as a shadow?

It copied Saint Peter's in Rome; it parodied it. This impulse to imitate became a mania—something to weep over.

Henceforth each century has its Roman Saint Peter's. In the seventeenth century, it was the Val-de-Grâce; in the eighteenth, Sainte-Geneviève. Every country has its Saint Peter's. London has hers; St. Petersburg, hers; Paris has two or three. A paltry legacy, the last drivels of a great but decrepit art, was falling into second childhood before dying.

If, instead of characteristic monuments, such as we have just mentioned, we examine art in general from the sixteenth to the eighteenth century, we would at once observe the same phenomenon of decrepitude and decay. From Francis II the dressing of the edifice is effaced more and more so lets the geometric design show through, like the bony framework of an emaciated invalid. The graceful lines of art give way to the cold, inexorable lines of geometry. A structure is no longer a structure; it is a polyhedron. Architecture, however, painfully tries to hide this nudity. Hence the Greek pediment set over the Roman pediment, and vice versa. It is forever the Pantheon on the Parthenon, Saint Peter's at Rome. Such are the brick houses with stone corners during the time of Henry IV; to wit, the Place Royale and the Place Dauphine. Such are the churches during the reign of Louis XIII, heavy, squat, top-heavy, laden down with a dome like a hump. Thus, too, the Mazarin architecture, the bad Italian *pasticcio* of the Quatre-Nations, the palaces of Louis XIV, long court barracks, stiff, cold, boring. Such are, lastly, the buildings of Louis XV, with chicory leaves and vermicelli ornaments, and all the warts and fungi which disfigure that aged, toothless, and debased coquette. From Francis II to Louis XV the disease progressed in geometric ratio. Art becomes nothing but skin clothing bones. It dies miserably.

Meanwhile, what of printing? All the life ebbing away from architecture, was being absorbed by printing. As architecture waned, printing waxed.

The store of strength spent hitherto by the human mind on buildings is now spent upon books. By the sixteenth century, the press, grown now to the stature of its fallen rival, wrestles with it and wins. In the seventeenth century, printing is already so dominant, so triumphant, so well-ensconced in the house of victory that it can give to the world the feast of a great literary era. In the eighteenth century, after a long sleep at the court of Louis XIV, it takes up again the old sword of Luther, arms Voltaire with it, and runs headlong to attack that ancient Europe whose architectural expression it has already destroyed. By the end of the eighteenth century, it has completely destroyed the remains. In the nineteenth century it begins to reconstruct.

Now, which of these two arts, we ask, better represents human thought during three centuries? Which of the two expresses, not only its literary and scholastic fancies, but its vast, profound, universal movement as well? Which of the two has superimposed itself, without break or gap, upon the human race, that thousand-footed, lumbering monster? Architecture or printing?

Printing! And make no mistake about it! Architecture is dead, irrevocably dead, killed by the printed book, killed because it is less durable, killed because it is more costly. Every cathedral costs millions. Imagine now the cost necessary to rewrite an architectural book; the cost of rebuilding those countless edifices and spreading them once more over the land; the cost of returning to those eras when their number was such that from the testimony of an eye witness, "You would have thought that the world was casting off its old dress to clothe itself in a white robe of churches." *Erat enim ut si mundus, ipse excutiendo semet, rejecta vetustate, candidam ecclesiarum vestem indueret* (Glaber Radulphus).

A book is so quickly made, costs so little, and can go so far! Is it any wonder that all human thought should use this conveyance? This is not to say that some architect will not make again, here or there, a beautiful monument, some isolated masterpiece. We shall have again, from time to time, during the reign of printing, an obelisk constructed, say, by an entire army out of melted cannons, as, during the reign of architecture, we had the Iliads, the Romanceros, the Mahabharatas, and the Nibelungen, built by whole nations with the welded fragments of a thousand rhapsodies. The great good fortune of having an architect of genius may befall the twentieth century, like a Dante in the thirteenth. But architecture will never be the social, collective, dominant art it was. The great poem, the great structure, the great masterwork of humanity will never again be built; it will be printed.

And, besides, if, by chance, architecture should be revived, it will never again be mistress. It will submit to the laws of literature which once received its laws from architecture. The respective position of the two arts will be reversed. It is certain that during the architectural epoch, the poems, rare, it is true, resemble monuments. The Indian Vyasa is leafy, strange, impenetrable like the pagoda. Egyptian poetry, like its edifices, has great, tranquil lines; in ancient Greece poetry had the beauty, serenity, and calm of its temples; in Christian Europe, writings show the majesty of Catholicism, the popular naïveté, the rich and luxuriant vegetation of an era of rebirth. The Bible resembles the pyramids; the Iliad, the Parthenon; Homer, Phidias. Dante in the thirteenth century is the last Romanesque church; Shakespeare, in the sixteenth, the last Gothic cathedral.

Thus, to recapitulate briefly, the human race has two books, two registers, two testaments: architecture and printing, the stone Bible and the paper Bible. Unquestionably, when one examines these two books, so widely read through the centuries, it is permissible to regret the visible majesty of the granite writing, those gigantic alphabets in colonnades, porches, and obelisks, those kinds of human mountains which cover the world and the past, from the pyramids to the church steeple, from Cheops to Strasbourg. One must read the past in these marble pages. One must admire and leaf though over and over again the book written by architecture; but one must not deny the grandeur of the edifice which printing has raised in its turn.

The edifice is colossal. I cannot name the statistician who calculated that, by piling one upon the other all the volumes issuing from the press since Gutenberg, one would fill the space between the earth and the moon; but it is not that kind of greatness of which we wish to speak. Nevertheless, if we try to form a collective picture of the combined results of printing down to modern times, does not this total picture seem to us like an immense structure, having the whole world for its foundation, a building upon which humanity has worked without cease and whose monstrous head is lost in the impenetrable mist of the future? This printed tower is the swarming ant-hill of intelligences. It is the beehive where all the imaginations, those golden bees, arrive with their honey. The building has a thousand stories. Here and there, opening up on its ramps, can be seen the mysterious caverns of science which intersect in its bowels. Everywhere on its surface art luxuriously exhibits its arabesques, its rose-windows, and its lacework. There every individual work, however capricious or isolated it may seem, has its place and its projection. The result of the ensemble is harmony. From Shakespeare's cathedral to Byron's mosque, a thousand bell-towers throng together pell-mell in this metropolis of universal thought. At its base, there have been recast several ancient titles of humanity which architecture had not registered. To the left of the entrance, there has been attached the old white-marble bas-relief of Homer, to the right the polyglot Bible raises its seven heads. The hydra of the Romancero stands forth further on, as well as several other hybrid forms, the Vedas and the Nibelungen. However, the prodigious building remains forever incomplete. The press, that giant engine, incessantly gorging all the intellectual sap of society, incessantly vomits new material for its work. The entire human race is its scaffolding. Every mind is its mason. Even the humblest may block a hole or lay a stone. Rétif de la Bretonne brings his hod of plaster. Every day a new tier is raised. Besides the original and individual contributions of separate writers, there were collective donations. The eighteenth century contributed the *Encyclopedia*; the Revolution the *Monitor*. Certainly, these too are structures, growing and piling themselves up in endless spirals; here, too, there is a confusion of languages, untiring labor, incessant activity, a furious competition of all humanity, a promised refuge for the intelligence against another deluge, against another submersion by the barbarians.

It is the second Tower of Babel of the human race.

23

In the holy year of 1482, a blessed, lucky creature was the valiant knight Robert d'Estouteville, sieur of Beyne, baron of Ivry and St. Audrey in La Marche, keeper of the provosty of Paris, and the councilor and chamberlain of the king. It was then nearly seventeen years since the king had, on November 7, 1465, the year of the great comet,* conferred on him the important appointment of Provost of Paris, which was considered more a dignity than an office. It was a marvelous thing that in that year there should still be a gentleman holding a commission under the king whose appointment dated from the time of the marriage of the natural daughter of Louis XI with the Bastard of Bourbon.

It was a small, low hall, with coved ceiling; at the farther end stood a table studded with fleurs-de-lis, a large

*This comet, against which Pope Calivtus ordered public prayers, is the same that was again visible in 1835.

empty armchair of carved oak, reserved for the provost, and on the left a stool for the auditor, Master Florian. Below was the clerk busily writing. In front were the people, and before the door and the table a posse of the provost's men in frocks of purple camlet with white crosses. Two sergeants of the Parloir aux Bourgeois, in their kersey jackets, half scarlet and half blue, stood sentry before a low closed door which was seen behind the table. A single pointed window, of scanty dimensions, encased in the thick wall, threw the faint light of a January morning on two grotesque figures; the fantastic demon of stone sculptured by way of ornament to the groining of the ceiling, and the judge seated at the extremity of the hall.

Figure to yourself seated at the provost's table, lolling upon his elbows between two piles of papers, his feet upon the skirt of his plain, brown cloth robe, furred with white lambskin, which encircled his jolly, rubicund visage and double chin, Master Florian Barbedienne, auditor to the Chatelet.

Now, the said auditor was deaf. A trifling defect this in an auditor. Master Florian, nevertheless, gave judgment without appeal, and very consistently too. It is most certain that it is quite sufficient for a judge to appear to listen; and this condition, the only essential one for strict justice, the venerable auditor fulfilled the more exactly, inasmuch as no noise could divert his attention.

For the rest, he had among the auditory a merciless comptroller of his sayings and doings in the person of our young friend, Jehan Frollo du Moulin, who was sure to be seen everywhere in Paris except before the professors' chairs.

"Look you," said he, in a low tone to his companion Robin Poussepain, who was grinning beside him while he commented on the scenes that were passing before them; "there is the pretty Jehanneton du Buisson of the Marche Neuf! Upon my soul, he condemns her too, the old brute! He must have no more eyes than ears. Fifteen sous four deniers parisis, for having worn two strings of beads! 'Tis paying rather dear, though—Soho! two gentlemen among these varlets! Aiglet de Soins and Hutin de Mailly—two esquires, *Corpus Christi*! Ha! they have been dicing. When shall we see our rector? To pay a fine of one hundred livres to the king! Bravo, Barbedienne!—May I be my brother the archdeacon, if this shall prevent me from gaming; gaming by day, gaming by night, gaming while I live, gaming till I die, and staking my soul after my shirt!—By 'r Lady, what damsels! one after another, pretty lambs! Ambroise Lecuyere, Isabeau la Paynette, Berarde Gironin, I know them all, by my fay! Fined, fined, fined! That will teach you to wear gilt belts! Ten sous parisis, coquettes! Oh! the old deaf imbecile! Oh! Florian, the blockhead! Oh! Barbedienne, the booby! There he is at his feast! Fines, costs, charges, damages, stocks, pillory, imprisonment, are to him Christmas cakes and St. John's march-pane! Look at him, the hog! Get on! what! another lewd woman! Thibaud la Thibaude, I declare! For being seen out of the Rue Glaigny!—Who is that young fellow? Gieffroy Mabonne, one of the bowmen of the guard—for swearing an oath, forsooth! A fine for you, La Thibaude! a fine for you, Gieffroy!—but ten to one the old stupid will confound the two charges, and make the woman pay for the oath, and the soldier for incontinence! Look, look, Robin! what are they bringing in now? By Jupiter, there are all the hounds in the pack! That must be a fine head of game! A wild boar, surely! And so it is, Robin, so it is! And a rare one too, God wot!—Gramercy! 'tis our prince, our Pope of Fools, our bell-ringer, our one-eyed, hunchbacked, bandy-legged Quasimodo!"

Sure enough it was Quasimodo, bound, corded, pinioned. The party of the provost's men who surrounded him were accompanied by the captain of the watch in person, having the arms of France embroidered on the breast of his coat, and those of the city on the back. At the same time there was nothing about Quasimodo, save and except his deformity, which could justify this display of halberts and arquebusses; he was silent, sullen, and quiet. His only eye merely gave from time to time an angry glance at the bonds which confined him.

Meanwhile Master Florian was intently perusing the endorsement of paper containing the charges alleged against Quasimodo, which had been handed to him by the clerk. By means of this precaution, which he was accustomed to take before he proceeded to an examination, he acquainted himself beforehand with the name, condition, and offense of the prisoner; was enabled to have in readiness replies to expected answers; and succeeded in extricating himself from all the sinuosities of the interrogatory, without too grossly exposing his infirmity. To him, therefore, the endorsement was like the dog to the blind man. If, however, his infirmity chanced to betray itself now and then by some incoherent apostrophe or some unintelligible question, with the many it passed for profoundness, with some few for imbecility. In either case the honor of the magistracy remained unimpeached; for it is better that a judge should be reputed profound or imbecile than deaf.

After ruminating a while on Quasimodo's affair, he threw back his head and half closed his eyes, to give himself a look of the more majesty and impartiality, so that at that moment he was both deaf and blind—a two-fold condition without which there is no perfect judge. In this magisterial attitude he commenced his examination.

"Your name?"

Now, here was a case which the law had not provided for—the deaf interrogating the deaf.

Quasimodo, unaware of the question addressed to him, continued to look steadfastly at the judge, without answering. The deaf judge, equally unaware of the deafness of the accused, conceiving that he had answered, as persons in his situation generally did, went on, agreeably to his mechanical routine: "Very well: your age?"

Quasimodo maintained the same silence as before. The judge again supposing that he had answered his question, continued. "Now your business?"

Still Quasimodo was silent. The people who witnessed

this curious scene began to whisper and to look at one another.

"That will do," rejoined the imperturbable auditor, when he presumed that the accused had finished his third answer. "You are accused before us, in the first place, of making a nocturnal disturbance; secondly, of an assault upon the person of a lewd woman; thirdly, of disloyalty, sedition, and resistance to the archers of the guard of our lord the king. What have you to say for yourself on these points? Clerk, have you taken down the prisoner's answers thus far?"

At this unlucky question, a roar of laughter burst from both clerk and audience, so vehement, so loud, so contagious, so universal, that neither of the deaf men could help noticing it. Quasimodo merely turned about and shrugged his hump with disdain; while Master Florian, equally astonished, and supposing that the mirth of the spectators had been provoked by some disrespectful reply of the prisoner's, rendered visible to him by the rising of his shoulders, indignantly exclaimed: "For that answer, fellow, you deserve a halter. Know you to whom you speak?"

This sally was not likely to check the explosion of the general mirth. So odd and so ridiculous did it appear to all, that the fit of laughter spread to the very sergeant of the Parloir aux Bourgeois, a sort of knave of spades, proverbial for stupidity. Quasimodo alone preserved his gravity, for this very sufficient reason, that he had not the least notion of what was passing around him. The judge, more and more exasperated, thought fit to proceed in the same strain, hoping thereby to strike the prisoner with a terror that should react upon the audience.

"How dare you insult the auditor of the Chatelet, the deputy superintendent of the police of Paris, appointed to inquire into crimes, offenses, and misdemeanors; to control all trades; to prevent forestalling and regrating; to cleanse the city of filth and the air of contagious diseases; to repair the pavements; in short to pay continual attention to the public welfare, and that too without wages or hope of salary! Do you know that I am Florian Barbedienne, own lieutenant of Monsieur, the provost, and moreover, commissary, comptroller, examiner?"

The Lord knows when Master Florian would have finished this flight of eloquence, had not the low door behind him suddenly opened and afforded passage to the provost himself. Master Florian did not stop short at his entrance, but, turning half round upon his heel, and abruptly directing to the provost the harangue which a moment before he was launching forth against Quasimodo: "Monsiegneur," said he, "I demand such punishment as it shall please you to pronounce upon the prisoner here present for audacious and heinous contempt of justice."

Out of breath with the exertion, he sat down and began to wipe off the perspiration which trickled from his forehead, and fell in big drops upon the parchments spread out before him. Messire Robert d'Estouteville knitted his brows, and commanded attention with a gesture so imperious and expressive that Quasimodo had some inkling of what was meant.

"What hast thou done to be brought hither, varlet?" said the provost, sternly.

The poor devil, supposing that the provost was inquiring his name, broke his habitual silence, and in a harsh and guttural voice replied, "Quasimodo."

The answer was so incongruous with the question as once more to excite the risibility of the bystanders, when Messire Robert, flushed with rage, exclaimed, "Art thou making thy game of me too, thou arrant knave?"

"Bell-ringer at Notre Dame," replied Quasimodo, conceiving that the judge had inquired his profession.

"Bell-ringer!"—roared the provost, who had got up that morning, as we have observed, in such an ill-humor as not to need the further provocation of these cross-grained answers—"bell-ringer! I'll have such a peal rung on thy back as shall make thee rue thy impertinence. Dost thou hear, varlet?"

"If you want to know my age," said Quasimodo, "I believe I shall be twenty, next Martinmas."

This was too provoking—the provost lost all patience. "What, wretch! dost thou defy the provost! Here, vergers, take this fellow to the pillory of the Greve; let him be flogged, and then turn him for an hour. 'S death, he shall pay for his insolence, and my pleasure is that this sentence be proclaimed by four trumpeters in the seven castellanies of the viscounty of Paris."

The clerk instantly fell to work to record the sentence.

"*Ventre Dieu!* but that's a just sentence!" cried Jehan Frollo du Moulin, from his corner.

The provost turned about, and again fixing his flashing eyes on Quasimodo, "I verily believe," said he, "that the knave has dared to swear in our presence. Clerk, add a fine of twelve deniers parisis for the oath, and let half of it be given to the church of St. Eustache."

In a few minutes the sentence was drawn up. The language was simple and concise. The practice of the provosty and viscounty of Paris had not been laid down by the present Thibaut Baillet, and Roger Bamme, king's advocate; it was not then obstructed by that forest of quirks, cavils, and quibbles, which these two lawyers planted before it at the commencement of the sixteenth century. Everything about it was clear, explicit, expeditious. It was all straightforward work, and you perceived at once at the end of every path, uninterrupted by bushes or roundabout ways, the pillory, the gibbet, and the wheel. You knew at least what you had to expect.

The clerk handed the sentence to the provost, who affixed his seal, and left the hall to continue his round of the courts, in a mood which was likely to increase the population of the jails of Paris. Jehan Frollo and Robin Poussepain laughed in their sleeve; while Quasimodo looked on with an air of calm indifference.

While Master Florian Barbedienne was in his turn reading the sentence, previously to his signing it, the clerk, feeling compassion for the wretched victim and hoping to obtain some mitigation of his punishment, approached as near as he could to the ear of the auditor, and said, pointing at the same time to Quasimodo—"The poor fellow is deaf."

He conceived that this community of infirmity might awaken Master's Florin's lenity in behalf of the culprit. But, in the first place, as we have already mentioned, Master Florian was by no means anxious to have it known that he was deaf; and, in the next, he was so hard of hearing as not to catch a single syllable of what the clerk said to him. Pretending, nevertheless, to hear, he replied, "Aha! that is a different thing, I did not know that. In this case let him have another hour in the pillory"; and he signed the sentence with this alteration.

"That's right!" cried Robin Poussepain, who owed Quasimodo a grudge: "this will teach him to handle people roughly."

24

With the reader's permission, we shall conduct him back to the Place de Greve, where we yesterday quitted Gringoire to follow La Esmeralda.

It is the hour of ten in the morning; the appearance of the Place indicates the morrow of a festival. The pavement is strewed with wrecks—rags, ribbons, feathers, drops of wax from the torches, fragments of the public banquet. A good many citizens are lounging about, kicking the half-consumed cases of the fireworks, admiring the Maison aux Piliers, extolling the beautiful hangings of the preceding day, and looking at the nails which had held them. The venders of cider and beer are trundling their barrels among the groups. A few pedestrians, urged by business, bustle along at a quick rate. The shopkeepers are calling to one another from their doors, and conversing together. The *fete*, the ambassadors, Coppenole, the Pope of Fools, were in every mouth, each striving to crack the best jokes and to laugh the loudest. And yet four sergeants on horseback, who have just posted themselves at the four sides of the pillory, have already gathered around them a considerable portion of the populace, who were kicking their heels about the Palace in the hopes of enjoying the amusement of an execution.

Now, if the reader, after surveying this lively and noisy scene which is performing all over the Palace, turns his eye toward the ancient half Gothic, half Roman building, called Rolande's Tower, which forms the corner of the quay to the west, he may perceive at the angle of the facade a large public breviary, richly illuminated, sheltered from the rain by a small penthouse, and secured from thieves by an iron grating, which, nevertheless, does not prevent your turning over the leaves. Beside this breviary is a narrow-pointed, unglazed window, looking out upon the Place, and defended by two crossbars of iron—the only aperture for the admission of air and light to a small cell without door, formed in the basement of the wall of the old building, and full of a quiet the more profound, silence the more melancholy, from its very contiguity to a public place, and that the most populous and the most noisy in Paris.

This cell had been noted in Paris for three centuries, ever since Madame Rolande, of Rolande's Tower, out of affection for her father, who had fallen in the Crusades, caused it to be cut out of the wall of her own house, for the purpose of shutting herself up in it forever, keeping no part of her mansion but this hole, the door of which was walled up, and the window open winter and summer, and giving all the rest to the poor and to God. In this anticipated tomb the disconsolate lady had awaited death for twenty years, praying night and day for the soul of her father, lying upon ashes, without so much as a stone for a pillow, habited in black sackcloth, and subsisting solely upon the bread and water which the pity of the passengers induced them to deposit on her windowsill, thus living upon charity, after giving away her all. At her death, at the moment of quitting this for her last sepulcher, she bequeathed it forever to afflicted females, maids, wives, or widows, who should have occasion to pray much for themselves or others, and who should wish to bury themselves alive, on account of some heavy calamity or some extraordinary penance.

In the cities of the Middle Ages tombs of this sort were not rare. In the most frequented street, in the most crowded and noisy market, in the midst of the highways, almost under the horses' feet and the cart-wheels, you frequently met with a cellar, a cave, a well, a walled and grated cabin, in which a human being, self-devoted to some everlasting sorrow, to some signal expiation, spent night and day, in prayer.

Besides the cell of the Greve, there was one at Montfaucon, another at the charnel-house of the Innocents; a third, I do not exactly remember where, at the logis Clichon, I believe; and others at various places, where you still find traces of them in traditions, though the buildings have been swept away. On the hill of St. Genevieve a kind of Job of the Middle Ages sang for thirty years the seven penitential psalms, upon a dunghill, at the bottom of a cistern, beginning afresh as soon as he had finished, and raising his voice highest at night; and to this day the antiquary imagines that he hears his voice, as he enters the street called *Puits qui parle*.

But to return to the cell of Rolande's Tower. It is right to mention that ever since the death of Madame Rolande it had seldom been for any length of time without a tenant. Many a woman had come to mourn, some their indiscretions, and others the loss of parents or lovers. Parisian scandal, which interferes in everything, even in such things as least concern it, pretended that very few widows had been seen among the number.

According to the fashion of the age, a Latin legend inscribed upon the wall indicated to the lettered passenger the pious destination of this cell. Down to the middle of the sixteenth century it was customary to explain the object of a building by a short motto placed over the door. Thus in France there may still be read over the postern of the seignorial house of Tourvile, *Sileto et Spera*; in Ireland, beneath the coat of arms over the grand entrance to Fortescue Castle, "Forte Scutum Salus Ducum"; in England, over the principal door of the hospitable mansion of Earl Cowper, "Tuum Est." In those days every building was a thought.

As there was no door to the cell of Rolande's Tower, there had been engraven in Roman capitals underneath the window, these two words:

TU ORA

Hence the people, whose plain common sense never looks for profound meanings in things, and who scruple not to attach to *Ludovico Magno* the signification of *Porte St. Denis*, gave to this dark, damp, loathsome hole the name of *Trou aux Rats*, an interpretation less sublime perhaps than the other, but certainly more picturesque.

25

At the period of which we are treating the cell of Rolande's Tower was occupied. If the reader is desirous of knowing by whom he has only to listen to the conversation of three honest gossips, who, at the moment at which we have directed his attention to the Trou aux Rats (rat-hole), were going to the very spot, proceeding from the chateau along the river-side toward the Greve.

Two of them were dressed like wives of respectable citizens of Paris. Their fine white neckerchief; their linsey-woolsey petticoat, striped red and blue; their white worsted stockings, with colored clocks, pulled up tight upon the leg; their square-toed shoes of tawny leather with black soles; and above all their headdress, a sort of high cap of tinsel loaded with ribbons and lace, still worn by the women of Champagne, and also by the grenadiers of the Russian Imperial guard, indicated that they belonged to that class of wealthy tradesfolk which comes between what lackeys call a woman and what they style a lady. They wore neither gold rings nor gold crosses, evidently not on account of poverty, but simply for fear of fine. Their companion was attired nearly in the same fashion, but in her dress and manner there was something which betrayed the country woman. The height of her belt above the hips told that she had not been long in Paris. Add to this a plaited neckerchief, bows of ribbons at her shoes, the stripes of her petticoat running breadthwise instead of lengthwise, and various other enormities equally abhorrent to good taste.

The first two walked with the step peculiar to the woman of Paris who are showing the lions to their provincial friends. The third held a big boy by one hand, while she carried a large cake in the other. The boy did not care to keep up with her, but suffered himself to be dragged along, and stumbled every morning, to the no small alarm of his mother. It is true that he paid much greater attention to the cake than to the pavement. Some weighty reason no doubt prevented his taking a bite, for he did no more than look wistfully at it. 'Twas cruel to make a Tantalus of the jolt-headed cub.

Meanwhile the three damoiselles—for the term dames was then reserved for noble females—were talking all at once.

"Let us make haste, damoiselle Mahiette," said the youngest, who was also the lustiest of the three, to her country friend. "I am afraid we shall be too late. We were told at the Chatelet that he was to be put in the pillory forthwith."

"Pooh! pooh! What are you talking of, damoiselle Oudarde Musnier?" replied the other Parisian. "He is to stay two hours in the pillory. We shall have plenty of time. Have you ever seen anyone in the pillory, my dear Mahiette?"

"Yes," answered Mahiette, "at Rheims."

"Your pillory at Rheims! why, 'tis not worth mentioning. A wretched cage, where they turn nothing but clodpoles!"

"Clodpoles, forsooth!" rejoined Mahiette, "in the Cloth Market at Rheims! We have had some noted criminals there, however—people who had murdered both father and mother. Clodpoles, indeed! what do you take us for, Gervaise?"

It is certain that the provincial lady felt somewhat nettled at the attack on the honor of their pillory. Luckily the discreet damoiselle Oudarde gave a seasonable turn to the conversation.

"What say you, Mahiette," she asked, "to our Flemish ambassadors? Have you ever had any like them at Rheims?"

"I confess," replied Mahiette, "that Paris is the only place for seeing Flemings such as they."

"And their horses, what beautiful animals, dressed out as they are in the fashion of their country!"

"Ah, my dear," exclaimed Mahiette, assuming in her turn an air of superiority, "what would you say had you been at Rheims at the coronation in the year '61, and seen the horses of the princes and of the king's retinue. There were housings and trappings of all sorts; some of damask cloth and fine cloth of gold garnished with sable; others of velvet furred with ermine; others all covered with jewelry, and large gold and silver bells. Think of the money that all this must have cost. And then the beautiful pages that were upon them."

"Heyday!" cried Oudarde, "what is there to do yonder? See what a crowd is collected at the foot of the bridge. There seems to be something in the midst of them that they are looking at."

"Surely I hear the sound of a tambourine," said Gervaise. "I dare say it is young Esmeralda playing her antics with her goat. Quick, Mahiette, and pull your boy along. You are come to see the curiosities of Paris. Yesterday you saw the Flemings; today you must see the Egyptian."

"The Egyptian" exclaimed Mahiette, starting back and forcibly grasping the arm of her son. "God forbid! she might steal my boy. Come, Eustache."

With these words she began to run along the quay toward the Greve, till she had left the bridge at a considerable distance behind her. Presently the boy, whom she drew after her, tripped and fell upon his knees; she stopped to recover breath, and Quadarde and Gervaise overtook her.

"That Egyptian steal your boy," said Gervaise; "beshrew me if this is not a strange fancy."

Mahiette shook her head with a pensive look.

"And what is still more strange," observed Oudarde, "Sister Gudule has the same notion of the Egyptians."

"Who is Sister Gudule?" inquired Mahiette.

"You must be vastly ignorant at your Rheims not to know that," replied Oudarde. "Why, the recluse of the Trou aux Rats."

"What, the poor woman to whom we are carrying the cake?"

Oudarde nodded affirmatively. "Just so. You will see her presently at her window in the Greve. She holds just the same opinion as you of those Egyptian vagabonds, who go about drumming on tambourines and telling fortunes. Nobody knows why she has such a horror of the Zingari and Egyptians. But you, Mahiette, wherefore should you take to your heels thus, at the mere sight of them?"

"Oh," said Mahiette, clasping her boy's head in both her hands, "I would not for the world that the same thing should happen to me as befell Pauqette la Chantefleurie."

"Ah, you must tell us that story, good Mahiette," said Gervaise, taking her by the arm.

"I will," answered Mahiette; "but how ignorant you must be in your Paris not to know that. But we need not stop while I tell you the story. You must know then, that Paquette la Chantefleurie was a handsome girl of eighteen, just when I was so myself, that is eighteen years ago, and it is her own fault that she is not at this day, like me, a hearty, comely mother of six-and-thirty, with a husband and a boy. She was the daughter of Guybertaut, minstrel of Rheims, the same that played before King Charles II at his coronation, when he went down our river Vesle from Sillery to Muison, and the Maid of Orleans was in the barge with him. Paquette's father died while she was quite an infant; so she had only her mother, who was the sister of Monsieur Matthieu Pradon, master-brazier here at Paris, in the Rue Parin-Gariln, who died only last year. You see she came of a good family. The mother was unluckily a kind, easy woman, and taught Paquette nothing but to do a little needlework and make herself finery, which helped to keep them very poor. They lived at Rheims, in the Rue Folle Peine. In '61, the year of the coronation of our King Louis XI, whom God preserve, Paquette was so lively and so handsome that everybody called her La Chantefleurie. Poor girl! what beautiful teeth she had! and how she would laugh that she might show them! Now a girl that laughs a great deal is in the way to cry; fine teeth spoil fine eyes. Chantefleurie and her mother had great difficulty to earn a livelihood; since the death of the old minstrel their circumstances had been getting worse and worse; their needlework produced them no more than six deniers a week. How different from the time when old Guybertaut received twelve sois parisis for a single song, as he did at the coronation! One winter—it as that of the same year, '61—when the poor creatures had neither cord-

wood nor fagots, the weather was very cold, which gave
Chantefleurie such a beautiful color that she was admired
by all the men, and this led to her ruin—Eustache, don't
meddle with the cake!—We all knew what had happened
as soon as we saw her come to church one Sunday with a
gold cross at her breast. And, look you, she was not fifteen
at the time. Her first lover was the young Viscount
deCormontreuil, whose castle is about three-quarters of a
league from Rheims; and when she was deserted by him
she took up first with one and then with another, till at last
all men became alike to her. Poor Chantefleurie!" sighed
Mahiette, brushing away a tear that started from her eye.

"There is nothing very extraordinary in this history,"
said Gervaise; "nor, as far as I can see, has it anything to
do with Egyptians or children."

"Have patience," replied Mahiette, "you will soon see
that it has. In '66, it will be sixteen years this very month
on St. Paul's day, Paquette was brought to bed of a little
girl. How delighted she was, poor thing! She had long
been wishing for a child. Her mother, good soul, who had
always winked at her faults, was now dead; so that
Paquette had nothing in the world to love, and none to
love her. For five years, ever since her fall, she had been
a miserable creature, poor Chantefleurie! She was alone,
alone in this life, pointed at and hooted in the streets,
cuffed by the beadles, teased by little ragged urchins. By
this time she was twenty—an age at which it is said lewd
women begin to be old. Her way of life scarcely brought
her in more than her needlework had formerly done; the
winter had set in sharp, and wood was again rare on her
hearth, and bread scarce in her cupboard. She was, of
course very sorrowful, very miserable, and her tears wore
deep channels in her cheeks. But in her degraded and forlorn condition it seemed to her that she should be less degraded and less forlorn, if she had anything or anyone else
in the world that she could love, and that could love her.
She felt that this must needs be a child, because nothing
but a child could be innocent enough for that. Women of

her class must have either a lover or a child to engage their affections, or they are very unhappy. Now as Paquette could not find a lover, she set her whole heart upon a child, and prayed to God night and day for one. And he took compassion on her, and gave her a little girl. Her joy is not to be described. How she did hug and fondle her infant! it was quite a tempest of tears and kisses. She suckled it herself, made it clothes out of her own, and thenceforward felt neither cold nor hunger. Her beauty returned. An old maid makes a young mother. In a short time she again betook herself to her former loose courses and she laid out all the money that she received on frocks and caps and lace and little satin bonnets, and all sorts of finery for her child. Monsieur Eustache, hav'n't I told you not to meddle with that cake? It is certain that little Anges—that was the name given to the child at her christening—was more bedizened with ribbons and embroidery than a princess. Among other things she had a pair of little shoes, such as I'll be bound Louis XI never had. Her mother had made and embroidered them herself, with the utmost art and skill of her needle. A prettier pair of little rose-colored shoes was never seen. They were not longer than my thumb, and you must have seen the child's tiny feet come out or you would never believe they could go into them. But then those feet were so small, so pretty, so rosy—more so than the satin of the shoes. When you have children, Oudarde, you will know that nothing is so pretty as those delicate little feet and hands."

"I desire nothing better," said Oudarde, with a sigh; "but I must wait till it is the good pleasure of Monsieur Andry Musnier."

"Paquette's baby," resumed Mahiette, "had not merely handsome feet. I saw it when but four months old. Oh! it was a love! Her eyes were larger than her mouth, and she had the most beautiful dark hair, which already began to curl. What a superb brunette she would have made at sixteen! Her mother became every day more and more dotingly fond of her. She hugged her, she kissed her, she tickled her, she washed her, she pranked her up—she was ready to eat her. In the wildness of her joy she thanked God for the gift. But it was her tiny rosy feet above all that she was never tired of admiring. She would pass whole hours in putting on them little shoes, taking them off again, gazing at them, and pressing them to her lips."

"The story is well enough," said Gervaise, in an undertone; "but where are the Egyptians?"

"Why, here," replied Mahiette. "One day a party of very strange-looking people on horseback arrived at Rheims. They were beggars and vagabonds, who roved about the country, headed by their duke and their counts. Their visage was tawny; they had curly hair, and wore silver rings in their ears. The women were uglier than the men. Their complexion was darker. They went bare-headed; a shabby mantle covered the body, an old piece of sackcloth was tied about the shoulders, and their hair was like a horse's tail. The children, who were tumbling about upon their laps, were enough to frighten an ape. These hideous people had come—so it was said—straightway from Egypt to Rheims through Poland; the pope had confessed them, and ordered them by way of penance to wander for seven years together through the world without lying in a bed; they claim ten livres tournis of all archbishops, bishops, and crosiered and mitred abbots, by virtue of a bull of the pope. They came to Rheims to tell fortunes in the name of the King of Algiers and the Emperor of Germany. This was quite enough, as you may suppose, to cause them to be forbidden to enter the city. The whole band then encamped without more ado on the mill-hill, by the old chalk-pits, and all Rheims went to see them. They looked at your palm and foretold wonderful things. At the same time there were various reports about their stealing children, cutting purses, and eating human flesh. Prudent persons said to the simple, 'Go not near them,' and yet went themselves in secret. It was quite the rage. The fact is, they told things which would have astonished a cardinal. Mothers were not a little proud of their children after the

Egyptians had read all sorts of marvels written in their hands in Pagan gibberish. One had an emperor, another a pope, a third a great captain. Poor Chanterfleurie was seized with curiosity; she was anxious to know her luck, and whether little Agnes should one day be Empress of Armenia or something of that sort. She carried her to the encampment of the Egyptians; the women admired the infant, they fondled her, they kissed her with their dark lips, they were astonished at her tiny hands, to the no small delight of the poor mother. But above all they extolled her delicate feet and her pretty little shoes. The child was not quite a year old. She had begun to lisp a word or two, laughed at her mother like a little madcap, and was plump and fat and played a thousand engaging antics. But she was frightened at the Egyptians and fell a-crying. Her mother kissed and cuddled her, and away she went overjoyed at the good luck which the fortune-tellers had promised her Agnes. She was to be a beauty, a virtue, a queen. She returned to her garret in the Rue Folle Penie quite proud of her burden. Next day she softly slipped out for a moment while the infant lay asleep on the bed, leaving the door ajar, and ran to tell an acquaintance in the Rue Sechesserie how that there would come a time when her dear little Agnes would have the King of England and the Archduke of Ethiopia to wait upon her at table, and a hundred other marvelous things. On her return, not hearing the child cry as she went up stairs, she said to herself, 'That's lucky! baby is asleep yet.' She found the door wider open than she had left it; she went in hastily and ran to the bed. Poor mother! the infant was gone, and nothing belonging to it was left except one of its pretty little shoes. She rushed out of the room, darted down stairs, screaming, 'My child! my child! who has taken my child?' The house stood by itself, the street was a lonely one; nobody could give her any clue. She went through the town, searching every street; she ran to and fro the whole day, distracted, maddened, glaring in at the doors and windows, like a wild beast that has lost her young. Her dress was in disorder, her hair hung loose down her back, she was fearful to look at, and there was a fire in her eyes that dried up her tears. She stopped the passengers, crying, 'My child! my child! my dear little child! Tell me where to find my child, and I will be your slave, and you shall do with me what you please.' It was quite cutting, Oudarde, and I assure you I saw a very hard-hearted man, Master Ponce Lucabre, the attorney, shed tears at it. Poor, poor mother! In the evening she went home. While she was away, a neighbor had seen two Egyptian women slip slyly up her stairs with a large bundle, and presently come down again, shut the door, and hurry off. After they were gone, cries as if of a child had been heard proceeding from Paquette's lodging. The mother laughed with joy, flew up stairs, dashed open the door, and went in. Only think, Oudarde, instead of her lovely baby, so smiling, and so plump, and so ruddy, there she found a sort of little monster, a hideous, deformed, one-eyed, limping thing, squalling, and creeping about the floor. She covered her eyes in horror. 'Oh,' said she, 'can it be that the witches have changed my Agnes into this frightful animal?' Her neighbor took the little imp away forthwith; he would have driven her mad. He was the misshapened child of some Egyptian or other, who had given herself up to the devil. He appeared to be about four years old, and talked a language which was not a human language—such words were never before heard in this world. Chantefleurie snatched up the tiny shoe, all that was left her of all that she had loved. She lay so long, without moving, without speaking, apparently without breathing, that everybody thought she was dead. All at once she trembled in every limb; she covered the precious relic with passionate kisses, and burst into a fit of sobs, as if her heart was going to break. I assure you we all wept along with her. 'Oh, my baby!' said she, 'my dear little baby! where art thou?' It made one's heart bleed. I can't help crying still at the thought of it. Our children, you see, are as the very marrow of our bone. Oh, my Eustache, my poor Eustache, if I were to lose thee, what would become

of me! At length Chantefleurie suddenly sprang up, and
ran through the streets of Rheims, shouting, 'To the camp
of the Egyptians! Let the witches be burnt!' The Egyptians
were gone. It was dark night; nobody could tell which way
they had gone. Next day, which was Sunday, there were
found on a heath between Gueux and Tilly, about two
leagues from Rheims, the remains of a large fire, bits of
ribbons which had belonged to the dress of Paquette's
child, and several drops of blood. There could be no further doubt that the Egyptians had the night before
held their sabbath on this heath, and feasted upon the child
in company with their master, Beelzebub. When Chantefleurie heard these horrid particulars, she did not weep;
she moved her lips, as if to speak, but could not. The day
after her hair was quite gray, and on the next she had
disappeared."

"A frightful story, indeed," exclaimed Oudarde, "and
enough to draw tears from a Burgundian!"

"I am no longer surprised," said Gervaise, "that you are
so dreadfully afraid of the Egyptians."

"You did quite right," replied Oudarde, "to get out of
their way with Eustache, especially as these are Egyptians
from Poland."

"Not so," said Gervaise; "it is said that they come from
Spain and Catalonia."

"At any rate," answered Oudarde, "it is certain that they
are Egyptians."

"And not less certain," continued Gervaise, "that their
teeth are long enough to eat little children. And I should
not be surprised if Esmeralda were to pick a bit now and
then, though she has such a small, pretty mouth. Her white
goat plays so many marvelous tricks that there must be
something wrong at bottom."

Mahiette walked on in silence. She was absorbed in that
reverie which is a sort of prolongation of a doleful story,
and which continues till it has communicated its vibration
to the inmost fibers of the heart. "And did you never know
what became of Chantefleurie?" asked Gervaise. Mahiette

made no reply. Gervaise repeated the question, gently shaking her arm and calling her by her name.

"What became of Chantefleurie?" said she, mechanically repeating the words whose impression was still fresh upon her ear. Then making an effort to recall her attention to the sense of those words: "Ah!" said she, sharply, "it was never known what became of her."

After a pause she added: "Some said they saw her leave Rheims in the dusk of the evening by the Porte Flechembault; and others at daybreak by the old Porte Basee. Her gold cross was found hanging on the stone cross in the field where the fair is held. It was this trinket that occasioned her fall in '61. It was a present from the handsome Viscount de Cormontreuil, her first admirer. Paquette never would part with it, distressed as she had often been. She clung to it as to life. Of course, when we heard how and where it was found, we all concluded that she was dead. Yet there were persons who declared they had seen her on the road to Paris walking barefoot upon the flints. But, in this case, she must have gone out at the gate of Vesle, not only out of the town, but out of the world."

"I don't understand you," said Gervaise.

"The Vesle," replied Mahiette, with a melancholy smile, "is our river."

"Poor Chantefleurie!" said Oudarde, shuddering; "drowned!"

"Drowned!" replied Mahiette. "Ah! how it would have spoiled good Father Guybertaut's singing, while floating in his bark beneath the bridge of Tinqueux, had he been told that his dear little Paquette would some day pass under that same bridge, but without song and without bark!"

"And the little shoe?" said Gervaise.

"Disappeared with the mother," replied Mahiette.

Oudarde, a comely, tenderhearted woman, would have been satisfied to sigh in company with Mahiette; but Gervaise, who was of a more inquisitive disposition, had not got to the end of her questions.

"And the monster?" said she, all at once, resuming her inquiries.

"What monster? asked Mahiette.

"The little Egyptian monster, left by the witches at Chantefleurie's in exchange for her child. What was done with it? I hope you drowned that too."

"Oh, no!" replied Mahiette.

"Burnt then, I suppose? The best thing too that could be done with a witch's child."

"Nor that either, Gervaise. The archbishop had compassion on the Egyptian boy; he carefully took the devil out of him, blessed him, and sent him to Paris to be exposed in the wooden cradle at Notre Dame as a foundling."

"Those bishops," said Gervaise, grumblingly, "because they are learned men, never do anything like other people. Only think, Oudarde, to pop the devil into the place of the foundlings! for it is quite certain that this little monster could be nothing else. Well, Mahiette, and what became of him at Paris? No charitable person would look at him, I reckon."

"I don't know," replied her country friend. "Just at that time my husband bought the place of notary at Beru, about two leagues from Rheims, and being fully engaged with our own business, we lost sight of the matter."

Amid such conversation the worthy trio reached the Place de Greve. Engrossed by the subject of their discourse, they had passed Rolande's Tower without being aware of it, and turned mechanically toward the pillory, around which the concourse of people was every moment increasing. It is probable that the scene which at this moment met their view would have made them completely forget the Trou aux Rats and their intention of calling there, had not Eustache, whom Mahiette still led by the hand, as if apprised by some instinct that they had passed the place of their destination, cried, "Mother, now may I eat the cake?"

Had the boy been less hasty, that is to say less greedy, he would have waited till the party had returned to the house of Master Andry Musnier, Rue Madame la Valence in the University, when there would have been the two branches of the Seine and the five bridges of the city between the cake and the Trou aux Rats, before he had ventured the timid question: "Mother, now may I eat the cake?"

That very question, an imprudent one at the moment when it was put by Eustache, roused Mahiette's attention.

"Upon my word," said she, "we are forgetting the recluse. Show me your Trou aux Rats, that I may carry her the cake."

"Let's go at once," said Oudarde; " 'tis a charity."

This was far from agreeable to Eustache. "She sha'n't have my cake," said he, dashing his head against his two shoulders by turns, which in a case of this kind is a signal token of displeasure.

The three women turned back, and having arrived at Rolande's Tower, Oudarde said to the other two: "We must not all look in at the hole at once lest we should frighten Sister Gudule. Do you pretend to be reading the *Dominus* in the breviary, while I peep in at the window—she knows something of me. I will tell you when to come."

She went up by herself to the window. The moment she looked in, profound pity took possession of every feature, and her open, good-humored face changed color and expression as suddenly as if it had passed out of the sunshine into the moonlight; a tear trembled in her eye and her mouth was contracted as when a person is going to weep. A moment afterward she put her finger upon her lips, and made a sign for Mahiette to come and look.

Mahiette went in silence on tiptoe, as though approaching the bed of a dying person. It was in truth a melancholy sight that presented itself to the two women while they looked in without stirring or breathing at the barred window of the Trou aux Rats.

The cell was small, wider than deep, with covered ceiling, and seen from within resembled the hollow of a large episcopal miter. Upon the stone floor, in one angle, a female was seated, or rather crouched. Her chin rested upon her knees, while her arms and clasped hands encircled her legs. Doubled up in this manner, wrapped in brown sackcloth, her long, lank, gray hair falling over her face down to her feet, she presented at first sight a strange figure standing out from the dark ground of the cell, a sort of dun triangle which the ray entering at the window showed like one of those specters seen in dreams, half shadow and half light, pale, motionless, gloomy, cowering upon a grave or before the grating of a dungeon. It was neither woman, nor man, nor living creature; it had no definite form; it was a shapeless figure, a sort of vision in which the real and the fantastic were contrasted like light and shade. Scarcely could there be distinguished under her streaming hair the forbidding profile of an attenuated face; scarcely did the ample robe of sackcloth which enfolded her permit the extremity of a bare foot to be seen peeping from beneath it and curling up on the hard, cold pavement. The faint likeness of the human form discernible under this garb of mourning made one shudder.

This figure, which you have supposed to be imbedded in the stone floor, appeared to have neither motion, nor breath, nor thought. Without other clothing save the sackcloth, in the month of January, barefoot upon a pavement of granite, without fire, in the gloom of a dungeon, the oblique aperture of which admitted only the chill blast but not the cheering sun, she seemed not to suffer, not even to feel. You would have thought that she had turned herself to stone with the dungeon, to ice with the season. Her hands were clasped, her eyes fixed. At the first glance you would have taken her for a specter, at the second for a statue.

At intervals, however, her livid lips opened for the purpose of breathing, and quivered; but they looked as dead and as will-less as leaves driven by the blast. Meanwhile, those haggard eyes cast a look, an ineffable look, a profound, melancholy, imperturbable look, steadfastly fixed on a corner of the cell which could not be seen from without; a look which seemed to connect all the gloomy thoughts of that afflicted spirit with some mysterious object.

Such was the creature to whom was given from her garb the familiar name of Sacky, and from her dwelling that of the Recluse.

The three women—for by this time Gervaise had rejoined Oudarde and Mahiette—peeped in at the window. Their heads intercepted the light that entered the dungeon, but yet the wretched being whom they deprived of it appeared not to notice them. "Let us not disturb her," said Oudarde, softly; "she is praying."

Mahiette scrutinized all this time that wan, withered, death-like face, under its veil of hair, with an anxiety that increased every moment, and her eyes filled with tears. "It would indeed be most extraordinary!" muttered she. Putting her head between the bars of the aperture she was enabled to see the corner upon which the eye of the unhappy recluse was still riveted. When she drew back her head from the window, her cheeks were bathed with tears.

"What do you call this woman?" said she to Oudarde, who replied: "We call her Sister Gudule."

"For my part," rejoined Mahiette, "I call her Paquette la Chantefleurie."

Then, laying her finger upon her lips, she made a sign to the astonished Oudarde to put her head through the aperture and look. Oudarde did so, and beheld in the corner upon which the eye of the recluse was fixed in gloomy ecstasy a tiny shoe of pink satin, embroidered all over with gold and silver. Gervaise looked in after Oudarde, and the three women fell a-weeping at the sight of the unfortunate mother. Neither their looks, however, nor their ears, were noticed by the recluse. Her hands remained clasped, her lips mute, her eyes fixed, and that look thus bent on the little shoe was enough to cut anyone who knew her story to the heart.

The three women gazed without uttering a word; they

durst not speak even in a whisper. This profound silence, this intense sorrow, this utter forgetfulness of all but one object, produced upon them the effect of a high altar at Easter or Christmas. It awed them too into silence, into devotion; they were ready to fall on their knees.

At length Gervaise, the most inquisitive, and of course the least tenderhearted of the three, called to the recluse, in hopes of making her speak, "Sister! Sister Gudule!" Thrice did she repeat the call, raising her voice every time. The recluse stirred not; it drew from her neither word, nor look, nor sigh, nor sign of life.

"Sister! Sister St. Gudule!" said Oudarde, in her turn, in a kinder and more soothing tone. The recluse was silent and motionless as before.

"A strange woman!" exclaimed Gervaise. "I verily believe that a bombard would not waken her."

"Perhaps she is deaf!" said Oudarde, sighing.

"Perhaps blind," added Gervaise.

"Perhaps dead," ejaculated Mahiette.

It is certain that if the spirit had not yet quitted that inert, lethargic, and apparently inanimate frame, it had at least retired to and shut itself up in recesses which the perceptions of the external organs could not reach.

"What shall we do to rouse her?" said Oudarde. "If we leave the cake in the window, some boy will run away with it."

Eustache, whose attention had till this moment been taken up by a little cart drawn by a great dog, which had just passed along, all at once perceived that his mother and her friends were looking through the window at something; and, curious to learn what it was, he clambered upon a post, and thrusting his red chubby face in at the aperture, he cried: "Only look, mother! who is that?"

At the sound of the child's clear, fresh, sonorous voice the recluse started. She instantly turned her head; her long, attenuated fingers drew back the hair from her brow, and she fixed her sad, astonished, distracted eyes upon the boy. That look was transient as lightning. "Oh, my God!" she instantly exclaimed, burying her face in her lap; and it seemed as if her harsh voice rent itself a passage from her chest, "at least keep those of others out of my sight!"

This shock, however, had, as it were, awakened the recluse. A long shudder thrilled her whole frame; her teeth chattered; she half raised her head, and, taking hold of her feet with her hands as if to warm them, she ejaculated, "Oh! how cold it is!"

"Poor creature," said Oudarde, with deep compassion, "would you like a little fire?"

She shook her head in token of refusal.

"Well, then," rejoined Oudarde, offering her a bottle, "here is some hippocras, which will warm you."

Again she shook her head, looked steadfastly at Oudarde, and said: "Water!"

Oudarde remonstrated. "No, sister," said she, "that is not a fit drink for January. Take some of this hippocras and a bit of the cake we have brought you."

She pushed aside the cake, which Mahiette held out to her. "Some brown bread," was her reply.

"Here," said Gervaise, catching the charitable spirit of her companions, and taking off her cloak; "here is something to keep you warm. Put it over your shoulders."

She refused the cloak as she had done the bottle and the cake, with the single word, "Sackcloth."

"But surely," resumed the kind-hearted Oudarde, "you must have perceived that yesterday was a day of public rejoicing."

"Ah! yes, I did," replied the recluse; "for the last two days I have had no water in my pitcher."

After a pause she added: "Why should the world think of me who do not think of it? When the fire is out the ashes get cold."

As if fatigued with the effort of speaking, she dropped her head upon her knees. The simple Oudarde conceived that in the concluding words she was again complaining of cold. "Do have a fire then," said she.

"Fire!" exclaimed the recluse, in a strange tone; "and

would you make one for the poor baby who has been underground these fifteen years?"

Her limbs shook, her voice trembled, her eyes flashed; she raised herself upon her knees; all at once she extended her white, skinny hand toward the boy. "Take away that child," cried she. "The Egyptians will presently pass."

She then sank upon her face, and her forehead struck the floor with a sound like that of a stone falling upon it. The three women concluded that she was dead. Presently, however, she began to stir, and they saw her crawl upon her hands and knees to the corner where the little shoe was. She was then out of their sight, and they durst not look after her; but they heard a thousand kisses and a thousand sighs, mingled with piercing shrieks, and dull heavy thumps, as if from a head striking against a wall; at last, after one of these blows, so violent as to make all three start, they heard nothing more.

"She must have killed herself!" said Gervaise, venturing to put her head in at the aperture: "Sister! Sister Gudule!"

"Sister Gudule!" repeated Oudarde.

"Good God!" exclaimed Gervaise—"she does not stir. She must be dead!—Gudule! Gudule!"

Mahiette, shocked to such a degree that she could scarcely speak, made an effort. "Wait a moment," said she. Then going close to the window, "Paquette!" she cried, "Paquette la Chantefleurie."

A boy who thoughtlessly blows a lighted cracker which hangs fire, and makes it explode in his eyes, is not more frightened than was Mahiette at the effect of this name thus abruptly pronounced.

The recluse shook all over, sprang upon her feet, and bounded to the window, her eyes at the same time flashing fire, with such vehemence, that the three women retreated to the parapet of the quay. The haggard face of the recluse appeared pressed against the bars of the window. "Aha!" she cried, with a horrid laugh, " 'tis the Egyptian that calls me!"

The scene which was just then passing at the pillory

caught her eye. Her brow wrinkled with horror, she stretched both her skeleton arms out of her cell, and cried with a voice unlike that of a human being: "So, it is thou, spawn of Egypt, it is thou, child-stealer, that callest me. Cursed be thou for thy pains! cursed—cursed—cursed."

26

These words were, if we may so express it, the point of junction of two scenes which had thus far been acting contemporaneously, each on its particular stage; the one, that which has just been detailed, at the Trou aux Rats; the other, which we are about to describe, at the pillory. The first had been witnessed only by the three females with whom the reader has just made acquaintance; the spectators of the other consisted of the crowd we some time since saw collecting in the Place de Greve around the pillory and the gallows.

The mob, accustomed to wait whole hours for public executions, did not manifest any vehement impatience. They amused themselves with gazing at the pillory, a very simple contrivance, consisting of a cube of masonry some ten feet high, hollow within. A rude flight of steps of rough stone led to the upper platform, upon which was seen a horizontal wheel of oak. Upon this wheel the culprit was bound upon his knees and with his hands tied behind him. An axle of timber, moved by a capstan concealed from sight within the little building, caused the wheel to revolve in the horizontal plane, and thus exhibited the culprit's face to every point of the Place in succession. This was called turning a criminal.

Thus, you see, the pillory of the Greve was by no means so interesting an object as the pillory of the Halles. There was nothing architectural, nothing monumental about it; it had no roof with iron cross, no octagon lantern, no slender pillars spreading at the margin of the roof into capitals of acanthi and flowers, no fantastic and monstrous water-spouts, no carved woodwork, no delicate sculpture deeply cut in stone.

The culprit, tied to the tail of a cart, was at length brought forward; and when he had been hoisted upon the platform, where he could be seen from all points of the Place, bound with cords and thongs upon the wheel of the pillory, a prodigious hooting, mingled with laughter and acclamations, burst from the mob. They had recognized Quasimodo.

It was a strange reverse for the poor fellow to be pilloried on the same spot, where the preceding day he had been hailed and proclaimed Pope and Prince of Fools, escorted by the Duke of Egypt, the King of Thunes, and the Emporor of Galilee. So much is certain, that there was not a creature in that concourse, not even himself, alternately the object of triumph and of punishment, who could clearly make out the connection between the two situations. Gringoire and his philosophy were lacking to the spectacle.

Presently Michel Noiret, sworn trumpeter of our lord the king, commanded silence and proclaimed the sentence agreeably to the ordinance of the provost. He then fell back behind the cart with his men in their official liveries.

Quasimodo never stirred; he did not so much as frown. All resistance, indeed, on his part was rendered impossible by what was then called in the language of criminal jurisprudence, "the vehemence and the firmness of the bonds," which means that the chains and the thongs probably cut into the very flesh. He had suffered himself to be led, and pushed, and carried, and lifted, and bound again and again. His face betrayed no other emotion than the astonishment of a savage or an idiot. He was known to be deaf; you would have supposed him to be blind also.

He was placed on his knees upon the circular floor. His

doublet and shirt were taken off and he allowed himself to be stripped to the waist without opposition. He was immersed in a fresh series of thongs; he suffered himself to be bound and buckled; only from time to time he breathed hard, like a calf whose head hangs dangling over the tale of a butcher's cart.

"The stupid oaf!" exclaimed Jehan Frollo du Moulin to his friend Robin Poussepain (for the two students had followed the culprit as a matter of course), "he has no more idea of what they are going to do than a ladybird shut up in a box."

A loud laugh burst from the mob, when they beheld Quasimodo's naked hump, his camel breast, and his scaly and hairy shoulders. Amid all this mirth, a man of short stature and robust frame, clad in the livery of the city, ascended the platform and placed himself by the side of the culprit. His name was quickly circulated among the crowd. It was Master Pierrat Torterue, sworn tormentor of the Chatelet.

The first thing he did was to set down upon one corner of the pillory an hourglass, the upper division of which was full of red sand, that dropped into the lower half. He then threw back his cloak, and over his left arm was seen hanging a whip composed of long white glistening thongs, knotted, twisted, and armed with sharp bits of metal. With his left hand he carelessly turned up the right sleeve of his shirt as high as the elbow. At length he stamped with his foot. The wheel began to turn. Quasimodo shook in his bonds. The amazement suddenly expressed in his hideous face drew fresh shouts of laughter from the spectators.

All at once, at the moment when the wheel in its revolution presented the mountain shoulders of Quasimodo to Master Pierrat, he raised his arms; the thin lashes hissed sharply in the air like so many vipers, and descended with fury upon the back of the unlucky wight.

Quasimodo started like one awakened from a dream. He began to comprehend the meaning of the scene, he writhed in his bonds; a violent contraction of surprise and pain distorted the muscles of his face, but he heaved not a single sigh. He merely turned his head, first one way, then the other, balancing it the while, like a bull stung in the flank by a gadfly.

A second stroke succeeded the first, then came a third, and another, and another. The wheel continued to turn and the blows to fall. The blood began to trickle in a hundred little streams down the swart shoulders of the hunchback; and the slender thongs, whistling in the air in their rotation, sprinkled it in drops over the gaping crowd.

Quasimodo had relapsed, in appearance at least, into his former apathy. He had endeavored at first quietly and without great external effort, to burst his bonds. His eye was seen to flash, his muscles to swell, his limbs to gather themselves up, and the thongs, cords, and chains to stretch. The effort was mighty, prodigious, desperate; but the old shackles of the provost proved too tough. They cracked and that was all. Quasimodo sank down exhausted. Stupor gave place in his countenance to an expression of deep despondency. He closed his only eye, dropped his head upon his breast, and counterfeited death.

Thence forward he stirred not. Nothing could make him flinch—neither the blood which oozed from his lacerated back, nor the lashes which fell with redoubled force, nor the fury of the executioner, roused and heated by the exercise, nor the hissing and whizzing of the horrible thongs. At length an usher of the Chatelet, habited in black, and mounted upon a black horse, who had taken his station by the steps at the commencement of the flogging, extended his ebony wand toward the hourglass. The executioner held his hand; the wheel stopped; Quasimodo's eye slowly opened.

Two attendants of the sworn tormentor's washed the bleeding back of the sufferer, rubbed it with a sort of ointment, which in an incredibly short time closed all the wounds, and threw over him a kind of yellow frock shaped like a priest's cope; while Pierrat Torterue drew through his fingers the thongs saturated with blood which he shook off upon the pavement.

Quasimodo's punishment was not yet over. He had still to remain in the pillory that hour which Master Florian Barbedienne had so judiciously added to the sentence of Messire Robert d'Estouteville; to the great glory of the old physiological pun—*Surdus absurdus.* The hourglass was therefore turned, and the hunchback left bound as before, that justice might be fully satisfied.

The populace, especially in a half-civilized era, are in society what the boy is in a family. So long as they continue in this state of primitive ignorance, of moral and intellectual minority, so long you may say of them as of the mischievous urchin, "That age is without pity." We have already shown that Quasimodo was generally hated, for more than one good reason, it is true. There was scarcely a spectator among the crowd, but either had or imagined that he had ground to complain of the malicious hunchback of Notre Dame. His appearance in the pillory had excited universal joy; and the severe punishment which he had undergone, and the pitiful condition in which it had left him, so far from softening the populace, had but rendered their hatred more malignant by arming it with the sting of mirth.

Thus when the "public vengeance" was once satisfied—according to the jargon still used by gownsmen—it was the turn of private revenge to seek gratification.

Here, as in the great hall, the women were most vehement. All bore him some grudge—some for his mischievous disposition, and others for his ugliness; the latter were the most furious. A shower of abuse was poured upon him, accompanied by hootings, and imprecations, and laughter, and here and there by stones.

Quasimodo was deaf, but he was sharpsighted, and the fury of the populace was expressed not less energetically in their countenances than in their words. Besides, the pelting of the stones explained the meaning of the bursts of laughter. This annoyance passed for a while unheeded;

but by degrees that patience, which had braced itself up
under the lash of the executioner, gave way under all these
stings of petty insects. The bull of the Asturias, which
scarcely deigns to notice the attacks of the picador, is exasperated by the dogs and the bar derillos.

At first he slowly rolled around a look of menace at the
crowd; but shackled as he was, this look could not drive
way the flies which galled his wounds. He then struggled
in his bonds, and his furious contortions made the old
wheel of the pillory creak upon its axis. This served only
to increase the jeers and the derisions of the populace.

The wretched sufferer, finding, like a chained beast, that
he could not break his collar, again became quiet; though
at times a sigh of rage heaved all the cavities of his chest.
Not a blush, not a trace of shame, was to be discerned in
his face. He was too far from the social state and too near
to the state of nature to know what shame is. Besides, is
it possible that disgrace can be felt by one cast in a mold
of such extreme deformity? But rage, hatred, despair,
slowly spread over that hideous face a cloud which gradually became more and more black, more and more
charged with an electricity that darted in a thousand
flashes from the eye of the Cyclop.

This cloud, however, cleared off for a moment at the appearance of a mule bearing a priest. The instant he caught
a glimpse of this mule and this priest in the distance, the
face of the poor sufferer assumed a look of gentleness.
The rage which had contracted it was succeeded by a
strange smile, full of ineffable meekness, kindness, tenderness. As the priest approached this smile became more expressive, more distinct, more radiant. The prisoner seemed
to be anticipating the arrival of a deliverer; but the moment the mule was near enough to the pillory for its rider
to recognize the sufferer, the priest cast down his eyes,
wheeled about, clapped spurs to his beast, as if in a hurry
to escape a humiliating appeal, and by no means desirous
of being known or addressed by a poor devil in such a situation. This priest was the archdeacon Claude Frollo.

Quasimodo's brow was overcast by a darker cloud than ever. For some time a smile mingled with the gloom, but it was a smile of bitterness, disappointment, and deep despondency. Time passed. For an hour and a half at least he had been exposed to incessant ill-usage—lacerated, jeered, and almost stoned. All at once he again struggled in his chains with a redoubled effort of despair that made the whole machine shake; and breaking the silence which he had hitherto kept, he cried in a hoarse and furious voice, more like the roaring of a wild beast than the articulate tones of a human tongue, "Water!"

This cry of distress, heard above the shouts and laughter of the crowd, so far from exciting compassion, served only to heighten the mirth of the good people of Paris, who surrounded the pillory, and who, to confess the truth, were in those days not much less cruel or less brutalized than the disgusting crew of vagabonds whom we have already introduced to the reader; these merely formed, in fact, the lowest stratum of the populace. Not a voice was raised around the unhappy sufferer, but in scorn and derision of his distress. It is certain that at this moment he was still more grotesque and repulsive than pitiable; his face empurpled, and trickling with perspiration, his eye glaring wildly, his mouth foaming with rage and agony, and his tongue lolling out of it. It must also be confessed that had any charitable soul of either sex been tempted to carry a draught of water to the wretched sufferer, so strongly was the notion of infamy and disgrace attached to the ignominious steps of the pillory, that it would have effectually deterred the good Samaritan.

In a few minutes Quasimodo surveyed the crowd with anxious eye, and repeated in a voice more rugged than before, "Water!" He was answered with peals of laughter.

"There is water for thee, deaf varlet," cried Robin Poussepain, throwing in his face a sponge soaked in the kennel. "I am in thy debt."

A woman hurled a stone at his head. "That will teach

thee to waken us at night," said she, "with thy cursed bells."

"Take that to drink thy liquor out of!" shouted a fellow, throwing at him a broken jug, which hit him upon the chest. "It was the sight of thy frightful figure that made my wife have a child with two heads."

"Water!" roared the panting Quasimodo, for the third time.

At that moment he saw the populace make way. A young female, in a strange garb, approached the pillory. She was followed by a little white goat, with gilt horns, and carried a tambourine in her hand. Quasimodo's eyes sparkled. It was the Bohemian whom he had attempted to carry off the preceding night, and he had a confused notion that for this prank he was suffering his present punishment, though in fact it was because he had the misfortune to be deaf and to be tried by a deaf judge. He thought that she was coming to take revenge also, and to give him her blow as well as the rest.

He watched her with nimble foot ascend the steps. He was choked with rage and vexation. Had the lightning of his eye possessed the power, it would have blasted the Egyptian before she reached the platform. Without uttering a word she approached the sufferer, who vainly writhed to avoid her; and loosing a gourd from her girdle, she gently lifted it to the parched lips of the exhausted wretch. A big tear was seen to start from his dry and bloodshot eye, and to trickle slowly down his deformed face so long contracted by despair. It was perhaps the first he had shed since he arrived at manhood.

Meanwhile he forgot to drink. The Egyptian pouted her pretty lip with impatience, and then put the neck of the gourd between Quasimodo's jagged teeth; he drank greedily, for his thirst was extreme.

When he finished the hunchback protruded his dark lips, no doubt to kiss the kind hand which had brought so welcome a relief; but the damsel, perhaps recollecting the violent assault of the foregoing night, quickly drew back her hand with the same start of terror that a child does from a dog which he fears will bite him. The poor fellow then fixed on her a look full of reproach and unutterable woe.

Under any circumstances it would have been a touching sight to see this girl, so fresh, so pure, so lovely, and at the same time so weak, humanely hastening to the relief of so much distress, deformity, and malice. On a pillory, this sight was sublime. The populace themselves were moved by it, and began clapping their hands and shouting, "Huzza! huzza!"

It was precisely at this moment that the recluse perceived from the window of her den the Egyptian on the pillory, and pronounced upon her that bitter imprecation: "Cursed by thou, spawn of Egypt! cursed! cursed! cursed!"

La Esmeralda turned pale, and with faltering step descended from the pillory. The voice of the recluse still pursued her: "Get thee down! get thee down, Egyptian child-stealer! thou wilt have to go up again one of these days!"

"Sacky is in her vagaries today," said the people, grumbling: and that was all they did. Women of her class were then deemed holy and reverenced accordingly. Nobody liked to attack persons who were praying night and day.

The time of Quasimodo's punishment having expired, he was released, and the mob dispersed.

Mahiette and her two companions had reached the foot of the Grand Pont on their return, when she suddenly stopped short. "Bless me!" she exclaimed, "what has become of the cake, Eustache?"

"Mother," said the boy, "while you were talking with the woman in that dark hole, a big dog came and bit a great piece of it, so I ate some too."

"What, sir," she asked, "have you eaten it all?"

"It was the dog, mother. I told him to let it alone, but he didn't mind me—so I just took a bite too."

" 'Tis a sad greedy boy!" said his mother, smiling and scolding at once. "Look you, Oudarde, not a cherry or an apple in our garden is safe from him; so his grandfather says he will make a rare captain. I'll trim you well, Master Eustache! Go along, you greedy glutton!"

27

Several weeks had elapsed. It was now the beginning of March. The sun, which Dubartes, that classic ancestor of periphrasis, had not yet styled "the grand-duke of candles," shone forth brightly and cheerily. It was one of those spring days which are so mild and so beautiful, that all Paris, pouring into the public places and promenades, keeps them as holidays. On days so brilliant, so warm, and so serene, there is a particular hour at which the curious spectators should go to admire the porch of Notre Dame. It is the moment when the sun, already sinking in the west, looks the cathedral almost full in the face. His rays, becoming more and more horizontal, slowly withdraw from the pavement of the Place, and mount along the pinnacled facade, causing its thousands of figures in relief to stand out from their shadows, while the great central rose-window glares like the eye of a Cyclop, tinged by the reflections of the forge. It was now just that hour.

Opposite to the lofty cathedral, glowing in the sunset, upon a stone balcony, over the porch of a rich Gothic building which formed the angle of the Place and the street of the Parvis, some young and handsome females were chatting, laughing, and disporting themselves. By the length of their veils, which fell from the top of their pointed caps, encircled with pearls, to their heels; by the fineness of the embroidered neckerchief which covered their shoulders, but without wholly concealing the delicate contours of their virgin bosoms; by the richness of their petticoats, which surpassed that of their upper garments; by the gauze, the silk, the velvet, with which their dress was trimmed; and above all by the whiteness of their hands, which showed them to be unused to labor; it was easy to guess that they belonged to noble and wealthy families. It was, in fact, Damoiselle Fleur de Lys de Gondelaurier and her companions, Diane de Christeuil, Amelotte de Montmichel, Colombe de Gaillefontaine, and little de Champchevriver, who were staying at the house of the Dame de Gondelaurier, a widow lady, on account of the expected visit of Monseigneur de Beaujeu, and his consort, who were to come to Paris in April, for the purpose of selecting ladies of honor for the Dauphiness Marguerite. Now all the gentry for a hundred miles round were anxious to obtain this favor for their daughters; and with this view numbers had already brought or sent them to Paris. Those mentioned above had been placed by their parents under the care of the discreet and venerable Dame Aloise de Gondelaurier, widow of an officer of the King's crossbowmen, who resided with her only daughter in her own house in the Place du Parvis.

The damsels were seated partly in the room, partly in the balcony, some on cushions of Utrecht velvet, others on oaken stools, carved with flowers and figures. Each of them held on her lap a portion of a large piece of tapestry, on which they were all working together, while the other part lay upon the matting that covered the floor.

They were chatting together in that low tone and with those titters so common in a young party of young females when there is a young man among them. He whose presence was sufficient to set at work the self-love of all this youthful company, appeared himself to care very little about it; and, while these beautiful girls were each striving to engage his attention, he seemed to be busily engaged himself in polishing the buckle of his belt with his leather glove.

Now and then the old lady spoke to him in a very low tone, and he answered as well as he could, with a sort of awkward and forced politeness. From her smiles, from various other little significant tokens, and from the nods and winks which Dame Aloise directed toward her daughter, Fleur de Lys, while softly speaking to the captain, it was easy to see that he was an accepted lover, and that a match was on foot and would no doubt be speedily concluded between the young officer and Fleur de Lys. It was easy too to see from his coldness and embarrassment that, on his side at least, it was anything but a love-match. The good lady, who, fond mother as she was, doted upon her daughter, did not perceive the indifference of the captain, and strove by her words and gestures to make him notice the grace with which Fleur de Lys plied her needle or her distaff.

"Look, nephew," said she, plucking him by the sleeve, in order to whisper in his ear—"look at her now, as she stoops."

"Yes, indeed," replied the young man, relapsing into his former cold and irksome silence.

A moment afterward he was required to stoop again. "Did you ever," said Dame Aloise, "behold a comelier or genteeler girl than your intended? Is it possible to be fairer? Are not her hands and arms perfect models? and her neck, has it not all the elegance of a swan's?"

"No doubt," he replied, thinking of something else all the while.

"Why don't you go and talk to her then?" retorted the lady, pushing him toward Fleur de Lys. "Go and say something to her. You are grown mighty shy all at once."

Now we can assure the reader that neither shyness nor modesty was to be numbered among the captain's defects. He attempted, however, to do as he was desired.

"Fair cousin," said he, stepping up to Fleur de Lys, "what is the subject of this tapestry which you are working?"

"Fair cousin," answered Fleur de Lys, in a peevish tone, "I have told you three times already that it is the grotto of Neptune."

It was evident that the captain's cold and absent manner had not escaped the keen observation of Fleur de Lys, though it was not perceived by her mother. He felt the necessity of making an attempt at conversation.

"And what is it intended for?" he inquired.

"For the abbey of St. Antoine des Champs," replied Fleur de Lys, without raising her eyes.

The captain lifted up a corner of the tapestry. "And pray, my fair cousin," said he, "who is this big fellow, in the disguise of a fish, blowing the trumpet with puffed-out cheeks?"

"That is Triton," answered she.

In the tone of Fleur de Lys' brief replies there was still something that betokened displeasure. The captain was more and more at a loss what to say. He stooped down over the tapestry. "A charming piece of work, by my fay!" cried he.

At this exclamation, Colombe de Gaillefontaine, another beautiful girl, of a delicately fair complexion, in a dress of blue damask, timidly ventured to address a question to Fleur de Lys, in the hope that the handsome captain would answer it. "My dear Gondelaurier," said she, "have you seen the tapestries in the hotel of La Roche-Guyon?"

"Is not that the building next to the garden of the Louvre?" asked Diane de Christeuil, with a laugh. This young lady, be it observed, had remarkably handsome teeth, and consequently never spoke without laughing.

"And near that great old tower of the ancient wall of Paris?" inquired Amelotte de Montmichel, a charming brunette, with ruddy cheek and dark curling hair, who had a habit of sighing as the other had of laughing, without knowing why.

At this moment Berangere de Champchevrier, a little sylph of seven years, looking down upon the Place, through the rails of the balcony, cried: "Oh! look, godmother Fleur de Lys! look at that pretty dancer dancing on the pavement and playing on the tambourine, among the people down yonder!"

"Some Egyptian I dare say," replied Fleur de Lys, carelessly turning her head toward the Place.

"Let's see! let's see!" cried her lively companions, running to the front of the balcony, while Fleur de Lys, thinking of the coldness of her lover, slowly followed, and the captain, released by this incident, which cut short a conversation that embarrassed him not a little, returned to the farther end of the apartment with the satisfaction of a soldier relieved from duty. The service of the gentle Fleur de Lys was nevertheless easy and delightful; and so it had formerly appeared to him—but now the prospect of a speedy marriage became every day more and more disagreeable. The fact is, he was of a rather inconstant disposition, and, if the truth must be told, rather vulgar in his tastes. Though of high birth, he had contracted more than one of the habits of the common soldier. He was fond of the tavern, and felt comfortable only among coarse language, military gallantries, easy beauties, and easy conquests.

The captain, then, had stood for some moments, lost in thought, or not thinking at all, leaning in silence on the carved mantel-piece, when Fleur de Lys, suddenly turning round, addressed him. After all, it went sorely against the grain with the poor girl to pout at him.

"Did you not tell us, cousin, of a little Bohemian, whom you rescued one night, about two months ago, from the hands of a dozen robbers?"

"I think I did, cousin," replied the captain.

"I should not wonder," she resumed, "if it was the Bohemian dancing yonder in the Parvis. Come and see whether you know her, Cousin Phœbus."

In this gentle invitation to come to her and the tone in which it was uttered he detected a secret desire of reconciliation. Captain Phœbus de Chateaupers—for this is the personage whom the reader has had before him since the commencement of this chapter—advanced with slow step toward the balcony. "Look," said Fleur de Lys, softly grasping the captain's arm—"look at yonder girl dancing in that circle. Is she your Bohemian?"

Phœbus looked. "Yes," said he, "I know her by her goat."

"Oh! what a pretty little goat!" exclaimed Amelotte, clapping her hands in admiration.

"Are its horns of real gold?" asked Berangere.

"Godmother," she began again, having all at once raised her bright eyes, which were in constant motion, to the top of the towers of Notre Dame—"who is the man in black up yonder?"

All the young ladies looked up. A man was indeed lolling his elbows on the topmost balustrade of the northern tower, overlooking the Greve. It was a priest, as might be known by his dress, which was clearly distinguishable, and his head was supported by both his hands. He was motionless as a statue. His eye was fixed on the Place as intently as that of a hawk on a starling's nest which it has discovered.

" 'Tis the archdeacon of Josas," said Fleur de Lys.

"You must have good eyes to know him at this distance," observed Gaillefontaine.

"How he looks at the dancing-girl!" exclaimed Diane de Christeuil.

"Let the Egyptian take care of herself!" said Fleur de Lys. "The archdeacon is not fond of Egypt."

" 'Tis a pity that man looks at her so," added Amelotte de Montmichel; "for she dances delightfully."

"Good Cousin Phœbus," abruptly cried Fleur de Lys, "since you know this Bohemian, just call her up. It will amuse us."

"Yes, do!" exclaimed all the young ladies, clapping their hands.

"Where is the use of it?" rejoined Phœbus. "She has no doubt forgotten me, and I know not even her name. However, as you wish it, ladies, I will try." Leaning over the balustrade of the balcony, he called out: "My girl!"

The dancer had paused for a moment. She turned her

head in the direction from which the voice proceeded; her sparkling eye fell upon Phœbus, and she stood motionless.

"My girl!" repeated the captain, beckoning her to come to him.

The girl still looked steadfastly at him; she then blushed deeply, as if every drop of her blood had rushed to her cheeks, and, taking her tambourine under her arm, she made her way through the circle of astonished spectators toward the house to which she was summoned, with slow, faltering step, and with the agitated look of a bird unable to withstand the fascination of a serpent.

A moment afterward the tapestry hung before the door was raised, and the Bohemian appeared at the threshold of the apartment, out of breath, flushed, flurried, with her large eyes fixed on the floor; she durst not advance a step farther. Berangere clapped her hands.

Meanwhile the dancer stood motionless at the door of the room. Her appearance had produced a singular effect upon the party of young ladies. It is certain that all of them were more or less influenced by a certain vague and indistinct desire of pleasing the handsome officer; that the splendid uniform was the point at which all their coquetries were aimed; and that ever since his entrance there had been a sort of secret rivalry among them, of which they were themselves scarcely conscious, but which nevertheless betrayed itself every moment in all they said and did. As, however, they all possessed nearly the same degree of beauty, they fought with equal weapons, and each might cherish a hope of victory. The coming of the Bohemian suddenly destroyed this equilibrium. Her beauty was so surpassing, that at the moment when she appeared at the entrance of the room, she seemed to shed over it a sort of light peculiar to herself. In this close apartment, overshadowed by hangings and carvings, she appeared incomparably more beautiful and radiant than in the public place—like a torch which is carried out of the broad daylight into the dark. In spite of themselves, the young ladies were dazzled. Each felt wounded, as it were, in her beauty.

Their battlefront—reader, excuse the term—was changed accordingly, though not a single word passed between them. The instincts of women apprehend the answer one another much more readily than the understandings of men. An enemy had come upon them; of this they were all sensible, and therefore they all rallied. One drop of wine is sufficient to redden a whole glass of water; to tinge a whole company of handsome women with a certain degree of ill-humor, merely introduce a female of superior beauty, especially when there is but one man in the party.

The reception of the Bohemian was of course marvelously cold. They surveyed her from head to foot, then looked at each other with an expression which told their meaning as plainly as words could have done. Meanwhile the stranger, daunted to such a degree that she durst not raise her eyes, stood waiting to be spoken to.

The captain was the first to break silence. "A charming creature, by my fay!" cried he, in his straightforward, blundering manner. "What think you of her, my pretty cousin?"

This ejaculation, which a more delicate admirer would at least have uttered in a less audible tone, was not likely to disperse the feminine jealousies arrayed against the Bohemian.

"Not amiss," replied Fleur de Lys to the captain's question, with affected disdain. The others whispered together.

At length Madame Aloise, who felt not the less jealousy because she was jealous on behalf of her daughter, accosted the dancer. "Come hither, my girl," said she. The Egyptian advanced to the lady.

"My pretty girl," said Phœbus, taking a few steps toward her, "I know not whether you recollect me——"

"Oh, yes!" said she, interrupting him, with a smile and a look of inexpressible kindness.

"She has a good memory," observed Fleur de Lys.

"How was it," resumed Phœbus, "that you slipped away in such a hurry the other night? Did I frighten you?"

"Oh, no!" said the Bohemian.

In the accent with which this "Oh, no!" was uttered immediately after the "Oh, yes!" there was an indefinable something which wounded Fleur de Lys to the quick.

"In your stead," continued the captain, whose tongue ran glibly enough in talking to one, whom from her occupation he took to be a girl of loose manners, "you left me a grim-faced, one-eyed, hunchbacked fellow—the bishop's bell-ringer, I think they say. Some will have it that the archdeacon, and others that the devil, is his father. He has a comical name—I have quite forgot what—taken from some festival or other. What the devil did that owl of a fellow want with you, hey?"

"I don't know," answered she.

"Curse his impudence!—a rascally bell-ringer run away with a girl like a viscount! A common fellow poach on the game of gentlemen! Who ever heard of such a thing! But he paid dearly for it. Master Pierrat Torterue is the roughest groom that ever trimmed a varlet; and I assure you, if that can do you any good, he curried the bell-ringer's hide most soundly."

"Poor fellow!" said the Bohemian, who at the captain's words could not help calling to mind the scene at the pillory.

"Zounds!" cried the captain, laughing outright, "that pity is as well bestowed as a feather on a pig's rump. May I be——" He stopped short. "I beg pardon, ladies, I had like to have forgotten myself."

"Fie, sir!" said Gaillefontaine.

"He is only talking to that creature in her own language," said Fleur de Lys in an undertone, her vexation increasing every moment. Nor was it diminished when she saw the captain, enchanted with the Bohemian and still more with himself, making a pirouette, repeating with blunt soldier-like gallantry—"A fine girl, upon my soul!"

"But very uncouthly dressed," said Diane de Christeuil, grinning and showing her beautiful teeth.

This remark was a new light to her companions. It

showed them the assailable side of the Egyptian; as they fell foul of her dress.

"How comes it, my girl," said Montmichel, "that you run about the streets in this manner, without neckerchief or stomacher?"

"And then, what a short petticoat!" exclaimed Gaillefontaine. "Quite shocking, I declare!"

"My dear," said Fleur de Lys, in a tone of anything but kindness, "the officers of the Chatelet will take you up for wearing that gilt belt."

"My girl," resumed Christeuil, with a bitter smile, "if you were to cover your arms decently with sleeves, they would not be so sunburnt."

It was in truth a sight worthy of a more intelligent spectator than Phœbus, to see how these fair damsels, with their keen and envenomed tongues, twisted, glided, and writhed around the dancing-girl; they were at once cruel and graceful; they spitefully fell foul of the poor but whimsical toilet of tinsel and spangles. There was no end to their laughs, and jeers, and sarcasms. You would have taken them for some of those young Roman ladies, who amused themselves with thrusting gold pins into the breasts of a beautiful slave; or they might be likened to elegant greyhounds, turning, with distended nostrils and glaring eyes, round a poor fawn, which the look of their master forbids them to devour.

What after all was a poor street-dancer to these scions of distinguished families! They seemed to take no account of her presence, and talked of her before her face, and even to herself, as of an object at once very disgusting, very mean, and very pretty.

The Bohemian was not insensible to their stinging remarks. From time to time the glow of shame or the flash of anger flushed her cheek or lit up her eye; a disdainful word seemed to hover upon her lips; her contempt expressed itself in that pout with which the reader is already acquainted; but she stood motionless, fixing upon Phœbus a look of resignation, sadness, and good nature. In that look there was also an expression of tenderness and anxiety. You would have said that she restrained her feelings for fear of being turned out.

Meanwhile Phœbus laughed and began to take the part of the Bohemian, with a mixture of impertinence and pity. "Let them talk as they like, my dear," said he, clanking his spurs; "your dress is certainly somewhat whimsical and out of the way, but, for such a charming creature as you are, what does that signify?"

"Dear me!" exclaimed the fair Gaillefontaine, bridling up, with a sarcastic smile, "how soon the gentlemen archers of the king's ordnance take fire at bright Egyptian eyes!"

"Why not?" said Phœbus.

At this reply, carelessly uttered by the captain, Colombe laughed, so did Diane, so did Amelotte, so did Fleur de Lys, though it is true that a tear started at the same time into the eye of the latter. The Bohemian, who had hung down her head at the remark of Colombe de Gaillefontaine, raised her eyes glistening with joy and pride, and again fixed them on Phœbus. She was passing beautiful at that moment.

The old lady, who watched this scene, felt offended, though she knew not why. "Holy Virgin!" cried she all at once, "what have I got about me? Ah! the nasty beast!"

It was the goat which, in springing toward her mistress, had entangled her horns in the load of drapery which fell upon the feet of the noble lady when she was seated. This was a diversion. The Bohemian without saying a word disengaged the animal.

"Oh! here is the pretty little goat with golden feet!" cried Berangere, leaping for joy.

The Bohemian crouched upon her knees, and pressed her cheek against the head of the fondling goat, while Diane, stooping to the ear of Colombe, whispered: "How very stupid of me not to think of it sooner! Why, it is the Egyptian with the goat. It is reported that she is a witch, and that her goat performs tricks absolutely miraculous."

"Well," said Colombe, "the goat must perform one of its miracles and amuse us in its turn."

Diane and Colombe eagerly addressed the Egyptian. "My girl," said they, "make your goat perform a miracle for us."

"I know not what you mean," replied the dancer.

"A miracle, a piece of magic, or witchcraft, in short."

"I don't understand you," she rejoined, and again began fondling the pretty creature, repeating, "Djali! Djali!"

At this moment Fleur de Lys remarked a small embroidered leathern bag hung round the neck of the goat. "What is that?" she asked the Egyptian.

The girl raised her large eyes toward her and gravely answered: "That is my secret."

"I should like to know what your secret is," thought Fleur de Lys.

The good lady had meanwhile risen. "Girl," said she, sharply, "if neither you nor your goat have any dance to show us, why do you stay here?"

The Bohemian, without making any reply, drew leisurely toward the door. The nearer she approached it, the more slowly she moved. An invincible loadstone seemed to detain her. All at once she turned her eyes glistening with tears toward Phœbus and stood still.

"By my fay!" cried the captain, "you sha'n't get off thus. Come back and give us a dance. By the by, what is your name, my pretty dear?"

"La Esmeralda," said the dancing-girl, whose eyes were still fixed upon him.

At this strange name, the young ladies burst into a loud laugh.

"A terrible name that for a damoiselle!" said Diane.

"You see plainly enough," observed Amelotte, "that she is a witch."

"My girl," said Dame Aloise in a solemn tone, "your parents never found that name for you in the font."

While this scene was passing, Berangere had enticed the goat into a corner of the room with a marchpane. They were at once the best friends in the world. The inquisitive girl loosed the little bag from the neck of the animal, opened it, and emptied its contents upon the mat; they consisted of an alphabet, each letter being separately inscribed upon a small piece of box-wood. No sooner were these playthings spread out upon the mat than, to the astonishment of the child, the goat—one of whose miracles this no doubt was—sorted out certain letters with her golden foot, arranged them and shuffled them gently together, in a particular order, so as to make a word, which the animal formed with such readiness that she seemed to have had a good deal of practice in putting it together. Berangere, clapping her hands in admiration, suddenly exclaimed: "Godmother Fleur de Lys, come and see what the goat has done!"

Fleur de Lys ran to her and shuddered. The letters which the goat had arranged upon the floor formed the name

PHŒBUS.

"Was it the goat that did this?" she asked, in a tremulous voice.

"Yes, indeed it was, godmother," replied Berangere. It was impossible to doubt the fact.

"The secret is out," thought Fleur de Lys. At the outcry of the child, all who were present, the mother and the young ladies, and the Bohemian, and the officer, hastened to the spot. The dancing-girl saw at once what a slippery trick the goat had played her. She changed color, and began to tremble, like one who had committed some crime, before the captain, who eyed her with a smile of astonishment and gratification.

For a moment the young ladies were struck dumb. "Phœbus!" they at length whispered one another, "why, that is the name of the captain!"

"You have a wonderful memory," said Fleur de Lys to the petrified Bohemian. Then bursting into sobs, "Oh!" she stammered, in a tone of anguish, covering her face with both her fair hands, "she is a sorceress!" the while a voice, in still more thrilling accents, cried in the recesses of her heart—"She is a rival!" She sank fainting on the floor.

"My daughter! my daughter!" shrieked the affrighted mother. "Get thee gone, child of perdition!" said she to the Bohemian.

La Esmeralda picked up the unlucky letters in the twinkling of an eye, made a sign to her Djali, and retired at one door, while Fleur de Lys was borne away by another.

Captain Phœbus, being left by himself, wavered for a moment between the two doors, and then followed the gypsy girl.

28

The priest, whom the young ladies had observed on the top of the north tower stooping over the Place, and intently watching the motions of the Bohemian, was in fact the Archdeacon Claude Frollo

Our readers have not forgotten the mysterious cell which the archdeacon had reserved for himself in that tower.

Every day, an hour before sunset, the archdeacon ascended the staircase of the tower, and shut himself up in this cell, where he frequently passed whole nights. On this day, just as he had reached the low door of his retreat, and put into the lock the little complicated key which he always carried with him in the pouch hanging at his side, the sounds of a tambourine and castanet struck his ear.

These sounds came from the Place du Parvis. The cell, as we have already stated, had but one window, looking upon the roof of the church. Claude Frollo hastily withdrew the key, and the next moment he was on the top of the tower, in the attitude of profound reverie in which the young ladies had perceived him.

There he was, grave, motionless, absorbed—all eyes, all ears, all thought. All Paris was at his feet with the thousand spires of its buildings, and its circular horizon of gentle hills, with its river winding beneath its bridges, and its population pouring through its streets, with its cloud of smoke, and its mountain-chain of roofs, crowding close upon Notre Dame, with their double slopes of mail; but in this whole city the archdeacon's eye sought but one point of the pavement, the Place du Parvis, and among the whole multitude but one figure, the Bohemian.

The Bohemian was dancing; she made her tambourine spin round on the tip of her finger, and threw it up in the air while she danced Provençal sarabands—light, agile, joyous, and not aware of the weight of that formidable look which fell plump upon her head.

The crowd thronged around her; from time to time a man habited in a yellow and red loose coat went round the circle of spectators to keep them back; he then seated himself in a chair, at the distance of a few paces from the dancer, taking the head of the goat upon his knees. This man seemed to be the companion of the Bohemian; but Claude Frollo could not from his elevated station distinguish his features.

From the moment that the archdeacon perceived this stranger, his attention seemed to be divided between the dancer and him, and the gloom which overspread his countenance became deeper and deeper. All at once, he started up, and a thrill shook his whole frame. "Who can that man be?" he muttered—"till now I have always seen her alone!"

He then darted beneath the winding vault of the spiral staircase and descended. In passing the door of the belfry, which was ajar, he beheld an object which struck him; it was Quasimodo, leaning out at one of the apertures of those slated penthouses which resemble enormous blinds, and intently looking down at the Place. So entirely was he engrossed by the scene that he was not aware of the passing of his foster-father. "Strange!" murmured Claude. "Can it be the Egyptian that he is watching so earnestly?" He continued to descend. In a few minutes the archdeacon, full of care, sallied forth into the Place by the door at the foot of the tower.

"What has become of the Bohemian?" he inquired, mingling with a group of spectators whom the tambourine had collected.

"I know not," replied one of them; "I have but just missed her. I rather think she is gone to give them a dance in yon house opposite, from which someone called to her."

Instead of the Egyptian, upon the same carpet on which but a moment before she had been cutting her capricious capers, the archdeacon now found only the man in the red and yellow surtout, who, to earn in his turn a few pieces of small coin, moved round the circle, with his elbows against his hips, his head thrown back, his face flushed, his neck stretched, and a chair between his teeth. On this chair was tied a cat, which a neighbor had lent for the purpose, and which, being frightened, was swearing lustily.

"By Our Lady!" exclaimed the archdeacon, at the moment when the mountebank passed him with his pyramid of chair and cat! "what is Pierre Gringoire about here?"

The stern voice of the archdeacon threw the poor fellow into such a commotion that he lost the balance of his edifice, and chair and cat tumbled pell-mell upon the heads of the persons nearest to him, amid the inextinguishable laughter of the rest.

In all probability Master Pierre Gringoire—for sure enough it was he—would have had an ugly account to settle with the mistress of the cat and the owners of all the bruised and scratched faces around him, had he not availed himself of the confusion to slip away to the church after the archdeacon, who had motioned him to follow.

The cathedral was already dark and deserted, and the lamps in the chapels began to twinkle like stars amid the gloom. The great rose-window of the front alone, whose thousand colors were lit up by a ray of the horizontal sun, glistened in the dark like a luster of diamonds, and threw its dazzling reflection on the farther extremity of the nave.

After they had advanced a few steps from the entrance, Dom Claude, stopping short with his back against a pillar, looked steadfastly at Gringoire. In this look there was nothing to excite dread in Gringoire, deeply as he was ashamed of having been caught by a grave and learned personage in that merry-andrew garb. The look of the priest had in it nothing sarcastic or ironical; it was serious, calm, and piercing. The archdeacon first broke silence.

"Come hither, Master Pierre. There are many things which I want you to explain. In the first place, how happens it that I have not seen you for these two months, and that I find you in the public streets, in goodly garb forsooth, half red and half yellow, like a Caudebec apple?"

"Messire," dolefully replied Gringoire, "it is indeed a strange accouterment; and one in which I feel about as comfortable as a cat in a cocoanut-shell cap. 'Tis a sad thing, I admit, to let the gentlemen of the watch run the risk of belaboring under this sorry disguise the shoulders of a Pythagorean philosopher. But how can I help it, my reverend master? The blame rests with my old coat, which basely forsook me in the depth of winter, upon pretext that it was dropping to tatters. What could I do? Civilization is not yet so far advanced that one may go stark naked, as Diogenes of old wished to do."

"A respectable profession truly, this that you have taken up!" replied the archdeacon.

"I allow, master, that it is better to philosophize or poetize, to blow up the flame in the furnace or to receive it from heaven, than to carry cats about the streets. Accordingly, when I heard your exclamation, I was struck as comical as an ass before a spit. But what would you have, messire? A poor devil must live one day as well as another; and the finest Alexandrines that ever were penned cannot stay the hungry stomach so well as a crust of bread.

You know, for example, that famous epithalamium which I composed for Madame Margaret of Flanders, and the city refuses to pay me for it on the ground that it was not good enough, as if one could furnish tragedies like those of Sophocles at four crowns apiece. Of course, I was ready to perish with hunger. Luckily, I knew that I was pretty strong of jaw, so says I to this jaw—Try feats of strength and balancing; work and keep thyself. A band of beggars, who are my very good friends, have taught me twenty different Herculean feats, and now I give to my teeth every night the bread which they have helped to earn in the day. After all, I grant that it is a sorry employment of my intellectual faculties, and that man was not made to play the tambourine and to carry chairs between his teeth. But, my reverend master, in order to live one must get a livelihood."

Dom Claude listened in silence. All at once his hollow eye assumed an expression so searching and so piercing that Gringoire felt that look penetrate to the inmost recesses of his soul.

"Well, Master Pierre; but how happens it that you are now in the company of that Egyptian dancing-girl?"

"Gramercy!" replied Gringoire, "it is because she is my wife and I am her husband."

The gloomy eye of the priest glared like fire. "Wretch! Is this really so?" cried he, furiously grasping Gringoire's arm. "Hast thou so completely forsaken thy God as to become the husband of that creature?"

"By my hope of paradise, monseigneur," answered Gringoire, trembling in every joint, "I swear that she allows me no more familiarity than if I were an utter stranger."

"What are you talking, then, about husband and wife?" rejoined the priest.

Gringoire lost no time in relating to him as concisely as possible the circumstances with which the reader is already acquainted, his adventure in the Cour des Miracles, his marriage with the broken jug, and the course of life

which he had since followed. From his account it appeared
that the Bohemian had never shown him more kindness
than she had done on the first night. " 'Tis a provoking
thing, though," said he, as he finished his story; "but it is
owing to a strange notion, which those Egyptians have put
into her head."

"What mean you?" asked the archdeacon, whose agitation had gradually subsided during this narrative.

"It is rather difficult to explain my meaning," replied
the poet. " 'Tis a superstition. My wife, as I am informed
by an old fellow whom we call among ourselves the Duke
of Egypt, is a child that has been either lost or found,
which is the same thing. She has a charm hung round her
neck to find her parents, but which would lose its virtue if
the girl were to lose hers."

"So then," rejoined Claude, whose face brightened up
more and more, "you really believe, Master Pierre, that
this creature is yet virtuous?"

"What chance, Dom Claude, can a man have against a
superstition? This, I tell you, is what she has got into her
head. I consider this nun-like chastity, which keeps itself
intact among those Bohemian females, who are not remarkable for that quality, as a very rare circumstance indeed. But she has three things to protect her: the Duke of
Egypt, who has taken her under his safeguard; her whole
tribe, who hold her in extraordinary veneration, like another Notre Dame; and a certain little dagger, which the
hussy always carries about her somewhere or other, notwithstanding the ordinances of the provost, and which is
sure to be in her hands if you but clasp her waist. She is
a saucy wasp, I can tell you."

The archdeacon pursued his cross-examination of Gringoire. In the estimation of the latter, La Esmeralda was a
handsome, fascinating, inoffensive creature, with the exception of the pout peculiar to her; a simple, warm-hearted
girl, exceedingly ignorant, and exceedingly enthusiastic;
fond above all things of dancing, of noise, of the open
air; a sort of human bee, having invisible wings at her feet,

and living in a perpetual whirl. She owed this disposition to the wandering life which she had always led. Gringoire had contrived to learn so much as this, that she had traveled over Spain and Catalonia, and as far as Sicily; nay, he believed that she had been carried by the caravan of Zingari to which she belonged into the kingdom of Algiers. The Bohemians, so Gringoire said, were vassals of the King of Algiers, as chief of the nation of the white Moors. So much was certain that La Esmeralda had come to France while very young by way of Hungary. From all these countries the girl had brought scraps of odd jargons, snatches of old songs, and foreign ideas, which made her language as curious a piece of patchwork as her dress, half Parisian and half African. For the rest, she was a favorite with the people of those quarters of the city which she frequented, for her sprightliness, her gracefulness, her personal attractions, her dancing, and her singing. She had a notion that in the whole city there were but two persons who hated her, and of whom she often spoke with terror— the wretched recluse of Rolande's Tower, who, for some reason or other, bore an implacable enmity to the Egyptians, and cursed the poor dancing-girl whenever she passed her cell, and a priest, whom she never met without being frightened by his looks and language. This last intimation disturbed the archdeacon not a little, though Gringoire scarcely noticed his agitation; so completely had the lapse of two months effaced from the memory of the thoughtless poet the singular circumstances of that night when he first met with the Egyptian, and the presence of the archdeacon on that occasion. There was nothing else that the young dancer had reason to be afraid of; she never told fortunes, so that she was safe from prosecutions for witchcraft, so frequently instituted against the gypsy women. And then Gringoire was as brother to her, if not a husband. After all, the philosopher bore this kind of Platonic marriage with great resignation. At any rate, he was sure of lodging and bread. Every morning he sallied forth from the headquarters of the Vagabonds, mostly in company with the Egyptian; he assisted her in collecting her harvest of small coin in the streets; at night he returned with her to the same room, allowed her to lock herself up in her own cell, and slept the sleep of the righteous, "a very easy life," said he, "considering all things, and very favorable to reverie."

And then, in his soul and conscience, the philosopher was not sure that he was not over head and ears in love with the Bohemian. He loved her goat almost as dearly. The animal had been trained by the girl, who was so extremely clever at the business that she had taken only two months to teach it to put together the word Phœbus.

"Phœbus!" exclaimed the priest; "why Phœbus?"

"God knows," replied Gringoire. "Possibly she may imagine that this word possesses some secret magic virtue. She frequently repeats it in an undertone when she thinks she is alone."

"Are you sure," inquired Claude, with his piercing look, "that is only a word, and not a name?"

"Name! whose name?" said the poet.

"How should I know?" rejoined the priest.

"I'll just tell you, messire, what I am thinking. These Bohemians are a sort of Guebres, and worship the sun— Dan Phœbus."

"That is not so clear to me as to you, Master Pierre."

"At any rate, 'tis a point which I care very little about. Let her mutter her Phœbus as much as she pleases. So much is certain that Djali is almost as fond of me as of her mistress."

"What is Djali?"

"Why, that is the goat."

The archdeacon rested his chin upon the points of his fingers, and for a moment appeared to be lost in thought. Then, suddenly turning toward Gringoire—"Thou wilt swear," said he, "that thou hast never touched her?"

"What! the goat?" asked Gringoire.

"No, the girl."

"Oh! my wife! I swear I never did."

"And thou art often alone with her?"

"Every evening for a full hour."

Dom Claude knitted his brow. "Oh! oh! *Solus cum sola non cogitabantur orare Pater-noster.*"

"Upon my life I might say the *Pater*, and the *Ave Maria*, and the *Credo in Deum Patrem ominpotentum* and she would take no more notice of me than a pig of a church."

"Swear to me, by the soul of thy mother," cried the archdeacon with vehemence, "that thou hast not touched this creature with the tip of thy finger."

"I am ready to swear it by the body of my father also. But, my reverenced master, allow me to ask a question in my turn."

"Speak."

"How can this concern you?"

The pale face of the archdeacon crimsoned like the cheek of a bashful girl. He paused for a moment before he replied, with visible embarrassment: "Listen, Master Pierre Gringoire. You are not yet eternally lost, as far as I know. I take an interest in your welfare. Let me tell you, then, that the moment you but lay a hand on that Egyptian, that child of the devil, you become the vassal of Satan. 'Tis the body, you know, that always plunges the soul into perdition. Woe betide you, if you approach this creature! That is all. Now get thee gone!" cried the priest with a terrible look; and pushing the astonished Gringoire from him by the shoulders, he retreated with hasty step beneath the gloomy arcades of the cathedral.

29

Ever since the morning that Quasimodo underwent the punishment of the pillory, the good people who dwelt in the neighborhood of Notre Dame fancied that they perceived a great abatement in his ardor for bell-ringing. Before that event, the bells were going on all occasions; there were long tollings which lasted from prime to compline, chimes for high mass, merry peals for a wedding or a christening, mingling in the air like an embroidery of all sorts of charming sounds. The old church, all quaking and all sonorous, seemed to keep up a perpetual rejoicing. You felt incessantly the presence of a spirit of noise and caprice speaking by all these brazen mouths. This spirit seemed now to have forsaken its abode.

It so happened that in this year of grace, 1482, the Annunciation fell upon Tuesday, March 25. On that day the air was so light and serene that Quasimodo felt some reviving affection for his bells. He went up therefore into the north tower, while below the bedel threw wide open the doors of the church, which were at that time formed of enormous slabs of oak, covered with hide, bordered with nails of iron gilt, and adorned with carvings, "most cunningly wrought."

Having reached the high loft of the belfry, Quasimodo gazed for some time at the six bells with a sad shake of the head, as if lamenting that some other object had intruded itself into his heart between them and him. But when he had set them in motion, when he felt this bunch of bells swinging in his hand; when he saw, for he could not hear, the palpitating octave running up and down that sonorous scale, like a bird hopping from twig to twig; when the demon of Music, that demon which shakes a glittering quiver of stretti, trills, and arpeggios, had taken possession of the poor deaf bell-ringer, he was once more happy, he forgot all his troubles, his heart expanded, and his face brightened up.

He paced to and fro, he clapped his hands, he ran from rope to rope, he encouraged the six chimers with voice and gesture, as the leader of an orchestra spurs on intelligent performers.

He was thus engaged in egging on his bells, which all

six bounded and shook their shining haunches, like a noisy team of Spanish mules, urged first this way, then that by the apostrophes of the driver. All at once, casting down his eye between the large slates which like scales cover the perpendicular wall of the belfry to a certain height, he descried in the Place a young female oddly accoutered, who stopped and spread upon the ground a carpet on which a little goat came and posted itself. A circle of spectators was soon formed round them. This sight suddenly changed the current of his ideas, and congealed his musical enthusiasm as a breath of air congeals melted rosin. He paused, turned his back to his bells, and, leaning forward from beneath the slated penthouse, espyed the dancing-girl with that pensive, kind, nay, tender look, which had once before astonished the archdeacon. Meanwhile the bells, left to themselves, abruptly ceased all at once, to the great disappointment of the lovers of this kind of music, who were listening with delight to the peals from the Pont au Change, and went away as sulky as a dog to which you have held a piece of meat and given a stone.

30

One fine morning in the same month of March, I believe it was Saturday, the 29th, the festival of St. Eustache, it so happened that our young friend Jehan Frollo du Moulin perceived, while dressing himself, that his breeches, containing his purse, gave out no metallic sound. "Poor purse!" said he, drawing it forth from his pocket; "not one little parisis. How cruelly thou hast been gutted by dice, Venus, and the tavern.

"There thou art, empty, wrinkled, flaccid. Thou art like the bosom of a fury. I would just ask you, Messer Cicero and Messer Seneca, whose dogeared works lie scattered on the floor, of what use is it to me to know, better than a master of the mint or a Jew of the Pont aux Chageurs, that a gold crown is worth thirty-five unzains, at twenty-five sous eight deniers' parisis each, if I have not a single miserable black liard to risk on the double six. Oh, Consul Cicero, this is not a calamity from which one may extricate one's self with periphrases, with *quemadmodum* and *verumenimveros*."

He began to put on his clothes in silent sadness. While lacing his buskins, a thought occurred to him, but he gave it up immediately. Again it presented itself, and he put on his vest the wrong side out, an evident sign of some violent inward struggle. At length, dashing his cap upon the ground, he exclaimed: "Yes, I will go to my brother; I shall get a lecture, but then I shall get a crown."

Then hastily throwing on his surcoat trimmed with fur, and picking up his cap, he rushed out of the room. He went down the Rue de la Harpe toward the City.

Having crossed the Petit Pont, Jehan at length found himself before Notre Dame. Again he wavered in his purpose, and he walked for a few moments round the statue of M. Legris, repeating to himself: "I am sure of the lecture, but shall I get the crown?"

He stopped a verger who was coming from the cloisters. "Where is the Archdeacon of Josas?" he inquired.

"I believe he is in his closet in the tower," replied the verger; "and I would not advise you to disturb him there, unless you have a message from some such person as the Pope or Monsieur the King."

Jehan capped his hands. "By Jupiter!" he exclaimed, "a fine opportunity for seeing that famous den of sorcery!"

Determined by this reflection, he resolutely entered at the little black door, and began to ascend the winding stairs leading to the upper stories of the tower. "We shall see," said he to himself by the way. "By the whiskers of the Blessed Virgin, it must be a curious place, that cell which my reverend brother keeps so carefully to himself.

They say that he has a roaring fire there sometimes to cook the philosopher's stone at. By my fay, I care no more about the philosopher's stone than any cobble-stone, and I would rather find a savory omelet on his furnace than the biggest philosopher's stone in the world!"

Having reached the pillar gallery, he stood puffing for a moment, and then swore at the endless stairs by I know not how many million cartloads of devils. Having somewhat vented his spleen, he recommenced his ascent by the little door of the north tower, which is now shut against the public. Just after he had passed the bell-room, he came to a lateral recess in which there was a low pointed door. "Humph!" said the scholar; "this must be the place, I suppose."

The key was in the lock, and the door not fastened; he gently pushed it open far enough to look in.

A scene not unlike the cell of Dr. Faustus presented itself to the view of Jehan, when he ventured to look in at the half-open door. This, too, was a gloomy hole into which the light was very sparingly admitted. It contained, too, a great armchair and a large table, compasses, alembics, skeletons of animals hanging from the ceiling, a globe lying upon the floor pell-mell with glass jars, filled with liquids of various colors, skulls placed on parchments scrawled over with figures and letters, thick manuscripts wide open and heaped one upon another—in short all the rubbish of science—and the whole covered with dust and cobwebs; but there was no circle of luminous letters, no doctor in ecstasy contemplating the flaming vision as the eagle gazes at the sun.

The cell, however, was not unoccupied. A man seated in an armchair was stooping over the table. His back was turned to Jehan, who could see no more than his shoulders and the hinder part of his head; but he had no difficulty to recognize that bald crown, on which Nature had made an everlasting tonsure, as if to mark by this outward symbol the irresistible clerical vocation of the archdeacon.

The door had opened so softly that Dom Claude was not

aware of the presence of his brother. The young scape-grace took advantage of this circumstance to explore the cell for a few moments. To the left of the arm-chair and beneath the small window was a large furnace, which he had not remarked at the first glance. The ray of light which entered at the aperture passed through a circular cobweb, in the center of which the motionless insect architect looked like the nave of this wheel of lace. On the furnace lay in disorder all sorts of vessels, glass vials, retorts, and matrasses. There was no fire in the furnace, nor did it appear to have been lighted for a considerable time. A glass mask, which Jehan observed among the implements of alchemy, and which no doubt served to protect the archdeacon's face when he was at work upon any dangerous substance, lay in one corner, covered with dust, and as it were forgotten. By its side was a pair of bellows equally dusty, the upper surface of which bore this legend inlaid in letters of copper: *Spira, Spera.*

Other mottoes in great number were inscribed, according to the custom of the hermetic philosophers, upon the walls, some written with ink and others cut as if with a graver. Gothic, Hebrew, Greek, and Roman letters were all mixed together; the inscriptions ran into one another, the more recent effacing the older, and all dovetailing like the boughs of a clump of trees, or pikes in a battle. They composed in fact a confused medley of all human philosophies, reveries, and knowledge.

In other respects the cell exhibited a general appearance of neglect and dilapidation; and from the state of the utensils it might be inferred that the master had long been diverted from his usual pursuits by other occupations.

This master, meanwhile, bending over a vast manuscript adorned by grotesque paintings, appeared to be tormented by an idea which incessantly obtruded itself upon his meditations. So at least Jehan judged, on hearing his utter this soliloquy, with the pensive pauses of one in a brown study who thinks aloud: "Yes, so Manou asserted and Zoroaster taught. The sun is the offspring of fire, the moon of the sun; fire is the soul of the universe. Its elementary atoms are incessantly overflowing and pouring upon the world in innumerable currents. At the points where these currents intersect one another in the atmosphere they produce light; at their points of intersection in the earth they produce gold. Light, gold—one and the same thing. From the state of fire to the concrete state. The difference between the visible and palpable, between the fluid and solid in the same substance, between steam and ice, nothing more. This is not a dream—'tis the general law of nature. But how is science to set about detecting the secret of this general law?"

"The devil!" said Jehan to himself—" 'tis a long while to wait for a crown!"

"Others have thought," continued the archdeacon, "that it would be better to operate upon a ray of Sirius. But it is very difficult to obtain one of his rays pure, on account of the simultaneous presence of the other stars whose light mingles with it. Flamel conceives that it is simple to operate upon a terrestrial fire. Flamel! what a name for an adept! *Flamma*—yes, fire. That is all. The diamond is in charcoal, gold is in fire. But how is it to be extracted? Magistri affirms that there are certain names of women possessing so sweet and so mysterious a charm, that it is sufficient to pronounce them during the operation."

He closed the book with violence. He passed his hand over his brow, as if to chase away the idea which annoyed him; and then took up a nail and a small hammer, the handle of which was curiously painted with cabalistic letters.

"For some time past," said he, with a bitter smile, "I have failed in all my experiments. One fixed idea haunts me and pierces my brain like a red-hot iron. I have not even been able to discover the secret of Cassiodorus, who made a lamp to burn without wick and without oil. A simple matter, nevertheless!"

"Peste!" muttered Jehan.

"One single miserable thought then," continued the priest, "is sufficient to make a man weak or mad! Oh! how

Claude Pernelle would laugh at me! She who could not for a moment divert Nicolas Flamel from the prosecution of the great work! But have I not in my hand the magic hammer of Zechiele! At every blow which the dread rabbi, in the recesses of his cell, struck upon this nail with this hammer, some one of his enemies whom he had doomed to destruction sank into the earth which swallowed him up.

"Let's see! let's try!" resumed the archdeacon with vehemence. "If I succeed, a blue spark will fly from the head of the nail—Emen Hetan! Emen Hetan!—That's not it— Sigeani! Sigeani!—May this nail open a grave for every man named Phœbus! Curses on it! forever and ever the same ideas!"

He angrily threw down the hammer, and then sunk forward in his armchair upon the table so that the enormous back completely hid him from Jehan's sight. For a few minutes he saw no part of him but his hand convulsively clenched upon a book. All at once Dom Claude rose, took up a pair of compasses, and engraved in silence on the wall in capital letters the Greek word

'ANATKH.

"My brother is mad," said Jehan to himself. "It would have been much more simple to write *Fatum*. Everybody is not obliged to understand Greek."

The archdeacon returned, seated himself again in his armchair, and laid his head on both his hands like one whose head aches to such a degree that he cannot hold it up.

The student watched his brother with astonishment.

Perceiving that the archdeacon had relapsed into his former stupor, he softly drew back his head and took several steps outside the door, that his footfall might apprise the archdeacon of his arrival.

"Come in," cried his brother, from within the cell; "I have been waiting for you. Come in, Master Jacques."

The scholar boldly entered. The archdeacon, to whom

such a visitor in such a place was anything but welcome, started at the sight of him. "What! is it you, Jehan?"

" 'Tis a J at any rate," said the student, with his ruddy, impudent, jovial face.

The countenance of Dom Claude resumed its stern expression. "What brings you hither?"

"Brother," replied the scholar, assuming as humble, modest, and decorous an air as he could, and twirling his cap on his fingers with a look of innocence, "I am come to ask of you—"

"What?"

"A little wholesome advice, which I much need." Jehan durst not add—"and a little money which I need still more." This last member of the sentence he forbore to utter.

"Sir," said the archdeacon, in an austere tone, "I am highly displeased with you."

"Alas!" sighed the student.

Dom Claude made his chair describe one fourth of a circle, and looked steadfastly at Jehan. "I wanted to see you," said he.

This was an ominous exordium. Jehan prepared himself for a fierce attack.

"Every day, Jehan, complaints are brought to me of your misconduct. What have you to say for yourself about that beating which you gave to the young Viscount Albert de Ramonchamp?"

"Oh!" replied Jehan, "a mere bagatelle! The scurvy page amused himself with making his horse run in the mud for the purpose of plashing the scholars."

"And what excuse have you to make," resumed the archdeacon, "about that affair with Mahiet Targel, whose gown you tore? *Tunicam dechiraverunt,* says the complaint."

"Pooh! only one of the sorry Montaigu hoods! that's all!"

"The complaint says *tunicam* and not *capettam.* Have you not learned Latin?"

Jehan made no reply.

"Yes," continued the priest, "the study of letters is at a low ebb now. The Latin language is scarcely understood, the Syriac unknown, the Greek so hateful that it is not accounted ignorance even in the greatest scholars to skip a Greek word without pronouncing it, and to say, *Græcum est, non legitur.*"

Jehan boldly raised his eyes. "Brother," said he, "would you like me to explain in simple French, the Greek word written there upon the wall?"

"Which word?"

" 'Anatkh!'"

A slight flush tinged the pallid cheek of the archdeacon, like the puff of smoke which betokens the secret commotions of a volcano. The student scarcely perceived it.

"Well, Jehan," stammered the elder brother with some effort, "what is the meaning of that word?"

"Fatality."

Dom Claude turned pale, and the scholar carelessly continued: "And that word underneath engraven by the same hand, signifies impurity. You see I do know something of Greek."

The archdeacon was silent. This Greek lesson had made him thoughtful. Young Jehan, who had all the art of a spoiled child, deemed it a favorable moment for hazarding his request. Assuming, therefore, as soothing a tone as possible, he thus began: "My good brother, surely you will not look morose and take a dislike to me, merely on account of a few petty bruises and thumps given in fair fight to a pack of little chits and monkeys—*quibusdam marmosetis.* You see, I do know something of Latin, brother Claude."

But this canting hypocrisy had not its accustomed effect upon the stern senior. It did not remove a single wrinkle from the brow of the archdeacon. "Come to the point," said he dryly.

"Well then," replied Jehan, screwing up his courage; "it is this—I want money."

At this straightforward declaration the countenance of the archdeacon all at once assumed a magisterial and paternal expression.

"You know, Monsieur Jehan," said he, "that our fief of Tirechappe produces no more, deducting ground-rent and other out-goings for the twenty-one houses, than thirty-nine livres, eleven sous, six deniers parisis. This is half as much again as in the time of the Paclets, but 'tis no great deal."

"I want money," repeated Jehan, stoically.

"You know that the official has decided that our twenty-one houses are liable to the payment of fines to the bishopric, and that to relieve ourselves from this homage we must pay the most reverend bishop two marks in silver gilt at the rate of six livres parisis. Now I have not yet been able to save these two marks, as you well know."

"I know that I want money," repeated Jehan for the third time.

"And what would you do with it?"

At this question a glimmer of hope danced before the eyes of Jehan. He resumed his soft and fawning manner.

"Look you, my dear brother Claude, it is not for any bad purpose that I make this application. It is not to play the gallant in taverns with your unzains, or to parade the streets of Paris in a suit of gold brocade with a lackey at my heels. No, brother; it is for an act of charity."

"What act of charity?" inquired Claude, with some surprise.

"There are two of my friends who have proposed to purchase baby-linen for the child of a poor widow in Haudry's alms-house: it is a real charity. It would cost three florins, and I wish to contribute my share."

"A likely story!" observed the sagacious Claude. "What sort of baby-linen must it be to cost three florins—and that too for the infant of one of the Haudry widows! Since when have those widows had young infants to provide clothes for?"

"Well then," cried Jehan, once more arming himself

with his usual impudence, "I want money to go at night to see Isabenau la Thierrye."

"Dissolute wretch!" exclaimed the priest.

" 'Impurity," said Jehan.

This word, which stared the scholar in the face on the wall of the cell, produced an extraordinary effect on the priest. He bit his lip, and his anger was extinguished in a deep blush.

"Get you gone!" said he to Jehan; "I expect someone."

Jehan made another attempt. "Brother Claude, give me at least one petit parisis to get something to eat."

"Where are you in Gratian's decretals?" asked Dom Claude.

"I have lost my exercises."

"Where are you in the Latin humanities?"

"Somebody has stolen my Horace."

"Where are you in Aristotle?"

"By my fay, brother!—which of the fathers of the Church is it who says that heretics have in all ages sought refuge under the briers of Aristotle's metaphysics? Faugh upon Aristotle's! I will not tear my religion to rags against his metaphysics."

"Young man," replied the archdeacon, "at the last entry of the king, there was a gentleman called Philippe de Comines, who had embroidered on the trappings of his horse this motto, which I counsel you to ponder well: *Qui non laborat non manducet.*" (He that will not work neither shall he eat.)

The scholar continued silent for a moment, with his finger on his ear, his eye fixed upon the floor, and a look of vexation. All at once turning toward Claude with the brisk motion of a water-wagtail, "Then, my good brother," said he, "you refuse me a sou to buy me a crust at the baker's?"

"Qui non laborat non manducet."

At this inflexible answer of the archdeacon's Jehan covered his face with his hands, sobbed like a woman, and cried in a tone of despair, *"O τo τo τo τo τoî!"*

"What is the meaning of that?" asked Claude, surprised at this vagary.

"Why," said the scholar, after rubbing his eyes with his knuckles to give them the appearance of weeping—"it is Greek—'tis an anapæst of Æschylus, which expresses grief to the life."

He then burst into a laugh so droll and so ungovernable that the archdeacon could not help smiling. It was in fact Claude's fault; why had he so utterly spoiled the boy?

"Nay now, my good brother Claude," resumed Jehan, "only look at my wornout buskins. Did you ever see a more lamentable sight?"

The archdeacon had quickly resumed his former sternness. "I will send you new buskins, but no money."

"Only one poor petit parisis, brother!" besought Jehan. "I will learn Gratian by heart, I will be a good Christian, a real Pythagoras of learning and virtue. One petit parisis, pray! Would you let me fall a prey to hunger which is staring me in the face?"

Dom Claude shook his wrinkled brow. *"Qui non laborat——"*

"Well then," cried Jehan, interrupting him, "jollity forever! I will game, I will fight, I will go to the tavern and the bordel!"

So saying he knew up his cap, and snapped his fingers like castanets. The archdeacon eyed him with gloomy look.

"Jehan," said he, "you are on a very slippery descent. Know you wither you are going?"

"To the tavern," said Jehan.

"The tavern leads to the pillory."

" 'Tis a lantern like any other; and it was perhaps the one with which Diogenes found his man."

"The pillory leads to the gallows."

"The gallows is a balance, which has a man at one end and all the world at the other. 'Tis a fine thing to be the man."

"The gallows leads to hell."

"That is a rousing fire."

"Jehan, Jehan, the end will be bad."

"The beginning at least will have been good."

At this moment the sound of a footfall was heard on the stairs.

"Silence!" said the archdeacon; "here is Master Jacques. Hark ye, Jehan," added he in a lower tone, "be sure not to mention what you shall have seen and heard here. Quick! hide yourself under this furnace, and don't so much as breathe."

The scholar crept under the furnace. Here an excellent idea occurred to him. "By the by, brother Claude, I must have a florin for not breathing."

"Silence! you shall have it."

"But give it me now."

"There, take it!" said the archdeacon angrily, throwing him his pouch. Jehan crawled as far as he could under the furnace and the door opened.

31

The person who entered had a black gown and a gloomy look. Our friend Jehan, who had contrived to arrange himself in his hiding place in such a manner as to hear and see all that passed, was struck at the first glance by the perfect sadness of the garb and the countenance of the visitor. A certain gentleness at the same time overspread that face; but it was the gentleness of a cat or a judge. The man was very gray, wrinkled, and hard upon sixty; with white eyebrows, hanging lip, and large hands. When Jehan saw that it was nobody, that is to say, in all probability some physician or magistrate, and that his nose was at a great distance from his mouth, a sure sign of stupidity, he shrank back in his hole, vexed at the prospect of having to pass an indefinite time in so confined a posture and in such scurvy company.

The archdeacon meanwhile had not even risen to this personage. He motioned to him to be seated on a stool near the door, and, after a few moments' silence, in which he seemed to be pursuing a previous meditation, he said with the tone of a patron to his client, "Good-morrow, Master Jacques."

"Good-morrow, master," replied the man in black.

In the two ways of pronouncing on the one hand that Master Jacques, and on the other that master, by way of eminence, there was as much difference as between monseigneur and monsieur; it clearly bespoke the teacher and the disciple.

"Well," resumed the archdeacon, after another silence, which Master Jacques took care not to interrupt, "have you succeeded?"

"Alas! master," said the other, with a sorrowful smile, "I keep puffing away. More ashes than I want, but not an atom of gold."

A gesture of displeasure escaped Dom Claude. "I was not talking of that, Master Jacques Charmolue, but of the proceedings against your sorcerer, Marc Cenaine, I think you called him, the butler of the Court of Accompts. Doth he confess his guilt. Has the torture produced the desired effect?"

"Alas! no," replied Master Jacques, still with his sad smile; "we have not that consolation. The man is as hard as a flint. We might boil him in the Swine Market before he would confess. However, we are sparing no pains to get at the truth; his joints are all dislocated. We are trying everything we can think of, as old Plautus says:

Advorsum, stimulos, laminas, crucesque, compedesque,
Nervos, catenas, carceres, numellas, pedicas, boias—

but all to no purpose. Oh! he is a terrible fellow. He fairly puzzles me."

"Have you found nothing further in his house?"

"Yes," said Master Jacques, groping in his pouch; "this parchment. There are words upon it which pass our comprehension; and yet Monsieur Philippe Lheulier, the criminal advocate, knows something of Hebrew, which he picked up in the affair of the Jews at Brussels."

As he thus spoke Master Jacques unrolled the parchment.

"Give it to me," said the archdeacon. He threw his eye over it. "Pure magic, Master Jacques!" he exclaimed. "*Emen Hetan*—that is the cry of the witches on their arrival at their Sabbath meetings. *Per ipsum et cum ipso, et in ipso*—that is the command which chains down the devil in hell. *Hax, pax, max*—that belongs to medicine—a form against the bite of mad dogs. Master Jacques, you are the king's proctor in the ecclesiastical court; this parchment is abominable."

"We will apply the torture again. But here is something else," added Master Jacques, fumbling a second time in his pouch, "that we have found at Marc Cenaine's."

It was a vessel of the same family as those which covered Dom Claude's furnace. "Aha!" said the archdeacon; "a crucible of alchemy!"

"I must confess," resumed Master Jacques, with his timid and awkward smile, "that I tried it upon the furnace, but with no better luck than with my own."

The archdeacon examined the vessel. "What has he engraved on his crucible? *Och, och*—the word that drives away fleas. This Marc Cenaine is an ignoramus. I can easily believe that you will not make gold with this. 'Tis fit to put in your alcove in summer, and that is all."

"Talking of blunders," said the king's proctor, "I have been examining the porch below before I came up; is your reverence quite sure that the one of the seven naked figures at the feet of Our Lady, with wings at his heels, is Mercury?"

"Certainly," replied the priest; "so it is stated by Augustin Nypho, the Italian doctor, who had a bearded demon that revealed everything to him. But we will go down presently, and I will explain this to you by the text."

"Many thanks, master," said Charmolue, with a very low obeisance. "But I had well-nigh forgotten—when doth it please you that I should order the young sorceress to be apprehended?"

"What sorceress?"

"That Bohemian, you know, who comes every day to dance in the Parvis, in despite of the prohibition of the official. She has a goat which is possessed, and has the devil's own horns, and reads, and writes, and understands mathematics, and would be enough to bring all Bohemia to the gallows. The indictment is quite ready. A handsome creature, upon my soul, that dancer; the brightest black eyes! a pair of Egyptian carbuncles! When shall we begin?"

The archdeacon turned pale as death. "I will tell you," stammered he, with a voice scarcely articulate. Then with an effort he added: "For the present go on with Marc Cenaine."

"Never fear," said Charmolue, smiling: "as soon as I get back, I will have him strapped down again to the leathern bed. But 'tis a devil of a fellow; he tires Pierrat Torterue himself, and his hands are bigger than mine. As saith the good Plautus:

Nudus vinctus centum pondo, es quando pendes per pedes.

The windlass will be the best thing to set to work upon him."

Dom Claude appeared to be absorbed in gloomy reverie. Suddenly turning to Charmolue: "Master Pierrat—Master Jacques, I would say, go on with Marc Cenaine."

"Ay, ay, Dom Claude. Poor man, he will have suffered a martyrdom. But then what an idea, to go to the Sabbath! a butler of the Court of Accompts, who ought to know the text of Charlemagne's ordinance, *Stryga vel masca*! As for the girl—Semlarda as they call her—I shall await your orders. Ah, true! and when we are at the porch, you will also explain to me what the gardener in low relief at the entrance of the church is meant for! Is it not the Sower? Hey, master! What think you?"

Dom Claude, engrossed by his own reflections, attended not to the speaker. Charmolue, following the direction of his eye, perceived that it was mechanically fixed upon a large spider's web stretched across the window. At that moment, a giddy fly attracted by the March sun, flew into the net and became entangled in it. At the shock given to his web, an enormous spider rushed forth from his central cell, and then at one leap sprang upon the fly, which he doubled up with his forelegs, while with his hideous sucker he attacked the head. "Poor fly!" said the proctor, and raised his hand to rescue it. The archdeacon, suddenly starting up, held back his arm with convulsive violence.

"Master Jacques!" cried he, "meddle not with fatality!"

The proctor turned about in alarm; it seemed as if his arm was held by iron pincers. The eye of the priest was fixed, wild, glaring, and gazed intently upon the horrible little group of the fly and the spider.

"Oh, yes, yes!" resumed the priest, with a voice that seemed to proceed from his very bowels—"this is an emblem of the whole affair. It is young, it flies about, it is merry, it seeks the open air, the spring sunshine, liberty. Oh, yes! But it is stopped at the fatal window; it is caught in the toils of the spider, the hideous spider! Poor dancing-girl! poor predestined fly! Be quiet, Master Jacques! it is fatality! Alas, Claude! thou art the spider. Claude, thou art the fly too! Thou didst seek science, the light, the sunshine; thou desirest only to reach the free air, the broad daylight of eternal truth; but, while darting toward the dazzling window, which opens into the other world, a world of brightness, intelligence, and science, blind fly, silly doctor, thou didst not perceive that subtle spider's web, spread by Fate between the light and thee; thou rushedst into it, and now, with mangled head and broken wings, thou strugglest in the iron grip of fatality! Master Jacques! Master Jacques! let the spider alone!"

"I assure you," said Charmolue, who stared at him without comprehending his meaning, "that I will not meddle with it. But, for mercy's sake, master, loose my arm! you have a hand like a vise."

The archdeacon heard him not. "Oh, fool! fool!" he began again, without taking his eyes for a moment off the window. "And if thou couldst have broken through those formidable meshes with thy delicate wings, dost thou imagine that thou couldst then have attained the light? How wouldst thou have passed that glass, which is beyond it, that transparent obstacle, that wall of crystal harder than brass, which separates all philosophies from truth? Oh, vanity of science! how many sages come fluttering from afar to dash their heads against it! how many systems come buzzing to rush pell-mell against this eternal window!"

He paused. The concluding reflections, which had insensibly diverted his mind from himself to science, appeared to have restored him to a degree of composure. Jacques Charmolue brought him back completely to a feeling of reality by asking him this question: "By the by, master, when will you come and help me to make gold? I am not lucky at it."

The archdeacon shook his head with a bitter smile. "Master Jacques," he replied, "read the *Dialogus de Energia et Operatione Dæmonum*, by Michel Psellus. What we are about is not absolutely innocent."

"Speak lower, master," said Charmolue. "I thought as much myself. But a man may be allowed to dabble a little in hermetics when he is but king's proctor in the ecclesiastical court at thirty crowns tournos per annum. Only let us speak lower."

At that moment sounds resembling those made in mastication, proceeding from beneath the furnace, struck the alarmed ear of Charmolue.

"What is that?" he asked.

It was the scholar, who, cramped in his hiding place and heartily weary of it, had there found a hard crust and a cube of moldy cheese, and fallen foul of them without ceremony, by way of consolation and breakfast. As he was very hungry he made a great noise, and smacked his chaps so audibly at every munch as to excite alarm in the proctor.

" 'Tis only my cat," said the archdeacon, sharply, "regaling herself under there with a mouse."

This explanation satisfied Charmolue. "In fact, master," he replied, with a respectful smile, "every great philosopher has had his familiar animal. As Servius says, you know: *Nullus emin lucus sine genio est.*"

Dom Claude, apprehensive of some new prank of Jehan's, reminded his worthy disciple that they had some figures on the porch to study together; and both left the cell, to the great relief of the scholar, who began seriously to fear that his knees and his chin would grow together.

32

"*Te Deum laudamus!*" exclaimed Master Jehan, sallying forth from his hole: "the two screech owls are gone. Och! och!—Hax! pax! max!—the fleas!—the made dogs!—the devil!—I've had quite enough of their talk! my head rings like a belfry. Let us be off too and turn my good brother's money into bottles!"

He cast a look of kindness and admiration into the interior of the precious pouch, adjusted his dress, wiped his buskins, brushed the ashes from his sleeves, whistled a tune, cut a caper, looked round to see if there was anything else in the cell that he could make free with, picked up here and there on the furnace some amulet of glass, fit to be given by way of trinket to Isbeau la Thierrye, opened the door which his brother as a last indulgence had left unlocked, and which he in his turn left open as the last trick he could play him, and descended the winding stairs, hopping like a bird.

He stamped with his foot when he found himself again on the ground. "Oh, good and honorable pavement of Paris!" he exclaimed—"cursed stairs that would give a breathing to the angels of Jacob's ladder themselves! What was I thinking of to squeeze myself into that stone gimlet which pierces the sky, and all to eat mouldy cheese and see the steeples of Paris through a loophole!"

He had moved but a few steps when he perceived the two screech owls, alias Dom Claude and Master Jacques Charmolue, contemplating one of the sculptures of the porch. He approached them on tiptoe, and heard the archdeacon say in a very low tone to his companion: "It was William of Paris who had a Job engraved upon that stone of the color of lapis lazuli, and gilt on the edges. Job represented the philosopher's stone, which must be tried and tortured in order to become perfect, as saith Raymond Lully: *Sub conservatione for mœ specificœ salva anima.*"

"What is that to me?" said Jehan to himself—"I have got the purse."

At this moment he heard a loud and sonorous voice behind him pour forth a formidable volley of oaths: "*Sang Dieu! Ventre Dieu! Bedieu! Corps de Dieu! Nombril de Belzequth! Nom d'un pape! Corne et tonnerre!*"

"Upon my soul," cried Jehan, "that can be nobody but my friend Captain Phœbus!"

The name Phœbus struck the ear of the archdeacon at the moment when he was explaining to the king's proctor the dragon hiding his tail in a bath whence issue smoke and a royal head. Dom Claude shuddered, stopped short, to the great surprise of Charmolue, turned round, and saw his brother Jehan accosting a tall officer at the door of the Gondalaurier mansion.

It was in fact Captain Phœbus de Chateaupers. He was leaning against the angle of the house and swearing like a pagan.

"By my fay, Captain Phœbus," said Jehan, grasping his hand, "you swear with marvelous emphasis."

"Blood and thunder!" replied the captain.

"Blood and thunder to you!" rejoined the scholar. "But I say, gentle captain, what has occasioned this overflow of fair words?"

"I beg your pardon, my good comrade Jehan," cried Phœbus, shaking him by the hand, "a horse at the top of his speed cannot stop short. Now I was swearing at full gallop. I have just come from these affected prudes, and whenever I leave them I have my throat full of oaths; I am forced to turn them out or they would choke me outright—blood and thunder!"

"Will you come and drink with me" asked the scholar.

This proposal pacified the captain. "I fain would," said he, "but I have no money."

"Well, but I have."

"Aha! let us see!"

Jehan exhibited the pouch to the wondering gaze of the captain. Meanwhile the archdeacon, who had left Charmolue quite astounded, had approached and stopped within a few paces of them, watching both without their being aware of it, so entirely was their attention engrossed by the pouch.

"A purse in your pocket, Jehan," cried Phœbus, "is like the moon in a bucket of water. You see it, but it is not there; 'tis only the shadow. Nothing but pebbles in it, I would wager."

"There are the pebbles that I pave my pocket with," replied Jehan, dryly; and so saying he emptied the pouch upon a post close by, with the air of a Roman saving his country.

"By heaven!" muttered Phœbus; "real money! 'tis absolutely dazzling."

Jehan retained his grave and dignified attitude. A few

liards had rolled into the mud; the captain in his enthusiasm, stooped to pick them up. He counted the pieces, and turning with a solemn look toward his companion, "Do you know, Jehan," said he, "that there are twenty-three sous parisis? Whom have you had the luck to lighten last night in the Rue Coupe-Gueule?"

Jehan threw back the long light hair that curled about his face, and half closed his disdainful eyes. " 'Tis a good thing," said he, "to have a brother who is an archdeacon and a simpleton."

"*Corne de Dieu!*" exclaimed Phœbus. "The worthy fellow!"

"Let us go and drink," said Jehan.

The two friends then bent their steps toward the tavern known by the sign of La Pomme d'Eve. It is superfluous to say that they had first picked up the money, and the archdeacon followed them.

The archdeacon followed them with wild and gloomy look. Was this the Phœbus whose accursed name had, ever since his interview with Gringoire, haunted all his thoughts? He knew not, but at any rate it was a Phœbus, and this magic name sufficed to lure the archdeacon to follow the two reckless companions with stealthy step, listening to their conversation, and watching their slightest gestures with intense anxiety. Indeed, nothing was more easy than to hear all they said, so loud was the tone in which they carried on their conversation about duels and doxies, flagons and drunken frolics.

At the turning of a street, the sound of a tambourine was wafted to them from a crossing at a little distance. Dom Claude heard the officer say to his brother: "Blood and thunder! let us quicken our pace!"

"Why, Phœbus?"

"I am afraid lest the Bohemian should see me."

"What Bohemian?"

"The girl with the goat."

"La Esmeralda?"

"The same, Jehan. I always forget her devil of a name.

Let us make haste; she would know me again. I don't wish
that girl to speak to me in the street."

"Are you then acquainted with her, Phœbus?"

Here the archdeacon saw Phœbus grin, stoop to Jehan's
ear, and whisper a few words in it. The captain then burst
into a loud laugh, and tossed his head with a triumphant
air.

"Indeed!" said Jehan.

"Upon my soul!" replied Phœbus.

"Tonight?"

"This very night."

"Are you sure she will come?"

"You must be silly, Jehan. Not the least doubt of it."

"Captain Phœbus, you are a lucky fellow!"

The archdeacon heard every syllable of this conversation. His teeth chattered. A shudder, visible to the eye,
thrilled his whole frame. He paused for a moment, leaned
against a post, like a drunken man, and again followed the
two boon companions.

33

The celebrated tavern, called La Pomme d'Eve, was situated in the University, at the corner of Rue de la
Rondelle and Rue du Batonnier. It was a very spacious but
very low room with a double roof, the central return of
which was supported by a massive wooden pillar painted
yellow; the floor covered with tables, bright tin jugs hanging up against the wall; plenty of topers, plenty of lewd
women, a window next to the street, a vine at the door,
and over the door a creaking square of sheet iron, upon
which were painted a woman and an apple, rusted with
rain and turning upon an iron spike. This kind of weather-

cock, which looked toward the pavement, was the sign of the house.

It was nightfall, and the tavern, full of candles, glared at a distance like a forge in the dark; the sounds of carousal, swearing, altercation, mixed with the jingle of glasses, issued from the broken panes. Through the haze which covered the window, in consequence of the heat of the room, might be discerned swarms of confused figures, from which burst from time to time roars of laughter. The pedestrians whose business called them that way, passed this noisy window without casting their eyes on it; but at intervals some little ragged urchin would stand on tiptoe to look in, and shout the old doggrel couplet with which it was usual in those days to greet drunkards:

> Aux Houls,
> Saouls, saouls, saouls!

One man, however, kept incessantly walking to and fro before the noisy tavern, narrowly watching all goers and comers, and never moving father from it than a sentry from his box. He was muffled up in a cloak to the very eyes. This cloak he had just bought at a shop contiguous to the tavern, no doubt as a protection from the cold of the March evenings, perhaps also to conceal his dress. From time to time he paused before the window, looked through the small lozenge-shaped panes bordered with lead, listened, and stamped.

At length the tavern door opened. It was this that he appeared to be waiting for. Two persons who had been drinking there came out. The ray of light which escaped at the door fell for a moment upon their jovial faces. The man in the cloak stationed himself under a porch on the other side of the street to watch them.

"The clock has just struck seven," exclaimed one of the topers; "that is the time for my appointment."

"I tell you," replied his companion, with an articulation far from distinct, "that I don't live in the Rue des Mauvaises Paroles—*indignus qui inter verba mala habitat.* I lodge in the Rue Jean-Pain-Mollet. You are more horned than a unicorn, if you say to the contrary."

"Jehan, my friend, you are drunk," said the other.

His companion rejoined, staggering; "That is what you are pleased to say, Phœbus; but it is proved that Pluto had the profile of a hound."

The reader has no doubt already recognized in the two jolly topers the captain and the scholar. The man who was watching them in the dark appeared also to have recognized them; for, with slow step, he followed all the zigzags into which the captain was drawn by his companion. The former, more inured to tipling, was none the worse for liquor. The man in the cloak, listening to them attentively, was enabled to catch the whole of the following interesting conversation.

"Body o' Bacchus! Mr. Bachelor, try to walk straight; you know I must leave you. It is seven o'clock, I tell you, and I have an appointment."

"Then go, leave me!—I see the stars and darts of fire. You are like the castle of Dampmartin, bursting with laughter."

"By my grandmother's warts, Jehan, the nonsense you talk is too absurd. By the by, Jehan, have you any money left?"

"Mr. Rector, there is no fault—the little shambles, *parva boucheria.*"

"Jehan, my friend, Jehan, you know I have an assignation with that damsel at the end of the Pont St. Michel. Surely, Jehan, we have not drunk all the parson's money. See if you have not one parisis left."

"The consciousness of having well spent the other hours is an excellent sauce to the table."

"Fire and fury! A truce to cross purposes, Jehan. Tell me, have you any money left? I must have some, or, by heaven, I will rifle your pockets."

"Why, sir, the Rue Galiache is a street that has the Rue

de la Verrerie at one end, and the Rue de la Thixeranderie at the other."

"Quite right, my dear friend Jehan, so it has. But, for heaven's sake! rally your senses. It is seven o'clock, and I want but one sou parisis."

"Silence, now—silence to the song, and attention to the chorus:

> " 'When it shall befall the cats
> To be eaten up by rats,
> Then the King of Arras city
> Shall be master—more's the pity!
> When at St. John's tide the sea,
> Wide and warm although it be,
> Shall be frozen firm and fast,
> As if done by winter's blast,
> Then the folks from Arras, they
> O'er the ice shall trudge away.' "

"Scholar of Antichrist!" cried Phœbus, "may thy brains be dashed out with thine own books!" At the same time he gave the intoxicated student a violent push which sent him reeling against the wall, where he presently sunk gently upon the pavement of Philip Augustus. From a relic of that brotherly compassion which is never wholly banished from the heart of a toper, Phœbus rolled Jehan with his foot upon one of those pillows of the poor which Providence keeps ready in the corners of the streets of Paris, and which the wealthy disdainfully stigmatize with the name of dunghills. The captain placed Jehan's head on an inclined plane of cabbage-stalks, and the scholar instantly began snoring in a magnificent bass. Yet was not the captain's heart wholly free from animosity. "So much the worse for thee if the devil's cart picks thee up as it passes!" said he to the sleeping scholar, and away he went.

The man in the cloak, who had kept following him paused for a moment before the helpless youth, as if undecided what to do; then, heaving a deep sigh, he continued to follow the captain.

Like them we will leave Jehan sleeping beneath the canopy of heaven, and speed after them, if it so please the reader.

On reaching the Rue St. Andre des Arcs, Captain Phœbus perceived that someone was following him. Chancing to turn his eyes, he saw a kind of shadow creeping behind him along the walls. He stopped; the figure stopped; he walked on; the figure walked on too. He felt but little alarm at this discovery. "Pooh!" said he to himself, "I have not a single sou."

He halted in front of the college of Autun, where he had commenced what he called his studies, close to the statue of Cardinal Pierre Bertrand, on the right of the porch, and looked around him. The street was absolutely deserted. Nothing was to be seen but the figure, which approached him with slow steps, so slow that he had abundant time to observe that it had a cloak and a hat. When very near to him, it stopped and remained motionless as the statue of Cardinal Bertrand; intently fixing upon him, however, a pair of eyes glaring with that vague light which issues at night from those of a cat.

The captain was brave and would not have cared a rush for a robber with a cudgel in his fist. But this walking statue, this petrified man, thrilled him with horror. There were at that time in circulation a number of stories of a goblin-monk who haunted at night the streets of Paris; these stories crowded confusedly upon his memory. He stood stupefied for some minutes, and at length broke silence by a forced laugh. "If you are a robber, as I hope," said he, "you are somewhat like a heron attacking a nutshell. I am the hopeful sprig of a ruined family, my dear fellow. Seek some better game. In the chapel of that college there is some wood of the true cross, which is kept in the treasure-room."

The hand of the figure was stretched from beneath the cloak, and grasped the arm of Phœbus with the force of an eagle's talons. "Captain Phœbus de Chateaupers!" said the specter at the same moment.

"What the devil!" cried Phœbus, "you know my name!"

"Not only your name," replied the mysterious stranger, in a sepulchral tone; "you have an assignation this evening."

"I have," answered the astounded Phœbus.

"At the hour of seven."

"In a quarter of an hour."

"At Falourdel's at the Pont St. Michel."

"Precisely so."

"To meet a female."

"I plead guilty."

"Whose name is—"

"La Esmeralda," said Phœbus, gayly, having by degrees recovered his levity.

At that name the specter shook the captain's arm with violence. "Captain Phœbus de Chateaupers, thou liest!"

Whoever could have seen at that moment the flushed face of the captain, the backward bound which he made with such force as to disengage his arm from the grip in which it was held, the fierce look with which he clapped his hand to the hilt of his sword, and the motionless attitude of the cloaked figure—whoever had witnessed this would have been frightened. It was something like the battle between Don Juan and the statue.

"Hell and fury!" cried the captain. "That is a word to which the ear of a Chateaupers is not accustomed. Thou darest not repeat it."

"Thou liest!" said the specter, dryly.

The captain gnashed his teeth. Goblin-monk, phantom, superstitious tales were all forgotten at the moment. In his eyes it was but a man and an insult. "Bravely said!" stammered he, half choked with rage. He drew his sword, and in a faltering voice—for rage makes one tremble, as well as fear—cried: "Here! on the spot! this very moment! draw—draw! The blood of one of us must dye this pavement!"

Meanwhile the other neither flinched nor stirred. When he saw his adversary on guard and ready for the combat: "Captain Phœbus," said he in a tone tremulous with vexation, "you forget your engagement."

In men like Phœbus gusts of passion are like boiling milk, the ebullition of which a drop of cold water is sufficient to allay. At those few simple words the captain dropped the weapon which glistened in his hand.

"Captain," continued the stranger, "tomorrow, the day after tomorrow, a month, a year, ten years hence, you will find me ready to cut your throat; but first go to your assignation."

"In fact," said Phœbus, as if seeking to capitulate with himself, "a sword and a girl are two delightful things to encounter in a meeting; but I don't see why I should give up one for the other when I may have both."

He returned his sword to the scabbard.

"Go to your assignation," repeated the unknown.

"Many thanks, sir, for your courtesy," replied Phœbus, with some embarrassment. "It is very true that it will be time enough tomorrow to slash and cut buttonholes in father Adam's doublet. I am beholden to you for allowing me one more agreeable quarter of an hour. I did hope, to be sure, to put you to bed in the kennel, and yet be in time for my appointment, especially as in such cases it is genteel to make the damsels wait a little. But you appear to be a hearty fellow, and it is safest to put off our meeting till tomorrow. So I shall go to my assignation, which is for the hour of seven, as you know." Here Phœbus tapped his forehead. "Ah! I forgot! I must have money, and I have not a single sou left."

"Here is money," said the stranger.

Phœbus felt the cold hand of the unknown slip into his a large piece of money. He could not help taking the coin, and pressing that hand.

"By heaven!" he exclaimed, "you are a good fellow!"

"On condition!" said the stranger. "Prove to me that I was wrong, that you spoke the truth. Conceal me in some corner where I may see whether the girl is really the same whose name you mentioned."

"Oh!" replied Phœbus, "that will make no difference to me."

"Come along then," rejoined the figure.

"At your service," said the captain. "For aught I know, you may be the devil in *propria persona*; but let us be good friends tonight; tomorrow I will pay you my debts, both of the purse and the sword."

They walked away with hasty steps. In a few minutes the noise of the river apprised them that they were on the bridge of St. Michel, at that time covered with houses. "I will first introduce you," said Phœbus to his companion, "and then go and fetch the wench, who is to wait for me near the Petit Chatelet." That companion made no reply; since they had been walking side by side he had not uttered a word. Phœbus stopped before a low door, against which he kicked violently. A light glimmered through the crevices of the door. "Who's there?" cried a mumbling voice. *"Corps-Dieu! Tete-Dieu! Ventre-Dieu!"* replied the captain. The door instantly opened, and discovered an old woman and a lamp, both of which trembled. The hag was bent almost double, and dressed in rags. Her head shook, and her hands, face, and neck were covered with wrinkles. She had very small eyes; her lips receded owing to the loss of her teeth, and all round her mouth she had long white hairs resembling the whiskers of a cat. The interior of her dwelling corresponded in appearance with herself. The walls were of plaster; the ceiling was formed of the black rafters and floor of the room above; the fireplace was dismantled, and every corner displayed a drapery of cobwebs. Two or three rickety tables and stools occupied the middle of the floor; a dirty boy was playing in the ashes, and at the farther end the stairs, or rather ladder, led up to a trap-door in the ceiling. On entering this den, the captain's mysterious companion drew his cloak up to his eyes, while Phœbus kept swearing like a Turk. He put into the hand of the old woman the coin which had been given to him by the stranger. The crone, who called him Monseigneur at every other word, deposited the crown in a drawer. While her back was turned, the ragged urchin rose from the hearth, slyly went to the drawer, took out the piece of money, and put a dry leaf which he had pulled from a fagot in its place.

The hag beckoned to the two gentlemen, as she called them to follow, and ascended the ladder before them. On reaching the room above, she set the lamp upon a coffer; and Phœbus opened a door that led to a dark closet. "This way, my good fellow," said he to his companion. The man in the cloak complied without uttering a word; the door closed upon him; he heard Phœbus bolt it, and a moment afterward go downstairs with the old woman. The light disappeared along with them.

34

Claude Frollo—for we presume that the reader, more intelligent than Phœbus, has discovered that the specter-monk was no other than the archdeacon—Claude Frollo groped about for a new moments in the dark hole in which the captain had bolted him. It was in fact a loft such as builders sometimes leave in the roof above the outer walls of a house. The vertical section of this kennel, as Phœbus had aptly called it, would have given a triangle. It had neither window nor loophole, and the inclined plane of the roof would not permit a person to stand upright in it. Claude therefore crouched in the dust and the mortar that cranched under him. His brain seemed to be on fire; but what passed at that moment in the dark soul of the archdeacon none but God and himself could ever know.

He waited a full quarter of an hour. To him this interval

appeared an age. All at once he heard the stairs creak; someone was coming up. The trap-door opened; a light was discernible. In the crazy door of the loft there was a crevice, to which he applied his eye. It was wide enough to allow him to see all that passed in the adjoining room. The hag first made her appearance, with the lamp in her hand, then Phœbus, turning up his whiskers, then a third face, that of the beautiful and graceful Esmeralda. The priest saw it rise above the floor like a dazzling apparition. Claude trembled; a cloud darkened his eyes; his arteries beat with violence; he was stunned with a rushing as of a mighty wind; everything about him seemed to whirl round; and presently sight and hearing forsook him.

When he came to himself, Phœbus and La Esmeralda were alone, sitting on the wooden coffer by the side of the lamp, which threw a strong light upon their two youthful faces, and enabled the archdeacon to discover a truckle-bed at the farther extremity of the garret.

Beides this bed was a window; through the panes of which, broken like a spider's web by a shower of rain, he could see a patch of sky, and the moon couched on a bed of light, fleecy clouds.

The damsel was flushed, confused, palpitating. Her long downcast eyelashes shaded her crimsoned cheeks. The face of the officer, to which she durst not raise her eyes, was radiant with delight. Unconsciously, and with a charming semblance of childishness, she traced unmeaning lines on the lid of the coffer with the tip of her finger, and then looked at the finger which had been thus employed. Her feet could not be seen; the little goat was cowering upon them.

An amorous chitchat is a very commonplace sort of thing. It is a perpetual I love you—a phrase musical enough to the parties concerned, but exceedingly bald and insipid to indifferent persons, when not adorned with a few *fiorituri*. Claude, however, was not an indifferent listener.

"Oh! despise me not, Monseigneur Phœbus," said the

girl, without raising her eyes. "I fear that what I am doing is wrong."

"Despise you, my pretty dear!" replied the officer, with a consequential air of gallantry; "despise you! and why?"

"For having accompanied you."

"I perceive, my beauty, that we don't understand one another. I ought, by rights, not to despise you, but to hate you."

The girl looked at him in alarm. "Hate me! what then have I done?"

"For wanting so much solicitation."

"Alas!" said she, "I am breaking a vow. I shall never find my parents again. The charm will lose its virtue. But no matter! what need have I at present of father or mother?"

As she thus spoke, she fixed on the captain her large dark eyes, moist with delight and tenderness.

"I declare I do not comprehend you!" exclaimed Phœbus.

La Esmeralda was silent for a moment; a tear then trickled from her eye, a sigh burst from her lips, and she said, "Oh, monseigneur, I love you."

There was around this young female such an odor of chastity, such a charm of virtue, that Phœbus did not feel quite at ease by her side. This confession, however, emboldened him. "You do love me!" said he, with transport, throwing his arm round the waist of the Egyptian, having only waited for such an occasion.

"Phœbus," resumed the Bohemian, gently removing from her waist the tenacious hand of the captain, "you are kind, you are generous, you are handsome; you saved me, who am but a poor foundling. I have long been dreaming about an officer saving my life. It was you that I dreamt of before I knew you; the officer of my dreams had a handsome uniform like you, the look of a gentleman, and a sword. Your name is Phœbus; 'tis a fine name; I love your name, I love your sword. Draw your sword, Phœbus—let me look at it."

"Strange girl!" said the captain, unsheathing his sword with a smile. The Egyptian looked at the handle, and at the blade, examined with especial curiosity the cipher on the hilt, and kissed the weapon, saying: "You belong to a brave man."

As she bent over it, Phœbus availed himself of this opportunity to imprint a kiss upon her beautiful neck. The girl suddenly raised her head, with a face crimsoned like a cherry. The priest gnashed his teeth in the dark.

"Captain Phœbus," the Egyptian again began, "let me talk to you. Just stand up and walk, and let me hear your spurs rattle. Gemini! how handsome you are!"

The captain rose in compliance with her wish, and said in a tone of rebuke, yet with a smile of satisfaction, "Why, how childish you are! But, my dear, did you ever see me in my state uniform?"

"Ah, no!" replied she.

"You would say that is handsome."

Phœbus went and again seated himself beside her, but much closer than before.

"Hark you, my dear."

The Egyptian patted his lips with her pretty hand, with the grace and playfulness of a child. "No, no, I won't hearken to you. Do you love me? I want you to tell me if you love me."

"Do I love thee, angel of my life?" exclaimed the captain, half sinking upon his knee. "I love thee, and never loved any but thee."

The captain had so often repeated this declaration in many a similar conjuncture, that he brought it out without boggling or making a single blunder. At this impassioned apostrophe, the Egyptian raised her eyes and a look of angelic happiness toward the dirty ceiling which here usurped the place of heaven. "Oh!" she softly murmured, "this is the moment at which one ought to die!"

Phœbus thought it a seasonable moment for stealing another kiss, which inflicted fresh torment on the miserable archdeacon in his hiding place.

"To die!" cried the amorous captain. "What are you talking of, my angel! Why, 'tis the very time to live, or Jupiter is a cheat! Die at such a moment as this! A good joke, by the devil's horns. No, no, that won't do. Hark ye, my dear Similar, I beg pardon, Esmenarda, but you have such a prodigiously outlandish name, that I can't beat it into my head."

"Good Heaven!" said the poor girl, "and I thought it a pretty name for its singularity. But, since you dislike it, I will change it to whatever you please."

"Nay, my darling, don't think about such trifles! 'tis a name one must get used to, that's all. When once I have learned it by heart, I shall say it offhand. But listen, my dear Similar; I passionately adore you. I cannot tell how much I love you; and I know a damsel who is bursting with rage about it."

"Who is that?" inquired the jealous girl.

"That is nothing to the purpose," said Phœbus. "Do you love me?"

"Do I?" said she.

"Well, that is enough. You shall see how I love you too. May the great devil Neptunus spit me upon his prong, if I don't make you the happiest girl in the world. We will have a pretty little box somewhere or other. My archers shall parade under your windows. They are all on horseback, and Captain Mignon's are fools to them. I will take you to the Grange de Rully—'tis a magnificent sight. Eighty thousand stand of arms; thirty thousand suits of bright armor, cuirasses or brigandines; the sixty-seven banners of the trades; the standards of the Parliament, the Chamber of Accompts, the workers of the mint—in short, a devil of a train. I will take you to see the lions in the King's Hotel, which all the women are very fond of."

For some moments the damsel, absorbed in her own charming thoughts, was drinking in the intoxicating tones of his voice, without attending to the meaning of his words.

"Oh! you shall be so happy!" continued the captain, at the same time examining the buckle of her belt.

"What are you about?" said she sharply, roused from her reverie.

"Nothing," replied Phœbus; "I was only saying that you must lay aside this strange mountebank dress when you are with me."

"When I am with you, my Phœbus!" said the girl, affectionately; and again she became silent and thoughtful. All at once she turned toward him. "Phœbus," said she, with an expression of infinite love, "instruct me in thy religion."

"My religion!" cried the captain, bursting into a hoarse laugh. "I instruct you in my religion! Blood and thunder! What do you want with my religion?"

"That we may be married," replied the Egyptian.

The captain's face assumed a mixed expression of surprise, disdain, and licentious passion. "Pooh!" said he; "what should we marry for?"

The Bohemian turned pale, and sorrowfully drooped her head.

"My sweet one," resumed Phœbus, tenderly, "these are silly notions. Of what use is marriage? Do people love one another less for not having mangled Latin in the shop of a priest?" As he thus spoke in his kindest tones, his eye glistened more and more.

Dom Claude, meanwhile, was watching all that passed. The planks of which the door was made were so decayed as to leave large chasms for his hawk's eyes. The priest quivered and boiled at the scene. The sight of the beauteous girl thus *tête-à-tête* with the ardent officer seemed to infuse molten lead into his veins. An extraordinary commotion took place within him. Whoever could have seen, at that moment, the face of the unhappy man closely pressed against the crevices of the door, would have taken it for the face of a tiger looking through the bars of a cage at some jackal devouring a gazelle. His eye flamed like a candle through the chasms.

All at once, Phœbus snatched away the neckerchief of the Egyptian. The poor girl, who had continued pale and thoughtful, started up, and hastily retreated from the enterprising officer. Casting a glance at her bare shoulders, blushing, confused, and dumb with shame, she crossed her two finely turned arms over her bosom to conceal it. But for the flush that crimsoned her cheeks, whoever had seen her thus silent, motionless, and with downcast eyes, would have taken her for a statue of Modesty.

This attack of the captain's upon her toilet had uncovered the mysterious amulet which she wore about her neck.

"What is that?" said he, seizing this pretext for approaching the beautiful creature whom his vehemence had just alarmed.

"Touch it not," answered she, sharply; " 'tis my protector. It is this that will enable me to find my family, if I do nothing unworthy of it. Oh, leave me, captain, I beseech you! Ah, mother! my poor mother! where art thou? Help, help thy child!—Pray, Captain Phœbus, give me my neckerchief!"

"Oh, mademoiselle!" said Phœbus, stepping back in a tone of indifference, "I see plainly that you love me not."

"Not love him!" exclaimed the unhappy girl, at the same time clinging to the captain, and making him sit down by her. "Not love thee, my Phœbus! Naughty man to say so! Wouldst thou break my heart? I am thine. Of what use to me is the amulet! what need have I of a mother! to me thou art father and mother, since I love thee! Phœbus, my beloved Phœbus, look, look at me; thou wilt not put away from thee one who comes to place herself in thy hands! My soul, my life, my all, are thine. So I am but loved, I shall be the proudest and the happiest of woman. And when I am grown old and ugly, Phœbus, when I shall be no longer fit for thee to love, then permit me to be thy servant. Others shall then embroider scarfs for thee, but thou wilt let me clean thy boots and thy spurs, and brush thy uniform. Thou wilt grant me that indulgence, wilt thou not, my Phœbus? Meanwhile take me; let me belong to thee, and be the only object of thy love! We Egyptians want nothing else but air and love."

As she thus spoke, she threw her arms round the neck of the officer, and with a sweet smile and tearful eye fixed upon him a beseeching look. The captain pressed his burning lips to her bosom.

All at once above the head of the captain she beheld another head—a livid, green convulsive face, with the look of one of the damned; close to this face was a hand holding a dagger. It was the face and hand of the priest. Unperceived by them, he had contrived to break open the crazy door, and there he was!

The girl was struck speechless and motionless with horror by this terrible apparition; like a dove raising her head at the moment when a falcon with glaring eyes is looking into her nest. She had not even the power to shriek. She saw the dagger descend upon the captain, and rise again reeking. "Perdition!" he exclaimed, and fell. She swooned.

At the moment when her eyes closed, and her senses were forsaking her, she thought that she felt a kiss, burning as a hot iron, impressed upon her lips. On coming to herself, she was surrounded by soldiers belonging to the watch. The captain was carried away bathed in his blood. The priest was gone. The window at the farther end of the chamber, which looked toward the river, was wide open. A cloak, supposed to belong to the officer, was picked up, and she heard the men saying to one another, " 'Tis a sorceress who has stabbed a captain."

35

For upward of a month Gringoire and the whole of the crew in the Cour des Miracles had been in a state of extreme anxiety. La Esmeralda was missing. They knew neither what had become of her, which sorely grieved the Duke of Egypt and his vagabond subjects, nor what had become of her goat, which redoubled Gringoire's sorrow. One night the girl had disappeared, and all researches had proved bootless; no traces of her could be discovered. Some of the mendicant tribe had told Gringoire that they had met her that evening, near the Pont St. Michel, walking along with an officer; but this husband after the fashion of Bohemia was an incredulous philosopher; and besides, he knew better than anyone else how well his wife could defend herself. He had had abundant opportunities of judging what invincible chastity resulted from the two combined virtues of the amulet and the Egyptian, and had mathematically calculated the resistance of that chastity to the second power. He was therefore quite easy on that point.

But for this very reason he was the more puzzled to account for her disappearance. So deeply did he take it to heart, that he would have fretted the flesh off his bones, had it been possible for him to become thinner than he was. He had forgotten everything else, even his literary pursuits, not excepting his great work *De Figuris regularibus et irregularibus*, which he intended to get printed with the first money he should have. For he was over head and ears in love with printing, ever since he had seen the *Didaskalon* of Huge St. Victor, printed with the celebrated types of Vindelin of Spire.

One day, while sorrowfully passing the Tournelle, a prison for criminals, he perceived a concourse of people about one of the doors of the Palace of Justice. "What is going forward here?" he asked a young man who was coming out.

"I know not, sir," answered the young man. "I am told that they are trying a woman for murdering an officer of the king's ordnance. As there seems to be something of sorcery in the business, the bishop and the official have interfered, and my brother, the archdeacon of Josas, devotes all his time to it. I wanted to speak to him, but could not get at him for the crowd, which vexed me exceedingly, as I am in great need of money."

"Alas sir!" said Gringoire, "I wish it was in my power to lend you some; but my breeches are all in holes, not with crowns or any other coin, I can assure you."

He durst not tell the young man that he knew his brother, the archdeacon, whom he had never called upon since the scene in the church—a neglect of which he felt ashamed.

The scholar went his way, and Gringoire followed the crowd who were ascending the great staircase. In his estimation there was nothing like a criminal trial for dispelling melancholy, the judges being in general so amusingly stupid. The people with whom he had mingled moved on and elbowed one another in silence. After a slow and tiresome shuffling along an endless passage, which ran winding through the palace like the intestinal canal of the old structure, he arrived at a low door opening into a hall, in which, from his tall stature, he was enabled to overlook above the undulating heads of the crowd.

The hall was spacious and dark, which made it appear still larger. The day was declining; the tall pointed windows admitted but a faint light, which expired before it reached the vaulted roof, an enormous trellis of carved woodwork, the thousand figures of which seemed to move confusedly in the dusk. There were already several lighted candles here and there upon the tables, which threw their rays upon the heads of clerks poring over heaps of papers. The anterior part of the hall was occupied by the crowd; on the right and left were lawyers seated at tables; at the farther end, upon a raised platform, a great number of judges, men with immovable and sinister-looking faces, the last rows of whom were scarcely discernible for the darkness. The walls were sprinkled with abundance of fleurs-de-lis. A large crucifix was indistinctly seen above the judges, and on every side an array of pikes and halberts, which the light of the candles seemed to tip with fire.

"Sir," said Gringoire to one of his neighbors, "who are all those persons ranged in rows yonder, like prelates in council?"

"Sir," answered the neighbor, "those are the counselors of the great chamber on the right, and the counselors of inquiry on the left; the masters in black gowns and the messires in red ones."

"And who is that great red porpoise above them?" inquired Gringoire.

"That is monsieur the president."

"And those rams behind him?" continued Gringoire, who, as we have already observed, was not fond of magistrates; perhaps owing to the grudge which he bore the Palace of Justice ever since his dramatic miscarriage.

"They are the masters of requests of the king's hotel."

"And that boar in front of them?"

"The clerk to the court of parliament."

"And that crocodile, on the right?"

"Master Philippe Lheulier, advocate extraordinary to the king."

"And that great black cat on the left?"

"Master Jacques Charmolue, the king's proctor in the ecclesiastical court, with the gentlemen of the officiality."

"But, I pray you, sir, what are all these worthy folks about here?"

"They are trying somebody."

"Who is it? I do not see the accused."

"It is a young woman, sir. She stands with her back toward us, and we can't see her for the crowd. Why there she is, where you see that group of halberts."

"Do you know her name?" asked Gringoire.

"No, sir, I am but just come; but I presume that there is sorcery in the case, as the official attends the trial."

"Come on!" said our philosopher—"let us watch all these lawyers banqueting on human flesh! 'Tis a sight as well as any other."

Here the bystanders imposed silence on the interlocutors. An important witness was under examination.

"Gentlemen," said an old woman in the middle of the hall, who was so muffled up as to look like a walking bundle of rags, "gentlemen, it is as true as that my name is Falourdel, and that I have kept house for forty years at the Pont St. Michel, and regularly paid rent, taxes, and rates. A poor old woman now, gentlemen, but once reckoned handsome, though I say it. One night I was spinning, when there comes a knock at my door. I asked, 'Who's there?' and there was such a swearing! I opened the door; two men came in; a man in black, with a comely officer. Nothing was to be seen of the man in black but his eyes, for all the world like two burning coals; all the rest of him was cloak and hat. 'St. Martha's room!' said they to me. That is my room upstairs, gentlemen, my best room. They gave me a crown. I put it into my drawer, saying to myself: It will serve tomorrow to buy tripe with at the shambles of the Gloriette. Well, we went upstairs, and while my back was turned, the man in black was gone. This staggered me a little. The officer, as handsome a gentleman as you would wish to set eyes on, went downstairs with me, and out he goes. By the time I had spun a quarter of a bobbin, in he comes again with a pretty poppet of a damsel, who would have dazzled you like the sun if she had been properly attired. She had with her a goat; a large goat; it might be black, it might be white, I don't recollect now. The girl—that was no concern of mine—but the goat put me out, I must say. I don't like those animals; they have got a beard and horns, too, like a man, and then the thing smells of witchcraft. However, I said nothing, and why should I? Had not I got the crown? And all right too, my lord, wasn't it? So I took the captain and the girl to the room upstairs, and left them alone, that is to say, with the goat. I went down, and fell to spinning again. But I ought to tell you that my house has a groundfloor and a floor above; the back of it looks to the river, like all the other houses on the bridge, and the windows both of the ground floor and the chamber open toward the water. Well, as I said just now, I began spinning again. I can't tell, not I, why I thought of the goblin-monk which the goat had put into my head—and then the girl was dressed in such a strange fashion! Well, all at once I heard such a scream upstairs, and something fall upon the floor, and the window open. I ran to mine which is below, and saw a black figure drop before my eyes, and tumble into the water. It was a specter in the habit of a priest. The moon was shining bright, so I saw it as plain as I see you now. It swam away toward the city. I was all over of a tremble, and called the watch. When those gentlemen came in, they did not know what to make of it at first, and being rather fuddled, they fell to beating me. I soon set them right. We went up, and what should we find but my best chamber drenched with blood, the captain laid at full length with a dagger in his bosom, the girl shamming dead, and the goat frightened out of its wits! 'A pretty job!' said I; 'it will take me a fortnight to get the floor clean again—scour and scrub it as I will.' They carried away the officer—poor young man!—and the girl with her bosom all bare. But, worse than all, next day, when I went to the drawer for the crown to buy tripe, lo and behold! I found nothing but a withered leaf where I had left it!"

The old woman ceased speaking. A murmur of horror arose from the auditory. "The specter, the goat, and all that, look very like sorcery," said Gringoire to a neighbor. "Ay, and the withered leaf," added another. "No doubt," observed a third, "it was a witch colleague with the goblin-monk to rob the officer." Gringoire himself could scarcely help thinking that there was some probability in the conjecture.

"Witness," said the president in a dignified manner, "have you nothing further to communicate to the court?"

"No, my lord," replied the old woman, "only that in the report my house is called a crazy, filthy hovel, which is a scandalous falsehood. To be sure the houses on the bridge are not so goodly as some, but yet the butchers like to live in them, and their wives are as proper, comely women as you would wish to see."

The magistrate whom Gringoire had likened to a crocodile now arose. "Silence!" said he. "I beg you my lord and gentlemen, to bear in mind that a dagger was found upon the accused. Witness, have you brought with you the leaf into which the crown given you by the demon was changed?"

"Yes, sir," she replied, "here it is."

An usher handed the dead leaf to the crocodile, who gave a sinister shake of the head, and passed it to the president; and the president sent it to the king's proctor in the ecclesiastical court; so that it went the round of the hall. "Upon my word, a birch leaf!" ejaculated Master Jacques Charmolue; "a fresh proof of sorcery!"

A counselor then rose and spoke. "Witness," said he, "two men went upstairs together at your house; a man in black, who immediately disappeared, and whom you afterward saw swimming in the Seine, in the habit of a priest, and the officer. Which of the two gave you the crown?"

The old woman considered for a moment. "It was the officer," said she.

A murmur again ran through the court. "Aha!" thought Gringoire, "that alters the case materially."

Master Phillippe Lheulier, advocate extraordinary to the king, again interposed. "Let me remind you, my lord and gentlemen, that the officer in his deposition, taken in writing by his bedside, while admitting that he had a confused idea at the moment when he was accosted by the man in black, that it might be the goblin-monk, added, that the phantom had strongly pressed him to keep his appointment with the accused; and, when the said captain observed that he had no money, he gave him the crown with which the officer paid the witness Falourdel. The crown therefore is a coin of hell."

This conclusive observation appeared to dispel all the lingering doubts of Gringoire and the other skeptics among the audience.

"Gentlemen are in possession of the papers," added the king's advocate, sitting down; "they can refer to the deposition of Captain Phœbus de Chateaupers."

At that name the accused rose. Her head was seen above the crowd. To his horror, Gringoire recognized La Esmeralda.

She was pale; her hair, once so gracefully plaited, and studded with sequins, was disheveled; her lips were livid, her eyes hollow. Alas! what a change!

"Phœbus!" exclaimed she, wildly, "where is he?—Oh, my lords, before you put me to death, for mercy's sake tell me if he still lives!"

"Silence, prisoner!" replied the president; "we have nothing to do with that."

"If you have any pity, tell me if he is alive!" she resumed, clasping her attenuated hands; and her chains were heard to rustle along her dress.

"Well," said the king's advocate, dryly, "he is dying. Are you satisfied?"

The unhappy girl sank down again upon her seat, voiceless, tearless, white as a waxen image.

The president stooped toward a man placed at his feet, who had a gold-laced cap, a black gown, a chain about his neck, and a wand in his hand. "Usher, bring in the second prisoner."

All eyes turned toward a small door which opened, and, to the extreme agitation of Gringoire, in walked a pretty goat with gilt horns and hoofs. The elegant creature stopped for a moment on the threshold, stretching out her neck, as if, perched on the point of some rock, she was overlooking a vast plain beneath her. All at once she descried the Bohemian, and, springing over the table and the head of a clerk of the court, in two leaps she was at her knees: she then nestled gracefully on the feet of her mistress, soliciting a word or a caress; but the prisoner remained motionless, and poor Djali herself could not obtain even a look.

"Nay, by my fay! 'tis the same nasty beast," cried old Falourdel. "I could swear positively to them both."

"If it so pleaseth you, my lord and gentlemen," began Charmolue, "we will proceed to the examination of the second prisoner."

The second prisoner was the goat, sure enough. Nothing was more common in those days than to indict animals for sorcery.

The proctor of the ecclesiastical court then pronounced this solemn denunciation: "If the demon which possesses this goat, and which has withstood all the exorcisms that have been tried, persists in his wicked courses, and shocks the court with them, we forewarn him that we shall be forced to demand that he be sentenced to the gallows or the stake."

Cold perspiration covered the face of Gringoire. Charmolue took from a table the tambourine of the Egyptian, held it in a particular way to the goat, and asked, "What hour is it?"

The goat eyed him with intelligent look, raised her gilt foot and struck seven strokes. It was actually seven o'clock. A shudder of terror thrilled the crowd. Gringoire could no longer contain himself.

"The creature will be her own destruction!" he exclaimed aloud. "See you not that she knows not what she does?"

"Silence among the lieges in the court!" cried the usher, sternly.

Jacques Charmolue, by shifting the tambourine in various ways, made the goat exhibit several other tricks respecting the day of the month, the month of the year, and so forth, which the reader has already witnessed; and, from an optical delusion peculiar to judicial proceedings, the very same spectators, who had perhaps many a time applauded the innocent pranks of Djali in the streets, were horror-stricken at them within the walls of the Palace of Justice. The goat was decidedly the devil.

But when the king's proctor had emptied out upon the table a little leathern bag filled with detached letters which Djali had about her neck, and the goat was seen sorting out with her foot the separate letters of the fatal name Phœbus, the spells to which the captain had fallen a victim appeared to be irresistibly demonstrated, in the opinion of all; and the Bohemian, that exquisite dancer, who had so often enchanted the gazers with her graceful performances, was an odious witch.

The poor girl, meanwhile, exhibited not the least sign of life; neither the fond evolutions of her Djali, nor the threats of the judges, nor the muttered imprecations of the audience, were noticed by her. In order to rouse her, a sergeant went to her, and shook her most unmercifully while the president, raising his voice in a solemn tone, thus spoke: "Girl, you are of Bohemian race, addicted to unrighteous deeds. In company with the bewitched goat, your accomplice, implicated in this indictment, you did, on the night of March 29 last, in concert with the powers of darkness, and by the aid of charms and unlawful practices, stab and slay Phœbus de Chateaupers, captain of the archers of the king's ordnance. Do you persist in denying this?"

"Oh horrors of horrors!" exclaimed the prisoner, covering her face with her hands. "Oh, my Phœbus! This is hell indeed!"

"Do you persist in denying it?" asked the president, coldly.

"I do deny it!" said she, in a tearful tone, and with flashing eye, as she rose from her seat.

"Then," proceeded the president, calmly, "how do you explain the facts laid to your charge?"

In broken accents, she replied: "I have already told you. I know not. It was a priest—a priest, a stranger to me—an infernal priest who haunts me!"

"There it his!" resumed the judge, "the goblin-monk."

"Oh, sirs, have pity upon me! I am but a poor girl."

"Of Egypt," continued the judge.

Master Jacques Charmolue, in his gentlest, softest tone, then said, "In consequence of the painful obstinacy of the prisoner, I demand the application of the torture."

"Granted," said the president.

The unhappy girl shook all over. She rose, however, at the order of the halberdiers, and, preceded by Charmolue and the officers of the officiality, walked with tolerably firm step, between two files of partisans, toward a low door, which suddenly opened, and closed after her. To Gringoire it seemed as though she had been swallowed up by the gaping jaws of some monster. As soon as she had disappeared, a plaintive bleating was heard. It was the poor goat bewailing the loss of her mistress.

The proceedings were suspended. A counselor observed that the judges must be fatigued, and that they would be detained a long time if they waited for the conclusion of the torture; to which the president replied, that a magistrate ought to have learned to sacrifice personal convenience to his duty.

"The provoking hussy!" said an old judge, "to bring the torture upon herself just now, when we ought to be at supper!"

36

Having ascended and descended some steps in passages so dark that they were lighted in broad day by lamps,

La Esmeralda, still surrounded by her dismal escort, was thrust by the sergeants of the place into a room of sinister aspect. This room, of circular shape, occupied the ground floor of one of the towers that at the present day still perforate the stratum of modern edifices with which new Paris has covered the old city. There were no windows in this dungeon, neither was there any other aperture than the low entrance closed by a strong iron door. At the same time there was no want of light; in the massive substance of the walls there was a furnace, in which burned a large fire, that threw a red glare over the den, and quite eclipsed the light of a miserable candle placed in a corner. The iron portcullis, which served as a door to the furnace, was drawn up at that moment, so that at its flaming mouth there were to be seen only the lower extremities of its bars, resembling a row of black, sharp, parted teeth; which made the furnace look like the mouth of one of those dragons of the legends vomiting fire and smoke. By the light which it diffused, the prisoner perceived around the room a variety of instruments, the uses of which were unknown to her. In the middle was a leathern mattress laid almost flat upon the floor on which hung a thong with a buckle fastened to a copper ring, which a grotesque monster sculptured in the keystone of the vaulted ceiling held between his teeth. Tongs, pincers, broad plowshares, lay pellmell, heating in the fire in the interior of the furnace. Its blood-red flare presented to the eye in the whole circumference of the chamber naught but an assemblage of fearful objects. This Tartarus was merely called the chamber of the question.

On the bed was carelessly seated Pierrat Torterue, the "sworn tormentor." His assistants, two square-faced gnomes, with leathern aprons and linen breeches, were stirring the coals under the iron implements.

The poor girl had need to muster her courage; on entering this den she was struck with horror. The sergeants of the bailiff of the place ranged themselves on one side, and the priests of the officiality on the other. In one corner was a table, at which sat a clerk with pen, ink, and paper.

Master Jacques Charmolue approached the Egyptian with one of his kindest smiles. "My dear girl," said he, "do you persist in your denial?"

"Yes," she replied, in a voice scarcely audible.

"In that case," rejoined Charmolue, "it will be very painful to us to question you more urgently than we would. Take the trouble to sit down on this bed. Master Pierrat, give place to this young woman, and shut the door."

Pierrat rose growling. "If I shut the door," muttered he, "my fire will go out."

"Well then, my good fellow," replied Charmolue, "leave it open."

Meanwhile La Esmeralda remained standing. That leathern bed, on which so many wretched creatures had writhed in agony, frightened her. Horror thrilled the very marrow of her bones; there she stood bewildered, stupefied. At a sign from Charmolue, the two assistants laid hold of her, and placed her in a sitting posture on the bed. Those men did not hurt her, but when they grasped her, when the leather touched her, she felt all her blood flow back to her heart. She looked wildly around the room. She fancied that she saw those ugly implements of torture—which were, among the instruments of all kinds that she had hitherto seen, what bats, millipedes, and spiders are among birds and reptiles—quitting their places and advancing from every part of the room toward her, to crawl over her, and to bite, pinch, and sting her.

"Where is the doctor?" asked Charmolue.

"Here," answered a man in a black gown, whom she had not yet noticed.

She shuddered.

"Damoiselle," resumed the smooth tongue of the proctor of the ecclesiastical court, "for the third time, do you persist in denying the charges preferred against you?"

This time her voice failed; she was able only to nod an affirmative.

"You persist!" cried Charmolue. "I am very sorry for it, but I am obliged to perform the duty of my office."

"Mr. Proctor," said Pierrat, abruptly, "what shall we begin with?"

Charmolue paused for a moment, with the ambiguous grimace of a poet at a loss for a rhyme.

"With the buskin," he at length replied.

The unfortunate girl felt herself so totally abandoned by God and man, that her head sank upon her bosom, like something inert and destitute of animation. The tormentor and the physician approached her together; at the same time the two assistants began to rummage in their hideous arsenal. At the clanking of the horrible irons, the unhappy girl shivered like a dead frog subjected to the action of galvanism. "Oh, my Phœbus!" murmured she, in so low a tone as to be inaudible. She then relapsed into her former insensibility and death-like silence. This sight would have rent any other heart than the hearts of judges. The wretched being to whom all this tremendous apparatus of saws, wheels, and pulleys was about to be applied; the being about to be consigned to the iron grip of executioners and pincers, was that gentle, tender, frail creature—poor grain of millet, given up by human justice to be ground in the horrible mill of the torture!

Meanwhile the horny hands of Pierrat's men had brutally stripped that beautiful leg, and that small elegant foot, which had so often delighted the bystanders with their gracefulness and agility in the streets of Paris. " 'Tis a pity!" muttered the tormentor, surveying those graceful and delicate forms. Had the archdeacon been present, he would assuredly have bethought him at that moment of his symbol of the spider and the fly. Presently the poor girl saw through the cloud that spread itself before her eyes the buskin approaching; presently her foot was hidden from sight in the iron-bound apparatus. Terror then restored her strength. "Take it off!" cried she wildly, at the same time

starting up. "For mercy's sake!" She sprang from the bed
with the intention of throwing herself at the feet of the
king's proctor; but, her leg being confined in the heavy
block of oak sheathed with iron, she sank down powerless
as a bee having its wings loaded with lead. On a sign from
Charmolue, she was replaced on the bed, and two coarse
hands fastened round her slender waist the thong that hung
from the ceiling.

"For the last time," said Charmolue, with his imperturbable benignity, "do you confess the crimes laid to your
charge?"

"I am innocent."

"Then how do you explain the circumstances alleged
against you?"

"Alas, sir, I know not."

"You deny them?"

"Everything!"

"Begin," said Charmolue to Pierrat.

Pierrat turned a screw; the buskin became more and
more contracted, and the wretched sufferer gave one of
those horrible shrieks which baffle the orthography of every human language.

"Hold!" said Charmolue to Pierrat. "Do you confess?"
he then asked the Egyptian.

"Everything!" cried the miserable girl. "I confess—
mercy! mercy!"

In defying the torture she had not calculated her
strength. Poor thing! her life had till then been so bright,
so cheery, so joyous!—the first pang overcame her.

"Humanity obliges me to inform you," observed the
king's proctor, "that, though you confess, you have nothing but death to expect."

"I wish for it," said she. And she sank back upon the
leathern bed, suspended, as if lifeless, by the thong buckled round her waist.

"So, my pretty!—hold up a little!" said Master Pierrat,
raising her. "You look like the golden sheep about the
neck of Monsieur of Burgundy."

Jacques Charmolue again raised his voice. "Clerk, write. Bohemian girl, you confess your participation in the feasts, sabbaths, and practices of hell, with demons, sorcerers, and witches? Answer."

"Yes," said she, in so low a tone as to be scarcely heard.

"You confess that you have seen the ram, which Beelzebub displays in the clouds to summon his children to their sabbath, and which is seen only by sorcerers?"

"Yes."

"You confess that you have had commerce with the devil in the shape of the goat implicated in these proceedings?"

"Yes."

"Lastly, you declare and confess that, instigated by, and with the assistance of the devil and the goblin-monk, you did, on the night of March 29 last, kill and slay a captain, named Phœbus de Chateaupers?"

She fixed her glazed eyes upon the magistrate, and replied, as if mechanically, without shock or convulsion, "Yes." It was evident that her spirit was utterly broken.

"Write, clerk," said Charmolue. Then turning to Pierrat's men: "Loose the prisoner," he proceeded, "and let her be taken back into court."

When the buskin was removed, the proctor examined her foot, still numbed with the pain. "Come, come," said he, " 'tis not much the worse. You cried out in time. You would soon be able to dance as well as ever, my beauty!" Then addressing the priests of the officiality. "Justice is enlightened at last," said he. " 'Tis a consolation, gentlemen! and the damsel will bear witness that we have shown her all possible lenity."

37

W hen she again entered the court, pale and halting, she was greeted with a general buzz of pleasure. On the part of the auditory, it arose from that feeling of gratified impatience which is experienced at the theater, at the conclusion of the last interlude of a play, when the curtain rises, and the fifth act begins; and on the part of the judges, from the prospect of being soon dismissed to their suppers. The poor little goat, too, bleated for joy. She would have run to her mistress, but she had been tied to a bench.

It was now dark night. The candles, having received no accession to their number, gave so faint a light that the walls of the court were not discernible. The darkness enveloped objects in a sort of haze. A few unfeeling faces of judges alone were with difficulty distinguishable. Opposite to them, at the other extremity of the long hall, they could perceive an undefined patch of white moving along the dark floor. It was the prisoner.

She advanced with faltering steps to her place. When Charmolue had magisterially resumed possession of his, he sat down; presently rising again, he said, without too strongly betraying the vanity of success: "The accused has confessed the crime."

"Bohemian girl," began the president, "you have confessed then all your misdeeds of magic, of prostitution, and of murder committed on the body of Phœbus de Chateaupers?"

Her heart was wrung, and she was heard to sob in the dark. "Whatever you please," answered she, faintly, "only put me to death soon!"

"Mr. Proctor," said the president, "the court is ready to hear your requisitions."

Master Charmolue produced a tremendous roll of paper, from which he began to read with abundant gesticulation, and the exaggerated emphasis of the bar, a Latin oration, in which all the evidence was built upon Ciceronian periphrases, flanked by quotations from Plautus, his favorite comic writer. We are sorry that we cannot treat the reader to this delectable composition. The orator delivered it with wonderful action. Before he had finished the exordium, big drops of perspiration trickled from his brow, and his eyes appeared to be starting from his head. All at once, he stopped short in the middle of a sentence. His look, which was wont to be so bland, nay even so stupid, became terrific. "Gentlemen," cried he—now deigning to speak in French, for it was not in his manuscript—"to such a degree is Satan mixed up in this business, that yonder he is personally present at our proceedings, and making a mock of their majesty!" As he thus spoke, he pointed with his finger at the little goat, which, observing the gesticulations of Charmolue, had seated herself upon her rump, and was imitating as well as she could, with her forepaw and her bearded head, the pathetic pantomime of the king's proctor in the ecclesiastical court. The reader will recollect that this was one of her most diverting tricks. This incident, the last proof, produced a powerful effect. To put an end to this scandal, the goat's legs were bound, and the king's proctor resumed the thread of his eloquent harangue. It was very long, but the winding-up was admirable. He concluded with requiring that the prisoner should be condemned, in the first place to pay a certain pecuniary indemnity; in the second, to do penance before the grand porch of Notre Dame; and thirdly, to be taken with her goat to the Place de Grève, and there executed.

He put on his cap and sat down.

A man in black gown, near the prisoner, then rose; it was her advocate. The judges, feeling in want of their supper, began to murmur.

"Be brief," said the president.

"My lord," replied the advocate, "since the prisoner has confessed the crime, I have but a few words to offer. In the Salic law there is this clause: 'If a witch have eaten a man, and she be convicted of it, she shall pay a fine of eight thousand deniers, which make two hundred sous in gold.' May it please the court then to sentence my client to pay this fine."

"That clause is become obselete," said the advocate extraordinary to the king.

"*Nego!*" replied the advocate of the prisoner.

"To the vote!" said a counselor; "the crime is proved, and it is late."

The question was put to the vote without leaving the court. The judges decided offhand; they were pressed for time. Their capped heads were seen uncovered one after another in the dusk, as the question was put to them successively in a low tone by the judge. The poor prisoner appeared to be looking at them; but her dim eye no longer saw the objects before it.

The clerk of the court began writing, and then handed a long parchment to the president. The unhappy girl heard a bustle among the people, pikes clashing together, and a chilling voice pronounced these words:

"Bohemian girl, on such a day as it shall please our lord the king, at the hour of noon, you shall be drawn in a tumbril, stripped to your chemise, barefoot, with a rope about your neck, to the great porch of the church of Notre Dame, and shall there do penance, holding in your hand a wax taper of two pounds' weight; and thence you shall be taken to the Place de Greve, and there hanged by the neck on the gallows of the city; and this your goat likewise; and you shall pay to the official three gold lions in reparation of the crimes by you committed and by you confessed, of sorcery, magic, incontinence, and murder done upon the body of Sieur Phœbus de Chateaupers. God receive your soul!"

"Oh! 'tis a dream!" murmured the prisoner, and she felt rough hands bearing her away.

38

In the Middle Ages, when a building was complete, there was almost as much of it underground as above. A palace, a fortress, a church, had always a double basement, unless it stood upon piles like Notre Dame. Under a cathedral there was a kind of subterraneous church, low, dark, mysterious, blind, and mute, beneath the upper nave, which was resplendent with light and rang with the pealing of organs and bells, night and day; sometimes it was a catacomb. In palaces, in bastiles, it was a prison, sometimes a sepulcher, and sometimes both together. These mighty edifices, the mode of whose formation and vegetation we have elsewhere described, had not merely foundations, but, as it were, roots, which shot out into the soil in chambers, in galleries, in staircases, like the building above them. Thus churches, palaces, bastiles, were buried up to the middle in the ground. The vaults of a building were another building, to which you descended instead of ascending, and which clapped its subterraneous stories beneath the exterior stories of the edifice, like those woods and mountains which appear reversed in the mirror of a lake beneath the woods and mountains rising from its banks.

At the Bastile St. Antoine, at the Palace of Justice, at the Louvre, these subterraneous edifices were prisons.

Into a dungeon of this kind—the *oubliettes* dug by Saint Louis, the *in pace* of the Tournelle—La Esmeralda was thrust after her condemnation, no doubt for fear of escape, with the colossal Palace of Justice over her head. Poor girl! she could not have stirred the smallest of the stones of which it was built. There needed not such a profusion of misery and torture to crush so frail a creature.

There she was, wrapped in darkness, buried, entombed, immured. Whoever had beheld her in this state, after having seen her sporting and dancing in the sun, would have shuddered. Cold as night, cold as death, not a breath of air in her dark locks, not a human sound in her ear, not a glimmer of light in her eyes, weighed down with chains, bent double, crouched beside a pitcher and a loaf of bread, on a little straw, in the pool formed beneath her by the water that dripped from the walls of her dungeon, motionless and scarcely breathing—what more could she suffer? Phœbus, the sun, the daylight, the free air, the streets of Paris, the dances which had won her such applause; her love-prattle with the officer; then the priest, the dagger, the blood, the torture, the gallows; all this had again passed before her mind, sometimes like a gay and golden vision, at others like a hideous nightmare; but it was now no more than a horrible and indistinct struggle, which was veiled in darkness, or than distant music played above on the earth, and which was not heard at the depth into which the unfortunate creature was sunk. Since she had been there, she had not walked, she had not slept. In this profound wretchedness, in the gloom of this dungeon, she could no more distinguish waking from sleeping, dream from reality than night from day. She had ceased to feel, to know, to think; at the utmost she mused. Never had living creature been plunged so deeply into nothingness.

Thus torpid, frozen, petrified, she had scarcely noticed the noise of a trap-door, which had opened twice or thrice somewhere near her, but without admitting a glimmer of light, and at which a hand had thrown down to her a crust of black bread. It was nevertheless the sole communication still left to her with mankind—the periodical visit of the jailer.

At length, one day, or one night—for midnight and noonday were of the same color in this sepulcher—she heard above her a louder noise than usually made by the jailer, when he brought her loaf and her pitcher of water. She raised her head, and saw a reddish ray entering through a cranny in a kind of trapdoor placed in the vaulted roof of the *in pace*. At the same time the heavy iron bars rattled; the door grated on its rusty hinges; it turned, and she saw a lantern, a hand, and the nether extremities of two figures, the door being too low for her to perceive their heads. The light so painfully affected her that she closed her eyes.

When she opened them again, the door was shut, a lantern was placed on one of the steps, and something like a human form stood before her. A black wrapper descended to its feet; a hood, of the same color concealed the face. Nothing was to be seen of the person, not even the hands. The figure looked like a long, black winding-sheet standing upright, under which something might be perceived moving. For some minutes she kept her eyes intently fixed on this spectral shape. Neither spoke. You would have taken them for two statues confronting each other. Two things only gave signs of life in the dungeon; the wick of the lantern which crackled owing to the dampness of the atmosphere, and the drip of the roof breaking this irregular crepitation by its monotonous plash, which caused the light of the lantern to dance in concentric rings on the oily surface of the pool.

At length the prisoner broke silence.

"Who are you?"

"A priest."

The word, the accent, the voice made her shudder.

"Are you prepared?" asked the priest, in a low tone.

"For what?"

"To die."

"Oh!" said she; "will it be soon?"

"Tomorrow."

Her head, which she had raised with a look of joy, again sank upon her bosom. " 'Tis a long time till then," murmured she. "Why not today? What difference could it have made to them?"

"You must be very unhappy, then?" said the priest after a moment's silence.

"I am very cold," she replied. She clasped her feet with her hands, and her teeth chattered.

The priest seemed from beneath the hood to cast his eyes around the dungeon. "Without light! without fire! in the water! 'Tis horrible!"

"Yes," answered she, with that air of timidity, which suffering had imparted; "everybody enjoys the light. Why should I be thrust into darkness?"

"Do you know," resumed the priest, after another pause, "why you are here?"

"I think I did know," said she, passing her attenuated fingers over her brow, as if to assist her memory, "but I don't now."

All at once, she burst out a-crying like a child. "I want to leave this place, sir. I am cold, I am afraid, and there are loathsome things which crawl up me."

"Well, come along with me."

With these words the priest took hold of her arm. The wretched girl was chilled to her inmost vitals, yet that hand produced a sensation of cold.

"Oh!" murmured she, "it is the icy hand of death! who are you then?"

The priest pushed back his hood. She looked at him. It was that sinister face which had so long haunted her, that demon-head which had appeared to her adored Phœbus, that eye which she had last seen glistening near a dagger.

This apparition, always so baneful to her, and which had thus hurried her on from misery to misery, roused her from her stupor. The thick veil which seemed to have spread itself over her memory was rent asunder. All the circumstances of her dismal adventure, from the night-scene at Falourdel's to her condemnation at La Tournelle, rushed at once upon her mind, not vague and confused as at the time of their occurrence, but distinct, fresh, palpitating, terrible. These recollections, almost obliterated by the excess of her sufferings, were revived by the somber figure before her, as the invisible words written with sympathetic ink upon white paper are brought out quite fresh on its being held to the fire. All the wounds of her heart seemed to be torn open afresh, and to bleed at once.

"Ha!" cried she, with a convulsive tremor, and holding her hands over her eyes, "it is the priest!" Presently dropping her enfeebled arms, she remained sitting, her head bent forward, her eye fixed on the ground, mute and trembling. The priest looked at her with the eye of a hawk, which has long been descending in silence from the topmost height of the heavens, in circles gradually more and more contracted around a poor lark squatting in the corn, and, having suddenly pounced like winged lightning upon his prey, clutches the panting victim in his talons.

She began to murmur in a faint tone: "Finish! finish! Give the last blow!" and she bowed down her head with terror, like the lamb awaiting the fatal stroke from the hand of the butcher.

At length he asked, "Are you afraid of me then?"

She made no reply.

"Are you afraid of me?" he repeated.

Her lips were compressed as though she smiled.

"Yes," said she, "the executioner jeers the condemned. For months he has been haunting, threatening, terrifying me! But for him, oh, God, how happy I should be! 'Tis he who killed him—who killed my Phœbus!" Sobbing vehemently, she raised her eyes to the priest. "Who are you, wretch?" she exclaimed. "What have I done to you? Why should you hate me thus? What grudge have you against me?"

"I love thee!" said the priest.

Her tears suddenly ceased. She eyed him with the vacant stare of an idiot. He had meanwhile sunk upon his knees, and gazed upon her with eye of fire.

"Dost thou hear? I love thee!" he repeated.

"Ah! what love?" ejaculated the unhappy creature, shuddering.

"The love of the damned," he replied.

Both remained silent for some minutes, overwhelmed by their emotions; he frantic, she stupid.

"Listen," at length said the priest, who had all at once recovered a wonderful degree of composure; "thou shalt know all. I will tell thee what hitherto I have scarcely dared to tell myself when I secretly examined my conscience, in those hours of night on which rests such thick darkness, that it seems as if God could no longer see us. Listen. Before I saw thee I was happy."

"And I!" she sighed forth faintly.

"Interrupt me not. Yes, I was happy, or at least I fancied that I was so. I was innocent. No head was lifted so high and so proudly as mine. Priests and doctors consulted me. Science was all in all to me; it was a sister, and a sister sufficed me. In spite, however, of my determination to acknowledge no other influence, that power of nature, which, silly youth as I was, I had hoped to crush for life, had more than once convulsively shaken the chain of those iron vows which bind me, miserable man that I am, to the cold stones of the altar. But, fasting, prayer, study, the mortifications of the cloister, restored to the spirit the dominion over the passions. I shunned the sex. Besides, I needed but to open a book, and all the impure vapors of my brain were dispelled by the splendor of science. In a few minutes the dark things of earth fled far away, and I found myself calm and serene in the soothing light of everlasting truth. So long as the demon sent only vague shadows of women to attack me, so long as they passed casually before my eyes, at church, in the streets, in the fields and scarcely recurred to my thoughts, I vanquished him with ease. Alas! if victory has not remained with me, it is the fault of God, who has not made man equal in strength to the demon. List to me. One day—"

The priest paused, and deep sighs burst from his bosom. He resumed:

"One day I was sitting at the window of my cell. I was reading. The window looked upon an open place. I heard the sound of a tambourine. Vexed at being disturbed in my reverie, I cast my eyes upon the place. What I there saw, and what others saw besides me, was not a sight made for human eye. There, in the middle of the pavement—it was noon—brilliant sunshine—a creature was dancing—a creature so beautiful that she might have served as a model for the mother of the Graces. Her eyes were black and splendid; amid her dark hair there were locks which, saturated, as it were, by the sun's beams, shone like threads of gold. Around her head, in her black tresses, there were pieces of metal, which sparkled in the sun, and formed a coronet of stars for her brow. I looked till I shuddered; I felt that the hand of Fate was upon me."

The priest, oppressed by emotion, again paused for a moment. He then proceeded:

"Half fascinated already, I endeavored to grasp at something to break my fall. I recollected the snares which Satan had previously spread for me. The creature before me possessed that superhuman beauty which can proceed only from heaven or from hell. She was not a mere girl, molded of our common clay, and faintly lighted within by the flickering ray of a female spirit. It was an angel, but an angel of darkness—of fire, not of light. At the moment when these thoughts were crossing my brain, I saw near her a goat, a beast which associates with witches. It looked at me and laughed. The noontide sun tipped its horns with flame. I then perceived the snare of the demon, and had no further doubt that thou wert come from hell, and come for my perdition. I believed so."

The priest here looked steadfastly in the face of the prisoner, and coldly added: "I believe so still."

"Meanwhile the charm began to operate by degrees. Thy dancing turned my brain. I felt the mysterious spell upon me. All that should have waked in my soul was lulled to sleep; and, like men perishing in the snow, I took pleasure in yielding to this slumber. All at once I heard thee begin to sing. What could I do? Thy singing was more fascinating than thy dancing. I would have fled. Impossible. I was riveted, rooted to the spot. I was forced to remain till thou hadst finished. My feet were ice, my head a furnace. At length, perhaps in pity to me, thy song

ceased, and I saw thee depart. The reflection of the dazzling vision, the sounds of the enchanting music, vanished
by degrees from my eyes, and died away in my ears. I
then sank into the corner of the window, stiff and helpless
as a fallen statue. The vesper bell awoke me; I fled; but
alas! something had fallen within me which I could not
raise up; something had come upon me, from which I
could not flee!"

He made another pause and thus proceeded:

"Yes, from that day I was possessed with a spirit that
was strange to me. I had recourse to my remedies—the
cloister, the altar, occupation, books. Follies! Oh, how hollow science sounds when you dash against it in despair a
head filled with passions. Knowest thou, maiden, what
thenceforth I always saw between the book and me? Thee,
thy shadow, the image of the luminous apparition which
had one day passed before me. But that image had no
longer the same color; it was somber, dark, gloomy, like
the black circle which long dances before the eye that has
been imprudent enough to gaze at the sun.

"Haunted by it incessantly, incessantly hearing thy song
ringing in my ears, incessantly seeing thy feet dancing
upon my breviary, my dreams by night, as well as my
thoughts by day, being full of thee. I was desirous to behold thee again, to touch thee, to know who thou wert, to
ascertain whether thou resemblest the ideal image impressed upon my mind, to dispel the phantasm by the reality. I waited for thee beneath porches, I lurked at the
corners of streets, I watched thee from my tower. Each
night, on examining myself, I found that I was more helpless, more spellbound, more bewitched, more undone.

"I learned who thou wert; Egyptian, Bohemian, gitana,
zingara. How could I longer doubt, that there was witchcraft in the case! I hoped that the law would break the
charm. A sorceress had bewitched Bruno d'Ast; he caused
her to be burned, and was cured. I knew him. I resolved
to try the same remedy. In the first place I obtained an ordinance forbidding thee to appear in the precincts of our

church, hoping to forget thee if I should see thee no more.
Reckless of this prohibition thou camest as usual. Then did
I conceive the idea of carrying thee off. One night I attempted to put it into execution. There were two of us. We
had thee already in our clutches, when that odious officer
came up and rescued thee. Thus did he commence thy sufferings, mine, and his own. At length, not knowing what
to do, I denounced thee to the official. I thought that I
should be cured, as Bruno d'Ast was. I had also a confused notion that a judicial process would deliver thee into
my power; that in a prison I should hold thee; that there
thou couldst not escape me. When one is doing evil 'tis
madness to stop halfway. The extremity of guilt has its de-
lirium of rapture.

"I should perhaps have renounced my design; my hideous idea would perhaps have evaporated from my brain
without producing any result. I imagined that it would de-
pend on me to follow up or to stop the proceedings whenever I pleased. But every wicked thought is inexorable,
and hurries to become a fact; and where I fancied myself
all-powerful, Fate proved more mighty than I. Alas! alas!
it was Fate that caught thee, and threw thee among the terrible works of the machine which I had secretly constructed. List to me. I have nearly done.

"One day—another day of lovely sunshine—I saw a
man walking before me, who pronounced thy name, who
laughed, and whose eyes glistened with unhallowed fire. I
followed him—thou knowest the rest."

He ceased speaking. "Oh, my Phœbus!" was all that the
poor girl could utter.

"Not that name!" said the priest, seizing her arm with
violence. "Name not that name! Wretched as we are, 'tis
that name which has undone us; or, rather, we are undoing
one another through the unaccountable freaks of fatality!
Thou art suffering, I know it. Thou art chilled; the darkness blinds thee; the dungeon clasps thee; but perhaps thou
hast still some light in the recesses of thy soul, were it but
thy childish love for that empty man who plays with thy

heart—while I, I carry a dungeon within me; within me is the chill of winter, the chill of despair; darkness enwraps my soul. Knowest thou all that I have suffered? I was present at thy trial. Yes, one of those priest's cowls covered torments unequaled but by those of the damned. I was there when that savage beast—oh—! I foreboded not the torture—bore thee off to his den. I saw thee stripped, and thy delicate limbs grasped by the infamous hands of the executioner. I saw thy foot, which I would have given an empire to kiss, that by which to have been trampled upon had been to me happiness, I saw it encased in the horrible buskin, which converts the members of a living being into a bloody jelly. At the shriek which was forced from thee, I plunged into my bosom a dagger that I carried beneath my wrapper. Look, it still bleeds."

He threw open his cassock. His breast was lacerated as by the claw of a tiger. The prisoner recoiled in horror.

"Oh, maiden!" said the priest; "take pity on me! Thou deemest thyself miserable. Alas! thou knowest not what misery is. It is to love a woman—to be a priest—to be hated—to love with all the energies of your soul—to feel that you would give for the least of her smiles your blood, your life, your character, your salvation, immortality and eternity, this world and the next—to regret that you are not a king, an emperor, an archangel, that you might throw a greater slave at her feet; to clasp her night and day in your sleeping and in your waking dreams—to see her fond of a soldier's uniform, and to have nothing to offer her but the squalid cassock, which is to her an object of fear and disgust—to be present, with heart bursting with jealousy and rage, while she lavishes on a silly braggart the treasures of love and beauty—to think of that delicious form till you writhe for whole nights on the floor of your cell, and to see all the endearments which you have reserved for her in imagination end in the torture—these, these are pincers heated in the fire of hell!"

The priest rolled in the water on the floor, and dashed his head against the stone steps of the dungeon. The Egyptian listened to him, looked at him. When he ceased speaking, breathless and exhausted, she repeated in a low tone: "Oh my Phœbus!"

The priest crawled toward her upon his knees. "I implore thee," he cried, "if thou hast any compassion, repulse me not. I love thee—I am miserable. When thou utterest that name, it is as if thou wert rending all the fibers of my heart. Only have pity. If thou goest to perdition, I must go with thee. All that I have done, I have done for this. The place where thou are wilt be to me a paradise; the sight of thee is more entrancing than that of heaven. Oh, say, wilt thou not have me? I should have thought that the day when a woman could reject such love the mountains would dissolve. Oh! if thou wouldst, how happy might we yet be! We would flee. I would enable thee to escape. We would seek that spot where there are the most trees, the most sunshine, the most azure sky."

She interrupted him with a loud thrilling laugh. "Look, father, you have blood upon your fingers!"

The priest, motionless for some moments, as if petrified, looked steadfastly at his hand.

"Why, yes," he at length replied with unwonted mildness, "abuse me, jeer me, overwhelm me!—but come, come! Let us lose no time. It will be tomorrow, I tell thee. The gibbet of the Greve—thou knowest the gibbet—it is always ready. It is horrible—to see thee drawn in that cart! Oh, mercy, mercy! Never did I feel as at this moment how dearly I love thee! Oh! come along with me. Thou shalt take thine own time to love me after I have saved thee. Thou shalt hate me as long as thou wilt. Only come. Tomorrow! tomorrow! the gallows! Oh, save thyself—spare me!"

In a state approaching to madness, he seized her arm, and would have hurried her along. She fixed her eyes intently upon him. "What is become of my Phœbus?" she inquired.

"Ah!" said the priest, loosing her arm from his grasp, "you have no pity!"

"What is become of Phœbus?" repeated she coolly.

"He is dead," replied the priest.

"Dead!" said she, still cold and passionless, "then why persuade me to live?"

He heard her not. "Oh, yes!" said he, as if talking to himself, "he must be dead. I struck home. The point must have reached his heart."

The girl rushed upon him like an enraged tigress, and thrust him toward the steps with supernatural force: "Begone, monster! begone, murderer! leave me to die! May the blood of us both mark thy brow with an everlasting stain! Be thine, priest! Never! never! Nothing shall bring us together, not even hell itself. Avaunt, accursed—never!"

The priest had stumbled upon the steps. Silently disengaging his feet from the skirts of his cassock, he picked up his lantern and began slowly to ascend to the door; he opened it and went forth. The prisoner gazed after him. All at once his head again appeared stooping over the stairs. His face was ghastly. With a rattle of rage and despair he cried: "I tell thee he is dead!"

She fell with her face to the ground; and no sound was then to be heard in the dungeon save the plash of the dropping water, which rippled the pool amid the profound darkness.

39

I cannot conceive anything in the world more delightful than the ideas awakened in the heart of a mother at the sight of her child's little shoe, especially if it be a holy day, a Sunday, a baptismal shoe; a shoe embroidered down to the very sole; a shoe upon which the infant has never yet stepped. This shoe is so small and so pretty; it is so

impossible for it to walk, that it seems to the mother as
though she saw her child. She smiles at it, she kisses it,
she talks to it; she asks herself if a foot can really be so
small; and, if the infant should be absent, the pretty shoe
is sufficient to set the sweet and tender creature before her
eyes. She fancies she sees it—she does see it—all alive,
all joyous, with its delicate hands, its round head, its pure
lips, its serene eyes, the white of which is blue. If it be
winter, there it is, crawling upon the carpet, climbing labo-
riously upon a stool, and the mother trembles lest it should
approach too near to the fire. If it be summer, it is creeping about in the court-yard or in the garden, looking inno-
cently and fearlessly at the big dogs and the big horses,
pulling up the grass growing between the stones, playing
with the shells and the flowers, and making the gardener
scold on finding sand on his borders and mold on his
paths. All about it is bright, joyous, and playful, like itself,
even to the very breeze and the sunshine, which sports together in the locks of its soft hair. All this the little shoe
sets before the mother, and it makes her heart melt like
wax before the fire.

But then the child is lost, these thousand images of joy,
delight, and affection, which crowd around the little shoe,
are transformed into as many frightful things. The pretty
little embroidered shoe then becomes but an instrument of
torture, which is incessantly racking the heart of the
mother. It is still the same fiber that vibrates— the deepest
and the most keenly sensitive fiber—not under the caresses of an angel, but in the grip of a demon.

One morning when the sun of May was rising in one of
these deep blue skies, beneath which Garofalo loved to
picture the taking down from the cross, the recluse of Rolande's Tower heard the rumbling of wheels, the tramp of
horses, and the clanking of iron in the Place de Greve. The
noise scarcely roused her; she tied her hair over her ears
that she might not hear it, and again fell to gaze upon her
knees at the inanimate object which she had thus adored
for fifteen years. To her this little shoe was, as we have al-

ready observed, the universe. Her thoughts were wrapped up in it, never to be parted from it but by death. How many bitter imprecations, how many touching complaints, how many earnest prayers she had addressed to Heaven on the subject of this charming little shoe of rose-colored satin, was known to the cell of Rolande's Tower alone. Never were keener sorrows poured forth over an object so pretty and so delicate. On this particular morning her grief seemed to burst forth with greater violence than usual; and she was heard from without bewailing herself with a loud and monotonous voice which wrung the heart.

"Oh, my child!" said she, "my child! my poor, dear little child!—never, no never shall I see thee more!—and still it seems as if it had happened but yesterday. Oh, my God! my God! better she had not been given to me at all than to have her taken from me so soon! And yet thou must know that our children are a part of ourselves, and that a mother who has lost her child is tempted not to be. Ah! wretch that I was, to go out that day! Oh, Lord! Lord! to snatch her from me thus, thou couldst never have seen me with her, when I warmed her, all glee, before the fire, when she ceased sucking to laugh in my face, when I made her little feet step up my bosom to my very lips! Hadst thou seen this, Oh, my God! thou wouldst have had pity on my joy; thou wouldst not have ravished from me the only love that was left in my heart! Was I then so vile a wretch, Oh, Lord! that thou couldst not look at me before condemning me! Alas! alas! there is the shoe, but where is the foot? where is the child? My child! I want my child! What is it to me that she is in Paradise? I want none of your angels; I want my child. Oh, that I could but once more, only once, put this pretty shoe on her rosy little foot, I would die blessing thee, Holy Virgin!—But no—fifteen years!—she must be grown up now!—Unfortunate girl! 'tis too certain that I shall never see thee more, not even in heaven, for there I shall never enter. Oh, what auguish!—to say, there is her shoe and that is all."

The wretched creature threw herself upon that shoe, a

source of solace and of sorrow for so many years; and she
sobbed as though her heart would break, just as she had
done on the very first day. Grief like this never grows old.
Though the garments of mourning become threadbare and
lose their color, the heart remains black as ever.

At this moment the brisk and merry voices of boys
passed before her cell. At the sight of the sound of children, the unhappy mother would always dart into the darkest nook of her sepulcher, with such precipitation that you
would think she was striving to bury her head in the wall,
in order that she might not hear them. On this occasion,
contrary to her custom, she started up and listened attentively. One of the boys was just saying to another, "They
are going to hang an Egyptian today."

With the sudden bound of the spider, that we lately saw
rushing upon the fly entangled in his net, she sprang to the
aperture which looked, as the reader knows, toward the
Place de Greve. A ladder was actually reared against
the permanent gallows, and the hangman was engaged in
adjusting the chains, which had become rusty with the wet.
A few people were standing around.

The laughing troop of boys was already far off. The recluse looked about for some passenger whom she might
question. She perceived close to her cell a priest, who
feigned to be reading in the public breviary, but whose
thoughts were must less engaged by the book than by the
gibbet, toward which he glanced from time to time with
wild and gloomy look. She recognized in him the Archdeacon of Josas, an austere and holy man.

"Father," she inquired, "whom are they going to hang
yonder?"

The priest looked at her without answering. She repeated the question. "I know not," said he.

"Some boys," rejoined the recluse, "said just now that
it was an Egyptian."

"I believe so," replied the priest.

Paquette la Chantefleurie burst into an hysterical laugh.

"Sister," said the archdeacon, "you seem to hate the Egyptians with all your heart."

"Hate them!" cried the recluse; "why, they are witches, child-stealers! They devoured my little girl, my child, my only child! They ate my heart along with her—I have none now!"

The priest eyed her coldly.

"There is one in particular," she resumed, "that I hate and that I have cursed; a young girl about the same age that my child would have been now had they not eaten her. Whenever this young viper passes my cell, she sets all my blood a-boiling."

"Well, then, sister, rejoice," said the priest, cold as the statue on a sepulcher; " 'tis for her that these preparations are making."

His head sunk upon his bosom and he slowly withdrew. The recluse waved her arms in triumph. "Thanks, sir priest," cried she. "I told her what she would come to."

She then began, with hurried step, to pace to and fro before her window, her hair disheveled, her eye glaring, dashing against the wall with her shoulder, with the wild air of a caged she-wolf which has long been hungry and is aware that the hour for her repast is approaching.

40

Phœbus, meanwhile, was not dead. Men of that kind are hard to kill. When Master Philippe Lheulier, advocate extraordinary to the king, said to poor Esmeralda, "He is dying"—he was either misinformed or joking. When the archdeacon repeated to her after condemnation, He his dying—the fact was that he knew nothing about the matter; but he believed it, he had no doubt of it, he made sure of it, he hoped it. It would have gone too much against the grain to give good tidings of his rival to the female of whom he was enamored. Every man in his place would have done the same.

Not that Phœbus' wound was not severe, but the injury was less serious than the archdeacon flattered himself it was. Now, the judges had evidence sufficient against Esmeralda. They believed Phœbus to be dead, and that was quite enough.

Phœbus, on his part, had not fled far. He had merely rejoined his company, in garrison at Queue-en-Brie, in the Isle of France, a few relays from Paris. He felt no inclination whatever to come forward personally in this process. He had a vague impression that he should cut a ridiculous figure in it. At bottom, he knew not what to think of the whole affair. Irreligious and superstitious, like every soldier who is nothing but a soldier, when he called to mind all the circumstances of this adventure, he could not tell what to make of the goat, of the odd way in which he had first met with La Esmeralda, of the not less strange manner in which she had betrayed her love, of her being an Egyptian, and, lastly, of the goblin-monk. He imagined that in this history there was much more of magic than of love, probably a sorceress, perhaps the devil; in short, a comedy, or to use the language of those days, a mystery of a very disagreeable nature, in which he played an extremely awkward part, that of the butt for blows and laughter. The captain was quite dashed; he felt the sort of shame which La Fontaine so admirably compares with that of a fox caught by a hen. He hoped besides that the affair would not be bruited abroad, that in his absence his name would scarcely be mentioned in connection with it, or at any rate not beyond the pleadings at the Tournelle. Neither was he far wrong in this expectation; there were then no newspapers; and scarcely a week passed but there was some coiner boiled, some witch hanged, or some heretic burned, at one of the numberless justices of Paris.

Phœbus therefore soon set his mind at ease respecting

the sorceress Esmeralda, or Similar, as he called her, the wound inflicted by the Bohemian or the goblin-monk—he cared not which—and the issue of the proceedings. But no sooner was his heart vacant on this score than the image of Fleur-de-Lys returned thither. The heart of Captain Phœbus, like the philosophy of those times, abhorred a vacuum.

Besides, Queue-en-Brie was a very stupid place, a village of blacksmiths and dairy women with chapped hands, a long line of crazy cottages bordering both sides of the high road for a mile. Fleur-de-Lys was his last passion but one, a handsome girl, with a good dowery. One fine morning, therefore, being quite convalescent, and presuming that the affair with the Bohemian must after the lapse of two months be completely blown over and forgotten, the amorous cavalier came swaggering to the door of the Gondelaurier mansion. He took no notice of a numerous concourse assembled in the Place du Parvis, before the porch of Notre Dame; he recollected that it was the month of May, and, supposing that the people might be drawn together by some religious holy day or procession, he fastened his horse to the ring at the gate and gayly went upstairs to his fair betrothed.

She was alone with her mother. Fleur-de-Lys had always felt sore about the scene with the sorceress, her goat, her cursed alphabet, and the long absences of Phœbus; nevertheless, at the entrance of her truant, he looked so well, had such a new uniform, such a smart shoulder-belt, and so impassioned an air, that she reddened with pleasure. The noble damoiselle was herself more charming than ever. Her magnificent light hair was admirably plaited; she was attired completely in sky-blue, which so well suits females of a fair complexion—a piece of coquetry which she had been taught by Colombe—and her eyes swam in that languor of love which suits them so much better.

Phœbus, who had so long set eyes on nothing superior in beauty to the wenches of Queue-en-Brie, was trans-

ported with Fleur-de-Lys; and this imparted such a warmth
and such a tone of gallantry to his manner that his peace
was instantly made. Madame de Gondelaurier herself, ma-
ternally seated as usual in her great armchair, had not the
heart to scold him; and as for the reproaches of Fleur-de-
Lys, they expired in accents of tenderness.

The young lady was seated near the window, still working away at her grotto of Neptune. The captain leant over
the back of her chair, and in an undertone she commenced
her half-caressing, half-scolding inquiries.

"What have you been doing with yourself for these two
months, you naughty man?"

"I swear," replied Phœbus, who did not relish the question, "you are so beautiful that an archbishop could not
help falling in love with you."

She could not forebear smiling. "Beautiful forsooth! My
beauty is nothing to the purpose, sir; I want an answer to
my question."

"Well, then, my dear cousin, I was ordered away to
keep garrison."

"Where, if you please? and why not come to bid me
adieu?"

"At Queue-en-Brie."

Phœbus was delighted that the first question enabled
him to shirk the second.

"But that is close by, sir. How is it that you have not
been once to see me?"

Here Phœbus was seriously embarrassed. "Why—our
duty—and, besides, charming cousin, I have been ill."

"Ill!" she exclaimed in alarm.

"Yes, wounded."

"Wounded!"

The poor girl was thunderstruck.

"Oh, you need not frighten yourself about it," said
Phœbus, carelessly; "it was nothing. A quarrel, a scratch
with a sword; how can that concern you?"

"Not concern me?" cried Fleur-de-Lys, raising her beautiful eyes swimming in tears. "Oh, in saying so you do not

say what you think. How came you by the scratch you talk of? I insist on knowing all."

"Well, then, my fair cousin, I had a squabble with Mahe Fedy—you know him—the lieutenant of St. Germain-en-Laye, and each of us ripped up a few inches of the other's skin. That is all."

The mendacious captain well knew that an affair of honor always raises a man in the estimation of a female. Accordingly, Fleur-de-Lys turned about and looked him in the face with emotions of fear, pleasure, and admiration. Still she was not completely satisfied.

"Ah, Phœbus," said she, "how I rejoice that you are quite well again! I do not know your Mahe Fedy—but he is a scurvy fellow. And what was the cause of this quarrel?"

Here Phœbus, whose imagination was not the most fertile, began to be puzzled how to get out of the dilemma.

"Oh, I hardly recollect—a mere nothing, a word about a horse—but, fair cousin," cried he, in order to change the conversation, "what is the occasion of this bustle in the Parvis? Only look," he continued, stepping to the window, "what a crowd there is in the Place!"

"I know not," replied Fleur-de-Lys. "I did hear that a witch is to do penance this morning before the church, and to be hung afterward."

The captain made so sure that the affair with La Esmeralda was long since over that he took but little interest in the information given to him by Fleur-de-Lys. He nevertheless asked her one or two questions.

"What is the name of this witch?"

"I know not," answered she.

"And what do they say she has done?"

"I know not," said she, with another shrug of her fair shoulders.

"Oh, my God!" said the mother, "there are nowadays so many sorcerers and witches, that they burn them, I verily believe, without knowing their names. You might as well ask the name of every cloud in the sky. But what need we

care? God Almighty will be sure to keep a correct list."
Here the venerable lady rose and advanced to the window.
"Bless me! there is indeed a crowd, as you say, Phœbus.
Why, the very roofs are covered with the populace."

The lovers were not listening to the worthy dowager. Phœbus had again planted himself behind his betrothed, and
was leaning over the back of her chair, wandering over so
much of her neck as was not covered by her dress. Dazzled by that skin which shone like satin, the captain said
within himself: "How can one love any but a fair
woman?" Both kept silence. The lady gave him from time
to time a look of delight and fondness; and their hair mingled together in the spring sunshine.

"Phœbus," said Fleur-de-Lys, abruptly, in a low tone,
"we are to be married in three months; swear that you
never loved any other but me."

"I do swear it, beautiful angel!" replied Phœbus, and his
impassioned look concurred with the emphatic accent of
his words to convince Fleur-de-Lys.

It is possible that at the moment he himself believed
what he asserted.

Meanwhile the good mother, pleased to see the young
people on such excellent terms, had left the apartment to
attend to some domestic matter or other. Phœbus perceived
her absence, which emboldened the enterprising captain.
Fleur-de-Lys loved him; she was betrothed to him; she was
alone with him; his former fondness for her was revived,
if not in all its freshness, at any rate in all its ardor. I know
not precisely what ideas crossed his mind; but so much is
certain, that Fleur-de-Lys became suddenly alarmed at the
expression of his countenance. She looked around her—
her mother was gone!

"Bless me!" said she, flushed and agitated. "I am very
hot!"

"Why," replied Phœbus, "I dare say it is almost noon.
The sun is troublesome. I will draw the curtains."

"No, no!" cried the trembling damsel; "on the contrary,

I have need of air"; and rising, she ran to the window, and stepped out on the balcony. Phœbus followed her thither.

The Place du Parvis, in front of Notre Dame into which, as the reader knows, this balcony looked, exhibited at this moment a sinister and singular spectacle, which quickly changed the nature of the timid Fleur-de-Lys' alarm. An immense crowd, which flowed back into all the adjacent streets, covered the Place, properly so called. The low wall which encompassed the Parvis would not have been sufficient to keep it clear, had it not been thickly lined by sergeants of the Onze-vingts and arquebusiers, with their pieces in their hands. The wide portals of the church were closed, contrasting with the numberless windows around the Place which, thrown open up to the very roofs, displayed thousands of heads heaped one above another, nearly like piles of cannon-balls in a park of artillery. The surface of this crowd was gray, squalid, dirty. The sight which it was awaiting was evidently one of those which have the privilege of calling together all that is most disgusting in the population. Nothing could be more hideous than the noise that arose from this assemblage of sallow caps and unkempt heads. In this concourse there were more women than men, more laughing than crying.

Ever and anon some harsh or shrill voice was heard above the general din to this effect:

"I say, Mahiet Baliffe, is she to be hanged yonder?"

"No, simpleton—only to do penance there in chemise. The priest is going to fling Latin in her face. 'Tis always done here, at noon precisely. If you want to see the hanging, you must e'en go to the Greve."

"I will go afterward."

"Is it true, La Boucandry, that she has refused a confessor?"

"I am told so, La Bechaigne."

"Only think! the Pagan!"

* * *

"It is the custom, sir. The bailiff of the Palace is bound to deliver over the culprit for execution—if of the laity to the provost of Paris; but if a clerk, to the official of the bishopric."

"I thank you, sir."

Such were the dialogues carried on at this moment among the spectators collected by the ceremony.

"Oh, my God! the poor creature!" exclaimed Fleur-de-Lys, surveying the populace with a sorrowful look. The captain was too much engaged with her to notice the rabble.

At this moment the clock of Notre Dame slowly struck twelve. A murmur of satisfaction pervaded the crowd. Scarcely had the last vibration of the twelfth stroke subsided, when the vast assemblage of heads was broken into waves like the sea in a gale of wind, and one immense shout of "There she is!" burst simultaneously from pavement, windows, and roofs.

Fleur-de-Lys covered her eyes with her hands that she might not see.

"Will you go in, charmer?" asked Phœbus.

"No," she replied; and those eyes which she had shut for fear she opened again out of curiosity.

A cart, drawn by a strong Norman bay, and completely surrounded by horsemen in purple livery, marked with white crosses, had just issued from the Rue St. Pierre-aux-Bœufs and entered the Place. The sergeants of the watch opened a passage for it through the populace with staves, with which they laid lustily about them. Beside the cart rode certain officers of justice and police, who might be known by their black dress, and the awkward manner in which they sat their horses. At their head paraded Master Jacques Charmolue. In the fatal vehicle was seated a young female, with her hands tied behind her, and no priest at her side. She was stripped to her chemise; her long black hair—for it was not then customary to cut it off till the culprit was at the foot of the gallows—fell loosely over her bosom and her half uncovered shoulders.

Through this flowing hair, more glossy than a raven's plumage, might be seen twisting a gray, knotty cord, which fretted her delicate skin, and twined itself around the neck of the poor girl like an earthworm upon a flower. Beneath this cord glistened a little amulet adorned with green beads, which had been left her no doubt because it is usual to refuse nothing to those who are going to die. The spectators in the windows could see at the bottom of the cart her naked legs, which she strove to conceal beneath her, as if by a last instinct of female modesty. At her feet there was a little goat, also bound. The prisoner held with her teeth her chemise, which was not properly fastened. Her misery seemed to be greatly aggravated by her being thus exposed nearly naked to the public gaze. Alas! is it not for such tremors that modesty is made!

"Only look, fair cousin," said Fleur-de-Lys, sharply to the captain, " 'tis that Bohemian hussy with the goat."

As she thus spoke, she turned round toward Phœbus. His eyes were fixed on the cart. He was unusually pale.

"What Bohemian with the goat?" said he, faltering.

"What!" rejoined Fleur-de-Lys, "don't you recollect?"

"I know not what you mean," said Phœbus, interrupting her.

He was stepping back to return to the room; but Fleur-de-Lys, whose jealousy, some time since so strongly excited by this same Egyptian, was anew awakened, cast on him a look full of penetration and mistrust. She had a confused recollection at the moment of having heard that a captain was implicated in the proceedings against this sorceress.

"What ails you?" said she to Phœbus; "one would suppose that the sight of this creature had given you a shock."

"Me! not the least in the world!" stammered Phœbus, with a forced grin.

"Then stay!" rejoined she imperiously, "and let us look on till all is over."

The unlucky captain was obliged to stay. He recovered somewhat of his assurance on observing that the prisoner never raised her eyes from the bottom of the cart. It was but too surely La Esmeralda. On this last step of misfortune and ignominy, she was still beautiful; her large black eyes appeared still larger, on account of the hollowness of her cheeks; her livid profile was pure and sublime. She resembled what she had been, as a Virgin of Masaccio's resembles a Virgin of Raphael's—feebler, thinner, more attenuated.

For the rest, there was nothing about her, excepting her modesty, but was left, as it were, to chance, so deeply was she overwhelmed by stupor and despair. At each jolt of the cart her form rebounded like an inanimate thing; her look was dull and silly. A tear glistened in her eye; but it was motionless, and looked as if it were frozen.

Meanwhile the somber cavalcade had passed through the crowd, amid shouts of joy and attitudes of curiosity. In order to deserve the character of faithful historians, we must nevertheless record that many of the mob, ay, and of the hardest-hearted too, on seeing her so beautiful and so forlorn, were moved with pity. The cart had now reached the Parvis.

It stopped before the central porch. The escort ranged itself on either side. The mob kept silence; and amid this silence, full of solemnity and anxiety, the folding doors of the great porch turned as if spontaneously upon their hinges, which creaked with a shrill sound like that of a fife, affording a view of the whole length of the church, vast, gloomy, hung with black, dimly lighted by a few tapers glimmering in the distance upon the high altar, and opening like the mouth of a cavern upon the Place resplendent with the glorious sunshine. At the farthest extremity, in the dusk of the chancel, was faintly seen a colossal silver cross relieved upon black cloth which fell behind it from the roof to the pavement. The whole nave was vacant. Heads of priests were, however, seen confusedly moving about in the distant stalls of the choir; and at the moment when the great door opened, there burst from the church a grave, loud, and monotonous chant, hurling, as it were, in gusts, fragments of doleful psalms at the head of the condemned one.

Non timebo millia populi circumdantis me: exsurge, Domine; salvum me fac, Deus!

Salvum me fac, Deus, quoniam intraverunt aquæ usque ad animam meam.

Infixus sum in limo profundi; et non est substantia.

At the same time another voice singly struck up on the steps of the high altar this melancholy offertory:

Qui verbum meum audit, et credit ei qui misit me, habet vitam æternam et in judicium non venit; sed transit a morte in vitam.

These chants sung by aged men, lost in the darkness, over that beautiful creature, full of youth and life, caressed by the warm air of spring, and inundated with the sunlight, belonged to the mass for the dead. The populace listened devoutly.

The terrified girl, fixing her eyes on the dark interior of the church, seemed to lose both sight and thought. Her pale lips moved, as if in prayer; and when the executioner's man went to assist her to alight from the cart, he heard her repeating in a faint voice the word Phœbus!

Her hands were unbound, and she alighted, accompanied by her goat, which had also been untied, and bleated for joy on finding itself at liberty; and she was then made to walk barefoot on the hard pavement to the foot of the steps leading to the porch. The rope which was fastened about her neck trailed behind her; you would have taken it for a snake that was following her.

The chanting in the church ceased. A large gold crucifix and a file of tapers began to move in the dusk. The sound of the halberts of the parti-colored Swiss was heard; and in a few moments a long procession of priests in copes, and deacons in dalmatics, slowly advanced chanting toward the

prisoner and expanded itself before her eyes and those of
the mob. But hers were riveted on him who walked at its
head immediately after the bearer of the crucifix. "Oh!"
she muttered to herself, shuddering, "there he his again;
the priest!"

It was actually the archdeacon. On his left was the sub-
chanter, and on his right the chanter bearing the staff of his
office. He advanced, with head thrown back, and eyes
fixed and open, chanting with a loud voice:

De ventre inferi clamavi, et exaudisti vocem meam.

Et projecisit me in profundum, in corde maris, et flumen
circumdedit me.

At the moment when he appeared in the broad daylight
beneath the lofty pointed arch of the portal, covered with
an ample cope of silver marked with a black cross, he was
so pale that sundry of the crowd imagined it must be one
of the marble bishops kneeling on the sepulchral monuments in the choir, who had risen and come to receive on
the brink of the tomb her who was about to die.

She, not less pale, not less statue-like, was scarcely
aware that a heavy lighted taper of yellow wax had been
put into her hand; she had not heard the squeaking voice
of the clerk reading the form of the penance, when told to
say Amen, she had said Amen. Neither did she recover
any life or any strength till she saw the priest make a sign
to those who had her in custody to retire, and advanced
alone toward her. She then felt the blood boil in her head,
and a spark of indignation was rekindled in that soul, already cold, benumbed, stupefied.

The archdeacon approached her slowly; even in this extremity she saw him survey her nearly naked form with an
eye sparkling with pleasure, desire, and jealousy. In a loud
voice he thus addressed she: "Bohemian girl, have you
prayed God to pardon your crimes and misdemeanors?"
Then stooping—as the spectators imagined, to receive her

last confession—he whispered, "Wilt thou be mine? I can even yet save thee!"

She eyed him steadfastly. "Go to the fiend, thy master, or I will inform of thee!"

He grinned horribly a ghastly smile. "They will not believe thee," he replied. "Thou wilt but add scandal to guilt. Answer quickly, wilt thou have me?"

"What hast thou done with my Phœbus?"

"He is dead," said the priest.

At that moment the wretched archdeacon raised his head mechanically, and saw on the other side of the Place the captain standing in the balcony with Fleur-de-Lys. He shuddered, passed his hand over his eyes, looked again, muttered a malediction, and all his features were violently contracted.

"Well then, die!" said he. "No one shall have thee."

Then, lifting his hand over the Egyptian, he pronounced these words in a loud and solemn tone: "*I nunc anima anceps, et sit tibi Deus misericors!*"

This was the dreadful form with which it was customary to conclude these gloomy ceremonies. It was the signal given by the priest to the executioner. The populace fell on their knees.

"*Kyrie Eleison!*" said the priests, who stopped beneath the porch.

"*Kyrie Eleison!*" repeated the crowd with a murmur that rose above their heads like the rumbling of an agitated sea.

"*Amen!*" said the archdeacon.

He turned his back on the prisoner; his head sank upon his bosom; his hands crossed each other; he rejoined the train of priests, and presently receded from sight with the crucifix, the tapers, and the copes beneath the dusky arches of the cathedral; and his sonorous voice expired by degrees in the choir while chanting this verse of anguish: "*Omnes gurgites tui et fluctus tui super me transierunt.*"

At the same time the intermitting stamp of the iron-shod shafts of the halberts of the Switzers dying away between the intercolumniations of the nave produced the effect of a clock-hammer striking the last hour of the doomed one.

Meanwhile the doors of Notre Dame were left open, displaying to view the church, empty, deserted, in mourning, taperless and voiceless. The condemned girl stood motionless in her place awaiting what was to be done with her. One of the vergers was obliged to intimate as much to Master Charmolue and at a sign which he made two men in yellow dresses, the executioner's assistants, approached the Egyptian to tie her hands again.

The unfortunate creature at the moment for reascending the fatal cart and setting out on her last stage was probably seized by some keen repining after life. She raised her dry but inflamed eyes toward heaven, toward the sun, toward the silvery clouds, studded here and there with trapeziums and triangles of azure, and then cast them down around her upon the earth, upon the crowd, upon the houses.

All at once while the men in yellow were pinioning her arms she gave a startling scream, a scream of joy. In the balcony at the corner of the Place she had descried him, her friend, her lord, her Phœbus just as he looked when alive. The judges had told her a falsehood! the priest had told her a falsehood! 'twas he himself—she could not possibly doubt it. There he stood living, moving, habited in his brilliant uniform, with the plume on his head and the sword by his side.

"Phœbus!" she cried; "my Phœbus!"—and she would have stretched out toward him her arms trembling with love and transport, but they were bound.

She then saw the captain knit his brow; a young and handsome female who leant upon him looked at him with disdainful lip and angry eye; Phœbus then uttered a few words, which she was too far off to hear; both hastily retired from the balcony into the room, and the window was immediately closed.

"Phœbus!" cried she, wildly, "dost thou too believe it?" A horrible idea had just flashed upon her. She recollected that she had been condemned for the murder of Captain

Phœbus de Chateaupers. She had borne up thus far against everything. This last shock was too violent. She fell senseless upon the pavement.

"Come!" said Charmolue, "carry her to the cart, and let us make an end of the business!"

No person had yet observed in the gallery of the royal statues, immediately above the pointed arches of the porch, a strange-looking spectator, who had till then been watching all that passed, with attitude so motionless, head so outstretched, visage so deformed, that, but for his apparel, half red and half purple, he might have been taken for one of those stone monsters, at whose mouths the long gutters of the cathedral have for these six hundred years disgorged themselves. This spectator had not lost a single incident of the tragedy that had been acting ever since noon before the porch of Notre Dame; and in the very first moments he had, unobserved, securely tied to one of the small pillars of the gallery a knotted rope, the end of which reached the pavement. This done, he had set himself to watch as quietly as before, hissing from time to time at the jackdaws as they flew past him. All at once, at the moment when the executioner's assistants were preparing to obey the phlegmatic order of Charmolue, he strode across the balustrade of the gallery, seized the rope with feet, knees, and hands, glided down the facade like a drop of rain down a pane of glass; ran up to the two men with the swiftness of a cat that has fallen from a roof; felled both of them to the ground with his enormous fists; bore off the Egyptian on one arm, as a girl would her doll, and at one bound he was in the church, holding up the young girl above his head and shouting with terrific voice: "Sanctuary! sanctuary!" This was all done with the rapidity of lightning.

"Sanctuary! sanctuary!" repeated the mob, and the clapping of ten thousand hands caused Quasimodo's only eye to sparkle with joy and exultation.

This shock brought La Esmeralda to her senses. She opened her eyes, looked at Quasimodo, and instantly closed them again, as if horror-stricken at the sight of her deliverer.

Charmolue stood stupefied—so did the executioners and the whole escort. Within the walls of Notre Dame the prisoner was secure from molestation. The cathedral was a place of refuge. Human justice dared not cross its threshold.

Quasimodo paused under the great porch. His large feet seemed as firmly rooted in the pavement of the church as the massive Roman pillars. His huge head, with its profuse covering of hair, appeared to be thrust down into his shoulders, like that of the lion, which, too, has a copious mane and neck. He held the damsel, palpitating all over, hanging from his horny hands like a white drapery; but he carried her with as much care as if he was fearful of bruising or disturbing her. He felt, you would have thought, that a thing so delicate, so exquisite, so precious, was not made for such hands as his. At times he looked as though he dared not touch her even with his breath. Then, all at once, he would clasp her closely in his arms, against his angular bosom, as his treasure, as his all, as the mother of that girl would herself have done. His cyclop eye bent down upon her, shed over her a flood of tenderness, of pity, of grief, and was suddenly raised flashing lightning. At this sight the women laughed and cried; the crowd stamped with enthusiasm, for at that moment Quasimodo was really beautiful.

After a triumph of a few minutes, however, Quasimodo hastened into the interior of the church with his burden. The people, fond of daring deeds, followed him with their eyes along the dusky nave, regretting that he had so soon withdrawn himself from their acclamations. All at once he was again descried at one of the extremities of the gallery of the kings of France; he ran along it, like a maniac, holding up his prize in his arms, and shouting: "Sanctuary!" The populace greeted him with fresh applause. Having traversed the gallery, he again penetrated into the interior of the church. Presently afterward he again appeared on the upper platform, still bearing the Egyptian in his arms, still running like one frantic, still shouting: "Sanctuary." Again the mob applauded. At length, he made his third appearance on the top of the tower of the great bell; there he seemed to show proudly to the whole city her whom he had saved, and this thundering voice—that voice which was heard so seldom, and which he himself never heard—made the air ring with the thrice-repeated shout of "Sanctuary! Sanctuary! Sanctuary!"

"Huzza! huzza!" cried the populace on their part; and this prodigous acclamation was heard on the other side of the river by the crowd collected in the Place de Greve, and by the recluse, who was still waiting with her eyes riveted on the gallows.

41

Claude Frollo was no longer in Notre Dame, when his foster-son cut thus abruptly the fatal noose in which the unhappy archdeacon had caught the Egyptian, and was himself caught. On returning to the sacristy he had stripped off the alb, the cope, and the stole, thrown them all into the hands of the stupefied bedel, hurried out at the private door of the cloisters, ordered a boatman of the Terrain to carry him across the river, and wandered among the hilly streets of the University, meeting at every step parties of men and women, hastening joyously toward the Pont St. Michel, "in hopes of being in time to see the sorceress hanged!" Pale and haggard, blinded and more bewildered than an owl let loose and pursued by a troop of boys in broad daylight, he knew not where he was, what he did, whether he was awake or dreaming. He walked, he ran, heedless whither, taking any street at random, still driven onward by the Greve, the horrible Greve, which he vaguely knew to be behind him.

In this manner he pursued his way along the hill of St. Genevieve, and left the town by the gate of St. Victor. So long as he could see, on turning round, the line of towers enclosing the University, and the scattered houses of the suburb, he continued to flee; but when, at length, the inequality of the ground had completely shut out that hateful Paris from his view, when he could fancy himself a hundred leagues off, in the country, in a desert, he paused, and felt as though he breathed once more.

A crowd of frightful ideas then rushed upon his mind. He saw plainly into the recesses of his soul, and shuddered. He thought of that unhappy girl who had undone him, and whom he had undone. With haggard eye he followed the double winding way along which fatality had urged their two destinies to the point of intersection, where it had pitilessly dashed them against one another. He thought of the folly of eternal vows, of the vanity of chastity, science, religion, and virtue. He willfully plunged into evil thoughts, and as he immersed himself in them he felt a satanic laugh arising within him.

And then he laughed again on bethinking him that Phœbus was not dead; that he was still alive, gay, and joyous; that he had a smarter uniform than ever, and a new mistress whom he took to see the old one hanged. He laughed still more heartily on reflecting that, among all the living beings whose death he had wished for, the Egyptian, the only creature whom he did not hate, was also the only one who had not escaped him.

This flight from Nature, from life, from himself, from man, from God, from everything, lasted till evening. Sometimes he threw himself on his face upon the earth and tore up the young corn with his fingers; at others he paused in some lone village street, and his thoughts were so insupportable, that he grasped his head with both hands, as though striving to wrench it from his shoulders in order to dash it upon the ground.

The sun was near setting when, on examining himself afresh he found that he was almost mad. The storm which had been raging within him from the moment when he had lost the hope and the will to save the Egyptian had not left in his mind a single sound thought or idea. His reason was laid prostrate, nay, almost utterly destroyed. His mind retained but two distinct images, La Esmeralda and the gibbet; all the rest was black. These two images formed a horrible group; and the more he fixed on them so much attention and thought as he was yet master of, the more they seemed to increase, according to a fantastic progression, the one in charm, in grace, in beauty, in light—the other in horror; so that at last La Esmeralda appeared like an enormous fleshless arm.

He proceeded along the Pre-aux-Clercs, took the lonely path which separated it from the *Dieu Neuf*, and at length reached the bank of the river. There Dom Claude found a boatman, who for a few deniers took him up the Seine to the point of the city, and set him ashore upon that vacant tongue of land where the reader has already seen Gringoire pondering, and which extended beyond the king's gardens parallel with the isle of the cattle-ferryman. The monotonous rocking of the boat and the murmur of the water had somewhat lulled the wretched Claude. When the boatman had left him, he remained standing stupidly upon the strand, looking straight forward. All the objects he beheld seemed to dance before his eyes, forming a sort of phantasmagoria. It is no uncommon thing for the fatigue of excessive grief to produce this effect upon the mind.

The sun had set behind the tall tower of Nesle. It was just twilight. The sky was white; the water of the river was white; and between these the left bank of the Seine, upon which his eyes were fixed, extended its somber mass, which, gradually diminished by the perspective, pierced the haze of the horizon like a black arrow. Lights began to glimmer here and there in the windows. This immense black obelisk, thus bounded by the two white sheets of the sky and the river, of great breadth at this place, produced on Dom Claude a singular effect, which may be compared with that which would be experienced by a man lying down on his back at the foot of the steeple of Strasburg cathedral, and looking at its enormous shaft piercing above his head the penumbra of the twilight; only in this case Claude was standing and the obelisk lying.

On entering the streets, the passengers who jostled one another by the light of the shopfronts appeared like specters incessantly going and coming around him. Strange noises rang in his ears; extraordinary fancies disturbed his mind. He saw neither houses nor pavement, neither men, women, nor carriages, but a chaos of confused objects blending one with another. At the corner of the Rue de la Barillerie there was a grocer's shop, the penthouse of which was hung all along, according to immemorial custom, with tin hoops, to which were attached imitation candles of wood; these, being shaken by the wind, clattered like castanets. He imagined that he heard the skeletons of Moutfaucon clashing together in the dark.

"Oh!" muttered he, "the night-wind is driving them one against another, and mingling the clank of their chains with the rattling of their bones. She is there too, perhaps, among them!"

Distracted, he knew not whither he went. Presently he was upon the Pont St. Michel. He perceived a light in the window of a ground-floor room; he approached it. Through a cracked pane he beheld a mean apartment, which awakened confused recollections in his mind. In this apartment, faintly lighted by a lamp, he saw a fair, fresh-colored, jovial-looking youth, who, loudly laughing the while, was toying with a young female whose dress was far from modest; and near the lamp was seated an old woman spinning and singing, or rather squalling, a song. In the intervals when the laughter ceased, snatches of the old woman's song reached the ear of the priest; the tenor of it was frightful and not very intelligible.

The old woman was Falourdel, the girl was a prostitute, and the youth was his brother Jehan. He continued to watch at the farther end of the room, open it, and look out on the quay, where a thousand illumined windows glanced in the distance; and he heard him saying while shutting the window: " 'Pon my soul, 'tis dark night. The citizens are lighting up their candles, and God Almighty his stars."

Jehan then went back to his companion, and held up a bottle which stood on the table. "Zounds!" he cried, "empty already! and I have no more money." So saying he came forth from the house. Dom Claude had but just time to throw himself on the ground that he might not be met, looked in the face, and recognized by his brother. Luckily the street was dark and the scholar not sober. "Oho!" said he; "here is one who has been enjoying himself today." With his foot he shook Dom Claude, who held in his breath.

"Dead drunk!" resumed Jehan. "Full enough, it seems. A proper leech loosed from a cask. Bald too!" added he, stooping—"an old man! *Fortunate senex!*"

Dom Claude then heard him move away, saying: "Never mind! Reason is a fine thing, though; and very lucky is my brother the archdeacon in being prudent and having money."

The archdeacon then rose, and ran without stopping toward Notre Dame, the enormous towers of which he saw lifting themselves in the dark above the houses.

The door of the cloisters was shut, but the archdeacon always carried about him the key of the tower in which was his laboratory. Availing himself of it, he entered the church. He found the interior dark and silent as the grave. From the large shadows which fell from all sides in broad sheets, he knew that the hangings put up for the morning's ceremony had not been removed. The great silver cross glistened amid the gloom, dotted with sparkling points, like the milky way of this sepulchral night. The tall windows of the choir showed above the black drapery the upper extremity of their pointed arches, the panes of which, admitting a faint ray of moonlight, had but those doubtful colors of night, a sort of violet, white, and blue, the tint of which is elsewhere found only on the faces of the dead. The archdeacon, perceiving all around the choir these livid points of arches, fancied that he beheld a circle of ghastly faces staring at him.

With hurried steps he began to flee across the church.

Thus the fever or the frenzy of the wretched priest had attained such a degree of intensity that to him the external world was but a kind of Apocalypse, visible, palpable, terrific.

For a moment he felt somewhat relieved. On entering one of the aisles he perceived a reddish light behind a cluster of pillars. He ran toward it as toward a star. It was the petty lamp on the public breviary of Notre Dame, beneath its iron grating. He hurried to the sacred book, in hopes of finding in it some consolation or encouragement. It was open at this passage of Job which caught his fixed eye: "Then a spirit passed before my face, and the hair of my flesh stood up."

On reading this fearful text, he felt much the same as a blind man whose fingers are pricked by the staff which he has picked up. His knees failed him, and he sank upon the pavement, thinking of her who had that day suffered death. Such volumes of blasting vapors enveloped his brain that it seemed as if his head had been turned to one of the chimneys of hell.

He must have remained for a long time in this attitude, neither thinking nor feeling, helpless and passive in the hand of the demon. At length, recovering some degree of consciousness, he thought of seeking refuge in the tower, near his trusty Quasimodo. He rose, and, being afraid, he took the lamp of the breviary to light him. This was a sacrilege; but he no longer regarded such a trifle as that.

He slowly ascended the staircase of the tower, filled with a secret dread, which was communicated to the passengers who now and then crossed the Parvis, on seeing the mysterious light of his lamp mounting so late from loophole to loophole to the top of the tower.

All at once he felt a cool air upon his face, and found

himself under the doorway of the uppermost gallery. At this moment the clock raised its loud and solemn voice. It was midnight. The priest thought of noon; it was again twelve o'clock. "Oh!" muttered he to himself, "she must be cold by this time!"

All at once a gust of wind extinguished his lamp, and at the same moment he saw something white, a shade, a human form, a female, appear at the opposite angle of the tower. He shuddered. By the side of this female there was a little goat, which mingled her bleating with the last tones of the bell. He had the courage to look at her—'twas she herself!

She was pale; she was sad. Her hair fell over her shoulders, as in the morning; but there was no rope about her neck; her hands were not bound; she was free, she was dead.

She was habited in white, and had a white veil over her head. She came toward him slowly, looking up at the sky, and followed by the supernatural goat. He was petrified; he would have fled, but was unable. All he could do was to recede a step for every one that she advanced. He retreated in this manner till he was beneath the dark vault of the staircase. His blood curdled at the idea that she might perhaps come that way too; if she had, he must have died of fright.

She did in fact approach so near as the door of the staircase, where she paused for a few moments; she cast a fixed look into the darkness, but without appearing to discern the priest, and passed on. She seemed to him taller than when alive; he saw the moonshine through her white robe; he heard her breath.

When she had gone, he began to descend the stairs, as slowly as he had seen the specter move. Horror-stricken, his hair erect, still holding the extinguished lamp in his hand, he fancied himself a specter and, while descending the winding stairs, he heard a voice laughing and repeating distinctly in his ear, "A spirit passed before my face, and the hair of my flesh stood up."

In the Middle Ages every town, and till the time of Louis XII, every town in France had its sanctuaries. Amid the deluge of penal laws and barbarous jurisdictions which inundated that division of Paris which we have specially called the City, these sanctuaries were a kind of islands, which rose above the level of human justice. Every criminal who took refuge there was saved. There were in a district almost as many sanctuaries as places of execution. It was the abuse of impunity going hand in hand with the abuse of punishment—two bad things, which strove to correct one another. The palaces of the king, the hotels of the princes, but above all, the churches, had the right of sanctuary. Sometimes that right was conferred for a time on a whole city which needed repeopling. Louis XI made Paris a sanctuary in 1467.

When he had once set foot in the sanctuary, the criminal was sacred, but he was obliged to beware of leaving it; one step out of the island-asylum plunged him again into the sea.

The churches had in general a cell appropriated to the reception of fugitives.

At Notre Dame it was a small cell on the top of the aisle, under the flying buttresses, facing the cloisters, on the very spot where the wife of the present keeper of the towers has made herself a garden, which is to the hanging gardens of Babylon what a lettuce is to a palm tree, or a portress to Semiramis.

Here it was that, after his wild and triumphant course through towers and galleries, Quasimodo deposited La Esmeralda. So long as this race lasted, the damsel had not recovered her senses; half stupefied, half awake, she was sensible of nothing but that she was mounting into the air, that she was floating, flying in it, that something was lifting her above the earth. From time to time she heard the loud laugh and the harsh voice of Quasimodo at her ear; she opened her eyes, and then beneath her she confusedly saw Paris speckled with its thousand roofs of slate and tile, like red and blue mosaic-work, and above her head the hideous but joyful face of Quasimodo. Again her eyes closed; she imagined that all was over, that she had been executed during her swoon, and that the deformed spirit who had governed her destiny had seized and borne her away.

But when the panting bell-ringer had laid her down in the cell of the sanctuary, when she felt his huge hands gently loosing the cord that galled her arms, she experienced that kind of shock which abruptly wakens those on board a ship that runs aground in the middle of a dark night. Her ideas awoke also and returned to her one by one. She saw that she was in the church; she recollected having been snatched out of the hands of the executioner; that Phœbus was alive, and that he no longer loved her; and these two ideas, one of which imparted such bitterness to the other, presenting themselves at once to the poor girl, she turned toward Quasimodo, who remained standing beside her, and whose aspect frightened her, saying, "Why did you save me?"

He looked anxiously at her, as if striving to guess what she said. She repeated the question. He then cast on her a look deeply sorrowful, and withdrew. She was lost in astonishment.

A few moments afterward he returned, bringing a bundle which he laid at her feet. It contained apparel which charitable women had left for her at the door of the church. She then cast down her eyes at herself, saw that she was almost naked, and blushed. Life had fully returned. Quasimodo seemed to participate in this feeling of

modesty Covering his face with his large hand, he again
retired, but with slow step.

She hastened to dress herself. It was a white robe with
a white veil—the habit of a novice of the Hotel Dieu.
She had scarcely finished before Quasimodo returned. He
brought a basket under one arm and a mattress under the
other. The basket contained a bottle, bread, and some other
provisions. He set down the basket, and said, "Eat!" He
spread the mattress on the floor, and said, "Sleep!" It was
his own dinner, his own bed, that the bellringer had
brought her.

The Egyptian lifted her eyes to his face to thank him;
but she could not utter a word. The poor fellow was absolutely hideous. She drooped her head with a thrill of horror. "Ah!" said he, "I frighten you, I see. I am ugly
enough, God wot. Do not look at me. In the daytime you
shall stay here; at night you can walk about all over the
church. But stir not a step out of it either by night or by
day, or they will catch you and kill you, and it will be the
death of me."

Moved at this address, she raised her head to reply, but
he was gone. Once more she was alone, pondering on the
singular words of this almost monstrous being, and struck
by the tone of his voice, at once so harsh and so gentle.
She then began to examine her cell. It was a chamber
some six feet square, with a small aperture for a window,
and a door opening upon the slightly inclined plane of the
roof, composed of flat stones. Several gutters terminating
in heads of animals, seemed to bend down over it, and to
stretch out their necks to look in at the hole. On a level
with its roof she perceived a thousand, chimney tops, disgorging the smoke of all the fires of Paris. Melancholy
prospect for the poor Egyptian, a foundling, rescued from
the gallows; an unfortunate young creature, who had neither country, nor family, nor home!

At the moment when the idea of her forlorn situation
wrung her heart more keenly than ever, she felt a hairy
shaggy head rubbing against her hands and her knees. She

shuddered—everything now alarmed her—and looked. It was the poor goat, the nimble Djali, which had escaped along with her at the moment when Quasimodo dispersed Charmolue's brigade, and had been at her feet nearly an hour, lavishing caresses on her mistress, without obtaining a single glance. The Egyptian covered the fond animal with kisses. "Oh, Djali!" said she, "how I have forgotten thee! And yet thou thinkest of me. Thou, for thy part, at least, art not ungrateful." At the same time, as if an invisible hand had removed the obstruction which had so long repressed her tears, she began to weep, and, as the big drops trickled down her cheeks, she felt the keenest and bitterest portion of her sorrows leaving her along with them.

Evening came on. The night was so beautiful, the moonlight so soft, that she ventured to take a turn in the high gallery which runs round the church. She felt somewhat refreshed by her walk, so calm did the earth appear to her, beheld from that elevation.

43

Next morning, she perceived on awaking that she had slept. This singular circumstance surprised her—it was so long that she had been unaccustomed to sleep! The sun, peeping in at her window, threw his cheering rays upon her face. But besides the sun she saw at this aperture an object that affrighted her—the unlucky face of Quasimodo. She involuntarily closed her eyes, but in vain; she still fancied that she saw through her rosy lids that visage so like an ugly mask. She kept her eyes shut. Presently she heard a hoarse voice saying very kindly: "Don't be afraid. I am your friend. I came to see you sleep. What harm can it do you, if I come to look at you when your eyes are shut? Well, well, I am going. There, now, I am behind the wall. Now you can open your eyes."

There was something still more plaintive than these words in the accent with which they were uttered. The Egyptian, affected by them, opened her eyes. He was actually no longer at the window. She went to it, looked out, and saw the poor hunchback cowering under the wall, in an attitude of grief and resignation. She made an effort to overcome the aversion which he excited. "Come!" said she kindly to him. Observing the motion of her lips, Quasimodo imagined that she was bidding him to go away. He then rose and retired, with slow and halting step and drooping head, without so much as daring to raise his eyes, filled with despair, to the damsel. "Come then!" she cried; but he continued to move off. She then darted out of the cell, ran to him, and took hold of his arm. On feeling her touch, Quasimodo trembled in every limb. He lifted his supplicating eye, and, finding that she drew him toward her, his whole face shone with joy and tenderness. She would have made him go into her cell, but he insisted on staying at her threshold. "No, no," said he, "the owl never enters the nest of the lark."

She then seated herself gracefully on her bed, with her goat at her feet. Both remained for some minutes motionless, contemplating in silence, he so much beauty, she so much ugliness. Every moment she discovered in Quasimodo some new deformity. Her look wandered from his knock-knees to his hunchback, from his hunchback to his only eye. She could not conceive how a creature so awkwardly put together could exist. At the same time an air of such sadness and gentleness pervaded his whole figure, that she began to be reconciled with it.

He was the first to break silence. "Did you not call me back?" said he.

"Yes!" replied she, with a nod of affirmation.

He understood the sign. "Alas!" said he, as if hesitating to finish, "you must know, I am deaf."

"Poor fellow!" exclaimed the Bohemian, with an expression of pity.

He smiled sadly. "You think nothing else was wanting, don't you? Yes, I am deaf. That is the way in which I am served. It is terrible, is it not?—while you—you are so beautiful!"

The tone of the poor fellow conveyed such a profound feeling of his wretchedness that she had not the heart to utter a word. Besides, he would not have heard her. He then resumed: "Never till now was I aware how hideous I am. When I compare myself with you, I cannot help pitying myself, poor unhappy monster that I am! I must appear to you like a beast. You, you are a sunbeam, a drop of dew, a bird's song!—I, I am something frightful, neither man nor brute, something harder, more shapeless, and more trampled upon, than a flint."

He then laughed, and scarcely could there be ought in the world more cutting than this laugh. He continued: "Yes, I am deaf: but you will speak to me by gestures, by signs. I have a master who talks to me in that way. And then, I shall soon know your meaning from the motion of your lips, from your look."

"Well, then," replied she, smiling, "tell me why you saved me?"

He looked steadfastly at her while she spoke.

"I understand," rejoined he; "you asked me why I saved you. You have forgotten a wretch to whom, the very next day, you brought relief on the ignominious pillory. A draught of water and a look of pity are more than I could repay with my life. You have forgotten that wretch—but he has not forgotten."

She listened to him with deep emotion. A tear started into the eye of the bell-ringer, but it did not fall. He appeared to make a point of repressing it. "Look you," he again began, when he no longer feared lest that tear should escape him—"we have very high towers here; a man falling from one of them would be dead almost before he reached the pavement. When you wish to be rid of me, tell me to throw myself from the top—you have but to say the word; nay, a look will be sufficient."

He then rose. Unhappy as was the Bohemian, this grotesque being awakened compassion even in her. She made him a sign to stay.

"No, no," said he, "I must not stay too long. I do not feel comfortable. It is out of pity that you do not turn your eyes from me. I will seek some place where I can look at you without your seeing me; that will be better."

He drew from his pocket a small metal whistle. "Take this," said he; "when you want me, when you wish me to come, when you have the courage to see me, whistle with this. I shall hear that sound."

He laid the whistle on the floor, and retired.

44

Time passed on. Tranquillity returned by degrees to the soul of La Esmeralda. Excessive grief, like excessive joy, is too violent to last. The human heart cannot continue long in either extremity. The Bohemian had suffered so much, that, of the feelings she had lately experienced, astonishment alone was left.

Along with security, hope began to revive within her. She was out of society, out of life, but she had a vague feeling that it might not be impossible for her to return to them. She was like one dead, keeping in reserve a key to her tomb.

The terrible images which had so long haunted her were leaving her by degrees. All the hideous phantoms, Pierrat Torterue, Jacques Charmolue, had faded from her mind— all of them, even the priest himself. And then, Phœbus was yet living; she was sure of it; she had seen him. To her the life of Phœbus was everything.

No doubt La Esmeralda did not think of the captain without pain. No doubt it was terrible that he too should have made such a mistake, that he should have thought the thing possible, that he too should have believed the wound to be inflicted by one who would have given a thousand lives for his sake. Still there was no great reason to be angry with him; had she not confessed the crime? had she not, frail creature as she was, yielded to the torture? All the fault was hers. She ought to have suffered them to tear her in pieces rather than make such an admission. After all, could she see Phœbus but once more, for a single minute; a word, a look would suffice to undeceive him and to bring back the truant. This she had not the least doubt of. There were, at the same time, several singular circumstances about which she was puzzled herself—the accident of Phœbus' presence at the penance; the young female in whose company he was. She was, no doubt, his sister. An improbable explanation, but she was satisfied with it, because she must needs believe that Phœbus still loved her, and loved but her. Had he not sworn it? What more could she require, simple and credulous as she was? And then, in this affair, were not appearances much more against her than against him? She waited therefore—she hoped.

When the thoughts of Phœbus allowed her time, the Egyptian would sometimes think of Quasimodo. He was the only bond, the only link, the only communication, that was left her with mankind, with the living. The unfortunate girl was more completely cut off from the world than Quasimodo. As for the strange friend whom chance had given her, she knew not what to make of him. She would frequently reproach herself for not feeling sufficient gratitude to blind her to his imperfections; but decidedly she could not accustom herself to the poor bell-ringer. He was too hideous.

She had left on the floor the whistle that he had given her. Quasimodo, nevertheless, looked in from time to time,

on the succeeding days. She strove as much as she could
to conceal her aversion, when he brought her the basket of
provisions or the pitcher of water; but he was sure to perceive the slightest movement of that kind, and then he
went sorrowfully away.

One day, he came just at the moment when she was fondling Djali. For a while he stood full of thought before the
graceful group of the goat and the Egyptian. At length,
shaking his huge misshapen head: "My misfortune," said
he, "is that I am too much like a human creature. Would
to God that I had been a downright beast, like that goat!"

She cast on him a look of astonishment. "Oh!" he replied to that look; "well do I know why," and immediately
retired.

Another time, when he came to the door of the cell,
which he never entered, La Esmeralda was singing an old
Spanish ballad; she knew not the meaning of her words,
but it dwelt upon her ear because the Bohemian women
had lulled her with it when quite a child. At the abrupt appearance of that ugly face the damsel stopped short, with
an involuntary start, in the middle of her song. The unhappy bell-ringer dropped upon his knees at the threshold
of the door, and with a beseeching look clasped his clumsy
shapeless hands. "Oh!" said he, sorrowfully, "go on, I pray
you, and drive me not away." Not wishing to vex him, the
trembling girl continued the ballad. By degrees her alarm
subsided, and she gave herself up entirely to the impression of the melancholy tune which she was singing; while
he remained upon his knees, with his hands joined as in
prayer, scarcely breathing, his look intently fixed on the
sparkling orbs of the Bohemian; you would have said that
he was listening to her song with his eyes.

On another occasion, he came to her with an awkward
and bashful air. "Hearken to me," said he, with effort; "I
have something to say to you." She made a sign to him
that she was listening. He then began to sigh, half opened
his lips, appeared for a moment ready to speak, looked at

her, shook his head, and slowly retired, pressing his hand
to his brow, and leaving the Egyptian in amazement.

Among the grotesque heads sculptured in the wall there
was one for which he showed a particular predilection, and
with which he seemed to exchange brotherly looks. The
Egyptian once heard him address it in these words: "Oh!
why am I not of stone, like thee?"

At length, one morning, La Esmeralda, having advanced
to the parapet of the roof, was looking at the Place, over
the sharp roof of St. Jean le Rond.

Quasimodo was behind her. He stationed himself there
on purpose to spare the damsel the disagreeable spectacle
of his ungainly person. On a sudden the Bohemian shuddered; a tear and flash of joy sparkled at once in her eyes;
she fell on her knees, and extended her arms in anguish toward the Place, crying, "Phœbus! come! come! one word,
a single word, for God's sake! Phœbus! Phœbus!" Her
voice, her face, her attitude, her whole figure had the ag-
onizing expression of a shipwrecked person who is making
signals gayly along in the sunshine.

Quasimodo, bending forward, perceived that the object
of this wild and tender appeal was a young and handsome
horseman, a captain, glistening with arms and accouterments, who passed caracoling through the Place, and bowing to a fair lady smiling in her balcony. The officer was
too far off to hear the call of the unhappy girl.

But the poor deaf bell-ringer understood it. A deep sigh
heaved his breast; he turned round, his heart was swollen
with the tears which he repressed; he dashed his convulsive fists against his head; and when he removed them
there was in each of them a handful of red hair.

The Egyptian paid no attention to him. Gnashing his
teeth, he said, in a low tone, "Perdition! That is how one
ought to look, then! One need but have a handsome outside!"

She continued meanwhile upon her knees, and cried,
with vehement agitation, "Oh! there he alights! He is going into that house! Phœbus! Phœbus! He does not hear

me! Phœbus! O! the spiteful woman to talk to him at the same time that I do! Phœbus! Phœbus!"

The deaf bell-ringer watched her. He comprehended this pantomime. The poor fellow's eye filled with tears, but he suffered none of them to escape.

All at once he gently pulled her sleeve. She turned round. He had assumed a look of composure, and said to her, "Shall I go and fetch him?"

She gave a cry of joy. "Oh! go, go! run! quick! that captain! that captain! bring him to me! I will love thee!" She clasped his knees. He could not help shaking his head sorrowfully. "I will go and bring him to you," said he, in a faint voice. He then retired and hurried down the staircase, stifled with sobs.

When he reached the Place, nothing was to be seen but the fine horse fastened to the gate of the Gondalaurier mansion. The captain had just entered. He looked up to the roof of the church. La Esmeralda was still at the same place, in the same posture. He made her a sad sign with his head, and leaned with his back against one of the pillars of the porch, determined to await the captain's departure.

In that house it was one of those festive days which precede a wedding. Quasimodo saw many persons enter, but nobody came out. Every now and then, he looked up at the roof; the Egyptian did not stir any more than he. A groom came and untied the horse, and led him to the stable. The whole day passed in this manner, Quasimodo at the pillar, La Esmeralda on the roof, and Phœbus no doubt at the feet of Fleur-de-Lys.

At length night arrived; a night without a moon, a dark night. To no purpose did Quasimodo keep his eye fixed on La Esmeralda; she soon appeared to be but a white spot in the twilight, which became more and more indistinct, till it was no longer discernible amid the darkness.

The windows of the Gondalaurier mansion, however, continued lighted, even after midnight. Quasimodo, motionless and attentive, saw a multitude of living and dancing shadows passing over the many-colored panes. Had he not been deaf, in proportion as the noises of Paris subsided, he would have heard more and more distinctly sounds of festivity, mirth, and music, within the mansion.

About one in the morning the company began to break up. Quasimodo, enveloped in darkness, watched all the guests as they came out under the porch lighted torches. The captain was not among them.

He was filled with sad thoughts. Ever and anon he looked up at the sky, as if tired of waiting. Large, heavy, ragged, black clouds hung like crape hammocks beneath the starry cope of night. You would have said that they were the cobwebs of the firmament. In one of those moments he all at once saw the glazed door of the balcony mysteriously open. Two persons came forth, and shut it after them without noise. It was a man and a woman. It was with some difficulty that Quasimodo recognized in the one the handsome captain, in the other the young lady whom he had seen in the morning welcoming the officer from the window. The Place was quite dark; and a double crimson curtain, which had collapsed again behind the door at the moment of its shutting, scarcely suffered a gleam of light from the apartment to reach the balcony.

The young captain and the lady, as far as our deaf watchman could judge—for he could not hear a word they said—appeared to indulge in a very tender *tête-à-tête*. The young lady seemed to have permitted the officer to throw his arm around her waist, and feebly withstood a kiss.

Quasimodo witnessed from below this scene, which it was the more delightful to see, inasmuch as it was not intended to be witnessed. He, however, contemplated that happiness, that beauty, with bitterness of soul. After all, Nature was not silent in the poor fellow, and his vertebral column, confoundedly twisted as it was, nevertheless thrilled like any other. He thought of the miserable portion which Providence had already allotted to him; that woman, love, and its pleasures, would be forever passing before his eyes, but that he should never do more than witness the felicity of others. But what afflicted him most in this sight, and mingled anger with his vexation, was, to think what the Egyptian must suffer if she beheld it. To be sure, the night was very dark; La Esmeralda, if she had stayed in the same place—and he had no doubt of that—was at a considerable distance; and it was quite as much as he could do himself to distinguish the lovers in the balcony. This was some consolation.

Meanwhile their conversation became more and more animated. The young lady appeared to beseech the officer not to require more of her. Quasimodo could discern her fair hands clasped, her smiles mingled with tears, her looks uplifted to heaven, and the eager eyes of the captain bent down upon her. Luckily, for the resistance of the female was becoming more and more feeble, the door of the balcony suddenly opened; an aged lady appeared; the fair one looked confused, the officer vexed, and all three went in.

A moment afterward, a horse was prancing beneath the porch, and the brilliant officer, wrapped in his cloak, passed swiftly before Quasimodo. The bell-ringer suffered him to turn the corner of the street, and then ran after him with the agility of a monkey, crying: "Ho! captain!"

The captain pulled up. "What would the varlet with me?" said he, on spying in the dark the uncouth figure limping toward him.

Quasimodo, on coming up to him, boldly laid hold of the horse's bridle. "Follow me, captain," said he; "there is one who would speak with you."

"By Mahound's horns!" muttered Phœbus; "methinks I have seen this rascally scarecrow somewhere or other. Halloo! fellow! let go the bridle."

"Captain," replied the deaf bell-ringer, "ask me not who it is."

"Loose my horse, I tell you," cried Phœbus, angrily. "What means the rogue, hanging thus from my bridle-rein? Dost thou take my horse for a gallows, knave?"

Quasimodo, so far from relaxing his hold of the bridle,

was preparing to turn the horse's head the contrary way. Unable to account for the opposition of the captain, he hastened to give him this explanation. "Come, captain; 'tis a female who is waiting for you—a female who loves you."

"A rare varlet!" said the captain; "to suppose that I am obliged to go to all the women who love me, or say they do. After all, perhaps, she is like thyself with that owl's face. Tell her who sent thee that I am going to be married, and that she may go to the devil."

"Hark ye, monseigneur," cried Quasimodo, thinking with a word to overcome his hesitation; " 'tis the Egyptian whom you are acquainted with."

This intimation made a strong impression upon Phœbus, but not of the kind that the speaker anticipated. It will be recollected that our gallant officer had retired with Fleur-de-Lys a few moments before Quasimodo rescued the condemned girl from the clutches of Charmolue.

"The Egyptian!" he exclaimed, with almost a feeling of terror. "What, then, art thou from the other world?" At the same time he clapped his hand to the hilt of his dagger.

"Quick! quick!" said the dwarf, striving to lead the horse; "this way!"

Phœbus dealt him a smart stroke with his whip across the arm. Quasimodo's eye flashed. He made a movement, as if to rush upon the captain; but, instantly restraining himself, he said: "Oh! how happy you are since there is somebody who loves you!" laying particular emphasis on the word somebody. "Get you gone!" added he, loosing the bridle.

Phœbus clapped spurs to his horse, at the same time swearing lustily. Quasimodo looked after him till he was lost in the darkness. "Oh!" said the poor fellow—"to refuse such a trifle as that!"

He returned to Notre Dame, lighted his lamp, and ascended the tower. As he expected, the Bohemian was still in the same place. The moment she saw him she ran to meet him. "Alone!" she exclaimed, sorrowfully clasping her hands.

"I could not meet with him," said Quasimodo dryly.

"You should have waited all night," she replied, angrily.

He saw her look of displeasure, and comprehended the reproach. "I will watch him better another time," said he, drooping his head.

"Go thy way!" cried she.

He left her. She was dissatisfied with him. He had rather be ill-used by her than give her pain. He therefore kept all the mortification to himself.

From that day he avoided the presence of the Egyptian. He ceased to come to her cell. At most she sometimes caught a glimpse of the bell-ringer on the top of a tower, with his eye fixed in melancholy mood upon her; but the moment he was aware that she saw him he was gone.

Truth obliges us to state that she grieved very little about this voluntary absence of the poor hunchback. At the bottom of her heart she was glad of it. Quasimodo did not deceive himself on this point.

She saw him not, but she felt the presence of a good genius around her. Her fresh supplies of provisions were brought by an invisible hand while she was asleep. One morning she found over her window a cage with birds. Above her cell there was a sculptured figure which frightened her, as she had more than once signified to Quasimodo. One morning—for all these things were done at night—it was gone; it had been broken off. Whoever had clambered up to this piece of sculpture must have risked his life.

Sometimes, in the evening, she heard the voice of some unseen person beneath the penthouse of the belfry singing a wild, sad strain, as if to lull her to sleep. They were verses without rhyme, such as a deaf man might make.

One morning, on opening her eyes, she saw two nose-gays standing in her window. One was in a bright handsome crystal vase, but cracked. The water with which it was filled had run out, and the flowers were faded. The other was a pot of coarse common stoneware, but which retained all the water, and the flowers in it were fresh and fragrant. I know not whether it was done intentionally, but La Esmeralda took the faded nosegay, and carried it all day at her bosom. On that day she heard not the voice singing from the tower—a circumstance that gave her very little concern. She passed whole days in fondling Djali, in watching the door of the logis Gondalaurier, in talking to herself of Phœbus, and in feeding the swallows with crumbs of bread.

For some time she had neither seen nor heard Quasimodo. The poor bell-ringer seemed to have entirely forsaken the church. One night, however, unable to sleep for thinking of her handsome captain, she heard a sigh near her cell. Somewhat alarmed, she rose, and by the light of the moon she saw a shapeless mass lying outside across the doorway. It was Quasimodo asleep upon the stones.

45

Meanwhile public rumor had communicated to the archdeacon the miraculous manner in which the Egyptian had been saved. When apprised of this, he knew not how he felt. He had made up his mind to the death of La Esmeralda, and was therefore easy on that point; he had drained the cup of misery to the dregs. The human heart—Dom Claude had deeply meditated on these matters—cannot contain more than a certain quantity of despair. When a sponge is thoroughly soaked, the sea may pass over it without introducing into it one additional drop.

Now, the sponge being filled by the death of La Esmeralda, Dom Claude could not experience keener suffering in this world. But to know that she was living, and

Phœbus too, was to be exposed anew to the vicissitudes, the shocks, the torments of life; and Claude was weary of them all.

On hearing these tidings, he shut himself up in his cell in the cloisters. He attended neither the conferences of the chapter nor the usual offices. He closed his door against all, not excepting the bishop, and continued to seclude himself in this manner for several weeks. It was reported that he was ill. So he really was.

What was he doing while thus shut up? Under what thoughts was the wretched archdeacon struggling? Was he engaged in a last conflict with his indomitable passion? Was he combining a final plan of death for her and perdition for himself?

His Jehan, his beloved brother, his spoilt child, came to his door, knocked, swore, entreated, mentioned his name ten times over—Claude would not open to him.

He passed whole days with his face close to the panes of his window. From that window, situated as we have said in the cloisters, he could see the cell of La Esmeralda; he perceived the girl herself with her goat, sometimes with Quasimodo. He remarked the little attentions of the scurvy hunchback, his respectful manners and his submissive demeanor toward the Egyptian. For the captain—it was not surprising; but for such an object as that! The idea distracted him.

Every night his frenzied imagination pictured to him La Esmeralda in all those attitudes which had made the blood boil most vehemently in his veins.

He saw her stretched upon the wounded captain, her eyes closed, her beautiful bosom covered with his blood, at the moment of transport, when the archdeacon had imprinted on her pale lips that kiss which had felt to the unfortunate girl, though half dead, like the touch of a burning coal. Again he saw her stripped by the rough hands of the torturers; he saw them expose her finely-shaped leg, and her white supple knee, while they encased her delicate little foot in the screw-buskin. He further saw that ivory knee alone left uncovered by the horrible apparatus. Lastly, he figured to himself the forlorn damsel, the rope about her neck, with bare feet, bare shoulders, bare bosom, as he had seen her on the day of penance. These images made his blood boil, and a thrill run through his whole frame.

One night, among others, they inflamed him to such a degree, that, leaping out of his bed, he threw a surplice over him, and quitted his cell, with his lamp in his hand, half naked, wild, and his eyes glaring like fire.

He knew where to find the key of the Porte Rouge, the communication between the cloisters and the church; and, as the reader knows, he always carried about him a key of the staircase to the towers.

46

On that night La Esmeralda had fallen asleep in her lodge, forgetful of the past, and full of hope and pleasing thoughts. She had slept for some time, dreaming, as she was wont, of Phœbus, when she seemed to hear a kind of noise about her. Her sleep was always light and unquiet—a bird's sleep; the least thing awoke her. She opened her eyes. The night was very dark. She nevertheless saw at the window a face looking at her; there was a lamp which threw a light upon this apparition. At the moment when the figure saw that it was perceived by La Esmeralda, it blew out the lamp. The girl, however, had had time to get a glimpse of it; her eyelids closed with affright. "Oh!" she cried in a faint voice—"the priest!"

All her past miseries flashed upon her again like lightning. She fell back on her bed frozen with horror. A moment afterward, she felt something touch her, which made her shudder. She raised herself furiously into a sitting posture. The priest clasped her in both his arms. She would have shrieked, but could not.

"Begone, murderer! begone, monster!" said she, in a voice faint and tremulous with rage and terror.

"Mercy! mercy!" muttered the priest, pressing his lips to her shoulders.

Seizing with both hands the hair remaining on his bald head, she strove to prevent his kisses, as though they had been the bites of a mad dog.

"Mercy! mercy!" repeated the wretched priest. "If thou didst but know what my love for thee is!—it is—fire; it is molten lead; it is a thousand daggers in my heart!" And he held her two arms with superhuman force.

"Loose me!" cried she, distractedly, "or I will spit in thy face!"

He loosed his hold. "Strike me; heap indignities upon me; do what thou wilt! but for mercy's sake, love me!"

She then struck him with childish rage. "Begone, demon!" said she, while her taper fingers bent in order to scratch his face.

"Love me! for pity love me!" cried the wretched priest, grappling her, and returning her blows with kisses.

She soon found that he was too strong for her. " 'Tis time to put an end to this!" said he, gnashing his teeth.

Palpitating, exhausted, vanquished, she made a last effort, and began to cry, "Help! help!—vampire! a vampire!"

No one came. Djali alone was awakened, and bleated with affright.

"Be silent," said the panting priest.

All at once, having fallen on the floor in the struggle, the hand of the Egyptian touched something cold, that felt like metal. It was Quasimodo's whistle. She seized it with a convulsion of hope, lifted it to her lips, and whistled with all the force she had left. The whistle gave out a clear, shrill, piercing sound.

"What is that?" inquired the priest.

Almost at the same moment he felt himself grasped by a vigorous arm. The cell was dark; he could not discern who held him thus; but he heard teeth gnashing with rage, and there was just sufficient light scattered amid the darkness to enable him to see the broad blade of a cutlass glistening above his head.

The priest imagined that he perceived the figure of Quasimodo. He supposed that it could be no other. He recollected having stumbled on entering against a bundle of something lying across the doorway outside. Still, as the newcomer uttered not a word, he knew not what to believe. He caught the arm which held the cutlass, crying, "Quasimodo!" forgetful, in this moment of distress, that Quasimodo was deaf.

In the twinkling of an eye, the priest was stretched on the floor, and felt a leaden knee pressing upon his breast. From the angular pressure of that knee he recognized Quasimodo; but what could he do? how was he to make himself known to the assailant? Night rendered the deaf monster blind.

He gave himself up for lost. The girl, with as little pity as an enraged tigress, interposed not to save him. The cutlass was descending upon his head. The moment was critical. All at once his adversary appeared to hesitate. "No," said a muttering voice: "no blood upon her!" It was actually the voice of Quasimodo.

The priest then felt a huge hand dragging him by the leg out of the cell; it was there that he was to die. Luckily for him, the moon had just burst forth. When they were past the door, her pale beams fell upon the head of the priest. Quasimodo looked at his face, was seized with a trembling, relaxed his grasp, and started back. The Egyptian, who had advanced to the threshold of the cell, saw with surprise the actors suddenly exchanging characters. It was now the priest's turn to threaten, Quasimodo's to supplicate. The priest, having furiously assailed the hunchback with gestures of anger and reproach, at length motioned him to retire. Quasimodo stood for a moment with bowed

head, and then, falling on his knees before the door of the
Egyptian, "Monseigneur," said he, in a tone of gravity and
resignation, "kill me first, and do what you please afterward."

As he thus spoke he offered his cutlass to the priest. Beside himself with rage the priest clutched at the weapon;
but La Esmeralda was too quick for him. Snatching the
cutlass from the hand of Quasimodo, and bursting into an
hysteric laugh, "Come on!" said she to the priest.

She held the blade uplifted. The priest wavered. She
would certainly have struck. "Thou darest not approach
now, coward," she cried. Then, with unpitying look, and
well aware that she should pierce the heart of the priest as
with a thousand red-hot irons, she added, "Ah! I know that
Phœbus is not dead!"

The priest, with a violent kick, overthrew Quasimodo,
and rushed quivering with rage to the vaulted staircase.
When he was gone, Quasimodo picked up the whistle
which had been the means of saving the Egyptian. "It was
getting rusty," said he, handing it to her. He then left her
to herself.

The damsel, vehemently agitated by this violent scene,
sank exhausted upon her bed, and sobbed aloud. Her horizon had again become overcast.

The priest, on his part, groped his way back to his cell.
The thing was conclusive. Dom Claude was jealous of
Quasimodo! With pensive look he repeated the fatal
phrase, "Nobody shall have her!"

47

As soon as Gringoire perceived the turn which this
whole affair was taking, and that decidedly halter,

gibbet, and other unpleasant things would be the lot of the principal characters of this comedy, he felt no sort of inclination to interfere in it. The vagabonds, with whom he had remained, considering that after all they were the best company in Paris, had continued to interest themselves for the Egyptian. This he thought perfectly natural in people who, like her, had no other prospect than Charmolue and Torterue, and who never soared like him into the regions of imagination between the two wings of Pegasus. From them he learned that she whom he had espoused over the broken jug had taken sanctuary in Notre Dame, and he was very glad of it. He thought sometimes of the little goat, and that was all. In the daytime he performed mountebank tricks for a livelihood, and at night he elucubrated a memorial against the Bishop of Paris.

One day he had stopped near St. Germain l'Auxerrois, at the corner of a building called the For-l'Eveque, which faced another named the For-le-Roi. At this For-l'Eveque there was a beautiful chapel of the fourteenth century, the choir of which looked toward the street. Gringoire was intently examining the sculptures on the outside. It was one of those moments of absorbing, exclusive, supreme enjoyment, when the artist sees nothing in the world but his art, and sees the world in his art. All at once he felt a hand fall heavily upon his shoulder. He turned about. It was his old friend, his old master, the archdeacon.

He was stupefied. It was a long time since he had seen the archdeacon, and Dom Claude was one of those solemn and impassioned personages, the meeting with whom always deranges the equilibrium of the skeptical philosopher.

The archdeacon kept silence for a few moments, during which Gringoire had leisure to observe him. He found Dom Claude greatly altered—pale as a winter morning, his eyes sunk, his hair almost white. The priest at length broke this silence, saying, but in a grave, freezing tone, "How goes it with you, Master Pierre?"

"As to my health?" said Gringoire, "why, I may say, so-

so. Upon the whole good. I take everything in moderation.
You know, master, the secret of health recommended by
Hippocrates—*cibi, potus, somni, venus, omnia moderata
sint*."

"Then you have no troubles, Master Pierre?" rejoined
the archdeacon, looking steadfastly at Gringoire.

"No, i' faith, not I."

"And what are you doing now?"

"You see, master, I am examining the cut of these
stones, and the way in which that basso-relievo is chiseled."

The priest smiled. It was one of those bitter smiles
which lift up but one of the corners of the mouth. "And
that amuses you?"

" 'Tis paradise!" exclaimed Gringoire. And, turning to
the sculptures, with the dazzled look of a demonstrator of
living phenomena, "Don't you think," said he, "that this
metamorphosis in low relief, for example, is executed with
great skill, patience, and delicacy? Look at this little pillar.
About what capital did you ever see foliage more elegant
and more highly finished?

Dom Claude interrupted him. "You are happy, then?"

"Yes, upon my honor," replied Gringoire, with warmth.
"At first I was fond of women, then of beasts, now of
stones. They are quite as amusing as women and beasts,
and much less treacherous."

The priest raised his hand to his brow. It was his habitual gesture. "Indeed!"

"Stay," said Gringoire, "you shall see that a man need
not want pleasure." He took the arm of the priest, who
made no resistance, and drew him into the staircase turret
of the For-l'Eveque. "There is a staircase for you! Whenever I look at it I am happy. It is the simplest of its kind,
and yet the most exquisite in Paris. Every step is rounded
off underneath. Its beauty and simplicity consist in the
overlapping parts, which for a foot or thereabout are let in,
mortised, imbedded, enchained, inchased, dovetailed one

into another, and bite in such a way as to be not less solid than goodly."

"And you wish for nothing?"

"No."

"And regret nothing?"

"Neither wishes nor regrets. I have arranged my life."

"Man arranges," said Claude; "circumstances derange."

"I am a Pyrrhonian philosopher," replied Gringoire, "and I keep everything in equilibrium."

"And how do you earn a livelihood?"

"I still make epics and tragedies now and then; but what brings in most money is the trade you have seen me follow—carrying pyramids of chairs and so forth between my teeth."

"A scurvy trade for a philosopher."

"It has to do with the equilibrium," said Gringoire. "When you take an idea into your head, you find it in everything."

"I know it," replied the archdeacon.

After a pause the priest resumed: "You are nevertheless as poor as ever?"

"Poor enough, I grant you, but not unhappy."

At this moment the dialogue was interrupted by the trampling of horses, and a company of archers of the king's ordnance, with raised lances, and an officer at their head, passed the end of the street. The cavalcade was brilliant, and the pavement rang beneath their tread.

"How you eye that officer," said Gringoire to the archdeacon.

"I rather think I know him."

"What is his name?"

"I believe," said Claude, "his name is Phœbus de Chateaupers."

"Phœbus, a curious name! There is also a Phœbus Comte de Foix. I once knew a girl who never swore but by Phœbus."

"Come this way!" said the priest, "I have something to say to you."

Ever since the appearance of the archers, some agitation was perceptible under the frozen exterior of the archdeacon. He walked on, followed by Gringoire, who was wont to obey him, like all who had ever approached him, such was the ascendency which he exercised. They proceeded in silence to the Rue des Bernardins, where a casual passenger only was at times to be seen. Here Dom Claude stopped short.

"What have you to say to me, master?" inquired Gringoire.

"Don't you think," said the archdeacon, with a look of deep reflection, "that the dress of those archers, who have just passed, is finer than yours or mine?"

Gringoire shook his head. "By my fay! I like my red and yellow jacket better than those shells of iron and steel. A sorry pleasure, to make at every step the same noise that the Ironmongers' Quay would do in an earthquake!"

"Then, Gringoire, you have never envied those comely fellows in their habiliments of war?"

"Envied them!—for what, Mr. Archdeacon?—for their strength, their armor, their discipline? Far preferable are philosophy and independence in rags. I had rather be the head of a fly than the tail of a lion."

"That is singular!" said the priest, thoughtfully. "A goodly uniform is nevertheless goodly."

Gringoire, seeing him absorbed in thought, left him, and went up to the porch of a neighboring house. Presently he returned, clapping his hands. "If you were not so deeply engaged with the goodly uniforms of the men-at-arms, Mr. Archdeacon, I would beg you to go and look at that door. I always said that the entrance to the Sieur Aubrey's house is not to be matched all the world over."

"Pierre Gringoire," said the archdeacon, "what have you done with the young Egyptian dancing-girl?"

"La Esmeralda? Why, how abruptly you change the conversation!"

"Was she not your wife?"

"Yes, after a fashion; by means of a broken jug we were

joined together for four years. By the by," added Gringoire, with a half bantering tone and look, "you seem to be always thinking of her."

"And do you never think of her now?"

"Very little. I am so busy! But what a charming little goat that was!"

"Did not that Bohemian save your life?"

"True enough, by'r Lady!"

"Well, what is become of her? What have you done with her?"

"I can't tell. I believe they hanged her!"

"You believe?"

"I am not sure. When I saw that they were determined to hang somebody, I got out of the way."

"Is that all you know about the matter?"

"Stop a moment! I was told that she had taken sanctuary in Notre Dame, and that she was safe there, which I was very glad to hear; but I have not been able to ascertain whether her goat was saved along with her—and that is all I know about the matter."

"I can tell you more, then," cried Dom Claude, his voice, hitherto low almost to a whisper, rising to the loudness of thunder. "She has actually taken sanctuary in Notre Dame. But in three days Justice will again seize her, and she will be hanged in the Greve. The parliament has issued a decree."

"That is a pity!" said Gringoire.

In the twinkling of an eye the priest had relapsed into his former coldness and tranquillity.

"And," resumed the poet, "who the devil has amused himself with soliciting an order of restitution? Why could they not let the parliament alone? What harm is there in it if a poor girl does seek shelter among the swallows' nests under the flying buttresses of Notre Dame?"

"There are Satans in the world," rejoined the archdeacon.

" 'Tis infernally cross-grained!" observed Gringoire.

"Then she did save your life?" resumed the archdeacon, after a pause.

"That was among my very good friends, the vagabonds. She came in the nick of time, or I should have been hanged. They would have been sorry for it now."

"Will you then not try to do something for her?"

"I desire no better, Dom Claude; but perhaps I may get my own neck into an ugly noose?"

"What signifies that?"

"What signifies it! You are exceedingly kind, master! I have just begun two great works."

The priest struck his forehead. Notwithstanding the composure which he affected, a violent gesture from time to time betrayed his inward convulsions. "What can be done to save her?"

"Master," said Gringoire, "I answer, *Il padelt,* which is Turkish for God is our hope."

"What can be done to save her?" repeated Claude, thoughtfully.

Gringoire, in his turn, struck his brow. "Hark ye, master, I have no lack of imagination; I will devise expedients. Suppose we solicit the king's pardon."

"Pardon! of Louis XI!"

"Why not?"

"Take the bone from the hungry tiger."

Gringoire cast about for other expedients. "Well, stop! Shall we make declaration that the girl is pregnant, and demand an examination of matrons?"

The pupil of the priest's hollow eye sparkled. "Pregnant, dolt! Knowest thou aught to that purpose?"

His look alarmed Gringoire. "Oh, no, not I!" he hastily replied. "Our marriage was literally *foris maritagium*—for I was shut out. At any rate we should obtain a respite."

"Stupid oaf! hold thy tongue!"

"Nay, don't be angry," muttered Gringoire. "One might obtain a respite; that would harm nobody, and would put forty deniers parisis into the pockets of the matrons, who are poor women."

The priest heard him not. "At any rate," he muttered, "she must go away! The order must be executed in three days! Besides, if there were no order, that Quasimodo! Who can account for the depraved tastes of women!" Then raising his voice: "Master Pierre," said he, "I have well weighed the matter; there is but one way to save her."

"And which?—I can see none for my part."

"Hark ye, Master Pierre; recollect that to her you owe your life. I will tell you frankly my idea. The church is watched night and day; such persons as have been seen to enter are suffered to go out again. Of course you would be allowed to go in. You must come. I will take you to her. You must change clothes with her."

"So far, so good," observed the philosopher. "And then?"

"Why then she will go away in your clothes, and you will remain in hers. You will be hanged perhaps; but she will escape."

Gringoire rubbed his brow with a profoundly serious look.

"I declare," said he, "that is an idea which would never come into my head of itself."

At this unlooked-for proposition of Dom Claude's, the open and good-humored countenance of the poet was overcast, like a smiling landscape of Italy, when some unlucky blast dashes a cloud upon the sun.

"Well, Gringoire, what say you to this expedient?"

"I say, master, they will not hang me perhaps, but they will hang me to a certainty."

"That does not concern us."

"The devil!" exclaimed Gringoire.

"She saved your life. You are only paying a debt."

"How many of my debts besides that are unpaid!"

"Master Pierre, you absolutely must comply."

The archdeacon spoke imperatively.

"Hark ye, Dom Claude," replied the dismayed poet, "you cling to this idea; but you are quite wrong. I see no

reason why I should thrust my head into the halter instead
of another."

"What is there then that so strongly attaches you to
life?"

"Why, a thousand things."

"What are they?—I would ask."

"What are they? The fresh air, the blue sky, morning
and evening, the warm sunshine, the moonlight, my good
friends the vagabonds, our romps with the good-natured
damsels, the beautiful architectural works of Paris to study,
three thick books to write—one of them against the bishop
and his mills—and I know not what besides."

"A head fit for a bell!" muttered the archdeacon. "Well,
but tell me, who saved this life which is so charming to
thee? To whom is it owing that thou yet breathest this air,
beholdest that sky, and canst amuse thy lark's spirit with
extravagances and follies? What wouldst thou be but for
her? And yet thou canst suffer her to die—her, to whom
thou owest thy life—her, that beautiful, lovely, adorable
creature, almost as necessary to the light of the world as
the sun himself; while thou, half-sage, half-madman, rough
sketch of something or other, species of vegetable, who
imaginest thou canst walk and think, thou wilt continue to
live with the life of which thou hast robbed her, as useless
as a candle at noonday! Nay, nay, have some feeling, Gringoire; be generous in thy turn. It was she who set the example."

The priest was warm. Gringoire listened to him at first
with a look of indecision; presently he began to soften,
and at last he put on a tragic grimace, which made his wan
face look like that of a newborn infant which has the colic.

"You are pathetic," said he, brushing away a tear. "Well,
I will think about it. 'Tis a droll idea, this of yours!" Pausing a while, he continued: "After all, who knows! perhaps
they will not hang me. Betrothal is not always followed by
marriage. When they find me up yonder in the little cell,
so grotesquely attired in cap and petticoat, perhaps they
will only laugh."

The priest interrupted him. "Are we agreed?"

"After all, what is death?" continued Gringoire, in the warmth of his excitement. "An unpleasant moment, a toll, a passage from little to nothing. When someone asked Cercidas of Megalopolis if he should like to die—'Why not?' he replied, 'for, after death, I shall see those great men, Pythagoras among the philosophers, Hecatæus among the historians, Homer among the poets, and Olympus among the musicians.'"

The archdeacon held out his hand. "It is settled, then; you will come tomorrow?"

This gesture, and the question which accompanied it, brought Gringoire back from his digression. "Beshrew me; no!" said he, in the tone of a man awakening from sleep. "Be hanged!—too absurd! I beg to be excused."

"Farewell then!" and the archdeacon added, muttering between his teeth, "I will find thee out again!"

"I don't wish that fellow to find me again," thought Gringoire, running after Dom Claude. "Hold, Mr. Archdeacon, no malice between old friends! You take an interest in that girl, my wife, I would say—quite right! You have devised a stratagem to withdraw her in safety from Notre Dame, but to me your expedient is extremely disagreeable. A capital idea has just occurred to me. If I could propose a method of extricating her from the dilemma without entangling my own neck in the smallest running noose whatever—what would you say to it? would that satisfy you? or must I absolutely be hanged before you are content?"

The priest tore off the buttons of his cassock with irritation. "Eternal babbler! what is thy proposal!"

"Yes," resumed Gringoire, talking to himself, and clapping his forefinger to his nose in the attitude of meditation—"that's it!—she is a favorite with the dark race. They will rise at the first word. Nothing easier. A sudden attack. In the confusion, carry her away! Tomorrow night—they will desire nothing better."

"Your proposal! Let us hear!" said the priest, shaking him.

Gringoire turned majestically toward him. "Leave me alone! you see I am composing." Having considered for a few moments longer, he clapped his hands in exultation, exclaiming, "Admirable! sure to succeed!"

"But the means?" inquired Claude, angrily. Gringoire's face beamed with triumph.

"Come hither, then, and lend me your ear. 'Tis a right bold counter-mine, which will get all of us out of our trouble. By heaven! it must be confessed that I am no fool."

He stopped short. "By the by, is the little goat with the girl?"

"Yes!—devil fetch thee!"

"They meant to have hanged her too—did they not?"

"What is that to me?"

"Yes, they meant to hang her. Why, it was only last month that they hanged a sow. The hangman likes that—he eats the meat afterward. Hang my pretty Djali! Poor, dear little lamb!"

"Malisons upon thee!" cried Dom Claude. "Thou thyself art the hangman. What means, dolt, hast thou devised for saving her? Must one tear thine idea from thee with pincers?"

"Gently, master, I will tell you."

Gringoire bent his lips to the archdeacon's ear, and whispered very softly, at the same time casting an uneasy look from one end of the street to the other though not a creature was passing. When he had finished, Dom Claude grasped his hand, and said coldly, "Good! to-morrow?"

"Tomorrow," repeated Gringoire. The archdeacon retired one way, while he went the other, saying to himself, in an undertone, "A rare business this, Monsieur Pierre Gringoire! No matter! It shall not be said, that because one is little one shrinks from great undertakings. Bito carried a full-grown bull upon his shoulders; the wagtail, the nightingale, the swallow, cross the ocean."

48

On returning to his cell, the archdeacon found his brother, Jehan du Moulin, who had passed the time while waiting by sketching his brother's profile in charcoal, with a caricature of a large nose.

Dom Claude's thoughts were so busy with other matters that he scarcely glanced at his brother. That happy-go-lucky, impish face, the brightness of which had so many times restored serenity to the gloomy physiognomy of the priest, was now incapable of dissipating the mist which each day was gathering thicker and thicker over a corrupted, mephitic, stagnant soul.

"Brother," said Jehan dryly, "I have come to see you."

The archdeacon didn't even raise his eyes.

"What do you want?"

"Brother," resumed the young hypocrite, "you are so good to me, and you give me such excellent advice, that I always come back to you."

"What now?"

"Alas, brother, you were right when you said to me, 'Jehan! Jehan! *cessat doctorum doctrina, discipulorum disciplina,* Jehan, be prudent! Jehan, be studious! Jehan, do not pass the night away from the college without just reason and the permission of your master. Do not beat the Picards, *noli, Joannes verberare Picardos.* Don't rot like an unlettered ass, *quasi asinus illitteratus,* upon the straw of the school. Jehan, submit to punishment at the discretion of the master. Jehan, go every evening to the chapel, and sing an anthem and pray to the glorious Blessed Virgin Mary!' Alas! this was very excellent advice."

"And so?"

"Brother, you see standing here a sinner, a criminal, a wretch, a libertine, a monstrous reprobate! My dear brother, Jehan has taken your gracious counsels as mere straw and dung to be trodden underfoot, and he has been well chastened for it. The good Lord is exceedingly just. So long as I had money, I squandered it in foolish, joyous living. Oh! how hideous and vile to look back upon that debauchery which seemed at the time so charming! Now I have not a single sou left; I have sold my linen, my shirt, and my towel. No more gay life for me. The burning candle has gone out, and I have only the poor wick that smokes under my nose. The girls make fun of me. I am drinking water. I am harassed by remorse and creditors."

"What else?" asked the archdeacon.

"Alas! my very dear brother, I would like to live a better life. I come to you, contrite of heart, penitent. I confess my evil ways. I beat my breast with heavy blows. You are very right to want me to become one day a licensee and submonitor of the college of Torchi. At this very moment I feel called to that office. But I have no ink left; I need to buy some; I have no pens, I must buy some; I have no paper, no book, I must buy some. To buy them I have need of a little money. And I come to you, brother, with my heart full of contrition."

"Is that all?"

"Yes," said the scholar. "A little money."

"I have none."

The scholar then said with an air at once grave and determined, "Well, my brother, I regret to inform you that I have received from other quarters very fine offers and propositions. You will not give me any money? No? In that case, I will become a Truand."

On pronouncing this monstrous word he assumed the stance of an Ajax expecting a thunderbolt to fall upon his head.

The archdeacon said to him coldly, "Then become a Truand."

Jehan made a low bow, and descended the cloister staircase whistling.

Just as he was passing through the court of the cloisters, under the window of his brother's cell, he heard the window open. Raising his head he saw the archdeacon's severe face looking through the opening.

"Go to the devil!" said Dom Claude. "This is the last money you will get from me."

So saying, the priest threw out a purse to Jehan, which made a large bump on his forehead. With that the youth set off, at once angry and pleased, like a dog that has been pelted with marrow-bones.

49

The reader has not perhaps forgotten that part of the Cour des Miracles was enclosed by the ancient wall surrounding the Ville, many of the towers of which had begun so early as this period to fall to ruin. One of these towers had been converted into a place of entertainment by the vagabonds.

The cellar, therefore, was the tavern. The descent to it was by a low door and stairs as rugged as a classic Alexandrine. Over the door there was by way of sign a wondrous daubing representing a number of new sous and dead chickens (*des sous neufs et de poulets tues*), with this pun underneath: *Aux sonneurs pourles trepasses.*

One evening, at the moment when the curfew-bell was ringing in every belfry in Paris, the sergeants of the watch, had they chanced to enter the redoubtable Cour des Miracles, might have remarked that there was a greater tumult than usual in the tavern of the vagabonds, and that the inmates were both drinking and swearing more lustily. In the open space without were numerous groups conversing in a subdued tone, as when some important enterprise is planning; and here and there a varlet was crouching, and whetting some rusty weapon or other upon a paving-stone.

In the tavern itself, however, wine, and gaming, were so powerful a diversion to the ideas which on that evening engrossed the vagabond crew, that it would have been difficult to discover from the conversation of the topers the nature of their project. They merely appeared to be in higher spirits than ordinary, and between the legs of each was seen glistening some weapon or other—a bill-book, a hatchet, a thick bludgeon, or the supporter of an old arquebuse.

The room, of circular form, was very spacious; but the tables were so close, and the customers so numerous, that all the contents of the tavern, men and women, benches and beer jugs, those who were drinking, those who were sleeping, those who were gaming, the able-bodied and the crippled, seemed to be tumbled together pell-mell, with just as much order and harmony as a heap of oyster shells.

Notwithstanding the confusion, after the first glance there might be distinguished, in this multitude, three principal groups crowding around three personages with whom the reader is already acquainted. One of these personages, grotesquely bedizened with many a piece of Eastern frippery, was Matthias Hunyadi Spicali, Duke of Egypt and Bohemia. The varlet was seated on a table, his legs crossed, his finger uplifted, imparting in a loud voice sundry lessons in black and white magic to many a gaping face round him. Another party had drawn closely about our old friend, the valiant king of Thunes, who was armed to the very teeth. Clopin Trouillefou, with grave look and in a low voice, was superintending the pillage of a large hogshead full of arms, which stood with head knocked out before him, and from which stores of hatchets, swords, coats of mail, hunting knives, spearheads, saws, augers, were disgorged like apples and grapes from a cornucopia. Each took from the heap what he pleased—one a helmet, another a long rapier, a third a cross or basket-hilted dagger. The very children armed themselves, and there were even little urchins cuirassed and accoutered, running between the legs of the topers like large beetles.

Amid all this din, upon the bench in the chimney corner was seated a philosopher absorbed in meditation, his feet in the ashes, and his eye fixed on the burning brands. It was Pierre Gringoire.

"Come, make haste, arm yourselves! we shall start in an hour!" said Clopin Trouillefou to his crew.

Two card players were quarreling. "Knave," cried the more rubicund of the two, holding up his fist at the other, "I will mark thee with the club. Thou shalt be qualified to succeed Mistigri in the card-parties of Monseigneur the King."

"Oaf," roared a Norman, who might easily be known by his nasal twang, "we are crammed together here like the saints of Callouville!"

"My sons," said the Duke of Egypt to his auditors, in his falsetto, "the witches of France go to the Sabbath without broom or aught else to ride on, merely with a few magical words; those of Italy always have a goat at the door waiting for them. They are all obliged to go out of the house through the chimney."

The voice of the young warrior in armor was heard above the uproar. "Huzza! huzza!" cried he, "my first feat of arms today! A vagabond! Zounds! what am I but a vagabond! Pour me out some drink! My friends, my name is Jehan Frollo du Moulin, and I am a gentleman. I could lay any wager that if Jupiter were a gendarme, he would be fond of plunder. We are going, brothers, on a rare expedition. We are valiant fellows. Lay siege to the church, break open the doors, carry off the damsel, rescue her from the judges, save her from the priests, and dismantle the cloisters, burn the bishop in his palace—why, we shall do it all in less time than a burgomaster takes to eat a basin of soup. Our cause is a righteous one; we'll plunder Notre Dame; that's flat. We'll hang Quasimodo. Do you know

Quasimodo, fair gentlewomen? Have ye seen him puffing
upon the great bell on a Whit Sunday? By Beelzebub's
horns, that is grand! you would take him for a devil astride
of a ghoul. I say, my friends, I am a vagabond to my
heart's core, a canter in my soul, a cadger born."

Meanwhile the rabble applauded with bursts of laughter;
and as the tumult swelled around him, the scholar shouted,
"How delightful!—*populi debacchantis populosa debac-
chatio!*" His eye swimming in ecstasy, he then fell
a-chanting, in the tone of a canon at vespers; but, suddenly
stopping short, he cried, "Here, you devil's taverner, give
me some supper!"

Then followed a moment of comparative quiet, during
which the Duke of Egypt raised his shrill voice, while in-
structing his Bohemians. "The weasel is called Aduine;
the fox, Bluefoot; the wolf, Grayfoot or Goldfoot; the bear,
the old man, or the grandfather. The cap of a gnome renders you invisible, and enables you to see invisible things.
Every toad that is baptized ought to be dressed in red or
black velvet, with a bell about its neck and a bell at each
foot. The godfather must take hold of the head; the godmother, of the rump."

Meanwhile the crew continued to arm themselves at the
other end of the tavern, amid such whispers as these:

"Poor Esmeralda!" said a Bohemian. "She is our
sister—we must release her."

"Is she still in Notre Dame?" asked a Jew-looking peddler.

"Ay, by the mass!"

"Well then, comrades!" cried the peddler, "to Notre
Dame! the sooner the better! In the chapel of St. Fereol
and St. Ferrutien there are two statues, one of St. John
Baptist, the other of St. Antony, both of gold, weighing together seventeen marks fifteen sterlings, and the pedestals
of silver gilt seventeen marks five ounces. I know this to
a certainty—I am by trade a goldsmith."

By this time Jehan's supper was set before him. Falling
to with an excellent appetite, he exclaimed, "By St. Voult-

de-Lucques!—the people call him St. Goguelu—I am the happiest fellow in Paris, though I have renounced the half of a house situate, lying, and being in Paradise, promised me by my brother the archdeacon. Look at that simpleton, gazing at me with the smooth look of an archduke. There is another on my left with tusks so long that they hide his chin. Body o' Mahound! comrade! thou hast the very air and odor of a bone-dealer, and yet hast the assurance to clap thyself down so near me! I am noble, my friend. Trade is incompatible with nobility. Go thy ways!—Soho! you there! what are ye fighting for?"

So saying, he dashed his plate on the pavement, and began singing with all his might one of the peculiar songs of the lawless crew of whom he had become a worthy associate.

Clopin Trouillefou had meanwhile finished his distribution of arms. He went up to Gringoire, who, with his feet on the andiron, appeared to be in a brown study. "Friend Pierre," said the King of Thunes, "what the devil art thou thinking of?"

Gringoire turned toward him with a melancholy smile. "I am fond of the fire, my dear sir," said he, "not for the trivial reason that it warms our feet or cooks our soup, but because there are sparks in it. Sometimes I pass whole hours watching those sparks. I discover a thousand things in those stars which sprinkle the black chimney-back. Those stars are worlds too."

"Thunder and death, if I understand thee!" cried the King of Thunes. "Dost know what hour it is?"

"Not I," answered Gringoire.

Clopin then went to the Duke of Egypt. "Comrade Matthias," said he, "it lacks not quite one quarter of an hour. I am told the king is in Paris."

"One reason more why we should get our sister out of their clutches," replied the old Bohemian.

"Thou speakest like a man, Matthias," rejoined Trouillefou. "Besides, we shall get on swimmingly. No resistance to fear in the church. The canons are mere hares,

and we are strong. The officers of the Parliament will be
finely taken in tomorrow when they go to look for her. By
the Pope's nose! they shall not hang the comely damsel."

With these words Clopin sallied forth from the tavern.

At that moment Clopin returned, and shouted with a
voice of thunder, "Midnight!"

At this signal, which had the effect of the sound to
horse upon a regiment in halt, all the vagabond crew, men,
women, and children, poured in a torrent out of the tavern,
with a loud noise of arms and the clanking of iron implements.

The moon was overcast. The Cour des Miracles was
quite dark. Not a light was to be seen. It was nevertheless
filled with a multitude of both sexes, who talked in low
tones together. A vast buzz was to be heard, and all sorts
of weapons will be seen glistening in the dark. Clopin
mounted a huge stone. "To your ranks, ye men of Cant,"
he cried. "To your ranks, Egypt! To your ranks, Galilee!"
A bustle ensued amid the darkness. The immense multitude appeared to be forming in column. In a few minutes
the King of Thunes again raised his voice. "Now, silence
in passing through the streets! No torch is to be lit till we
are at Notre Dame. March!"

In less than ten minutes the horsemen of the watch fled
panic-stricken before a long black procession descending
in profound silence toward the Pont-au-Change, along the
winding streets which run in all directions through the
massive quarter of the Halles.

50

That same night Quasimodo slept not. He had just gone
his last round in the church. He had not remarked that,

at the moment when he was fastening the doors, the archdeacon had passed, or the ill-humor he had shown on seeing him employed in carefully bolting and padlocking the
immense iron bars, which gave to the large folding doors
the solidity of a wall. Dom Claude appeared that night to
be more deeply absorbed in thought than usual. Ever since
the nocturnal adventure in the cell, he had treated Quasimodo with great harshness; but, in spite of this usage, nay,
even though he sometimes went so far as to strike him,
nothing could shake the submission, the patience, the de-
voted resignation of the faithful bell-ringer. From the archdeacon he would take anything, abuse, threats, blows,
without murmuring a reproach, without uttering a complaint. The utmost that he did was to watch the archdeacon
with anxiety when he ascended the staircase of the tower;
but Claude had of himself cautiously abstained from appearing again in the presence of the Egyptian.

That night, then, Quasimodo, after taking a glance at his
bells began to take a survey of Paris.

While his eye ranged over this expanse of haze and
darkness, an unaccountable feeling of apprehension and
uneasiness gained upon him. For several days past he had
been upon his guard. He had observed suspicious looking
men prowling incessantly about the church, and keeping
their eyes fixed on the young girl's asylum. He imagined
that some plot against the unfortunate refugee might be on
foot, and that the hatred of the people might be directed
against her as it was against himself. So he stood on the
watch, upon his tower, *revant dans son revoir,* as Rabelais
expresses it, gazing by turns at the cell and at the city,
making sure guard, like a good dog, with a heart full of
distrust.

All at once, while he was scrutinizing the great city with
the eye which Nature, by way of compensation, had made
so piercing that it almost supplied the deficiency of the
other organs, it seemed to him that the outline of the quay
of La Vielle Peelleterhie had an extraordinary appearance;
that there was a motion at that point; that the black line of

the parapet, defined upon the white surface of the water, was not straight and steady like that of the other quays; but that it undulated to the eye, like the waves of a river, or like the heads of a moving multitude. This struck him as strange. He redoubled his attention. The movement appeared to be toward the City. It lasted some time on the quay, then subsided by degrees, as if that which caused it were entering the interior of the Isle; it afterward ceased entirely, and the outline of the quay again became straight and motionless.

While Quasimodo was forming all sorts of conjectures, the movement seemed to reappear in the Rue du Parvis, which runs into the City, perpendicularly to the facade of Notre Dame. At last, notwithstanding the intense darkness, he perceived the head of a column approaching through this street, and the next moment a crowd spread itself over the Place du Parvis, where nothing could be distinguished but that it was a crowd.

This sight was alarming. It is probable that this singular procession, which seemed to make a point of avoiding observation, was equally careful to maintain profound silence; yet it could not help making some noise, were it only by the trampling of feet. But even this sound reached not the ear of Quasimodo; and this vast multitude of which he could scarcely see anything, and of which he heard absolutely nothing, though all was bustle and motion so near to him, must have had the effect of an army of the dead, mute, impalpable, and shrouded in vapor. It appeared to him as if a mist full of human beings was approaching, and that what he saw moving were shadows of the shades.

Then were his apprehensions revived, and the idea of an attempt against the gypsy girl again occurred to his mind. He had a confused foreboding of mischief. At this critical moment he began to consider what course he had best pursue, and with more judgment and decision than might have been expected from a brain so imperfectly organized. Ought he to wake the Egyptian? to assist her to escape? How? which way? the streets were invested; the church was backed by the river. There was no boat, no outlet. He had, therefore, but one course—to die on the threshold of Notre Dame; at any rate to make all the resistance in his power until succor should arrive, and not to disturb the slumbers of La Esmeralda; the unfortunate creature would be awakened time enough to die. This resolution once taken, he set about examining the enemy with greater composure.

The crowd seemed to increase every moment in the Parvis. He presumed, however, that the noise they made must be very slight, because the windows in the streets and the Place remained closed.

Clopin Trouillefou, on his arrival before the lofty portal of Notre Dame, had, in fact, ranged his troops in order of battle. Though he expected no resistance, yet he resolved, like a prudent general, to preserve such order as would enable him to face about in case of need against any sudden attack of the watch or of the *onze-vingts*. Accordingly, he drew up his brigade in such a way that, had you seen it from above, or at a distance, you would have taken it for the Roman triangle at the battle of Ecnomus, the boar's head of Alexander, or the famous wedge of Gustavus Adolphus. The base of this triangle rested upon the farthest side of the Place, so as to block up the Rue du Parvis; one of its sides faced the Hotel Dieu, and the other the Rue Saint Pierre-aux-Bœufs. Trouillefou had placed himself at the apex, with the Duke of Egypt, our friend Jehan, and the boldest of the vagabonds.

As soon as the first arrangements were terminated—and we must say, for the honor of the vagabond discipline, that Clopin's orders were executed in silence, and with admirable precision—the worthy chief of the band mounted upon the parapet of the Parvis, and raised his harsh and husky voice, turning his face toward Notre Dame, and at the same time waving his torch, the flame of which, blown about by the wind, and ever and anon almost drowned in its own smoke, now reddened the facade of the church, and presently left it buried in darkness.

"To thee, Louis de Beaumont, Bishop of Paris, counselor to the court of parliament, I, Clopin Trouillefou, King of Thunes, grand Cæsar, prince of Slang, bishop of Fools, give this notice: Our sister, falsely condemned for magic, has taken sanctuary in thy church. Thou owest her safeguard and protection. Now, the court of parliament wishes to lay hold of her again, and thou consentest thereto; therefore, oh, bishop, are we come to thee. If thy church is sacred, our sister is sacred also; if our sister is not sacred, neither is thy church. We summon thee, then, to surrender the girl to us if thou wouldst save thy church, or we will take the girl ourselves and plunder thy church. This will be still better. In testimony whereof I here plant my banner. So God keep thee, Bishop of Paris!"

Unluckily, Quasimodo could not hear these words, which were pronounced with a sort of wild and somber majesty. One of the vagabonds delivered his banner to Clopin, who solemnly planted it between two paving-stones. It was a pitchfork, on the tines of which hung a lump of bleeding carrion.

This done, the King of Thunes turned round and surveyed his army, a savage throng, whose eyes glistened almost as much as their pikes. After a moment's pause, he gave the word of onset: "Forward! my lads! To your business, blackguards!" was the cry of Clopin Trouillefou.

Thirty stout men, fellows with brawny limbs and the faces of blacksmiths, sprang from the ranks, bearing sledgehammers, pincers, and crowbars in their hands and on their shoulders. They made for the great door of the church, ascended the steps, and were presently crouching down beneath the arch, at work with their pincers and their levers. A crowd of the vagabonds followed to assist or to look on. The eleven steps of the porch were thronged by them. The door, however, held firm. "Devil!" said one, "it is tough and obstinate!"—"'Tis old, and its joints are stiff," said another.—"Courage, comrades," replied Clopin. "I'll wager my head against an old shoe that you will have opened the door, taken the girl, and stripped the high altar before there is a beadle awake. Hold, I think the lock is giving way."

Clopin was interrupted at this moment by a tremendous crash behind him. He turned round. An enormous beam had fallen from the sky; it had crushed a dozen of the vagabonds on the steps of the church, and rebounded on the pavement with the noise of a cannon, breaking a score or two of legs among the crowd of beggars, who, with cries of horror, scampered off in every direction. The area of the Parvis was cleared in a twinkling. The blacksmiths, though protected by the depth of the porch, abandoned the door, and Clopin himself fell back to a respectful distance from the church. "I have had a narrow escape," cried Jehan: "I was in the wind of it, by Jove! but Peter the Butcher is butchered."

It is impossible to describe the fright and consternation which fell with that beam upon the banditti. For some minutes they stood staring up at the sky, more astounded at the piece of timber than they would have been by the arrival of twenty thousand of the king's archers. "The devil!" exclaimed the Duke of Egypt, "this does look like magic!"—"It must surely be the moon that has thrown us this log," said Andry the Red. "Why then, methinks, the moon is a good friend to our Lady the Virgin," observed Francois Chanteprune. "Thousand popes!" cried Clopin, "ye are a parcel of fools!" but still he knew not how to account for the fall of the beam.

Meanwhile nothing was to be seen on the facade, the top of which was too high for the light of the torches to reach it. The ponderous beam lay in the middle of the Parvis, and nothing was heard save the groans of the wretches who had been mangled by its shock upon the steps. The first panic over, the King of Thunes at length fancied that he had made a discovery, which appeared plausible to his companions. *"Ventre Dieu!"* cried he, "are the canons defending themselves? If so, sack! sack!"—Sack! sack!" responded the whole crew, with a tremendous hurrah; and a

furious discharge of cross-bows and arquebuses was lev-
eled at the facade of the church.

The report of the firearms awoke the peaceful inhabitants of the neighboring houses; sundry windows might be
seen opening, nightcaps popping out, and hands holding
candles. "Fire at the windows!" roared out Clopin. The
windows were shut in an instant, and the poor citizens,
who had scarcely had time to cast a hasty but timid glance
upon this scene of flash and tumult, returned to perspire
with fright by the sides of their spouses, asking themselves
whether the witches' sabbath was now held in the Parvis,
or whether there was another attack of the Burgundians, as
in '64. The men were apprehensive of robbery, the women
of rape, and all trembled.

"Sack! sack!" repeated the men of Slang, but they durst
not advance. They looked first at the church and then at
the beam. The beam did not stir, and the church retained
its calm and lonely air, but something had frozen the courage of the vagabonds.

"To work, then, scoundrels!" cried Trouillefou. "Force
the door!" Not a soul moved a finger. "Pretty fellows,
these," said Clopin, "who are frightened out of their wits
by a bit of wood!"—"Captain," rejoined an old smith, "it
is not the bit of wood that frightens us, but the door is all
clamped with iron bars. The pincers are of no use."—
"What want you then to break it open?" inquired
Clopin.—"We want battering rams."—"Here it is then,"
cried the King of Thunes, stepping boldly up to the formidable beam, and setting his foot upon it; "the canons
themselves have sent you one. Thank you, canons," he
added, making a mock obeisance toward the church.

This bravado produced the desired effect. The charm of
the beam was broken; picked up like a feather by two hundred vigorous arms it was dashed with fury against the
great door, which the vagabonds had in vain attempted to
force. In the dim light thrown by the few torches upon the
Place, this long beam and its supporters might have been

taken for an immense beast with hundreds of legs butting at a giant of stone.

At the shock of the beam the half-metallic door resounded like an immense drum; it yielded not, but the whole cathedral shook and the innermost cavities of the edifice were heard to groan. At the same instant a shower of stones began to rain upon the assailants. "Hell and the devil!" cried Jehan; "are the towers shaking their balustrade upon us?" But the impulse was given; the King of Thunes was right; it was decidedly the bishop defending his citadel, and the vagabonds only battered the door with the more fury, in spite of the stones which were cracking skulls in all directions. It is remarkable that these stones fell one by one, but so closely did they follow each other, that the assailants always felt two at a time, one at their legs, the other on their heads. There were few of them that did not tell; already a large heap of killed and wounded lay bleeding and palpitating under the feet of their comrades who, nothing daunted, filled up their ranks as fast as they were thinned. The long beam continued to batter at regular intervals, the door to groan, and the stones to shower down. The reader need not be told that this unexpected resistance, which so exasperated the vagabonds, proceeded from Quasimodo. Chance had unluckily favored the courageous hunchback.

All at once he recollected that workmen had been engaged the whole day in repairing the wall, timbers, and roof of the southern tower. To that tower Quasimodo hastened. The lower rooms were full of materials. There were piles of stones, rolls of lead, bundles of laths, massive beams, and heaps of gravel; it was, in short, a complete arsenal.

There was no time to be lost. The crowbars and hammers were at work below. With a strength increased tenfold by the sense of danger, he hoisted up the heaviest and longest beam that he could find, shoved it out of a small window, and over the angle of the balustrade surrounding the platform, and fairly launched it into the abyss. The enormous mass in this fall of one hundred and sixty feet, grazed the wall, breaking the sculptures, and turned over and over several times in its descent. At length it reached the ground; horrid shrieks succeeded; and the black beam, rebounding on the pavement, looked like a serpent writhing and darting upon its prey.

Quasimodo saw the vagabonds scattered by the fall of the beam, like ashes before the wind. He took advantage of their consternation; and while they fixed a superstitious stare upon the log fallen as they thought from the sky, and put out the eyes of the stone saints of the porch by the discharge of their arrows and firearms, Quasimodo fell to work in silence to carry stones, rubbish, gravel, and even the bags of tools belonging to the masons, to the edge of the balustrade over which he had already hoisted the beam. As soon as they commenced battering the door, the shower of stones began to fall, and the vagabonds imagined that the church was tumbling about their ears. Anyone who could have seen Quasimodo at that moment would have been seized with dread.

The vagabonds, however, were nothing daunted. More than twenty times the massive door against which their attack was directed had trembled under the weight of the oaken ram, multiplied by the force of a hundred men. The panels were cracked, the carving flew off in shivers, the hinges at every blow sprang up from their pivots, the planks began to start, and the wood was pounded to powder between the braces of iron; luckily for Quasimodo there was more iron than wood. He was aware, nevertheless, that the door could not hold out long. Though he could not hear it, yet every stroke of the ram reverberated in the caverns, and in the inmost recesses of the church. From his lofty station he saw the assailants, flushed with triumph and with rage, shaking their fists at the gloomy facade, and, for his own sake, as well as for the Egyptian's, he coveted the wings of the daws, which flew off in flocks above his head. His ammunition was not effective enough to repel the assailants.

At this moment of anguish he remarked, a little lower down than the balustrade from which he crushed the men of Slang, two long gutters of stone which disgorged themselves immediately over the great door. The inner orifice of these gutters opened on the level of the platform. An idea struck him. He ran to his bell-ringer's lodge for a fagot, placed it over the hole of the two spouts, laid upon it several bundles of laths and rolls of lead, a kind of ammunition to which he had not yet resorted; and, as soon as all was arranged, he set fire to the fagot with his lantern.

During this interval, as the stones had ceased falling, the vagabonds no longer looked up; and the ruffians, panting like dogs baying the wild boar in his den, crowded tumultuously round the great door, shattered by the battering engines, but still standing. They awaited, with a thrill of impatience, the last grand blow, the blow that was to shiver it in pieces. Each was striving to get nearest to the door, that he might be first to dart into the rich magazine of treasures, which had been accumulating in the cathedral for three centuries.

All of a sudden, while they were grouping themselves for a last effort about the engine, each holding his breath and stiffening his muscles to throw all his strength into the decisive blow, a howling, more hideous than that which followed the fall of the fatal beam, burst forth from among them. Those who were not yet yelling and yet alive looked round. Two streams of molten lead were pouring from the building upon the thickest part of the crowd. This sea of men had subsided beneath the boiling metal, which had made, at the points where it fell, two black and smoking holes in the rabble, such as hot water would make in a snowdrift. Here the dying were writhing half calcined and roaring with agony. All around these two principal streams a shower of this horrible rain was scattered over the assailants, and the drops pierced their skulls like gimlets of fire. The clamor was horrible. The vagabonds, throwing the beam upon the dead and dying, fled, pell-mell, the bold and the timid together, and the Parvis was cleared a second time.

All eyes were raised to the top of the building. They beheld a sight of an extraordinary kind. In the uppermost gallery, above the central rose window, a vast body of flame, accompanied by showers of sparks, ascended between the two towers—a fierce and irregular flame, patches of which were every now and then carried off by the wind along with the smoke. Below this fire, below the somber balustrade, with its glowing red open-work ornaments, two spouts, in the shape of the jaws of monsters, vomited without cessation those silver streams, which stood out distinctly against the dark mass of the lower facade. As they approached the ground, those two streams spread like water poured through the holes of the rose of a watering pot.

A silence of terror fell upon the arms of vagabonds, during which might be heard the cries of the canons shut up in their cloisters, and more alarmed than horses in a stable that is on fire, together with the sound of windows steathily opened and more quickly shut, a bustle in the interior of the houses and in the Hotel Dieu, the wind in the flame, the last rattle of the dying, and the continuous pattering of the leaden rain upon the pavement.

Meanwhile, the principals of the vagabonds had retired to the porch of the Gondelaurier mansion, and were holding consultation. The duke of Egypt, seated on a post contemplated with religious awe the resplendent blaze burning at the height of two hundred feet in the air. Clopin Trouillefou struck his clumsy fists together with rage. "Impossible to break in!" muttered he to himself. "An enchanted church!" grumbled the old Bohemian, Matthias Hunyadi Spicali. "By the pope's whiskers," exclaimed a gray-headed ragamuffin who had been a soldier, "those two church gutters beat the portcullis of Lectoure at spewing lead out and out!" "Do you see that demon passing to and fro, before the fire?" cried the Duke of Egypt. "Egad," said Clopin, " 'tis that cursed bell-ringer, that Quasimodo."

"And I tell you," replied the Bohemian, shaking his head, "it is the spirit Sabnac, the demon of fortification. He appears in the form of an armed soldier with a lion's head. He changes men into stones, and builds towers with them. He has the command of fifty legions. I know him well— 'tis he, sure enough."

"Is there then no way of forcing that infernal door?" cried the King of Thunes, stamping violently on the pavement. The Duke of Egypt pointed mournfully to the two streams of boiling lead, which still continued to stripe the dark facade. "Churches have been known," observed he with a sigh, "to defend themselves in this manner, without the aid of men. It is now about forty years since St. Sophia at Constantinople threw down three times running the crescent of Mahomet by shaking her domes, which are her heads. William of Paris, who built this, was a magician."

"Shall we then give it up for a bad job, like a scurvy set of poltroons?" said Clopin. "Shall we leave our sister behind, to be hanged tomorrow by these cowled wolves?"

"And the sacristy too, where there are cartloads of gold?" added a rapscallion whose name we regret our inability to record.

"Beard of Mahound!" ejaculated Trouillefou.

"Let us make one more trial," said the preceding speaker.

Again Matthias Hunyadi shook his head. "We shall not get in at the door, that's certain."

"I shall go back," said Clopin. "Who will come with me? By the by, where is little Jehan, the student, who had cased himself up to the eyes in steel?"

"Dead, no doubt," replied someone. "I have not heard his laugh for some time."

The King of Thunes knitted his brow.

"More's the pity! He carried a bold heart under that iron shell. And Master Pierre Gringoire, what is become of him?"

"Captain Clopin," said Andry the Red, "he sneaked off as soon as we had reached the Pontaux-Changeurs."

Clopin stamped. " 'Sdeath! the coward! To urge us into this affair and then leave us in the lurch!"

"Captain," cried Andry the Red, who was looking down the Rue du Parvis, "yonder comes the little scholar."

"Thanks be to Pluto!" rejoined Clopin. "But what the devil is he dragging after him?"

It was actually Jehan, who was advancing as expeditiously as he could for his heavy warlike accouterments and a long ladder which, with the aid of half a dozen of the gang, he was trailing along the pavement, more out of breath than a pismire dragging a blade of grass twenty times as long as itself.

"Victory! *Te Deum!*" shouted the scholar.

Clopin went up to him. "What, in the devil's name, are you going at with that ladder?"

"I have got it," replied Jehan, panting and blowing. "I knew where it was kept—under the shed belonging to the lieutenant's house. I am acquainted with one of the maids there, who thinks me a perfect Cupid. The poor girl came down half-naked to let me in—and here is the ladder."

"I see," said Clopin; "but what are you going to do with it?"

Jehan eyed him with a look of spite and importance, and snapped his fingers like castanets. At that moment he was really sublime. His head was cased in one of those surcharged helmets of the fifteenth century, which daunted the enemy by their fantastic appendages. His was bestudded with ten iron beaks, so that he might have disputed the formidable epithet δεηεμϑολος with Nestor's Homeric ship.

"What am I going to do with it, august King of Thunes? Do you see that row of statues, which look so like idiots, there, above the three porches?"

"Yes, what then?"

"That is the gallery of the kings of France."

"And what of that?" said Clopin.

"Just listen. At the end of that gallery there is a door,

which is always on the latch. With this ladder I will mount to it, and then I am in the church."

"Let me go up first, boy."

"No, no, comrade. I brought the ladder. You shall be second, if you will."

"May Beelzebub strangle thee!" cried Clopin, peevishly. "I will not be second to any man."

"Then, my dear fellow, seek a ladder for yourself."

Jehan started again, dragging his ladder along and shouting, "This way, my lads!"

In an instant the ladder was raised and placed against the balustrade of the lower gallery, above one of the side doors, amid loud acclamations from the crowd of the vagabonds, who thronged to the foot of it to ascend. Jehan maintained his right to go up first. The gallery of the kings of France is at this present time about sixty feet above the pavement. The eleven steps up to the porch increased the height. Jehan mounted slowly, being impeded by his heavy armor, laying hold of the ladder with one hand, and having his arbalist in the other. When he was about half-way up he cast a melancholy look at the dead bodies that covered the steps and the pavement. "By my fay," said he, "a heap of carcasses that would not disgrace the fifth book of the *Iliad*." He then continued to ascend, followed by the vagabonds. Had you seen this line of cuirassed backs undulating in the dark, you would have taken it for an immense serpent with iron scales raising itself against the church.

The scholar at length touched the balcony and nimbly leaped upon it. He was greeted by a general shout from the whole gang. Thus master of the citadel he joined in the hurrahs, but all at once he was struck dumb with horror. He perceived Quasimodo crouching in the dark behind one of the royal statutes and his eye flashing fire.

Before a second of the besiegers could set foot on the gallery, the formidable hunchback sprang to the top of the ladder, and, without uttering a word, caught hold of the two sides with his nervous hands, and pushed them from the wall with superhuman force. The long ladder, bending under the load of the escalading party, whose piercing shrieks rent the air, stood upright for a moment, and seemed to hesitate; then, all at once taking a tremendous lurch, it fell with its load of banditti more swiftly than a drawbridge when the chains that held it have broken. An immense imprecation ensued; presently all was silent, here and there a mangled wretch crawled forth from beneath the heap of the dead. Quasimodo, leaning with his two elbows upon the balustrade, looked quietly on.

Jehan Frollo found himself in a critical situation. Separated from his comrades by a perpendicular wall of eighty feet, he was alone in the gallery with the formidable bell-ringer. While Quasimodo was playing with the ladder, the scholar had run to the postern, which he expected to find upon the latch. He was disappointed. The dwarf had locked it after him when he went down to the gallery. Jehan then hid himself behind one of the stone kings, holding his breath, and eyeing the monstrous hunchback with a look of horror, like the man who, having scraped acquaintance with the wife of a keeper of wild beasts, went one night in pursuance of an assignation, and, climbing over the wrong wall, found himself all at once face to face with a prodigious white bear. For some moments he was not observed by Quasimodo, who at length chancing to turn his head, and perceiving the scholar, suddenly started up.

Jehan prepared himself for a rude encounter, but the hunchback stood stock still, merely fixing his eye intently upon the scholar. "Hoho!" said Jehan, "why dost thou look at me so spitefully?" With these words the hair-brained youth slyly adjusted his arbalist. "Quasimodo," cried he, "I will change thy surname; instead of the deaf thou shalt henceforth be called the blind." The feathered shaft whizzed and pierced the left arm of the bell-ringer. Quasimodo heeded it no more than he would have done the scratch of a pin. He laid hold of the quarrel, drew it from his arm, and calmly broke it upon his massive knee; he then dropped rather then threw the pieces over the balustrade. Jehan had not time to discharge a second. Quasimodo having broken the arrow, suddenly drew in his breath, leaped like a grasshopper, and fell upon the scholar, whose armor was flattened against the wall by the shock. A tremendous sight was then seen in the *chiaroscuro* produced by the faint light of the torches.

Quasimodo grasped with his left hand the two arms of the scholar, who forbore even to struggle, so completely did he feel himself overpowered. With his right the hunchback took off in silence, and with ominous deliberation, the different parts of his armor one after another—helmet, cuirass, armpieces, sword, daggers. He looked for all the world like an ape picking a walnut. He threw the iron shell of the scholar, piece by piece, at his feet.

When Jehan found himself stripped, disarmed, powerless in the hands of his irresistible antagonist, he began to laugh him impudently in the face, with all the thoughtless gaiety of a boy of sixteen. But he did not laugh long. Quasimodo was seen standing upon the parapet of the gallery, holding the scholar by the leg with one hand, and swinging him round over the abyss like a sling. Presently was heard a sound like that of a coconut broken by being dashed against a wall; something was seen falling, but it was stopped one third of the way down by a projecting part of the building. It was a dead body that stuck there, bent double, the back broken, and the skull empty.

A cry of horror burst from the vagabonds. "Revenge!" shouted Clopin. "Sack! sack!" responded the multitude. "Storm! storm!" Then followed prodigious yells, intermingled with all languages, all dialects, all accents. The death of poor Jehan kindled a fury in the crowd. They were filled with shame and indignation at having been so long held in check before a church by a hunchback. Rage found ladders and multiplied the torches; and, in a few moments, Quasimodo beheld with consternation a fearful rabble mounting on all sides to the assault of Notre Dame. Some had ladders, others knotted rope, while such as could not procure either scrambled up by the aid of the sculptures,

holding by each other's rags. There were no means of
withstanding this rising tide of grim faces, to which rage
gave a look of twofold ferocity. The perspiration trickled
down their begrimed brows; their eyes flashed; all these
hideous figures were now closing in upon Quasimodo.
You would have imagined that some other church had sent
its gorgons, its demons, its dragons, its most fantastic
monsters, to the assault of Notre Dame.

Meanwhile, the Place was illumined with a thousand
torches. A flood of light suddenly burst upon the scene of
confusion, which had till then been buried in darkness.
The fire kindled on the platform was still burning, and illumined the city to a considerable distance. The enormous
outline of the two towers, projected afar upon the roofs of
the houses, formed a large patch of shadows amidst all this
light. The city seemed to be in a bustle. Distant alarm bells
were proclaiming that there was something amiss. The
vagabonds were shouting, yelling, swearing, climbing; and
Quasimodo, powerless against such a host of enemies,
shuddering for the Egyptian, seeing so many ferocious
faces approaching nearer and nearer to the gallery, prayed
to Heaven for a miracle, at the same time wringing his
hands in despair.

51

One has doubtless not forgotten that, on the night that
Notre Dame was raided, as Quasimodo studied Paris
from his vantage at the top of the tower, he saw a solitary
light shining from a top floor window of a tall, gloomy
building, located near the Gate Saint-Antoine. The light
was the flicker of Louis XI's candle in the Bastille.

King Louis XI had, in fact, been in Paris for two days. He was to leave again on the day after the morrow for his fortress of Montilz-les-Tours. His visits to the good city of Paris were rare and always of short duration because he felt there was a lack of personal security, due to an insufficient number of trapdoors, gibbets, and Scottish archers.

He had arranged to sleep that night in the Bastille. He disliked the great chamber at the Louvre, thirty feet square, with its massive chimney piece adorned with twelve great beasts and thirteen great prophets, and its huge bed, twelve feet by eleven. He, a good bourgeois king, felt lost in all that grandeur; he preferred the Bastille with its smaller room and smaller bed. And besides, the Bastille was more impregnable than the Louvre.

This chamber which the king had reserved for himself in the famous state-prison was, however, quite spacious; it occupied the uppermost floor of a turret forming part of the dungeon keep. It was circular room; the floor was covered with shiny straw matting; gilded pewter fleurs-de-lis adorned the rafters of the ceiling, while the spaces between them were colorful, being wainscoted with rich wood, sprinkled with rosettes of white powder, and painted a fine light green made of crushed orpine.

There was only one long and pointed window, covered with brass wire and latticed with iron bars. It admitted little light because of the beautiful stained glass, portraying the arms of the king and those of the queen, each pane of which cost twenty-two sols.

There was but one entrance, a modern door, under an overhanging circular arch, furnished inside with tapestry, and outside with one of those porches of Irish wood, frail structures of curious workmanship, which still were plentiful in old French mansions a hundred and fifty years ago. "Although they disfigure and encumber the places," says Sauval disparagingly, "nevertheless our old people don't want them removed, but keep them in spite of everyone."

In this chamber there was none of the furniture of ordinary apartments, neither benches, nor trestles, nor common box stools, nor fine stools supported by pillars and counter-pillars at four sols apiece. There was only one magnificent folding armchair, whose wood was painted with roses upon a red background, and whose seat was of red morocco, decorated with long silken fringe and studded with a thousand gold-headed nails. The absence of other chairs testified that one person alone had a right to be seated in this chamber. Next to the chair, and near the window, there was a table covered with a cloth embroidered with birds. On the table sat an inkstand, spotted with ink, some parchment scrolls, pens, and a chased silver goblet. A little removed from this table stood a chafing dish on a pedestal. A prie-dieu, covered with crimson velvet embossed with studs of gold, was near the bed at the far end of the room. This was a simple bed, spread with a yellow and flesh-toned damask counterpane without any decoration of any sort except a plain fringe. This bed became famous for having borne the sleep or the sleeplessness of Louis XI, and was still to be seen two hundred years ago in the house of a councillor of state, where it was seen by the aged Madame Pilou, celebrated in the great romance of "Cyrus" under the name of *Arricidie* and that of *La Morale Vivante*.

Such was the chamber referred to as, "The retreat where Monsieur Louis of France prays."

At this time in our story, as we said, it was very dark. Curfew had tolled an hour ago. In this room there was but one flickering candle on the table to illumine the five persons standing in groups.

One of these was a lord superbly attired in doublet and hose of scarlet striped with silver. His cloak, with large puffy sleeves, was made of cloth of gold with black figures. This splendid costume, as the light played upon it, glittered with every movement. This man wore upon his breast his coat of arms embroidered in brilliant colors: a chevron, with a deer passant in the base of the shield. The escutcheon was supported on the right by an olive branch, and on the left by a stag's horn. In his girdle was an expensive dagger, its silver-gilt molded like a crest surmounted by a count's coronet. This gentleman carried his head high; his bearing was haughty, and his look, wicked. At first glance you read arrogance in his face, at the second, cunning.

He stood bareheaded, with a long scroll in his hand, behind the comfortable armchair, upon which was seated, with his body ungracefully bent double, his knees crossed, and his elbow resting on the table, a person very shabbily dressed. Imagine, indeed, seated on the rich Cordovan leather, a pair of crooked joints, a pair of lean thighs poorly covered by black worsted, a trunk wrapped in a loose coat of fustian the fur lining of which had much more leather left than hair; and to crown the whole, an old greasy hat of the meanest black cloth, banded by small leaden figures. This, over a dirty skullcap, beneath which hardly a single hair was visible, was all that could be distinguished of the sitting personage. He kept his head so much bent over his chest that of his face, thus thrown into shadow, nothing could be seen but the end of his long nose, upon which a ray of light fell. The thinness of his wrinkled hand evidenced that he was an old man. This was Louis XI.

Some distance from them, talking in low voices, stood two men dressed in Flemish fashion, who were not so completely in shadow but that anyone who had attended the performance of Gringoire's mystery could not recognize them as the two principal Flemish envoys, Guillaume Rym, the sagacious pensionary of Ghent, and Jacques Coppenole, the popular hosier. It will be remembered that these two men were mixed up with the secret politics of Louis XI.

Lastly, near the door, behind all the rest, there stood in the dark, motionless like a statue, a stout, brawny, thickset man in military dress, with coat emblazoned, whose square face, with its prominent eyes, its immense mouth, its ears concealed under a great mat of hair, and with scarcely any forehead, seemed a sort of mixture of dog and tiger.

All were hatless except the king.

The lord standing by His Majesty was reading to him a long official paper, to which the king seemed to listen attentively.

The two Flemings were whispering to each other.

"By the rood!" muttered Coppenole, "I'm tired of standing. Aren't there any other chairs here?"

Rym answered him negatively, with a circumspect smile.

"By the rood!" said Coppenole again, very much discomfited that he had to speak thus in a whisper, 'I'm terribly tempted to sit on the floor, with my legs crossed, like the hosier that I am, as I do in my own shop."

"You had better not, Master Jacques."

"Whew! Master Guillaume, can only one stand here?"

"Or kneel," said Rym.

At that moment the king raised his voice and they stopped talking.

"Fifty sols for the gowns of our valets, and twelve livres for the mantles of the clerks of our crown! Is that right? You're spending gold by the tons! Are you mad, Olivier?"

As he spoke the old man raised his head, and you could see gleaming around his neck the golden shells of the collar of Saint-Michel. The candle shone full upon his meager and morose profile. He snatched the paper from the hands of the other.

"You are ruining us," he cried, scanning the ledger with his hollow eyes. "What is all this? Why do we need such a heavy complement of household personnel? Two chaplains at the rate of ten livres a month each, and a chapel clerk at a hundred sols. A chamber valet at ninety livres a year! Four squires of the kitchen at a hundred and twenty livres each a year! A roaster, a soup cook, a sauce cook, a head cook, a butler, and two assistants, at the rate of ten livres a month each! Two turn-spits at eight livres! A porter, a pastry cook, a baker, two carters, each sixty livres a year! And the marshal of the forges a hundred and twenty livres! And the marshal of our exchequer twelve hundred livres! And the comptroller five hundred! And I know not who else besides! Why this is preposterous! The wages of our domestics are pillaging France! All the gold in the Louvre will melt away in such a blaze of expenditures! We shall have to sell our plateware! And next year, if God and Our Lady (here he raised his cap) grant us life, we shall drink our tisanes from a pewter mug."

When he said this, he glanced at the silver goblet that was glittering on the table. He coughed, and continued, "Master Olivier, princes who reign over great seigneuries, as kings and emperors, ought not to allow extravagance to creep into their households, for 'tis a fire that will spread thence into the provinces. So, Master Olivier, let me not have to repeat this. Our expenses are increasing every year. And this much displeases us. Why, *Pasque Dieu*, till '79 it never exceeded thirty-six thousand livres; in '80, it rose to forty-three thousand six hundred and nineteen livres—I have these figures in my head—in '81 it came to sixty-six thousand six hundred and eighty; and this year, by the faith in my body, it will amount to eighty thousand livres! Doubled in four years! Monstrous!"

He stopped, out of breath, then resumed with vehemence.

"I see all around me nothing but people who are getting fat on my leanness. You are sucking money from my every pore!"

Everyone remained silent. It was one of his fits of passion which had to run its course.

He continued, "It's just like that petition in Latin from the French nobility, requesting us to re-establish what they call the great charges of the crown! Charges, indeed! Charges that would rush us! Ah, gentlemen, you say that we are not a king to reign 'without steward or cup-bearer'! But we'll show you, by God! whether we are king or not!"

Here he smiled, conscious of his power; his ill-humor was allayed by it, and he turned to the Flemings.

"Look you, Compère Guillaume, the grand master of the pantry, the grand butler, the grand chamberlain, the grand seneschal are not so useful as the meanest valet. Remember that, Compère Coppenole. They serve absolutely no purpose. Keeping themselves thus useless, around the king, they remind me of the four evangelists around the face of the great clock of the Palace, and that Philippe Brille has just now been renovating. They're gilt, yes, but they don't mark the hour, and the hand of the clock can do well without them."

He remained thoughtful for a moment and then added, shaking his aged head, "Ho, ho! by Our Lady, but I'm not Philippe Brille, and I am not going to regild the great vassals. I agree with King Edward: Save the people and kill the lords. Proceed, Olivier."

The person whom he so addressed again took the ledger in his hands and went on reading aloud:

". . . to Adam Tenon, the keeper of the seals of provostry of Paris, for silver, making and engraving said seals, which have been made new, because the former ones, by reason of their being old and worn out, could not any longer be used, twelve livres parisis.

"To Guillaume and brother, the sum of four livres four sols parisis, for his trouble and cost in having fed and nourished the pigeons of the two pigeon houses at Hotel des Tournelles during the months of January, February, and March of this year, for the which he has furnished seven quarters of barley.

"To a Gray Friar, for confessing a criminal, four sols parisis."

The king listened in silence. Occasionally he coughed; then he would lift the goblet to his lips and swallow a draught, after which he would make a wry face.

"In this year have been made," continued the reader, "by judicial order, by sound of trumpet, through the streets of Pairs, fifty-six cries—costs to be determined.

"For search made in divers places, in Paris and elsewhere, after treasure said to have been concealed in said places, but nothing has been found, forty-five livres parisis."

"Burying an écu to dig up a sou!" said the king.

"For putting in at the Hotel des Tournelles six panes of white glass, at the place where the iron cage is, thirteen sols.

"For making and delivering, by the king's order, on the day of the musters, four escutcheons, bearing the arms of our said lord, and wreathed all around with chaplets of roses, six livres.

"For two new sleeves for the king's old doublet, twenty sols.

"For a box of grease to grease the king's boots, fifteen deniers.

"For a new sty to keep the king's black swine, thirty livres parisis.

"Divers partitions, planks, and trapdoors, for the safe-keeping of the lions at the Hotel Saint-Paul, twenty-two livres."

"They are costly beasts!" said Louis XI. "But no matter; it's a fair piece of royal magnificence. There is a great red lion which I am very fond of for his engaging ways. Have you seen him, Master Guillaume? Princes should have those remarkable animals. We kings ought to have lions for our dogs and tigers for our cats. The great beasts befit a crown. In the time of the pagans of Jupiter, when the people offered up at the holy places a hundred oxen and a hundred sheep, the emperors gave a hundred lions and a hundred eagles. That was very fierce and very noble. The kings of France have always had those roarings about their throne. Nevertheless, people must do me the justice to say that I spend less money in that way than my predecessors, and that I am exceedingly moderate on the score of lions, bears, elephants, and leopards. Go on, Master Olivier. We wanted to mention this to our Flemish friends."

Guillaume Rym made a low bow, while Coppenole, with his surly countenance, looked much like one of those bears which His Majesty had been talking of. The king did not notice. He had just then put his goblet to his lips, and

was spitting out what remained in his mouth of the unsa-
vory beverage, saying, "Bah! that horrid tisane!"

The reader continued. "For the food of a rogue and a
vagabond, kept for the last six months in the lock-up of
the slaughterhouse, till it should be decided what is to be
done with him, six livres four sols."

"What's that?" interrupted the king. "Feeding something
that ought to be hanged! *Pasque Dieu!* I'll not contribute
a single sol toward such feeding. Olivier, you'll arrange
that matter with Monsieur d'Estouteville. And this very
night you'll make preparations for uniting this gentleman
in holy matrimony with the gallows. Now, go on!"

Olivier made a mark with his thumb nail at the rogue
and vagabond item, and went on.

"To Henriet Cousin, master executioner of Paris, the
sum of sixty sous parisis, to him adjudged by Monseigneur
the Provost of Paris, for having brought, by order of the
said lord the provost, a large, broad-bladed sword, to be
used in beheading persons judicially condemned for their
crimes, and for having it furnished with a scabbard and all
other appurtenances, and also for repairing and putting in
order the old sword, which had been splintered and jagged
by executing justice upon Messire Louis of Luxembourg,
as can be more fully made to appear—"

Here the king interrupted him. "Enough," he said. "I
shall give the order for that payment with all my heart.
These are expenses I don't so much think about. I have
never begrudged money so spent. Proceed."

"For making a large, new cage . . ."

"Ha!" said the king, putting a hand on each arm of the
chair, "I knew I had come to this Bastille for something.
Stop, Master Olivier. I want to see that cage myself. You
can read the cost of it to me while I am inspecting it. Messieurs the Flemings, come see it. It is curious."

He then rose, leaned upon the arm of his interlocutor,
made a sign to the sort of mute standing by the doorway
to go before him, made another to the two Flemings to follow him, and went out of the chamber.

The royal train was recruited at the door by men at arms ponderous with steel, and slender pages carrying torches. It proceeded for some time through the interior of the gloomy dungeon, perforated by staircases and corridors even into the thickness of the walls. The captain of the Bastille walked ahead, and directed the opening of the successive narrow doors before the sickly, old, and stooped king, who coughed as he walked along.

At each doorway, everyone was obliged to stoop in order to pass except only the man bent with aged. "Hum!" he said between his gums, for he had not teeth left, "we're quite ready for the door of the sepulcher. A low door needs a stooped person."

At length after making their way through the last door of all, so loaded with complicated locks that it took a full quarter of an hour to open it, they entered a spacious and lofty chamber, of Gothic vaulting, in the center of which was discernible by the light of the torches a great cubical mass of masonry, iron, and woodwork. The interior was hollow. It was one of those infamous cages for state prisoners which are called euphemistically *les fillettes du roi*, the king's daughters. In its walls there were two or three small windows, so thickly latticed with massive iron bars as to leave no glass visible. The door consisted of a single large flat stone, like that of a tomb—one of those doors that serve for entrance only. But in this case the tenant was alive.

The king went and paced slowly around this small edifice, examining it carefully, while Master Olivier, following him, read aloud the expenses.

"For making a great new wooden cage of heavy beams, joists, and rafters, measuring inside nine feet by eight feet, and seven feet high between the planks; mortised and bolted with great iron bolts, which cage has been fixed in a certain chamber in one of the towers of the Bastille Saint-Antoine, where, in said cage is to be kept, by command of our lord the king, a prisoner who before inhabited an old, decayed, and broken-down cage. Used in making

Victor Hugo

the said new cage, ninety-six horizontal beams and fifty-two perpendicular; ten joists, each eighteen feet long. Employed, in squaring, planing, and fitting all the said woodwork in the yard of the Bastille, nine carpenters for twenty days—"

"Very fine oak too!" said the king, rapping his knuckles on the timbers.

"Used in this cage," continued the other, "two hundred and twenty great iron bolts, of eight and nine feet, the rest of medium length—together with the plates and nuts for fastening said bolts—the said irons weighing altogether three thousand seven hundred and thirty-five pounds; besides eight heavy iron clamps for fixing the said cage in its place, with clamp irons and nails, weighing altogether two hundred and eighteen pounds—without counting the iron for the trellis work of the windows of the chamber in which the said cage has been placed, the iron bars of the door of the chamber, and other articles—"

"There's enough ironwork there to restrain the levity of any spirit," observed the king.

"The whole comes to three hundred and seventeen livres five sols seven deniers."

"Pasque-Dieu!" cried the king.

With this swear word, which was King Louis XI's favorite, someone stirred inside the cage. There was a rattle of chains being dragged across the floor, and a voice, so feeble that it might have come from a tomb, exclaimed, "Sire! sire! mercy!"

He who spoke could not be seen.

"Three hundred and seventeen livres five sols seven deniers!" repeated the king.

The piteous voice which had come from the cage had chilled the blood of all but one present, even that of Master Olivier. Only the king appeared not to have heard it.

Upon his order, Master Olivier continued with reading and His Majesty cooling continued his inspection of the cage.

"Besides the above, there has been paid to a mason who

made the holes to receive the bars of the windows, and the bars to support the floor of the chamber where the cage is, because the floor could not have upheld such a weight, twenty-seven livres fourteen sols parisis . . ."

Again there was a moan inside the cage, followed by the same voice saying, "Mercy, sire! I swear to you it was Monsieur the Cardinal of Angers who committed the treason, not I."

"The mason's price is high," said the king. "Proceed."

Olivier continued, ". . . to the carpenter for windows, beds, closet stools, and other things, twenty livres two sols parisis . . ."

The weak voice continued too.

"Alas! Sire! Will you not hear me? I declare it was not I who wrote that thing to Monseigneur de Guyenne, but Cardinal La Balue!"

"The carpenter is expensive," observed the king. "Is that all?"

"No, sire. To the glazier for the window glass of said chamber, forty-six sols eight deniers parisis."

"Have mercy, sire! Is it not enough that all my property has been given to my judges, my plateware to Monsieur de Torcy, my library to Master Pierre Doriolle, and my tapestry to the governor of Roussillon? I am innocent. It is fourteen years that I have shivered in this iron cage. Have mercy, sire, and you will meet mercy in heaven."

"Master Olivier," said the king, "what is the total bill?"

"Three hundred and sixty-seven livres eight sols three deniers parisis."

"Blessed Lady!" exclaimed the king. "An outrageously expensive cage!"

He snatched the ledger from the hands of Master Olivier, and began to add the figures for himself with his fingers' help, examining by turn the pages and the cage.

Meanwhile the prisoner was heard sobbing. In the dark the sound was doleful indeed; those accompanying the king looked at one another and turned pale.

"Fourteen years, sire! Since April, 1469, fourteen years!

In the name of God's holy Mother, sire, hear me! You have enjoyed all this time the warmth of the sun. Shall I never again see the light of day? Mercy, sire! Be merciful! Clemency in a king is a noble virtue that turneth away wrath. Does Your Majesty believe that at the hour of death it will be a great satisfaction for a king to have left no offense unpunished? Besides, sire, it was not I who betrayed Your Majesty, it was Monsieur of Angers. But I have a very heavy chain about my feet, with a huge iron ball at the end of it, much heavier than is needed. Oh, sire! have pity on me!"

"Olivier," said the king, shaking his head, "I notice that they have put down a bushel of plaster at twenty sols, thought it's worth only twelve. Will you send back this account?"

He turned his back on the cage, and began to move toward the door of the chamber. The wretched prisoner judged, by the dimming torchlight and the receding footsteps, that the king was leaving.

"Sire, sire!" he cried in despair.

But the door closed again; and he could hear nothing but faintly the hoarse voice of the turnkey, singing a popular song.

> Master Jean Balue
> Has lost sight
> Of his bishoprics;
> Mister de Verdun
> Has not one
> All are gone.

The king returned in silence to his retreat, followed by his train, who were horror-stricken by the pleas of the condemned. All at once His Majesty turned around to the governor of the Bastille.

"By the way," he said, "wasn't there someone in that cage?"

"*Pardieu*, yes, sire," replied the governor, astonished by the question.

"Who was it?"

"Monsieur the Bishop of Verdun."

The king knew this better than anybody else, but it was a way he had.

"Ah!" he said naively, as if he were thinking about it for the first time, "Guillaume de Harancourt, the friend of Monsieur the Cardinal La Balue. A good devil of a bishop!"

A few minutes later, the door of the retreat opened and then closed upon the five personages whom the reader found there at the beginning of this chapter. All resumed their places, their postures, and their whispered conversations.

During the king's absence, there had been placed on his table several dispatches, whose seals he immediately broke. He began to read them hastily one after the other. He then motioned to Master Olivier, who seemed to be acting in the capacity of a secretary, to take up a pen, and after communicating to him the content of each dispatch, began in a low voice to dictate his answers, which Olivier wrote, kneeling very uncomfortably at the table.

Guillaume Rym was watching closely.

The king dictated with such a low voice that the Flemings could catch nothing, except here and there some isolated, scarcely intelligible fragments like—"to maintain the fertile places by commerce, the sterile ones by manufacturers ... To show the English lords our four cannons, the London, the Brabant, the Bourg-en-Bresse, and the Saint-Omer ... It is because of the artillery that war is now more judiciously carried on ... To our friend Monsieur de Bressuire ... The armies cannot be maintained without taxes."

Once he raised his voice, "*Pasque-Dieu!* Monsieur the King of Sicily seals his letters with yellow wax like a king of France! Perhaps we are wrong to allow him to do so." Then, examining the seal, he continued, "My fair cousin of Burgundy authorized no arms on a red field with parallel lines. The greatness of a house is assured by maintaining the integrity of its prerogatives. Note that, Compère Olivier."

Then reading another, "Oh, oh," he said, "an audacious message! What is our brother the emperor asking of us?" On casting his eyes more carefully over the dispatch, he interrupted his perusal here and there with brief interjections. "Of course Germany is so large and so powerful that it's hardly credible! But we don't forget that old proverb, 'The finest country is Flanders; the finest duchy, Milan; the finest kingdom, France.' Is it not so, Messieurs the Flemings?"

This time Coppenole bowed as well as Guillaume Rym. The hoiser's patriotism was aroused.

The last dispatch made Louis XI frown. "What's this?" he exclaimed. "Complaints and petitions against our garrisons in Picardy! Olivier, write with all speed to Monsieur the Marshal de Rouault: that discipline has relaxed; that the gendarmes of the guard, the nobles, the free archers, the Swiss archers, are doing infinite mischief to the inhabitants; that the military establishment, not content with what they find in the houses of the husbandmen, compel them, with heavy blows with stones or sticks, to go and fetch from the town wine, fish, groceries, and other luxuries; that the king knows all these things; that we intend to protect our people against annoyance, theft, and pillage; that such is our will, by Our Lady! And furthermore, that it does not please us that any musician, barber, or servant at arms should go clad like a prince, in velvet, silk, and gold rings; that such vanities are despicable to God; that we, who are gentlemen, content ourselves with a doublet made of cloth at sixteen sols parisis an ell; that messieurs the soldiers' lackeys may even come down to that price, too. Order and command. To our friend, Monsieur de Rouault. Good."

He dictated this letter aloud, in a firm tone, and in short, abrupt sentences.

When he had finished, the door opened to admit a messenger, who rushed in, frightened and out of breath, crying, "Sire, sire, there's an uprising in Paris!"

The grave countenance of Louis XI contracted, but whatever emotion he experienced left no visible sign. He contained himself, and said with a tone and look of quiet severity, "Compère Jacques, you come storming in rather abruptly!"

"Sire, sire! there is a revolt!" Compère Jacques repeated, still panting.

The king, who had risen from his chair, seized him roughly by the arm, and, with eyes flashing angrily, yet glancing obliquely at the Flemings, whispered in his ear, so as not to be heard by anyone else, "Hold your tongue or speak low."

The newcomer understood, and, in a restrained manner, told the king a terrifying story, to which the monarch listened calmly.

Meanwhile Guillaume Rym was quietly calling Coppenole's attention to the face and dress of the courier—to his furred cap, his short cloak, his black velvet gown, which bespoke a comptroller

No sooner had this person given the king some details than Louis XI exclaimed, with a burst of laughter, "Indeed? Speak louder, Coictier! What have you to whisper about? Our Lady knows we have nothing to hide from our good Flemish friends."

"But, sire . . ."

"Speak up!"

"Compère." Coictier remained dumbfounded.

"Come, come," insisted the king, "speak up, sir. There's a commotion among the inhabitants in our fair city of Paris?"

"Yes, sire."

"Which is directed, say you, against Monsieur the Bailiff of the Palace of Justice?"

"So it seems," stammered the compère, quite confounded at the sudden and inexplicable change in the king's manner.

Louis XI resumed, "Where did the watch encounter the mob?"

"Coming along from the great truandry toward the Pont-aux-Changeurs, sire. I met the crowd myself as I was coming here in obedience to Your Majesty's command. I heard some of them shouting: 'Down with the bailiff of the Palace!' "

"And what grievances have they against the bailiff?"

"Ah," said Compère Jacques, "that he is their seigneur."

"Really!"

"Yes, sire. They are the rabble from the Court of Miracles. They have been complaining about the bailiff whose vassals they are. They don't want him either for a justiciary or as keeper of the highways."

"So, so!" said the king, with a satisfied smile which he strove in vain to disguise.

"In all their petitions to parliament," continued Compère Jacques, "they claim that they have only two masters: Your Majesty and their god, who I think is the devil."

"Hee, hee!" chuckled the king.

He rubbed his hands, laughed with that inward mirth which lightens the countenance. He was quite unable to dissemble his joy, though he now and then strove to compose himself. None of those present could understand—not even Master Olivier. At length, His Majesty remained silent for a moment, with a thoughtful and satisfied air.

All at once he asked, "Are there great numbers of them?"

"Yes, sire, there certainly are," answered Compère Jacques.

"How many?"

"At least six thousand."

The king could not help saying, "Good!" He went on, "Are they armed?"

"Yes, sire, with scythes, pikes, hackbuts, pickaxes—all sorts of dangerous weapons."

The king seemed not at all disturbed by this detail. Compère Jacques thought proper to add, "Unless Your Majesty sends help quickly to the bailiff, he is lost."

"We shall do so," said the king, with a look of affected gravity. "Good! We certainly will. Monsieur the Bailiff is our friend. Six thousand! They are determined rascals. Their boldness is magnificent, and we are very angry about it. But we have few men with us tonight. There will be time enough tomorrow morning."

Compère Jacques' voice rose again. "Immediately, sire! They'll have time to sack the bailiff's house twenty times over, violate the seigneurie, and hang the bailiff himself. For God's sake, sire send help before tomorrow!"

The king eyed him sternly and said, "I have told you tomorrow morning!"

It was one of those looks to which there is no reply.

After a pause, Louis XI again spoke, "My Compère Jacques, you must know what was," he corrected himself, "what is the feudal jurisdiction of the bailiff?"

"Sire, the bailiff of the Palace has the Rue de la Calandre, as far as the Rue de l'Herberie, the square Saint-Michel, and the squares commonly called Les Mureaux, situated near the church of Notre Dame-des-Champs" (here the king lifted the brim of his hat), "which mansions amount to thirteen; besides the Court of Miracles, and the lazaretto called the Banlieu, and all the highway beginning at that lazaretto and ending at the Porte Saint-Jacques. Of those several places he is the overseer—in charge of high, middle, and low justice—a full and entire lord."

"So ho!" said the king, scratching his left ear with his right hand, "that covers a good slice of my town! So Monsieur the Bailiff *was* the king of all that, eh?"

This time he did not correct himself. He continued, ruminating as if talking to himself, "Softly, Monsieur the Bailiff, you had a pretty piece of our Paris."

Suddenly he exploded.

"*Pasque-Dieu!* Who, among our people, are all these persons that pretend to be highway-keepers, justices, lords,

and masters, along with us—who have their tollgate at the
corner of every field, their court of justice and their executioner at every crossroad? So that, as the Greek thought he
had as many gods as he saw stars, so the Frenchman reck-
ons up as many kings as he see gibbets. *Pardieu!* This is
a terrible state of affairs and all this confusion displeases
me. I should like to know now whether it be God's pleasure that there should be in Paris no highway-keeper but
the king—no justiciary but our parliament—no emperor
but ourself in this empire! By the faith of my soul, the day
must come when there will be in France but one king, one
lord, one judge, one headsman, as there is but one God in
heaven!"

He again lifted his cap, and continued, still ruminating,
and in the manner of a huntsman cheering on his pack,
"Good! my people! Well done! Crush these false lords! Do
your work! At them! Sack them! Hang them! Pillage! Ah,
so you want to be kings, messeigneurs!"

Here he abruptly stopped himself, bit his lip, as if to recall his half-formulated thoughts, and fixed his piercing
eye in turn upon each of the five person around him. Then
suddenly taking his hat between his hands, and looking
steadfastly at it, he said, "Oh, I would burn you if you
knew what I have in my head!"

Then, once casting around him the cautious, anxious
look of a fox stealing back into his hole, "No matter," he
said, "we will send help to Monsieur the Bailiff. Unfortunately, at this time we have very few troops to oppose
such a number of the populace. We must wait until tomorrow. Order then shall be restored in the city, and all who
are taken shall be forthwith hanged."

"That reminds me, sire," said Coictier, "I forgot in my
first perturbation that the watch has arrested two stragglers
belonging to the band. If it be Your Majesty's pleasure to
see these men, they are here."

"If it be my pleasure!" exclaimed the king. "Indeed!
Pasque-Dieu! How could you forget such a thing? Run,
quick, Olivier. Bring them here!"

Master Olivier left and returned a moment later with the two prisoners surrounded by the archers of the ordnance. The first captive had a huge, idiotic face; he was drunk and befuddled. His clothing was in rags. He walked with one knee bent and the foot dragging. The other had a pale, half-smiling face, with which the reader is already acquainted.

The king scrutinized them for a moment, saying nothing. Then abruptly he addressed the first.

"What is your name?"

"Gieffroy Pincebourde."

"Your trade?"

"A Truand."

"What were you hoping to gain by that damnable sedition?"

Swinging his arms stupidly, the Truand fixed his eyes on the king. His was one of those heads, all out of shape, in which the intellect is about as effective as a light under a water extinguisher.

"I don't know," he said. "Everybody was going, so I went."

"Were you not going to outrageously attack and plunder your lord the Bailiff of the Palace?"

"I know they were going to take something from somebody, that's all."

A soldier showed the king a pruning hook which had been seized from the Truand.

"Do you recognize this weapon?" questioned the king.

"Yes, it's my pruning hook. I work in a vineyard."

"And is this man your comrade?" asked Louis XI, pointing to the other prisoner.

"No. I don't know him at all."

"Enough," said the king; and, motioning with his finger to the silent person standing motionless by the door, whom we have already pointed out to the reader, "Compère Tristan, there's a man for you!"

Tristan the Hermit bowed. In a low voice he gave an order to the archers who led the poor Truand away.

Meanwhile the king was questioning the second prisoner, who was perspiring profusely.

"Your name?"

"Sire, Pierre Gringoire."

"Your profession?"

"A philosopher, sire."

"How comes it, knave, that you have the audacity to go and beset our friend Monsieur the Bailiff of the Palace? And what have you to say about this popular commotion?"

"Sire, I had nothing to do with that."

"How now, varlet! Have you not been arrested by the watch in that bad company?"

"No, sire, there's a mistake. It was by chance. I write tragedies, sire. I beg Your Majesty to hear me. I am a poet. It's the hard lot of men of my profession to wander about the streets at night. By ill luck I happened to be strolling this evening. They arrested me without cause, I am an innocent party in this civil storm. Your Majesty saw that the Truand did not recognize me. I entreat Your Majesty . . ."

"Silence," said the king, between two swallows of his tisane. "You talk too much."

Tristan the Hermit stepped forward, and said, pointing to Gringoire, "Sire, shall we hang this one too?"

These were the first words he had uttered.

"Oh, why not," answered the king carelessly, "I don't see any objections."

"But I see a lot," said Gringoire.

At this moment, our philosopher's face was greener than an olive. He saw, by the cool and indifferent manner of the king, that his only help lay in something dramatic; so he threw himself at the feet of Louis XI with gestures of despair.

"Sire, will Your Majesty deign to hear me? Sire, vent not your wrath on such a poor creature as I. God's lightning does not strike a lettuce plant. Sire, you are an august and all-powerful monarch. Have pity on a poor, honest man, as incapable of fanning the flame of revolt as in icicle of striking a spark. Most gracious sire, mildness is the virtue of a lion and of a king. Alas! severity does but exasperate the minds of men. The fierce blasts of the north wind do not make the traveler lay aside his cloak; but the sun's rays little by little warm him so that at length he will gladly strip himself. I swear to you, my sovereign lord and master, that I am not one of the Truands, a thief, or a disorderly person. Sedition and robbery belong not in the train of Apollo. I am not a man to mingle with those clouds which burst into seditious clamor. I am a faithful vassal of Your Majesty. The same jealousy which the husband has for the honor of his wife—the affection with which a son should requite his father's love—a good vassal should feel for the glory of his king. He should exhaust himself in upholding his king's house and in promoting his service. Any other passion that might possess him would be mere frenzy. Such, sire, is my political creed. Do not, then, judge me to be seditious and plundering because my garment is out at the elbows. If you show me mercy, sire, on my knees I will pray to God, night and day, for you. Alas! I am not very rich, it is true. Indeed I am rather poor, but I am not wicked because I am poverty-stricken. That isn't my fault. Everyone knows that great wealth is not acquired by letters, and that the most accomplished writers have not always a warm hearth in wintertime. The lawyers take all the wheat for themselves and leave nothing but chaff for the other learned professions. There are forty most excellent proverbs about the philosopher's threadbare cloak. Oh, sire, clemency is the only light that can enlighten the interior of a great soul. Clemency carries the torch before all the other virtues. Without her they are blind, and grope for God in the dark. Mercy, which is the same thing as clemency, produces loving subjects, who are the most powerful bodyguard of the prince. What can it matter to Your Majesty, by whom all faces are dazzled, that there be one poor man more upon earth, a poor, innocent philosopher, creeping about in the darkness of calamity, with his empty watch pocket flat upon his empty stomach? Besides, sire, I am a man of letters. Great kings add a jewel to their crown by patronizing letters. Hercules did not disdain the title of Musagète. Mathias Corvin favored Jean de Monroyal, the ornament of mathematics. Now, it would be an ill way of patronizing letters to hang the lettered! What a stain to Alexander if he had had Aristotle hanged! Such an act would not have embellished his reputation by even a small patch; but it would have been a virulent ulcer to disfigure it. Sire, I wrote a very appropriate epithalamium for Mademoiselle of Flanders and Monseigneur the most august Dauphin. That was not like a firebrand of rebellion. Your Majesty sees that I am no dunce—that I have studied excellently—and that I have much natural eloquence. Grant me mercy, sire. By so doing, you will do an act in honor of Our Lady; and I assure you, sire, that I am very much frightened at the idea of being hanged."

So say, the desolate Gringoire kissed the king's slippers, while Guillaume Rym whispered to Coppenole, "He does well to crawl upon the floor. Kings are like the Jupiter of Crete—they hear only through their feet."

But, quite inattentive to the Cretan Jupiter, the hosier, his eyes upon Gringoire, answered with a heavy smile, "Ah, that's good! I could fancy I heard the Chancellor Hugonet asking me for mercy."

When at last Gringoire finished, quite out of breath, trembling, he raised his eyes toward the king, who was scratching with his fingernail a spot which he saw upon the knee of his breeches, after which His Majesty took another swallow from his goblet. But he uttered not a syllable—and this silence kept Gringoire in torture.

At last the king looked at him. "Here's a terrible prater," said he. Then, turning to Tristan the Hermit, he ordered, "Bah! let him go!"

Gringoire fell back on his rear, quite overcome with joy.

"Let him go?" grumbled Tristan. "Will Your Majesty not have him put in the cage for a while?"

"Compère," returned Louis XI, "do you think it is for birds like these that we have cages made at three hundred and sixty-seven livres eight sols three deniers a piece? Let the knave go immediately, put him out with a beating."

"Oh," exclaimed Gringoire in ecstasy, "this is indeed a great king!"

Then, for fear of a countermand, he rushed toward the door, which Tristan opened for him with very ill grace. The soldiers went out after him, belaboring him violently with their fists, which Gringoire endured like a true stoic philosopher.

The good humor of the king, ever since the revolt against the bailiff had been announced to him, manifested itself in everything. This unusual clemency of his was no small sign of it. Tristan the Hermit, in his corner, was looking as surly as a mastiff denied his bone.

Meanwhile the king was gaily tapping with his fingers on the arm of his chair the Pont-Audemer march. Though a dissembling prince, he was much better able to conceal his sorrow than his rejoicing. These external manifestations of joy, on the receipt of any good news, sometimes carried him great lengths; as, for instance, on the death of Charles the Bold of Burgundy, he ordered balustrades of silver added to Saint-Martin of Tours; and on his accession to the throne, he forgot to make arrangements for his father's funeral.

"Ha, sire," suddenly put in Jacques Coictier, "what have become of the sharp pains which made Your Majesty send for me?"

"Oh," said the king, "truly, my compère, I am in great pain. I hear a ringing in my ear, and red-hot rakes furrow my breast.

Coictier took the king's hand, and felt his pulse with a knowing look.

"Look, Coppenole," said Rym in a whisper, "there he is between Coictier and Tristan. That is his whole court—a physician for himself, and a hangman for the rest of his kingdom."

While taking the king's pulse, Coictier was assuming a look of greater and greater alarm. Louis XI watched him with some anxiety; while the physician's face grew more and more grave. The king's bad health was the only estate the good man had to cultivate, and accordingly he made the most of it.

"Oh! oh!" he muttered at length. "This is serious, indeed."

"Yes?" said the king uneasily.

"Pulse quick, irregular, intermittent," continued the physician.

"*Pasque-Dieu!*"

"In three days this could carry off a man."

"Notre Dame!" cried the king. "And the remedy, compère?"

"I am thinking, sire."

He made the king stick out his tongue, shook his head, made a face, and in the midst of this grimacing exclaimed, "By God, sire, I must tell you that there is a receivership of episcopal revenues vacant, and that I have a nephew . . ."

"Compère Jacques, I give the receivership to your nephew," answered the king, "but get this burning sensation off my chest."

"Since Your Majesty is so kind," resumed the physician, "I am sure you will not refuse to assist me a little in the building of my house on the Rue Saint-André-des-Arct."

"Hmm!" said the king.

"I'm at the end of my finances," said the doctor, "and it would really be a pity that the house should be left without a roof—not for the sake of the house itself, which is quite plain and homely, but for the sake of the paintings by Jehan Fourbault that adorn its wainscoting. There's a Diana flying through the air—so excellently done, so tender, so delicate, in action so artless, her head so well dressed, and crowned with a crescent, her flesh so white that she leads into temptation those who examine her too curiously. Then there's a Ceres, and she too is a very beautiful goddess. She sits upon cornhusks, and is crowned with a handsome wreath of ears of corn intertwined with goatsbeard and other flowers. Never were seen more amorous eyes, rounder legs, a nobler air, or a flowing robe more graceful. She's one of the most innocent and most exquisite beauties ever produced by brush."

"Cutthroat!" grumbled the king. "What are you after now?"

"I want a roof over these paintings, sire; and although it is but a trifle, I have no money."

"How much would it cost, your roof?"

"Why, uh, a copper roof, figured and gilded, two thousand pounds at the most."

"Wretched thief!" cried the king. "He never draws me a tooth but he makes a diamond of it!"

"May I have my roof?" said Coictier.

"Yes, and the devil take you! But cure me!"

Bowing low, Jacques Coictier said, "Sire, it is a repellent that will save you. We will apply to your loins the great deterrent concocted of cerate, Armenian bole, white of eggs, oil and vinegar. You are to continue with your tisane, and we will answer for Your Majesty's safety."

A lighted candle never attracts one gnat only. Master Olivier, seeing the king in a generous mood, and deeming the moment opportune, approached in his turn.

"Sire."

"What now?" said Louis XI.

"Sire, Your Majesty is undoubtedly aware that Master Simon Radin died."

"So?"

"He was the king's comptroller."

"Well?"

"Sire, his post is vacant."

While thus speaking, Master Olivier's haughty countenance had exchanged its arrogance for a fawning expression—the only alternation that ever takes place in the aspect of a courtier.

The king looked him full in the face and said dryly, "I understand.

"Master Olivier, the Marshal de Boucicaut used to say,

'There's no gift but from a king; there's no good fishing but in the sea.' I see that you are of the marshal's opinion. Now be this understood: our memory is good; in '68, we made you groom of our chambers; in '69, castellan at the bridge of Saint-Cloud, with a salary of a hundred livres tournois, (you wanted them in parisis); in November '73, by letters given at Gergeole, we appointed you keeper of the Bois de Vincennes, instead of Gilbert Acle, Esquire; in '75, warden of the forest of Rouvray-lez-Saint-Cloud, in place of Jacques le Maire; in '76, we graciously bequeathed to you, by letters-patent sealed with green wax, an annuity of ten livres parisis, to you and your wife, upon the Place-aux-Marchands, situated at the Ecole Saint-Germain; in '79, we made you warden of the forest of Senart, in place of that poor Jehan Daiz; then captain of the Château of Loches; then governor of Saint-Quentin; next captain of the bridge of Meulan, because of which you call yourself count. Moreover, out of the fine of five sols paid by every barber who shaves you on a holiday you get three sols, and we get only two. Also, we were pleased to change your name of Le Mauvais, which was too much like your countenance. In '74 we granted you, to the great displeasure of our nobility, an armorial shield of a thousand colors, that gives you a breast like a peacock's. *Pasque-Dieu!* Aren't you satisfied? Is not the net full of fishes fine and miraculous enough? Are you not afraid that a single salmon more would be sufficient to sink your boat? Pride will be your ruination, compère. Pride is ever followed close behind by ruin and shame. Consider all this and be silent."

These words, uttered in a tone of severity, brought back to the momentarily chagrined physiognomy of Master Olivier its former insolent expression. "Good," he muttered, almost aloud. "It's plain enough that the king is ill today, for he gives everything to his physician."

Louis XI, far from being annoyed by this remark, resumed with some mildness, "Wait, I forgot to add that I made you ambassador to Madame Marie at Ghent. Yes, gentlemen," added the king, turning to the Flemings, "this man has been an ambassador. There, compère," he continued, addressing himself again to Master Olivier, "let us not quarrel; we're old friends. It's very late. We've finished our work. Shave me!"

Our readers have undoubtedly already recognized in Master Olivier that terrible Figaro whom Providence, that greatest dramatist of all, so artfully mixed up in the long and sanguinary play of Louis XI's reign. We shall not here undertake to develop at full length that singular character. This barber to the king had three names. At court he was called politely Olivier le Daim; among the people, Olivier le Diable. But his real name was Olivier le Marvais; or the Bad.

Olivier le Mauvais, therefore, stood motionless, looking sulkily at the king, and enviously at Jacques Coictier.

"Yes, yes! the physician!" he muttered.

"Well, yes, the physician!" resumed Louis XI with singular good humor; "the physician has yet more influence than you. It's all very simple. He has got our whole body in his hands, and you do but hold us by the chin. Come, come, my poor barber, there's nothing wrong. What would you say, and what would become of your position, if I were a king like King Chilpéric, whose way it was to hold his beard with one hand? Come, compère, perform your office, and shave me. Go get what you need."

Olivier, seeing that the king had resolved to take the matter in jest, and that there was no way even to provoke him, went out grumbling to execute his commands.

The king rose from his chair, went to the window, and suddenly opened it in extraordinary agitation, exclaiming, "Oh, yes!" Then, clapping his hands, he continued, "There's a glare in the sky over the City. It's the bailiff burning; it can't be anything else. Hah! my good people, so you help me, then, at last, to do away with these seigneuries!"

Then turning to the Flemings, "Gentlemen," he said, "come and see. Is not that a fire that glares so red?"

The two Flemings came forward to look.

"A large fire," said Guillaume Rym.

"Oh," added Coppenole, whose eyes all at once sparkled, "that reminds me of the burning of the house of the Seigneur d'Hymbercourt. There must be a big revolt there."

"You think so, Master Coppenole?" interjected the king. And he looked almost as pleased as the hosier himself. "Don't you think it will be difficult to quell it?"

"By the rood! Sire, it may cost Your Majesty a good company of soldiers."

"Ha! cost me! That's different," returned the king. "If I chose . . ."

The hosier rejoined boldly. "If that revolt be what I think it is, you would choose in vain, sire."

"Compère," said Louis XI, "two companies from my ordnance and one discharge from a cannon are quite enough to rout this mob of common people."

The hosier, in spite of the signs that Guillaume Rym was making to him, seemed determined to provoke the king.

"Sire," he said, "the Swiss were common people too. Monsieur the Duke of Burgundy was a great gentleman, and made no account of the rabble. At the battle of Grandson, sire, he called out, 'Cannoneers, fire on those villains!' and he swore by Saint George. But the avenger, Scharnachtal, with his club, rushed upon the goodly duke and his people; and at the attack of the peasants, with their bull hides, the shining Burgundian army was shattered like a windowpane by a stone. Many a knight was killed there by those lowly knaves, and Monsieur de Château-Guyon, the most powerful lord in Burgundy, was found dead, with his great gray horse, in a small marshy meadow."

"Friend," returned the king, "you're talking about a battle. But this is only a riot, and I can put an end to it with a single frown when I please."

The other replied indifferently, "That may be, sire. In that case the people's hour has not yet come."

Guillaume Rym thought he must intervene.

"Master Coppenole," he said, "you are talking to a mighty king."

"I know it," answered the hosier gravely.

"Let him speak, Monsieur Rym, my friend," said the king. "I like his speaking plainly. My father, Charles VII, used to say the truth was sick. For my part I thought it was dead, and had found no confessor. But Master Coppenole shows me I was mistaken."

Then putting his hand familiarly on Coppenole's shoulder, "You were saying then, Master Jacques? . . ."

"I was saying, sire, that perhaps you are right; that, with you, the people's hour has not yet arrived."

Louis XI looked at him with his penetrating eye.

"And when will that hour come, master?"

"You will hear it strike."

"By what clock, please?"

Coppenole, his plain face calm, motioned the king to come to the window.

"Listen, sire. Here is a dungeon, an alarm-bell, cannons, people, soldiers. When the bell-tower rings out, when the cannons roar, when, with a great noise, the dungeon walls crumble and fall, when the townspeople and the soldiers shout and kill each other; then the hour will have struck."

Louis' face became gloomy and pensive. For a moment, he was silent, then gently caressing with his hand the thick wall of the dungeon, as if patting the shoulder of a war horse, "Ah no!" he said, "thou wilt not so easily crumble, wilt thou, my good Bastille!"

Then, turning around abruptly to the bold Fleming, he said, "Have you ever seen a revolt, Master Jacques?"

"Sire, I caused one," answered the hosier.

"What does one do to cause one?" asked the king.

"Oh," replied Coppenole, "it's not very hard to do. There are a hundred ways. First of all, there must be unrest in the town, which often there is. And then, the character of the inhabitants is important. The people of Ghent are ever inclined to revolt. They always like the son of the prince, but never the prince himself. Well, one morning, let's suppose, somebody comes into my shop, and says, Father Coppenole, there's this or that; for example, the Lady of Flanders wants to save her ministers, the high bailiff is doubling the tool on vegetables, or something else— anything you like. Me, I leave my work, go out of my shop into the street and cry: 'Revolt!' There's always a convenient barrel. I climb on it, and shout the first words that come into my head about whatever has been on my mind; for, when one is of the people, sire, one has always something on his mind. A crowd gathers. They shout. They sound the alarm. They arm themselves with weapons they have taken from the soldiers; the market people join us, and then the revolt is on. It will always be thus, as long as there are seigneurs in the seigneuries, townspeople in towns, and peasants in the country."

"And against whom do you rebel like that?" asked the king. "Against your bailiffs? Against your lords?"

"Sometimes. That depends. Against the duke, too, sometimes."

Louis XI took his seat again, and said with a smile, "Ah! but here they have gotten no further than the bailiff!"

Just then Olivier le Daim returned, followed by two pages carrying the king's toilet articles; but what surprised Louis XI was to see him also accompanied by the Provost of Paris and a knight of the watch, both of whom seemed alarmed. The face of the cantankerous barber also betrayed alarm, but satisfaction was also there. He was the first to speak.

"Sire, I ask Your Majesty's pardon for the calamitous news I bring you."

The king turned so quickly that he tore the floor matting with the legs of his heavy chair.

"What is it?"

"Sire," replied Olivier with the evil look of a man rejoicing that he is about to deal a violent blow, "it is not against the bailiff of the Palace that the mob is rebelling."

"Against whom then?"

"Against you, sire!"

The old king sprang to his feet, and stood erect like a young man.

"Explain yourself, Olivier! Explain; and beware of your head, compère, for I swear, by the cross of Saint-Lô, that if you lie to us in this matter, the sword that cut Monsieur of Luxembourg's throat is not so notched but it can saw your head too!"

The oath was formidable. Louis XI had never but twice in his life sworn by the cross of Saint-Lô.

Olivier opened his mouth to reply. "Sire . . ."

"On your knees!" interrupted the king violently. "Tristan, watch this man carefully."

Olivier fell to his knees and tersely reported.

"Sire, a witch has been condemned to death by your parliament. She has taken sanctuary in Notre Dame. The people want to take her from there by force. Monsieur the Provost and Monsieur the Knight of the Watch, who have just come from the spot, are here to correct me if I speak not the truth. The people are laying siege to Notre Dame."

"Ah, yes?" said the king in a low voice, pale and trembling with rage. "Notre Dame! So they are besieging Our Lady, my good mistress, in her own cathedral! Get up, Olivier. You are right. I give you Simon Radin's office. You are right. It is I whom they are attacking. The witch is safeguarded by the church. The church is under my protection. And I thought they were rioting against the bailiff. But it's against me!"

Then, as if rejuvenated by his fury, he began to stride up and down the room. He was no longer laughing. His mien was frightening. He paced back and forth. The fox had changed into a hyena. He seemed choked with rage. His lips moved but no words came. He wrung his bony hands. All at once he raised his head, his hollow eyes seemed full of light, and his voice shrilled like a clarion.

"Attack them! Tristan, attack these blackguards. Go, Tristan, my friend! Kill them! Kill them!"

When he had controlled himself, he sat again in his chair, and spoke calmly but with emphasis.

"Here, Tristan! There are right here in this Bastille fifty lances of the Viscount de Gif, and three hundred horses. Take them. There is also Monsieur de Châteauper's company of archers of our ordnance. You will take them. You are the provost marshal and have the men of your provostry. Take them. At the Hotel Saint-Pol you will find forty archers of Monsieur the Dauphin's new guard. You will take them. With all these forces, you will go in haste to Notre Dame. Ah, gentlemen of the mob of Paris, so you would throw yourselves against the crown of France, and at the holiness of Our Lady, and at the peace of this commonwealth! Exterminate them, Tristan! Exterminate them! And let not one escape except to be hanged at Montfaucon!"

Tristan bowed. "Very good, sire." But after a pause, he added, "What shall I do with the witch?"

The king thought.

"Ah! the witch! Monsieur d'Estouteville, what do the people want do with her?"

"Sire," answered the Provost of Paris, "I suppose that, since the people are come to drag her away from her sanctuary in Notre Dame, it is her impunity that offends them, and that they want to hang her."

The king seemed in deep thought: then he addressed Tristan the Hermit, "Well, then, compère, wipe out the people and hang the witch."

"That's a fine thing!" whispered Rym to Coppenole. "Punish the people for their intentions, and then do what they wished to do!"

"Enough, sire," answered Tristan. "If the witch is still in Notre Dame, must we take her away in spite of the sanctuary?"

"*Pasque-Dieu!* the sanctuary!" said the king, scratching his ear. "And yet that woman must be hanged."

Here, as if seized with a sudden thought, he knelt in front of his chair, took off his hat, put it upon the seat, and

looking devoutly at one of the leaden figures with which
it was adorned, "Oh," he said, joining his hands, "Our
Lady of Paris, my gracious patroness, pardon me. I will
only do it this one time. That sorceress must be punished.
I assure you, O Lady Virgin, my worthy mistress, that a
witch is unworthy of your kind protection. You know,
Lady, that many very pious princes have trespassed upon
the privilege of the churches, for the glory of God and the
necessity of the State. Saint Hugh, bishop of England, allowed King Edward to seize a magician in his church. My
master, Saint Louis of France, transgressed for the same
reason in the church of Saint-Paul. And Monsieur Al-
phonse, son of the king of Jerusalem, so profaned the
Church of the Holy Sepulcher itself. Pardon me, then, this
once, Our Lady of Paris. I will not do it again. And I will
give you a beautiful statue of silver like that which I gave
last year to Our Lady of Ecouys. Amen!"

He crossed himself, rose, put on his hat, and said to
Tristan, "With all speed, compère. Take Monsieur de
Châteaupers with you. Ring the alarm. Crush the mob.
Hang the witch. I have spoken. You will defray all the
costs of the execution and bring me an account of them.
Come, Olivier, I shall not go to bed tonight. Shave me."

Tristan the Hermit bowed and left. Then the king, motioning to Rym and Coppenole to retire, said, "God keep
you, gentlemen, my good Flemish friends! Go and take
some rest. Night is far spent; we are nearer to morning
than evening."

Both retired, escorted by the captain of the Bastille.

Upon reaching their apartment, Coppenole said to
Guillaume Rym, "Humph! I've had enough of this coughing king. I have seen Charles of Burgundy drunk, but he
was not as evil as this sick Louis XI."

"Master Jacques," replied Rym, "that is because a king
finds less cruelty in his wine than in his tisane."

52

O n leaving the Bastile, where he had been taken by the guard, Gringoire scudded down the Rue St. Antoine with the swiftness of a runaway horse. When he had reached the Baudoyer gate, he walked straight up to the stone cross which stood in the middle of the open space, as though he had been able to discern in the dark the figure of a man in a black dress and cowl, seated on the steps of the cross. "Is it you, master?" said Gringoire.

The black figure started up. "Death and perdition! You make my blood boil, Gringoire. The warder on the tower of St. Gervais has just cried half-past one."

"Why," replied Gringoire, " 'tis not my fault, but that of the watch and the king. I have had a narrow escape. I was on the point of being hanged. I am predestined to it, I fancy."

"Thou art never in time for anything," said the other; "but let us be gone. Hast thou the watchword?"

"Only think, master—I have seen the king! I have just come from him. He wears fustian breeches. 'Tis quite an adventure!"

"Eternal babbler! What care I for thy adventure! Hast thou the watchword of the vagabonds?"

"Be easy; I have."

" 'Tis well. We should not else be able to reach the church. The rabble block up all the streets. Luckily, they seem to have met with resistance. We shall perhaps yet arrive in time."

"Yes, master, but how are we to get into the church?"

"I have a key to the towers."

"And how shall we get out?"

"Behind the cloisters there is a postern opening upon the Terrain, and so to the river. I have taken the key of it, and I moored a boat there this morning."

"I have had a most lucky escape from the gallows indeed!" said Gringoire, exultingly.

"Never mind that now! come along, quick!" rejoined the other.

Both then proceeded at a rapid pace toward the city.

53

The reader probably recollects the critical situation in which we left Quasimodo. The brave hunchback, assailed on all sides, had lost, if not all courage, at least all hope of saving, not himself—he never once thought of himself—but the Egyptian. He ran in consternation to the gallery. The church was on the point of being carried by the mob. All at once the tramp of horses in full gallop was heard in the neighboring streets; and presently a wide column of horsemen riding at speed and a long file of torches poured with tremendous noise into the Place like a hurricane. "France! France for ever! Chateaupers to the rescue! Down with the rascals!" The affrighted vagabonds faced about.

Quasimodo, who could not hear the din, saw the naked swords, the torches, the pikeheads, the whole column of cavalry at the head of which he recognized Captain Phœbus. He observed the confusion of the rabble, the consternation of some and the alarm of the stoutest; and at the sight of this unexpected succor he mustered strength enough to throw down the foremost of the assailants who were already striding over into the gallery.

The conflict was terrible. As Father Mathiu observes,

"Wolf's flesh requires dogs' teeth." The king's troops amid whom Phœbus de Chateaupers conducted himself valiantly, gave no quarter; what escaped the point of the sword was cut down by the edge. The rabble, badly armed, foamed and bit. Men, women, children, darting at the flanks and chests of the horses, clung to them like cats with tooth and nail. Some thrust torches into the faces of the archers; while others, catching them by the neck with iron hooks, pulled them from their horses and cut them in pieces. One in particular was remarked with a huge scythe, mowing away at the legs of the horses. It was a fearful sight. Snuffling a stave with nasal twang, he kept his scythe incessantly going. At each stroke he formed about him a large semicircle of dismembered limbs. In this manner he wrought his way into the thickest of the cavalry with the deliberate movement, the swaying of the head, the regular expiration of a mower cutting a field of clover. It was Clopin Trouillefou. The tire of an arquebuse laid him prostrate.

Meanwhile windows were thrown open. The neighbors, hearing the shouts of men-at-arms, took part in the affair, and showers of balls were discharged from every story upon the rabble. The Parvis was filled with a dense smoke, which the musketry streaked ever and anon with fire. Through this smoke were faintly seen the facade of Notre Dame, and the decrepit Hotel Dieu, with a number of pale-faced patients gazing from the top of its roof studded with dormer windows.

The vagabonds at length gave way, discomfited by weariness, the want of proper weapons, the consternation of that surprise, the firing from the windows, and the furious onslaught of the king's troops. Forcing the line of their assailants, they fled in all directions, leaving the Parvis strewed with dead.

When Quasimodo, who had been busily engaged the whole time, perceived their defeat, he fell on his knees and lifted his hands to heaven; then, frantic with joy, he flew with the swiftness of a bird to the little cell, the access to which he had so gallantly defended. He had now but one thought—to throw himself at the feet of her whom he had saved for the second time. When he reached the cell, he found it empty.

54

At the moment when the vagabonds attacked the church, La Esmeralda was asleep. It was not long before she was roused by the constantly increasing noise around the cathedral and the uneasy bleating of her goat, which had awoke before her. She sat up, listening and looking about; then, alarmed by the light and the uproar, she hurried out of the cell to see what was the matter. The aspect of the Place, the scene exhibited there, the confusion of this nocturnal assault, the hideous appearance of the rabble, hopping about like a host of frogs, faintly discerned in the dark, the harsh croaking of this coarse mob, the few torches dancing to and fro in the obscurity, like those meteors of night gamboling over the misty surface of bogs, produced all together the effect of a mysterious battle between the phantoms of the witches' sabbath and the stone monsters of the church. Imbued from infancy with the superstitions of the gypsy tribe, her first idea was that she had caught the strange beings peculiar to night in their unhallowed pranks. She then hurried back in affright to her cell, to bury her face in the bedclothes, and to shut out if possible the terrific vision.

In an attitude of prayer she remained for a considerable time, trembling indeed more than she prayed, her blood curdling at the indications of the nearer and nearer approach of that infuriated multitude, utterly at a loss to account for their proceedings, ignorant of what they were doing and what they meant to do, but anticipating some terrible catastrophe.

Amid this anguish she heard a footstep close to her. She looked up. Two men, one of whom carried a lantern, had just entered her cell. She gave a faint shriek.

"Fear nothing," said a voice, which was not unknown to her; "it is I."

"And who are you?" she inquired.

"Pierre Gringoire."

That name gave her fresh courage. She lifted her eyes and saw that it actually was the poet. But at his side stood a black figure, muffled up from head to foot, which struck her mute.

"Ah!" resumed Gringoire, in a tone of reproach, "Djali knew me before you did!"

The little goat had, in fact, not waited for Gringoire to mention his name. No sooner did he enter than she fondly rubbed against his knees, covering the poet with endearments and white hair; for she was shedding her coat. Gringoire returned her caresses.

"Who is that with you?" said the Egyptian in a low tone.

"Be easy," answered Gringoire. " 'Tis one of my friends."

The philosopher, setting down the lantern, crouched upon the floor, clasped Djali in his arms, and cried with enthusiasm: "Oh! 'tis a darling creature, with its engaging ways, and withal shrewd, ingenious, and learned as a grammarian! Come, my Djali, let us see if thou hast not forgotten they diverting tricks. How does Master Jacques Charmolue do—?"

The man in black would not suffer him to finish. He stepped up to Gringoire, and roughly pushed him on the shoulder. Gringoire rose. "Ah! true!" said he; "I had well-nigh forgotten that we are in haste. But yet, master, that is no reason for hurting people so. My dear girl, your life is in danger, and Djali's too. They mean to hang you again.

We are your friends, and are come to save you. Follow us."

"Is it true?" cried she in extreme agitation.

"Quite true, I assure you. Come quick!"

"I will," stammered she. "But how is it that your friend does not speak?"

"Why," said Gringoire, "the fact is, that his father and mother were fantastic people, and made him a reserved disposition."

She was obliged to be satisfied with this explanation. Gringoire took her by the hand; his companion picked up the lantern and walked on before. The young creature was stupefied with fear. She suffered Gringoire to lead her away. The goat went with them, frisking about, and so overjoyed to see the poet again, that she thrust her head every moment against his legs with such force as to make him stagger. "Such is life," said the philosopher, whenever he had well-nigh fallen; "it is often our best friends that throw us down!"

They rapidly descended the tower stairs, passed through the church, dark, solitary, but ringing with the uproar, which produced a fearful contrast, and went out by the Porte Rouge into the cloister court. The cloisters were deserted; the canons had fled to the bishop's palace, where they were praying together; the court was empty, with the exception of a few affrighted servingmen, squatting in the dark corners. Gringoire and his companions proceeded toward the postern leading out of that court to the Terrain. The man in black unlocked it with a key which he brought with him. The reader is aware that the Terrain was a slip of land enclosed with walls, belonging to the chapter of Notre Dame, forming the eastern extremity of the island, in the rear of the cathedral. They found this spot entirely deserted.

The man with the lantern proceeded directly to the point of the Terrain. At that spot there was, at the water's edge, a decayed fence composed of stakes crossed with laths, upon which a few sickly branches of a low vine were

spread like the fingers of an open hand. Behind, and in the
shade cast by this trellis, lay a small skiff. The man made
a sign to Gringoire and his companion to get in. The goat
followed him. The man then stepped in himself, cut the
rope which moored the skiff, pushed off from the shore
with a long pole, seated himself in the forepart, and taking
up two oars, began to row out toward the middle of the
river. In this place the Seine is very rapid, so that he had
some difficulty to work off from the point of the island.

The skiff slowly pursued its way toward the right bank.
The girl watched the mysterious unknown with secret terror. He had carefully masked the light of his dark lantern;
and he was faintly seen in the forepart of the skiff, like a
specter. His cowl still down, formed a sort of visor, and
every time that, in rowing, he opened his arms, from
which hung wide black sleeves, they looked like two prodigious bats' wings. He had not yet uttered a word, or suffered a breath to escape him. He made no other noise in
the boat than what proceeded from the working of the
oars, which blended with the rush of the thousand ripples
against the side of the vessel.

The unknown suddenly ceased rowing, his arms sank, as
if broken, his head drooped upon his breast, and La Esmeralda heard him sigh convulsively. She had heard sighs of
that kind before.

The skiff, left to itself, drifted for some moments at the
will of the current. At length, the man in black roused
himself, and again began pulling against the stream. He
doubled the point of the isle of Notre Dame, and rowed toward the landing place of the Port-au-Foin.

The tumult around Notre Dame was raging with increased vehemence. They listened. Shouts of victory were
distinctly heard. All at once, a hundred torches, which
made the helmets of the men-at-arms glisten, appeared on
all parts of the church, on the towers, the galleries, the flying buttresses. These torches seemed to be employed in
searching after something; and presently distant shouts of,

"The Egyptian! the sorceress!—death to the Egyptian!"
were plainly heard by the fugitives.

The unhappy girl drooped her head upon her hands, and
the unknown began to row furiously toward the shore. Our
philosopher was meanwhile musing. He hugged the goat
in his arms, and sidled gently away from the Bohemian,
who pressed closer and closer to him, as to the only asylum that was now left her.

It is certain that Gringoire was in a cruel dilemma. He
considered that, as the law then stood, the goat would be
hanged too if she were retaken; that it would be a great
pity—poor dear Djali!—that two condemned ones thus
clinging to him were more than he could thus manage;
that, besides, his companion desired nothing better than to
take charge of the Egyptian. A violent conflict ensued
among this thoughts, in which, like Homer's Jupiter, he
weighed by turns the Egyptian and the goat; and he looked
first at one and then at the other with eyes brimful of tears,
muttering at the same time between his teeth: "And yet I
cannot save you both!"

A shock apprised them that the skiff had reached the
shore. The city still rang with the appalling uproar. The
unknown rose, stepped up to the Egyptian, and offered her
his arm to assist her to land. She refused it and clung to
the sleeve of Gringoire, who, on his part, engaged with the
goat, almost pushed her away. She then sprang without
help out of the boat. She was so alarmed that she knew not
what she was doing or whither she was going. She stood
stupefied for a moment, with her eyes fixed on the water.
When she came to herself a little she was alone on the
quay with the unknown. It appeared that Gringoire had
taken advantage of the instant of landing to steal away
with the goat among the cluster of houses composing the
Rue Grenier-sure-l'Eau.

The poor Egyptian shuddered on finding herself alone
with that man. She strove to speak, to cry out, to call Gringoire; but her tongue refused its office, and not a sound issued from her lips. All at once, she felt the hand of the

unknown upon hers. Her teeth chattered and she turned paler than the moon's ray which fell upon her. The man spoke not a word. With hasty step he began to move toward the Place de Greve, drawing her slowly by the hand. At that moment she had a vague feeling that Fate is an irresistible power. She had lost all elasticity, and followed mechanically, running while he walked. The quay at this spot is rising ground; to her it seemed as if she were going down hill.

She looked around at all sides. Not a passenger was to be seen.

Meanwhile, the unknown continued to drag her along with the same silence and the same rapidity. She had no recollection of the places through which he took her. In passing a lighted window she suddenly made an effort to resist, and cried: "Help! help!"

The window opened; the inmate of the room appeared at it in his shirt and nightcap, with a lamp in his hand, looked out with drowsy eyes upon the quay, muttered a few words, which she could not catch, and reclosed the window. She felt as though the last glimmer of hope was extinguished.

From time to time she mustered a little strength, and in a voice broken from the jolting of the rugged pavement and from her being out of breath, owing to the rapid rate at which she was drawn along, she asked: "Who are you?—who are you?" He made no reply.

Proceeding thus along the quay, they arrived at a large open space. The moon shone faintly. It was the Greve. In the middle of it stood a sort of black cross—it was the gibbet. She now knew where she was.

The man stopped, turned toward her, and raised his cowl. "Oh!" stammered she, petrified with horror, "I knew that it must be he!"

It was in truth the priest. He looked like a ghost. Moonlight produces this effect. It seems as if by that light one beholds only the specters of objects.

"List to me!" said he; and she shuddered at the sound of

that fatal voice, which she had not heard for so long a time. He continued, with frequent pauses and in broken sentences which betokened violent inward agitation—"List to me! Here we are. I would speak to thee. This is the Greve. We go no farther. Fate delivers us up into the hands of each other. Thy life is at my disposal; my soul at thine. Here is a place and a night beyond which one sees nothing. List to me then. I would tell thee—but not a word about thy Phœbus"; as he spoke he paced to and fro, like a man who cannot remain on one spot, and drew her after him—"talk not to me of him. If thou but utterest that name, I know not what I shall do; but it will be terrible."

Having proceeded thus far, like a body recovering its center of gravity, he stood still, but his words betrayed not the less perturbation. His voice became more and more faint.

"Turn not thy head from me thus. List to me. 'Tis a serious business. First, I would tell thee what has passed. It is not a thing to laugh at, I protest to thee. But what was I saying? Ah, yes! An order has been issued by the Parliament which consigns thee again to the gallows. I have rescued thee from their hands. But yonder they are searching for thee. Look."

He pointed toward the City. It was evident, in fact, that the search was continued. The noise drew nearer. The tower of the lieutenant's house, facing the Greve, was full of bustle and lights; and soldiers might be seen running on the opposite quay with torches shouting: "The Egyptian! where is the Egyptian? Death! death!"

"Thou seest that they are in pursuit of thee, and that I am not deceiving thee. Maiden, I love thee! Open not thy lips; answer me not, if it is to tell me that thou hatest me. I am determined not to hear that. I have aided thine escape. Let me complete the work. I can save thee. Everything is prepared. All depends on thy will. Whatever thou wilt shall be done."

He interrupted himself with vehemence—"No! that is not what I meant to say."

Then running, and drawing her along with him, for he still kept hold of her, he went straight to the foot of the gibbet, and, pointing to it, said coldly: "Choose between us."

She tore herself from his grip, and, throwing herself on the pavement, clasped the foot of the fatal machine; then, half turning her head, she looked over her shoulder at the priest. The priest stood motionless, his finger still raised toward the gibbet, like a statue.

"I feel less horror of that than of you," at length said the Egyptian.

He slowly dropped his arm, and cast his eyes upon the pavement in deep dejection. "Yes," said he; "if these stones could speak, they would say—'There is the most miserable of men!'"

"I love you," he again began. The girl, kneeling before the gibbet, covered by her long flowing hair, allowed him to proceed without interruption. His accent was now soft and plaintive, woefully contrasting with the lofty sternness of his features.

"I love you. Nothing can be more true. No fire can be fiercer than that which consumes my heart. Ah! maiden, night and day—yes, night and day—doth this claim no pity? 'Tis a love, a torture, night and day, I tell thee. Oh! my dear girl, 'tis an agony worthy of compassion, I assure thee. I would speak kindly to thee, thou seest. I would have thee not feel such horror of me. And then, if a man loves a woman it is not his fault. What! thou wilt never take compassion on me, then? Thou wilt hate me for ever? 'Tis this that makes me cruel—ay, hateful to myself! Thou wilt not even deign to look at me. Thou art thinking perhaps of something else, while I am talking to thee and trembling on the brink of the eternity of both. At any rate, talk not to me of thine officer! Were I to throw myself at thy knees; were I to kiss, not thy feet—thous wouldst not suffer me—but the ground beneath them; were I to sob like a child, and to tear from my bosom not words, but my heart and my entrails, to tell thee how I love thee, all would be in vain—all! And yet thou hast in thy soul nought but what is kind and tender. Thou art all goodness, all gentleness, all compassion, all charms. Alas! to me alone art thou unfeeling. Oh! what a fatality!"

He buried his face in his hands. La Esmeralda heard him weep; it was for the first time. His figure, thus upright and shaken by sobs, was more pitiable and more humble than if he had knelt. He continued to weep thus for some time.

"Alas!" he proceeded, this first paroxysm over, "I am at a loss for words. And yet I had well pondered what I should say to thee. Now I tremble and shudder; I shrink back at the decisive moment; I feel some superior power that overwhelms me and makes me stammer. Oh! I shall sink on the pavement unless thou take pity on me, on thyself. Condemn not both of us. Would that thou knewest how I love thee, and what a heart is mine. Oh! what an abandonment of all virtue, what a desperate desertion of myself! A doctor, I make a mock at science; a gentleman, I disgrace my name; a priest, I violate the most solemn vows, and renounce my God!—and all for thy sake, enchantress; and thou rejectest the wretched one! Oh! I must tell thee all—still more, something even yet more horrible—most horrible!"

As he uttered the concluded words, his look became quite wild. He kept silence for a moment, and then began again, as if speaking to himself, in a loud tone: "Cain, what hast thou done with thy brother?"

Again he paused, and then continued: "What have I done with him, Lord? I have taken him unto me, I have fed him, I have brought him up, I have loved him, I have idolized him, and, I have slain him! Yes, Lord, he it was whose head was but now dashed before mine eyes against the stones of thy temple, and it was on my account and on account of this female, on her account."

His eye glared wildly. His voice became more and more faint; he repeated several times, and with pauses of some length, like a bell prolonging its vibration; "On her account—" "On her account." His lips continued to move, but his tongue ceased to articulate any audible sound. All at once, he sank down and remained motionless upon the ground, with his head bowed to his knees. A slight movement made by the girl to draw her foot from under him brought him to himself. He passed his hand slowly over his hollow cheeks and looked vacantly for some moments at his fingers, which were wet. "What!" he muttered; "have I wept?"

Turning abruptly toward the Egyptian, with irrepressible anguish, he said: "And hast thou coldly beheld me weep? Knowest thou, girl, that those tears are lava? Is it then true that thy sex are not moved by anything that can befall the man they hate? Wert thou to see me die, thou wouldst laugh. But I—I wish not thy death! One word! a single word of kindness! Tell me not that thou lovest me; say only that thou wishest me well; it shall suffice—I will save thee. Otherwise—Oh! the time passes. I implore thee by all that is sacred, wait not till I am again transformed into stone, like that gibbet which also claims thee! Consider that I hold both our fates in my hand, that I am mad—oh! it is terrible—that I may let all drop, and that there is beneath us a bottomless abyss, down which I shall follow thee in thy fall to all eternity! One kind word! one word! but a single word!"

She opened her lips to answer. He fell on his knees before her, to catch with adoration the words, perhaps of sympathy, which should drop from her mouth. "You are an assassin!" said she.

The priest clasped her furiously in his arms, and burst forth into a terrific laugh. "Assassin though I be," cried he, "I will have thee. Thou wilt not have me for a slave; thou shalt have me for a master. Thou shalt be mine. I have a den to which I will drag thee. Thou shalt come, thou must come with me, or I will deliver thee up! Thou must die, girl, or be mine—be the priest's, the apostate's, the assassin's! The choice rests with thyself—decide instantly; for I will not submit to further humiliations."

His eye sparkled with passion and rage. The damsel's neck was flushed beneath the touch of his burning lips.

"Loose me, monsieur!" cried she. "Oh! the hateful, poisonous monk! Loose me, or I will tear out thy scurvy gray hair and dash it in thy face!"

He reddened, turned pale, released her from his grip, and eyed her with a gloomy look. She deemed herself victorious, and continued: "I tell thee I belong to my Phœbus, that 'tis Phœbus I love, that 'tis Phœbus who is handsome! As for thee, priest, thou art old, thou art ugly! Go thy way!"

He gave a violent shriek, like a wretch to whose flesh a red-hot iron is applied. "Die then!" said he, gnashing his teeth. She noticed the infernal malignity of his look, and would have fled. He caught her again, shook her, threw her down, and with rapid strides proceeded toward the angle of Roland's Tower, dragging her after him along the pavement by her beautiful arms.

On reaching that point he turned toward her. "Once more," said he, "wilt thou be mine?"

She replied firmly, "No."

He then cried aloud: "Gudule! Sister Gudule! Here is the Egyptian! Revenge thyself on her!"

The damsel felt herself suddenly seized by the wrist. She looked: it was a skeleton arm thrust through a hole in the wall which held her like a vice.

"Hold fast!" said the priest, " 'tis the Egyptian, who has run away. Let her not escape. I will fetch the sergeants; thou shalt see her hanged."

These inhuman words were answered by a guttural laugh from within the wall: "Ha! ha! ha!" The Egyptian saw the priest run off toward the bridge of Notre Dame. The tramp of horses was heard in that direction.

The girl presently recognized the malicious recluse. Panting with terror, she strove to release herself. She writhed, she made many a bound of agony and despair, but the recluse held her with supernatural force. The bony fingers meeting round her wrist clasped her firmly as if that

hand had been riveted to her arm. More efficient than a
chain or ring of iron, it was a pair of living and intelligent
pincers issuing from a wall.

Against the wall La Esmeralda sank exhausted, and then
the fear of death came over her. She thought of the pleasure of life, of youth, of the aspect of the sky, of the sce-
nery of nature, of love, of Phœbus, of all that was past and
all that was to come, of the priest who was gone to de-
nounce her, of the gibbet which stood there, and the hangman who would presently arrive. Then did she feel horror
mounting to the very roots of her hair, and she heard the
sinister laugh of the recluse, who said in a low tone:
"Thou art going to be hanged! ha! ha! ha!"

She turned half-dead toward the aperture and saw the
sallow face of the recluse between the bars. "What harm
have I done to you?" said she in a faint voice.

The recluse made no reply, but began to mutter, with a
singing, irritating, and jeering intonation: "Gypsy girl!
gypsy girl! gypsy girl!"

The wretched Esmeralda drooped her head, conceiving
that it was not a human being with which she had to deal.

Suddenly the recluse exclaimed, as if the girl's question
had taken all the intermediate time to reach her under-
standing: "What harm hast thou done me, dost thou ask?
What harm hast thou done me, Egyptian! Why, listen. I
had a child, seest thou? a little child, an infant, I tell
thee—a pretty little girl. My Agnes," she resumed, kissing
something in the dark. "Well, they stole my child; they
took my child away! they ate my child. That is the harm
thou hast done me."

The damsel replied, like the lamb in the fable: "Most
probably I was not even born then."

"Oh yes!" rejoined the recluse, "thou must have been
born. Thou were one of them. She would be about thy age.
Just! 'Tis fifteen years that I have been here; fifteen years
have I suffered; fifteen years have I prayed; fifteen years
have I dashed my head against these four walls. I tell
thee it was Egyptians who stole my baby, and ate her af-

terward. Hast thou a heart? then fancy to thyself what it is to have a child that sucks, that sleeps, that plays! 'Tis so innocent! Well, it was such an infant that they stole from me and killed, God wot. Now it is my turn; I will feast on the Egyptian. Oh, how I would bite thee if I could get my head between the bars! Only think—while the poor little thing was asleep. And if they had even wakened her when they took her up, her crying would have been to no purpose. I was not there. Ah, ye Egyptian mothers! ye ate my child! Come and see how I will serve yours."

She then began to laugh or to gnash her teeth—for both had really the same expression on that furious face. The day began to dawn. A gray light faintly illumined this scene, and the gibbet in the middle of the Place became more and more distinct. On the other side, toward the bridge of Notre Dame, the poor condemned one imagined that she heard the tramp of horses approaching.

"Mistress!" cried she, clasping her hands and sinking on her knees, dishevelled, overwhelmed, distracted with terror, "take pity on me. They are coming. I never harmed you. Would you have me die that horrid death before your face? You are compassionate, I am sure. 'Tis too frightful! Loose me—let me try to escape. Have mercy I should not like to die thus!"

"Give me back my child," said the recluse.

"Mercy! Mercy!"

"Give me my child."

"Let me go, for heaven's sake!"

"Give me my child."

The poor girl sank down, overcome, exhausted, with the glazed eye of one who is already in the grave. "Alas!" stammered she, "you seek your child, and I seek my parents!"

"Give me my little Agnes," continued Gudule. "Thou knowest not where she is?—then die!—I tell thee, I was a lewd woman; I had a child; they took it away—those accursed Egyptians! 'Tis plain then thou must die. When the Egyptian mother comes to ask for thee, I will say to her,

'Mother, look at that gibbet!' Or, give me back my child—knowest thou where she is, where my little daughter is? Stay, I will show thee. There is her shoe, all that is left me of her. Knowest thou where is its fellow? If thou dost tell me, and if it is at the end of the world, I will fetch it, if I crawl thither on hands and knees."

As she thus spoke, putting her other hand out at the aperture, she showed the little embroidered shoe to the Egyptian. It was already light enough for her to distinguish its form and colors.

"Let me look at that shoe," said the girl, shuddering. "Gracious God!" At the same time, with the hand that was at liberty, she tore open the little bag adorned with green beads which she still wore about her neck.

"Go to! go to!" muttered Gudule; "fumble away in thy infernal amulet!" Then stopping short, and trembling in every joint, she cried with a voice hissing from her very bowels—"My child! my child!"

The Egyptian had taken out of the bag a little shoe that was the precise fellow to the other. To this little shoe was attached a piece of parchment, upon which was written this legend:

> "When the fellow thou shalt find,
> Thy mother is not far behind."

In the twinkling of an eye the recluse had compared the two shoes, read the inscription upon the parchment, and, thrusting her face, beaming with celestial joy, against the bars of the window, shouted: "My daughter! my daughter!"

"My mother! my mother!" responded the Egyptian.

Here we stop short in our delineation.

The wall and the iron bars were between them.

"Oh! this wall!" cried the recluse. "To see her yet not be able to clasp her to my heart! Thy hand! give me thy hand!"

The girl put her hand through the window; the recluse

seized it, fastened her lips to it and stood absorbed in that kiss, giving no other sign of life but a sigh which from time to time heaved her bosom. Meanwhile tears gushed from her eyes in silence, and in the dusk, like a shower at night. The poor mother poured forth upon that adored hand the dark, deep well-spring of tears which was within her, and from which her sorrows had been oozing drop by drop for fifteen years.

All at once she raised her head, threw back the long, gray hair from her face, and, without saying a word, began to pull and thrust at the bars of her window more furiously than a lioness. The bars defied her utmost strength. She then went to a corner of her cell, fetched a large paving stone which served her for a pillow, and dashed it against them with such violence as to shiver one of them into several pieces. A second blow drove out the old iron cross which barricaded the window. With both hands she then pulled out the rusty fragments of the bars. There are moments when the hands of a woman possess superhuman force.

The passage being cleared—and this was accomplished in less than a minute—she clasped her daughter in her arms and drew her into the cell. "Come!" murmured she; "let me drag thee from the abyss!"

She set her down gently upon the floor, then caught her up again, and, carrying her in her arms, as if she had still been her infant Agnes, she paced her narrow cell, intoxicated, frantic with joy, shouting, singing, kissing the girl, talking to her, laughing, weeping, all at once and with vehemence.

"My child! my dear child!" cried she. "I have got my child! here she is! The gracious God has restored her to me. Come, all of you, and see that I have got my daughter again! Lord Jesus, how beautiful she is! The Almighty made me wait fifteen years, but it was to give her back to me in beauty. After all then the Egyptians did not eat thee? Who could have said so? My child, my dear little child, kiss me! Oh, those good Egyptians! How I love the Egyp-

tians! And it is thou thyself! And this was the reason why
my heart always leaped within me whenever thou were
passing. Fool that I was to take this for hatred! Forgive
me, my Agnes, forgive me! Thou must have thought me
very spiteful, didst thou not Ah! how I love thee! And the
pretty mark on thy neck! hast thou it still? Let us see. Yes,
there it is! Oh! how handsome thou art grown. It was from
thy mother thou hadst those large, bright eyes! Kiss me,
darling! I do love thee! What care I whether other mothers
have children! I can laugh at them now. Let them come.
Here is mine. Here is her neck, her eyes, her hair, her
hand. Show me anything more charming than this! Yes,
yes, she will have plenty of lovers, I will answer for it. I
have sorrowed for fifteen years. All my beauty has left me
and gone to her. Kiss me, love!"

"Oh mother!" said the girl, at length recovering power
to speak amid her emotion, "the Egyptian women told me
this. There was a good woman of our tribe who died last
year, and who always took care of me like a nurse. It was
she who fastened this little bag about my neck. She always
said: 'My dear, never part with this trinket. It is a treasure.
It will enable thee to find thy mother again. Thou carriest
thy mother about thy neck.' The Egyptian foretold it, you
see."

The recluse again clasped her daughter in her arms.
"Come, let me kiss thee! how sweetly thou saidst that!
When we go into the country we will give those little
shoes to an infant Jesus in the church. We certainly owe so
much as that to the kind, Holy Virgin. But what a charming voice thou hast! When thou wert speaking to me just
now, it was like music. Ah! Lord God! I have found my
child again! And yet who would believe the story! Surely
nothing can kill one, since I have not died of joy."

She then began to clap her hands, laughing, and exclaiming: "How happy we shall be!"

At that moment the cell rang with the clank of arms and
the tramp of horses, which seemed to be advancing from
the bridge of Notre Dame along the quay. The Egyptian

threw herself in unutterable anguish into the arms of the recluse.

"Save me!" she shrieked; "save me, mother! They are coming!"

The recluse turned pale. "Oh heavens! what sayst thou! I had forgotten! they are searching for thee! What hast thou done, then?"

"I know not," answered the unfortunate girl; "but I am condemned to die."

"Die!" cried Gudule, reeling as if stricken by a thunder-bolt. "Die!" she slowly repeated, fixing her glazed eye upon her daughter.

"Yes, mother," replied the affrighted girl, "they mean to put me to death. They are coming to take me. That gibbet is for me. Save me! save me! They are coming! Save me!"

For some moments the recluse remained motionless as a statue; she then shook her head doubtingly, and suddenly burst into a loud laugh, her old terrific laugh; "No, no, thou must be dreaming. It cannot be. To lose her for fif-teen years, and then to find her for a single minute! And they would take her from me again, now that she is grown up and handsome, and talks to me and loves me! They would now come to devour her before my face—mine, who am her mother! Oh no! such things are not possible. God Almighty would not permit such doings."

By this time the cavalcade had apparently halted. A dis-tant voice was heard calling out: "This way Messire Tris-tan! The priest says that we shall find her at the Trou-aux-Rats." The tramp of the horses began again.

The recluse started up with a shriek of despair. "Away! begone, my child! I now recollect it all. Thou art right. 'Tis for thy death. Curses on them! Away!"

She put her head out at the window and quickly drew it back again. "Stay!" said she, in a low, doleful voice, con-vulsively grasping the hand of the Egyptian, who was more dead than alive. "Stay! hold thy breath! The Place is full of soldiers. Thou canst not get away. It is too light."

Her eyes were dry and inflamed. For a moment she re-

mained silent; but with hurried steps she paced up and
down her cell, stopping now and then, and tearing out
handfuls of her gray hair, which she dashed upon the floor.

"They are coming!" she exclaimed all at once. "I will
talk to them. Hide thyself in this corner. They will not see
thee. I will tell them that I let thee go; that thou hast run
away—that I will!"

Catching up the girl in her arms, she carried her to a
corner of the cell which could not be seen from without.
Here she made her crouch down, taking care that neither
foot nor hand should protrude beyond the dark shadow,
loosed her black hair, which she spread over her white
robe to conceal it, and placed before her the water jug and
paving stone, the only movables that she possessed, fondly
imagining that they would help to hide her. This done, she
was more calm, knelt down, and prayed. Day had not yet
so far broken but that dim obscurity still pervaded the
Trou-aux-Rats.

At that moment, the voice passed very close to the cell,
crying: "This way, Captain Phœbus de Chateaupers!"

At that name, at that voice, La Esmeralda made a slight
movement. "Stir not!" said Gudule. She had scarcely uttered the words when a tumult of horses and men was
heard outside the cell. The mother hastily rose and posted
herself before the window to intercept the view of the interior. She beheld a numerous body of armed men, foot
and horse, drawn up in the Greve. Their commander
alighted and advanced toward her. He was a man of truc-
ulent aspect. "Old woman," said he, "we are seeking a
sorceress to hang her; we were told that thou hadst her."

The poor mother, assuming a look of as much indifference as she could, answered, "I know not what you
mean."

"Tete Dieu!" cried the other, "what kind of story did
that crazed archdeacon tell us? Where is he?"

"Monseigneur," said one of the soldiers, "he has slipped
away."

"Come, come, old crone," resumed the commandant,

"let us have the truth! A sorceress was given to thee to hold. What has thou done with her?"

The recluse, apprehensive lest denying everything she might awaken suspicion, replied in a tone of affected sincerity and surliness, "If you mean a young girl that I was desired to hold just now, all I can tell you is that she bit me, and I let her go. Leave me along, I pray you."

The countenance of the commandant betrayed a feeling of disappointment.

"Tell me no lies, old scarecrow," rejoined he. "I am Tristan, the Hermit, the *compere* of the king. Tristan, the Hermit, dost hear? 'Tis a name," he added, looking round at the Place de Greve, "which has an echo here."

"If you were Satan the Hermit," replied Gudule, regaining some hope, "I should have nothing else to tell you, neither should I be afraid of you."

"*Tete Dieu!*" cried Tristan, "there's a hag for you! So, the young sorceress has escaped! And which way is she gone?"

"Down the Rue du Mouton, I believe," answered Gulude in a careless tone.

Tristan turned his head, and motioned to his troops to prepare to start. The recluse began to breathe again.

"Monseigneur'" said one of the archers, all at once, "ask the old witch why the bars of her window are broken in this fashion."

That question once more overwhelmed the heart of the wretched mother with anguish. She nevertheless retained some presence of mind. "They were always so," stammered she.

"Pooh!" replied the archer, "they formed but yesterday a fair black cross, fit to remind a man of his prayers."

Tristan cast a sidelong glance at the recluse. "By my fay," said he, "the hag does begin to look confused."

The wretched woman felt that all depended on keeping up a bold face, and, while her soul was racked with mortal anguish, she fell a-laughing. Mothers have this kind of force. "Pshaw!" said she, "that fellow is drunk. It is more than a year since the tail of a cart laden with stones was backed against my window, and broke the grating. How I did abuse the driver!"

" 'Tis true enough," said another archer; "I was present."

Wherever you may be you are sure to meet with people who have seen everything. This unexpected testimony somewhat revived the recluse, who felt during this interrogatory like one forced to cross an abyss on the edge of a knife; but she was doomed to a continual alternation of hope and alarm.

"If it was a cart that did this," replied the first soldier, "the stumps of the bars would be driven inward, whereas these are bent outward."

"Aha!" said Tristan to the archer, "thou hast a nose like an inquisitor to the Chatelet. What hast thou to say to that, woman?"

"Good God!" she exclaimed, driven to extremity, and in a voice in spite of herself akin to that of weeping, "I assure you, Monseigneur, that it was a cart which broke those bars. That man saw it, you hear. Besides, what has this to do with your Egyptian"

"Hum!" grumbled Tristan.

"The devil!" resumed the first soldier, flattered by the commendation of the provost; "the fractures of the iron are quite fresh."

Tristan shook his head. She turned pale. "How long is it, say you, since this affair of the cart?"

"A month—a fortnight, perhaps—Monseigneur. I cannot recollect exactly."

"She said at first above a year," observed the soldier.

"That looks suspicious," said the provost.

"Monseigneur," she exclaimed, still standing close to the window and trembling lest they should think of putting in their heads and looking about the cell; "Monseigneur, I swear to you that it was a cart which broke this ironwork. I swear it by the angels in paradise. If it was not a cart, may I deny God, and may eternal perdition be my lot!"

"Thou art in good earnest in that oath," said Tristan, with a scrutinizing look.

The poor creature felt her assurance forsaking her by degrees. She was so confounded as to make awkward blunders, and she perceived with terror that she was not saying what she ought to have said.

A soldier now came up, crying: "Monseigneur, the old witch lies. The girl has not been in the Rue du Mouton. The chain has been up all night, and the keeper has not seen a creature pass."

Tristan, whose look became every moment more threatening, turned to the recluse. "What hast thou to say to this?"

"I know not, Monseigneur," replied she, still striving to make head against this new incident; "I may be mistaken. In fact I almost think she must have crossed the water."

"Why, that is the very contrary way," said the provost. "Besides, 'tis not likely that she would have gone back to the city, where search was making for her. Thou liest, hag!"

"And then," added the first soldier, "there is no boat either on this side of the water or on the other."

"She must have swum over," replied the recluse, defending the ground inch by inch.

"Who ever heard of women swimming!" cried the soldier.

"*Tete Dieu!* old woman! Thou liest! thou liest!" exclaimed Tristan, with vehemence. "I have a good mind to let the young sorceress go, and to take thee instead. A quarter of an hour's torture will bring the truth out of thy throat. Come, thou shalt go along with us."

"As you please, Monseigneur," said she, eagerly catching at these words. "Go to, go to! The torture! I am ready. Take me. Let us be gone forthwith!" Meanwhile, thought she, my daughter will have opportunity to escape.

" 'Sblood!" cried the provost, "what greediness of torture! The mad creature completely puzzles me."

An old gray-headed sergeant of the watch advanced

from ranks. "Mad indeed! Monseigneur," said he, addressing the provost: "If she has let loose the Egyptian, 'tis not her fault, for she is not fond of the Egyptians. For these fifteen years that I have belonged to the watch I have heard her every night cursing the Bohemian women with bitter and endless execrations. If the one we are seeking be, as I suppose, the dancing girl, with the goat, I know that she hates her above all."

Gulude made an effort, and repeated, "Above all."

The unanimous testimony of the men belonging to the watch confirmed the presentation of the old sergeant. Tristan the Hermit, despairing of being able to extract any information from the recluse, turned his back upon her, and with inexpressible anxiety she beheld him slowly proceeding toward his horse. "Come," muttered he between his teeth, "let us be off and pursue our search. I will not sleep till the Egyptian is hanged."

He nevertheless paused for some time before he mounted his horse. Gudule wavered between life and death, on seeing him cast around the Place the restless look of a hound, which is aware that the lair of the game is near at hand and is unwilling to leave the spot. At length he shook his head and vaulted into the saddle. The heart of Gulude, so cruelly oppressed, once more expanded, and, casting an eye upon her daughter, at whom she had not dared to look while the soldiers were there, she ejaculated in a low tone, "Saved!"

At this moment she heard a voice saying to the provost, "*Corbœuf!* Mr. Provost, 'tis no business of mine, who am a soldier, to hang witches. The beggarly crew are beneath one. I leave you to attend to it alone. You must permit me to go and rejoin my company, because it is without a captain."

That voice was the voice of Phœbus de Chateaupers. What she then felt is not to be described. He was there, then, her friend, her protector, her refuge, her Phœbus. She sprang up, and, before her mother could prevent her, darted to the window, crying, "Phœbus! my Phœbus! come hither!"

Phœbus was gone; he had just turned at a gallop the corner of the Rue de la Coutellerie. But Tristan was there still.

The recluse rushed upon her daughter with the roar of a wild beast. Striking her nails into her neck, she drew her back with violence. A mother tigress is not very particular. But it was too late. Tristan had seen her.

"Eigh! eigh!" cried he, with a grin which discovered all his teeth, and made his face resemble the muzzle of a wolf, "two mice in the trap!"

"I suspected as much," said the soldier.

"Thou art an excellent cat!" replied Tristan, patting him on the shoulder. "Come," he added "where is Henriet Cousin?"

A man who had neither the garb nor look of soldier stepped forth from the ranks. He wore a dress half gray and half brown, and leathern sleeves; had lank hair, and carried a coil of rope in his huge fist. This man always accompanied Tristan, who always accompanied Louis XI.

"My friend," said Tristan the Hermit, "I presume that yonder is the sorceress whom we are seeking. Thou wilt hang her forthwith. Hast thou thy ladder?"

"There is one under the shed of the Maison-aux-Piliers," replied the man. "Is it at this *justice* that we are to do the business?" continued he, pointing to the stone gibbet.

"Yes."

"Ho! ho! ho!" rejoined the man, with a more vulgar, more bestial grin that even that of the provost, "we sha'n't have far to go."

"Make haste," said Tristan, "and laugh after."

Ever since Tristan had espied the girl, and all hope was at an end, the recluse had not uttered a word. She had thrown the poor Egyptian, half dead, in the corner of the cell, and posted herself again at the window, with her two hands like claws resting upon the corner of the entablature. In this attitude, her eyes which had again become wild and fierce, were seen to wander fearlessly over the surrounding soldiers. At the moment when Henriet Cousin reached the cell, her look was so ferocious, that he started back.

"Monseigneur," said he, returning to the provost, "which are we to take?"

"The young one."

"So much the better; for yon old hag looks like a Tartar."

"Poor dancing girl with the goat!" sighed the veteran sergeant of the watch.

Once more Henriet Cousin approached the window. His eye quailed before that of the mother. "Madam," he began very timidly.

"What wouldst thou?" cried she, interrupting him, in a low but resolute tone.

" 'Tis not you I want," said he; " 'tis the other."

"What other?"

"The young one."

She shook her head, crying: "There is nobody, I tell thee—nobody!—nobody!"

"There is," replied the executioner, "and well you know it. Let me take the girl. I will not harm you."

"Oh! thou wilt not harm me!" said she with a strange sneer.

"Let me take the other, madam; 'tis by the order of Monsieur the provost."

With a frantic air she repeated: "There is nobody!— nobody!"

"I tell you there is," replied the executioner. "We all saw that there were two of you."

"Look then!" said the recluse, grinning. "Put thy head in at the hole."

The hangman eyed her nails, and durst not venture.

"Make haste!" cried Tristan, who had drawn up his men in a semicircle round the Trou-aux-Rats, and posted himself on horseback near the gibbet.

Henriet returned once more to the provost, quite at a loss how to proceed. He had laid his rope upon the ground, and, with a clownish air, twirling his hat upon his hand, "Monseigneur," he asked, "how are we to get in?"

"By the door."

"There is none."

"By the window."

"It is too small."

"Enlarge it then," said Tristan, angrily. "Hast thou not pickaxes?"

The mother watched them from her den, still leaning against the windowsill. She had ceased to hope; she knew not what she would have, but she would not have them take her daughter from her.

Henriet Cousin went to the shed of the Maison-aux-Piliers to fetch his tools. He also brought from the same place a ladder, which he immediately set up against the gibbet. Five or six of the provost's men armed themselves with mattocks and crowbars and Tristan proceeded with them to the cell.

"Old woman," said the provost, in a stern voice, "yield up the girl to us quietly."

She gave him such a look as though she understood not what he said.

"Tete Dieu!" resumed Tristan, "what reason canst thou have for preventing this sorceress from being hanged according to the king's pleasure?"

The wretched woman burst into one of her wild laughs. "What reason have I? 'Tis my daughter!" The accent with which she uttered that word made even Henriet Cousin himself shudder.

"I am sorry for it," replied the provost, "but it is the good pleasure of the king."

"What is thy king to me?" cried she, redoubling her terrible laugh. "I tell thee it is my daughter."

"Break down the wall," said Tristan.

Nothing more was required to make the opening sufficiently wider than to displace one massive stone under the window. When the mother heard the mattocks and the crowbars sapping her fortress, she gave a terrific scream;

and then began to run round her cell with frightful swiftness—one of the habits of a wild beast, which she had contracted from confinement. She said nothing, but her eyes flashed fire. The soldiers were thrilled to their hearts' core. All at once she caught up her paving stone in both hands, laughed, and hurled it at the workmen. The stone, feebly thrown, for her hands trembled—missed them all and rolled to the feet of Tristan's horse. She gnashed her teeth.

The recluse had sat down in front of her daughter, covering her with her body, listening with fixed eye to the poor girl, who stirred not, who spoke not, save that she murmured in a low tone: "Phœbus! Phœbus!"

In proportion as the work of the besiegers seemed to advance, the mother mechanically drew back, and pressed the girl closer and closer against the wall. All at once she saw the stone shake—for she kept strict watch, and never took her eyes from it—and she heard the voice of Tristan encouraging the laborers. This roused her from the stupor into which she had sunk for some minutes, and she cried—the while her voice sometimes rent the air like a saw, sometimes stammered as if all the maledictions thronging forth at once were jostling one another upon her lips—"Ho! ho! ho! But this is horrible. Robbers, do ye really mean to take my daughter from me? I tell you it is my daughter! Oh! the cowards! Oh! the hangman's lackeys! Oh! the journeymen murderers! Help! help! fire! But will they rob me of my child in this manner? Can such a thing be suffered by the Almighty?"

Then turning to Tristan, with foaming lips, glaring eyes, on all fours like a panther, and bristling with rage: "Come a little nearer to rob me of my daughter! Dost thou not comprehend that this woman tells thee it is her daughter! Knowest thou what it is to be the mother of a child? And if thou hast young ones, when they howl, hast thou not within thee something that yearns at their cry?"

"Down with the stone!" said Tristan; "it is loosened."

The crowbars displaced the ponderous stone. It was, as

we have said, the mother's last rampart. She threw herself upon it; she would have held it fast; she scratched it with her nails; but the massive block, set in motion by six men, slipped from her grasp, and glided gently to the ground along the iron levers.

The mother, seeing an entry made, threw herself athwart the aperture, barricading the breach with her body, waving her arms, striking her head against the top of the window, and shouting with a voice so husky with fatigue that it could scarcely be heard: "Help! fire! fire!"

"Now take the girl," said Tristan, cool as ever.

The mother scowled at the soldiers in so formidable a manner that they were much more disposed to fall back than to advance.

"On, there!" shouted the provost. "Henriet Cousin, on!"

Not a creature stirred a step.

The provost exclaimed, "What! men-at-arms afraid of a woman!"

"Monseigneur," said Henriet, "call you that a woman?"

"She has the mane of a lion," said another.

"Advance!" replied the provost, "the gap is large enough. Enter three abreast, as at the breach of Pontoise. Let us finish the business. By the death of Mahound! the first that recoils I will cut in two."

Placed between the provost and the mother, and threatened by both, the soldiers hesitated for a moment; then making their choice, they advanced toward the Trou-aux-Rats.

When the recluse saw this she suddenly raised herself upon her knees, threw back her long hair from her face, and dropped her lank and lacerated hands upon her thighs. Big tears started from her eyes, trickling one by one down the wrinkles in her cheeks, like a torrent along the bed which it has wrought for itself. At the same time she began to speak, but in a voice so suppliant, so meek, so subdued, so cutting, that more than one old trooper who could have eaten human flesh had to wipe his eyes.

"Gentlemen, and messieurs sergeants, one word! There

is one thing that I must tell you. It is my daughter, look
you—my dear little girl, whom I had lost. Listen—'tis
quite a history. I am no stranger to monsieurs the sergeants. They were always very kind to me at the time
when the boys in the streets pelted me with stones, because I led a loose life. You will leave me my child when
you know all. I was a poor unfortunate girl. The Bohemians stole my infant. Stay, here is her shoe, which I have
kept for fifteen years. Her foot was no bigger than that. La
Chantefleurie, Rue Folle-Peine, at Rheims—perhaps you
know that name. Well, I was the person. You will take pity
one me, will you not, gentlemen? The Egyptians stole her
from me, and hid her away for these fifteen years. I concluded she was dead. Only think, my good friends, I
thought she was dead. I have lived here these fifteen years,
in this den, without fire in winter. 'Tis hard, is it not? The
poor dear little shoe! I have prayed so earnestly that God
Almighty has heard me. This morning he has restored my
daughter to me. 'Tis a miracle of his doing. She was not
dead, you see. You will not take her from me, I am sure.
If it were myself I should not say a word—but as for her,
a girl of sixteen, give her time to see the sun! What harm
has she done to you? None whatever. Nor I either. Did you
but know, that I have none but her, that I am getting old,
that she was a blessing bestowed on me by the Holy Virgin herself! And then you are so kindhearted! You knew
not that it was my daughter, till I told you. Oh! how I love
her! I will be gone; we will both go. Who would stop two
weak women, one of them the mother, the other the
daughter? Let us pass, then! We are from Rheims. Oh! you
are very kind, messeurs sergeants; I love you all. You will
not take my darling from me—'tis impossible. Is it not?
quite impossible! My child! My own dear child!"

When she had done, Tristan the Hermit knitted his brow,
but it was to conceal a tear which started into his tiger-
eye. Conquering this weakness, however, he said in a dry
tone: "The king wills it."

Then, bending to the ear of Henriet Cousin, he whispered: "Finish out of hand!" The redoubtable provost himself perhaps felt even his heart fail him.

The hangman and the sergeants entered the cell. The mother made no resistance: she merely crawled toward her daughter, and threw herself headlong upon her. The Egyptian saw the soldiers approaching. The horror of death roused her. "Mother," cried she, in a tone of inexpressible anguish, "mother they are coming; defend me!"

"Yes, my love, I will defend thee," replied the mother in a faint voice; and, clasping her closely in her arms, she covered her with kisses. Mother and daughter, as they thus lay on the ground, presented a sight that was truly pitiable.

Henriet Cousin laid hold of the girl round the body. When she felt the touch of his hand she shuddered, "Heugh!" and fainted. The hangman, from whose eyes big tears fell drop by drop upon her, attempted to lift her, but was prevented by the mother, who had entwined her arms round her daughter's waist, and clung so firmly to her child, that it was impossible to part them. Henriet Cousin, therefore, dragged the girl out of the cell, and the mother after her—the latter, too, with her eyes shut, and apparently insensible.

Then sun was just then rising, and a considerable number of people collected thus early in the Place were striving to make out what it was that the hangman was thus dragging along the pavement toward the gibbet; for it was Tristan's way to prevent the near approach of spectators at executions.

There was not a creature at the windows. There were only to be seen on the top of that tower of Notre Dame which overlooks the Greve, two men standing out in dark relief from the clear morning sky, who appeared to be looking on.

Henriet Cousin stopped with what he was dragging at the foot of the fatal ladder, and scarcely breathing, so deeply was he affected, he slipped the cord about the lovely neck of the girl. The unfortunate creature felt the horrid touch of the rope. She opened her eyes, and beheld

the hideous arm of the stone gibbet extended over her
head. Rousing herself she cried in a loud and heart-rending
voice, "No! no, I will not." The mother, whose face was
buried in her daughter's garments, uttered not a word; her
whole body was seen to tremble, and she was heard to kiss
her child with redoubled fervency. The hangman took advantage of this moment to wrench asunder her arms with
which she had clung to the condemned girl. Either from
exhaustion, or despair, she made no resistance. He then
lifted the damsel on his shoulder, from which the charming
creature hung gracefully on either side, and began to ascend the ladder.

At that moment the mother, crouched on the pavement,
opened her eyes. Without uttering any cry, she sprang up
with a terrific look; then, like a beast of prey, she seized
the hand of the hangman and bit him. It was like lightning.
The executioner roared with pain. Some of the sergeants
ran to him. With difficulty they extricated his bleeding
hand from the teeth of the mother. She maintained profound silence. They thrust her back in a brutal manner, and
it was remarked that her head fell heavily upon the pavement. They lifted her up, but again she sank to the ground.
She was dead.

The hangman, who had not set down the girl, continued
to mount the ladder.

55

When Quasimodo ascertained that the cell was vacant,
that the Egyptian was not there, and that while he
was defending her she had been taken away, he grasped
his head with both hands, and stamped with rage and astonishment; he then began to run all over the church in

quest of the Bohemian, setting up strange shouts at every corner, and strewing his red hair upon the pavement. It was the very moment when the king's archers entered the cathedral victorious, also seeking the Egyptian. Quasimodo assisted them, having no suspicion—poor deaf creature!—of their fatal intentions; it was the vagabond crew whom he regarded as the enemies of the Egyptian. He himself conducted Tristan the Hermit to every possible place of concealment, opened for him all the secret doors, the double-bottomed altars, and the back sacristies. Had the unfortunate girl been still there he must inevitably have betrayed her. When Tristan was tired of the unsuccessful search—and on such occasions he was not soon tired— Quasimodo continued it alone. He traversed the church twenty times, a hundred times, lengthwise and breadthwise, from top to bottom, mounting, descending, running, calling, crying, shouting, ferreting, rummaging, poking his head into every hole, thrusting a torch into every dark corner, distracted, mad. At length, when he was sure, quite sure, that she was no longer there, that she had been stolen away from him, he slowly ascended the tower stairs, those stairs which he had mounted with such transport and exultation on the day that he saved her. He again passed that way, with drooping head, voiceless, tearless, almost unbreathing. The church was once more clear, and silence again reigned within it.

He then shook his head, and remained for a while in a state of stupor. All at once he furiously trampled upon his torch, and without word or sign he frantically dashed his head against the wall and fell swooning on the pavement.

When his senses returned, he threw himself upon the bed, he rolled upon it, he wildly kissed the spot where the damsel had lain; he remained thus for some minutes as motionless as if life had fled; he then rose, bathed in perspiration, panting, beside himself, and began to beat his head against the wall with the frightful regularity of a pendulum, and the resolution of one who is determined to dash out his brains. At length he fell a second time exhausted. Presently he crawled on his knees out of the cell, and crouched opposite to the door in an attitude of despair.

It appears that then, seeking in his doleful reverie to discover who could thus unexpectedly have carried off the Egyptian, he bethought himself of the archdeacon. He recollected that none but Dom Claude had a key to the staircase leading to the cell; he called to mind his nocturnal attempts upon the damsel, in the first of which he, Quasimodo, himself had assisted, and the second of which he had frustrated; he called to mind a thousand other circumstances, and soon felt not the least doubt that it was the archdeacon who had taken the girl from him. Such, however, was his respect for the priest, so deeply had gratitude, affection, love for that man struck root in his heart, that even at this moment they withstood the tugs of jealousy and despair.

He considered that the archdeacon had done this, and instead of the mortal rancor with which the thought would have filled his heart for any other, the moment it fixed upon Claude Frollo, it only aggravated his grief. At this moment, when the dawn began to whiten the flying buttresses, he descried on a higher story of the cathedral, at the angle formed by the outer balustrade which runs round the apsis, a figure in motion. The face of this figure was turned toward him. He recognized the person. It was the archdeacon. Claude's step was grave and deliberate. He looked not before him as he walked toward the north tower; but his face was turned askance toward the right bank of the Seine, as if he were striving to see something over the intervening roofs. The owl frequently has this oblique attitude, flying in one direction and looking in another. The priest thus passed on above Quasimodo without perceiving him.

The hunchback, petrified by this sudden apparition, watched till he lost sight of him at the door of the staircase of the north tower. The reader already knows that this is the tower which commands a view of the Hotel de Ville. Quasimodo rose and followed the archdeacon.

He went up the stairs to ascend the tower, for the purpose of ascertaining why the priest ascended it; if indeed the poor bell-ringer, who knew not what he did, or what he wished, could be said to have any purpose. He was full of rage and full of apprehension. The archdeacon and the Egyptian clashed together in his heart.

When he had reached the top of the tower, before he had issued from the darkness of the staircase and stepped out upon the platform, he looked cautiously about to discover where the priest was. Claude had backed toward him. A balustrade of open work surrounds the platform of the steeple. The priest, whose eyes were bent upon the town, was leaning with his breast against that corner of the balustrade which looks down upon the bridge of Notre Dame.

Quasimodo stole with wolf's step behind him, to see what he was thus looking at. The attention of the priest was so completely engrossed that he perceived not the approach of the hunchback.

He now perceived what the priest was looking at. The ladder was set up against the permanent gibbet. There were a few people in the Place and a great number of soldiers. A man was dragging along the pavement something white to which something black was clinging. This man stopped at the foot of the gibbet. What then took place he could not clearly discern: not that the sight of his only eye was at all impaired, but a party of soldiers prevented his distinguishing what was going forward. Besides, at that moment the sun burst forth and poured such a flood of light above the horizon, that every point of Paris, steeples, chimneys, gables, seemed to be set on fire at one and the same moment.

Meanwhile the man began to mount the ladder. Quasimodo now saw distinctly again. He carried across his shoulder a female dressed in white; this young female had a rope about her neck. Quasimodo knew her. It was the Egyptian!

The man reached the top of the ladder. There he arranged the rope. The priest, in order to see the better, now knelt down upon the balustrade.

The man suddenly kicked away the ladder, and Quasimodo, who had not breathed for some moments, saw the unfortunate girl, with the man crouched upon her shoulders, dangling at the end of the rope within two or three yards of the pavement. The rope made several revolutions, and Quasimodo saw the body of the victim writhe in frightful convulsions. The priest, on his part, with outstretched neck and eyes starting from his head, contemplated the terrific group of the man and the young girl, the spider and the fly.

At this most awful moment, a demon laugh, a laugh such as one only who has ceased to be human is capable of, burst forth upon the livid face of the priest. Quasimodo heard not this laugh, but he saw it. The bell-ringer recoiled a few steps from the archdeacon, then suddenly rushing furiously upon him, thrust him with his two huge hands into the abyss, over which Dom Claude was leaning. "Damnation!" cried the priest as he fell.

The gutter beneath caught him and broke the fall. He clung to it with eager hands, and was just opening his mouth to give a second cry, when he beheld the formidable and avenging face of Quasimodo protruded over the balustrade above his head. He was then silent.

The abyss was beneath him—a fall of more than two hundred feet and the pavement! In this terrible situation, the archdeacon uttered neither word nor groan. Suspended from the gutter, he wriggled, and made incredible efforts to raise himself upon it; but his hands had no hold of the granite, and his toes merely streaked the blackened wall without finding the least support. All who have ever been up the towers of Notre Dame know that the stone bellies immediately under the balustrade. It was against the retreating slope that the wretched archdeacon exhausted himself in fruitless efforts. He had not to do with a perpendicular wall, but a wall that receded from him.

Quasimodo might have withdrawn him from the gulf by

merely reaching him his hand; but he did not so much as look at him. He looked at the Greve. He looked at the Egyptian. He looked at the gibbet. The hunchback was leaning upon the balustrade, at the very spot which the archdeacon had just before occupied; and there, never turning his eye from the only object which existed for him at that moment, he was motionless and mute as one thunderstruck; while a stream flowed in silence from that eye, which till then had not shed a single tear.

The archdeacon meanwhile began to pant. The perspiration trickled from his bald brow, the blood oozed from his fingers' ends; the skin was rubbed from his knees against the wall. He heard his cassock, which hung by the gutter, crack and rip at every movement that he made. To crown his misery, that gutter terminated in a leaden pipe which bent with his weight. The archdeacon felt it slowly giving way. The wretched man said to himself, that when his cassock should be rent, when the leaden pipe should yield, he must fall, and horror thrilled his entrails. At times he wildly eyed a sort of narrow ledge, formed about ten feet below him by the architectural embellishments of the church, and in his distress he prayed to Heaven, in the recesses of his soul, to permit him to end his life on this space of two square feet were it even to last a hundred years. Once he glanced at the abyss beneath him; when he raised his head his eyes were closed and his hair standing erect.

There was something frightful in the silence of those two persons. While the archdeacon, at the distance of a few feet, was experiencing the most horrible agonies, Quasimodo kept his eye fixed on the Greve and wept.

The archdeacon, perceiving that all his exertions served but to shake the only frail support that was left him, determined to stir no more. There he was clasping the gutter, scarcely breathing, absolutely motionless save that mechanical convulsion of the abdomen which supervenes in sleep, when you dream that you are falling. His fixed eyes glared in a wild and ghastly manner. Meanwhile he began to lose his hold; his fingers slipped down the gutter; he felt his arms becoming weaker and weaker, and his body heavier and heavier. The leaden pipe which supported him bent more and more every moment toward the abyss. Beneath him he beheld—horrid sight!—the roof of St. Jean-le-Rond, diminutive as a card bent in two. He eyed one after another the passionless sculptures of the tower, suspended like himself over the abyss, but without fear for themselves or pity for him. All about him was stone; before his eyes gaping monsters; under him, at the bottom of the gulf, the pavement; over his head Quasimodo weeping.

In the Parvis several groups of curious spectators were calmly puzzling their brains to divine who could be the maniac that was amusing himself in this strange manner. The priest heard them say, for their voices reached him, clear and sharp, "By'r Lady, he must break his neck!"

Quasimodo wept.

At length the archdeacon, foaming with rage and terror, became sensible that all was useless. He nevertheless mustered all his remaining strength for a last effort. Setting both his knees against the wall, he hooked his hands into a cleft in the stones, and succeeded in raising himself about a foot; but this struggle caused the leaden beak which supported him to give way suddenly. His cassock was ripped up from the same cause. Feeling himself sinking, having only his stiffened and crippled hand to hold by, the wretched man closed his eyes, and presently his fingers relaxed their grasp. Down he fell!

Quasimodo watched him falling.

A fall from such a height is rarely perpendicular. The archdeacon, launched into the abyss, fell at first head downward and with outstretched arms, and then whirled several times over and over; dropping upon the roof of a house, and breaking some of his bones. He was not dead when he reached it, for the bell-ringer saw him strive to grapple the ridge with his fingers; but the steeple was too steep, and his strength utterly failed him. Sliding rapidly down the roof, like a tile that has got loose, down he went, and rebounded on the pavement. He never stirred more.

Quasimodo then raised his eye to the Egyptian, dangling from the gallows. At that distance he could see her quiver beneath her white robe in the last, convulsive agonies of death; he then looked down at the archdeacon, stretched at the foot of the tower, with scarcely a vestige of the human form about him, and, heaving a deep sigh, he cried, "There is all I ever loved!"

56

Toward the evening of the same day, when the judcial officers of the bishop came to remove the mangled corpse of the archdeacon from the pavement of the Parvis, Quasimodo was not to be found in Notre Dame.

Many rumors were circulated respecting this affair. The general opinion was that the day had arrived when, according to agreement, Quasimodo, or the devil, was to carry away Claude Frollo, the sorcerer. It was presumed that he had smashed the body to get at the soul, just as monkeys crack the shell of a nut to get at the kernel. For this reason the archdeacon was not interred in consecrated ground.

Louis XI died in the month of August in the following year, 1483.

As for Pierre Gringoire, he contrived to save the goat, and to gain applause as a tragic writer. It appears that, after dabbling in astrology, philosophy, architecture, alchemy, and all sorts of silly pursuits, he reverted to tragedy, which is the silliest of all. This he called "having come to a tragic end." In the accompts of the Ordinary for 1483 may be found the following entry relative to his dramatic triumphs: "To Jehan Marchand and Pierre Gringoire, carpenter and composer, who made and composed the mystery enacted at the Chatelet of Paris at the entry of Monsieur the legate and arranged the characters, habited and equipped as by the said mystery was required; and also for having made the scaffolds which were necessary thereto, one hundred livres."

Phœbus de Chateaupers likewise "came to a tragic end:" he married.

57

We have just said that, on the day when the Egyptian and the archdeacon died, Quasimodo was not to be found in Notre Dame. He was never seen afterward, nor was it ever known what became of him.

In the night following the execution of La Esmeralda, the hangman and his assistants took down the body from the gibbet, and conveyed it, according to custom, to the vault of Montfaucon.

Montfaucon, as we are told by Saval, was "the most ancient and the most superb gallows in the kingdom." Between the faubourgs of the Temple and St. Martin, about one hundred and sixty fathoms from the walls of Paris, and a few crossbow shots from la Courtille, was seen at the top of a gentle, imperceptible rise, yet sufficiently elevated to be seen for several leagues around, a building of strange form, nearly resembling a Celtic cromlech, and where also human victims were sacrificed.

Figure to yourself on the top of a mound of chalk a clumsy parallelopipedon of masonry, fifteen feet high, forty long, and thirty wide, with a door, an outer railing, and a platform; upon this platform sixteen massive pillars of unhewn stone, thirty feet high, ranged in form of a colonnade round three of the four sides of the masonry which supports them, connected at the top by strong beams, from which at certain distances hang chains, each having a skeleton dangling at the end of it; round about it in the plain a stone cross and two gibbets of secondary rank, which seem to spring up like shoots from the central stock; above all these in the atmosphere crows perpetually flying!—and you will have a picture of Montfaucon.

At the conclusion of the fifteen century, this formidable gibbet, which dated from 1320, was already very decrepit; the beams were rotten; the chains eaten up with rust; the pillars green with moss; there were wide interstices between the courses of the stone; and grass grew upon the untrodden platform. The profile of this edifice upon the sky was a horrible one, especially at night, when the faint moonlight fell upon those bleached skulls, or when the night breeze, shaking the chains and the skeletons, made them rattle in the dark. The presence of this gibbet was sufficient to induce a belief that all the environs were haunted.

The stonework which served as a base to the odious edifice was hollow. Here had been formed a vast vault, closed by an old crazy, iron gate, into which were thrown not only the human remains taken from the chains of Montfaucon, but the bodies of all the wretches executed at the other permanent gibbets of Paris. In this vast charnelhouse, in which so many human carcases and so many crimes have mouldered together, many of the great of the world, and many innocent persons, have successively laid their bones, from Enguerraud de Marigni, who made a present of Montfaucon, and who was a good man, to Admiral de Coligni with whom it was closed, and who was also a good man.

Respecting the mysterious disappearance of Quasimodo, all that we have been able to discover is this:

About a year and a half or two years after the events with which this history concludes, when search was made

in the vault of Montfaucon for the body of Olivier le Daim
who had been hung two days previously, and to whom
Charles VIII had granted the favor to be interred in better
company at St. Laurent, among these hideous carcases
were found two skeletons in a singular posture. One of
these skeletons, which was that of a female, had still upon
it some fragments of a dress that had once been white; and
about the neck was a necklace of the seeds of adrezarach,
and a little silk bag braided with green beads, which was
open and empty. These things were of so little value that
the hangman no doubt had not thought it worth his while
to take them. The other, by which this first was closely
embraced, was the skeleton of a male. It was remarked
that the spine was crooked, the head depressed between
the shoulders, and one leg shorter than the other. There
was, however, no rupture of the vertebræ of the neck, and
it was evident that the person to whom it belonged had not
been hanged. He must have come hither and died in the
place. When those who found this skeleton attempted to
disengage it from which it held in its grasp, it crumbled to
dust.

Afterword

Paris in *The Hunchback of Notre Dame* is populated by outcasts. Esmeralda and Quasimodo live outside the protective arms of society, and are therefore easily removed from it. Gringoire, though he freely admits that he doesn't really fit in anywhere, manages to muddle along, trying to stay out of trouble. He lives his life the best he can, never sticking his neck out too far, never standing up for anything, and so, as far as we know, manages to escape the gallows. He disappears into the night, perhaps to find his place among the truants at last. But you might well ask, Where would you fit into Parisian life in 1482? Better yet, where would you *want* to fit in? Let's look at some of the options:

First, there's the mob—the normal, everyday denizens of medieval Paris. They usually go about their business, in all likelihood pursuing the trades that their families have plied for generations, seldom traveling outside the city walls. They thrive on celebrations, including all the morbid ceremony connected with an execution. A hanging will draw as large a crowd as a religious pageant or a royal procession. They are a superstitious group: they are convinced that Satan hunts among them for human souls and that witches are commonplace and should be burned or hung when their wickedness is discovered. There aren't many independent thinkers among them; at least, there are few who would admit to independent thought. Who wants to suffer the fate of a witch or a blasphemer?

Another option is the military. Captain Phoebus is certainly a valued member of Paris society. He is a handsome, dashing young officer. Fleur-de-Lis, his betrothed, is the envy of all her friends. And yet, how does he manage to fit in so well? Because he is in the army, he lives by a strict code of honor: he must defend a lady of society's honor. But he also leads a debauched, drunken life, because that is what has always been expected of soldiers. Men like Phoebus protect the people who "matter," and use the people who don't. That's his reward for "fitting in."

What about the Church? The religious life is even more rigid than the military in that it prohibits its members a normal family life. Claude Frollo, intended for the priesthood from his earliest years, was sent away to study when he was just a small boy. He never knew what a true family was, never understood the workings of human love, so he is unable to set a good example for his orphaned brother. He is kind to Quasimodo, but feels more pity for him than real love. The emphasis of his education was on scholarly success, not on compassion. In time, he becomes such a prideful scholar that he ignores the teachings of the church and loses himself in the study of alchemy. And, having never been tempted by the love of a woman, he falls utterly and depravedly for Esmeralda's outer beauty. It is not love, but pure lust that overtakes him. The all-encompassing, rigid requirements of a priestly life twist Dom Claude Frollo into the most horrible monster of the novel. Outwardly, he is "normal." Inwardly, his soul is more hideous than Quasimodo's malformed shell.

And finally, what of the government and the king—the person who actually defines the society over which he rules? Every example of "justice" we see in this novel is a miscarriage of justice. Quasimodo's punishment for accosting Esmeralda (at Claude Frollo's behest, we might add), is much harsher than the crime warrants, simply because the judge is as deaf as the man whose case he's trying. Justice should be blind; it should not be deaf. Esmeralda is tortured into confessing to the murder of a man who is perfectly healthy. And is Louis XI, the King of France, the fountain of all wealth and justice in French society? He's a whining, miserly hypochondriac who is completely deaf to the pleas of his subjects, not because he cannot hear, but because he *chooses* not to hear. Given these options, is there any part of this society you would like to claim as your own?

In fact, the only milieu that offers any succor to anyone in *The Hunchback of Notre Dame* is the cathedral itself. It is the only place Quasimodo feels at home, and it houses the bells, his only friends. Even Esmeralda, when she claims sanctuary within its walls, is soothed by the cool solidity of the church and the ethereal singing of the choir. It is the geographic center of Paris and, in this novel, stands as its emotional heart, as well. It is the one place that welcomes, that embraces the outcast with the same protection offered to those society deems "worthy," and, in the end, it shakes off those who have betrayed its sanctity.

—Elizabeth Massie